Dear Reader:

It is my pleasure to present *Nothing Stays the Same*, the dramatic sequel to *EX-Terminator: Life After Marriage*, which centered around the hot topic of divorce.

It is a peek three years later at the lives of Marvin Thomas; his wife, Rachel; and their friends. They've left divorce court and are now living in the world of high society…but the good life doesn't last forever.

Readers will relate to the world of a man fighting to save his profitable electronics firm during a failing economy. Not only does he struggle to save his company but his family, home and friends…a sign of today's turbulent times.

Author Suzetta Perkins, now with her fifth novel, has established herself as a provocative, engaging novelist of the new millennium.

Thanks for supporting the work of Suzetta Perkins, one of my authors under Strebor Books. I appreciate you giving this book a chance and if you enjoy it, I hope that you will read Suzetta's other books: *Behind the Veil*, *A Love So Deep*, *EX-Terminator: Life After Marriage* and *Déjà Vu*.

Peace and Many Blessings,

Publisher
Strebor Books International
www.simonandschuster.com/streborbooks

## ALSO BY SUZETTA PERKINS
*Déjà Vu*
*EX-Terminator: Life After Marriage*
*A Love So Deep*
*Behind the Veil*

ZANE PRESENTS

# NOTHING
## STAYS THE
# SAME

## Suzetta Perkins

SBI

STREBOR BOOKS

NEW YORK LONDON TORONTO SYDNEY

SBI

Strebor Books
P.O. Box 6505
Largo, MD 20792
http://www.streborbooks.com

ISBN 978-1-59309-375-4
LCCN 2009942986

First Strebor Books trade paperback edition March 2010

Cover design: www.mariondesigns.com
Cover photograph: © Keith Saunders/Marion Designs

10  9  8  7  6  5  4  3  2  1

Manufactured in the United States of America

For information regarding special discounts for bulk purchases,
please contact Simon & Schuster Special Sales at 1-866-506-1949
or business@simonandschuster.com

The Simon & Schuster Speakers Bureau can bring authors to your
live event. For more information or to book an event, contact the
Simon & Schuster Speakers Bureau at 1-866-248-3049 or visit our
website at www.simonspeakers.com.

*To my husband, Jerry*
*Although we're not together, I still love you.*

# ACKNOWLEDGMENTS

I can't believe this is book number five. God is awesome.

I believe I understand the meaning of the words Michael Jackson sang when he said, *you are not alone.* I know that my writing career hasn't been by happenstance and I could not have done it alone. The many faces, new and old, I've met throughout my travels across the country...the faces of people who've em-braced my work; given me encouragement and said continue to write those stories of hope and faith, betrayal and redemption; told me how much *EX-Terminator* helped them to heal or move forward with their lives, who told me that *A Love So Deep* prepared them for transitional love, unconditional love, love they were not deserving of; told me I needed a sequel for *Behind the Veil* and rushed out to buy *Déjà Vu* when it was released and told others about it because it was a doggone good story...those faces have carried me. And it is because of you I write. I want to thank you from the bottom of my heart for the countless emails and letters of support. And a special thank you to the wonderful friends in my life, who've stood by my side and made my dream worth living.

As always, my family has been there—through the thick and thin, loving, supporting, inspiring, and promoting me in every way they knew how. From my dad, Calvin Sr., who devoured *Déjà Vu* in practically one sitting and rendering a verdict of GOOD BOOK, to my children, Teliza and Gerald Jr. (JR), who hustle my work as hard as I do—I love you. To all my family members who've supported me—especially my niece, Candace, who paraded me all over Facebook, along with my son, JR, thanks a million.

Zane, thank you for continuing to believe in my abilities as a writer. Strebor Books/Simon and Schuster have meant so much to me because they gave me the opportunity to showcase my talent. I will never forget. And thank you Charmaine, for being there every step of the way, helping me to make deadlines or facilitate book signings. And to Keith of Marion Designs, thank you so much for my outstanding book covers. Smooches.

To Maxine Thompson, my agent, I never would have made it without you. Not only do you represent me well, you take out time to promote. Thank you for the airtime on ArtistFirst and allowing me to connect with readers everywhere.

To LaTricia Smith and Jackie Thomas, thank you for giving me an opportunity to showcase my work on your blog radio show *Off the Pages*. It was great being your first guest.

To Edrina Bailey, an avid supporter and my reader, thank you for giving me your honest opinion and feedback. I've trusted your judgment from day one—your straight-from-the-hip critiques. It's only made me better.

My heartfelt love and thanks goes out to Alberta Lampkins, Melvin Lewis, and Althea Boone (Black Pearl's Book Club) for loving and celebrating a sistah, so much so that you helped to place me in positions to share with others. For that, I'm deeply grateful.

To the countless book clubs and readers that I've been privileged to meet, thank you for being a part of my experience. And because of you, I have never been alone on this journey. It is my prayer that I continue to write stories that you can touch and feel, with my own brand of seasoning, that will inspire, console, make you laugh, or maybe make you cry, and with an added pinch of the right spice make those stories hot or sizzle just a little.

Now sit back, relax, and ready yourself for another good read in *Nothing Stays the Same*. Being on top of the world is great, but a fall to the bottom can be disastrous—you know the story of Humpty Dumpty who couldn't be put back together again, especially in these economic times. There's hope, though, as the story ends on the day Barack Obama is elected president. Blessings.

# CHAPTER ONE

LANCASTER, BOSCHE, AND COLEMAN AT LAW was boldly engraved on a bronze plate outside the office with the double glass doors. Marvin Thomas touched his moustache and ran his hand over his head as he stared at the law firm's name on the wall. This was the last place he wanted to be, but he was about to lose everything—his company, possibly his marriage, and for sure his sanity. A frizzy-haired blonde woman, wearing black, diamond-encrusted horn-rimmed glasses, who sat behind a maple desk, jerked her head upward when the glass door opened. Marvin walked through the foyer and stood in front of her.

"Good afternoon. My name is Marvin Thomas, and I have an appointment with Attorney Cecil Coleman."

The receptionist ran her eyes over the handsome gentleman, who stood in front of her dressed in an expensive suit with manicured nails and eyes to die for. "Yes, Mr. Coleman is expecting you," the receptionist said, her eyes steadily slicing and dicing. "I'll let him know you're here."

"Thank you," Marvin said, ignoring her furtive glances while he continued to pace. He wrung his hands together and paced back and forth, tension etched in his face. Although there was a lot on his mind, Marvin didn't fail to notice the open-air terrarium filled with a variety of exotic plants and a small brook running on a pump that traveled through it. Track lights extended from the ceiling overhead to help provide photosynthesis for the greenery. Marvin jerked around at the sound of his name and walked the few feet to greet Cecil Coleman.

Long, sinewy fingers grasped Marvin's in a brotherly handshake that lasted twenty seconds. "Good to see you, Thomas. How long has it been—ten, fifteen years?"

"Ten years for sure since we finished undergrad."

"Come on back so we can talk," Coleman said. "Gretchen, hold my calls."

"Yes, Mr. Coleman."

Marvin followed the lanky-legged Cecil down a long corridor flanked on either side by offices until they reached an elevator. Although Marvin stood at six feet, two inches tall, Cecil had him by an inch. They both played basketball at Clark-Atlanta, however, neither was destined for star status.

They marched into the open elevator and Cecil pushed the button for the twenty-ninth floor, both gentlemen remaining quiet for the duration of the ride. The elevator boasted a panoramic view of the city and the ride up reminded Marvin of the first time he rode a Ferris wheel, his feet extending over a little bucket that lifted him high in the air. The elevator stopped, and they got off and walked a few feet to a carved oak door with CECIL COLEMAN, ATTORNEY AT LAW engraved on the plate.

Cecil's office was massive. An expansive cherrywood desk stood in the middle of the room with a high-backed mahogany-colored Italian executive chair sitting behind it. A large cherrywood credenza and bookcase blanketed the back wall, and to the right of the desk was an extensive built-in library filled with law books, State of Georgia statutes, LexisNexis, and case studies of well-publicized business takeovers, mergers, you name it. To the left of the desk was an executive conference table that sat fifteen, with matching Italian leather chairs. With hands in his pocket, Marvin crossed the length of the office and looked out the window. Tall skyscrapers littered the Atlanta skyline, and Interstates 75 and 85 snaked through the city like runaway children.

Cecil stood back and smiled as his old friend admired his accomplishments—a corner office that was four-hundred and fifty-square feet on the twenty-ninth floor of one of the most prestigious law firms in Atlanta. He was a Princeton man; his finest hour was graduating with his Juris Doctorate. After grad school, he interned at a smaller law firm, and met and married the woman who completed him. She was also an attorney, having completed her law degree a couple of years earlier.

Marvin turned from the window and looked at Cecil,

trying not to size him up, although the large Princeton class ring, and the diamond-encrusted Rolex that sat on the edge of the starched-white cuff of the Armani shirt made him take notice. "Nice."

"Thanks," Cecil said. "One of the perks of being partner. So what you've been up to?"

"Depends on where I start. After grad school, I worked for several software companies before starting my own. I don't know if you remember my cousin Harold, but we started out as business partners. Due to a family crisis, he resigned. My new partner, Kenny Richmond—"

"Richmond...Kenny Richmond. That name sounds familiar."

"Well, Kenny Richmond and I earned Fortune 500 status and have built a very lucrative business in the last three years. During all of that, I got married then divorced, but I'm now married to the most wonderful woman named Rachel. We have a two-year-old daughter named Serena, and she looks just like her father." Marvin smiled.

"So you're enjoying a life similar to mine," Cecil said with a hint of jealousy in his voice. As if seeing Marvin for the first time, he gave him a once-over and was mildly surprised that his friend probably shopped at the same clothiers he did.

"Well, I'm not sitting on the twenty-ninth floor, but...until a few months ago, we were doing great."

"Sit down, Marvin, and let's talk about what brought you here today. On second thought, let's go over to the conference table where we have more room. You want a drink?"

"No," Marvin said, as he watched Cecil reveal a hidden bar that was housed in the middle of his library. Although it was not illegal to have a bar in the privacy of one's office, it struck Marvin as strange because of constant reminders on television about our responsibility as law abiding citizens to not drink and drive. Maybe it was because Marvin no longer drank. Anyway, he was not here to condemn Cecil Coleman. This man was one of the best negotiators and business attorneys in the nation...the man who might save his life.

"So what can I do for you, Marvin?"

# CHAPTER TWO

Rachel Thomas got up from the couch and walked to the entertainment center that held Sylvia's family pictures. There were pictures of Sylvia, Kenny Sr., and Kenny Jr.; Kenny Sr. and Kenny Jr.; Kenny Jr. and his big sister, Maya; the whole Richmond clan including Sylvia's mother; and Sylvia and Kenny's wedding photo taken on a beach on what was a beautiful and sunny day in Jamaica.

Rachel picked up the picture of Kenny, Sylvia, and Kenny Jr. and stared at it. Kenny was tall, dark, and handsome, quite the contrast to Sylvia's caramel frappuccino color. Baby fat still grabbed Sylvia's curves, but the result was well worth the extra weight because Kenny Jr. had been a beautiful baby and would be more handsome than his father.

"Girl, can you believe that a little over three years have gone by since we were at Mona and Michael's engagement party?" Rachel hollered into the kitchen where Sylvia was putting the final touches on Kenny Jr.'s extra birthday cake.

"And Adonis had the audacity to show up talking about he wanted his wife back..." Sylvia interjected.

"And your behind passed out cold on the floor..."

Rachel and Sylvia laughed at the memory. "Look, we can reminisce later," Sylvia said. "Today is my baby's birthday. I tell you, Kenny Jr. is as handsome as his dad."

"And remember the look on my face, Sylvia, when you told me you were pregnant, and I didn't even know that you and Kenny had done anything?"

"Rachel, you weren't supposed to know everything. I believe we were feeling so bad about Ashley getting arrested for poisoning and killing William that I didn't want to be alone, and the moment happened."

"Yeah, right. Tell me anything, you crazy girl. I just know it messed up our plans to have a double wedding."

"You didn't need me and Kenny to double with you and Marvin. That day was meant just for the two of you. Rachel, you were so gorgeous in that Vera Wang gown. It looked beautiful against your cocoa brown skin. And I've never seen Marvin grin so much. He acted like someone who had just won the lottery."

"'Cuz that man was happy, and so was I. When I looked into those hazel eyes of his and saw all the love staring back, girl, I couldn't keep the tear well dry."

"I remember, and so does everyone else who was at the church that day."

"Sylvia, God finally blessed me with a real man, a true man—a God-fearing man. I don't think I even deserved him."

"I'll tell you this one thing, Denise would have been right there to scoop Marvin up like a bowl of Raisin Bran if you hadn't held on tight. Do you remember when Denise snatched her wig off at the Ex-Files meeting, talking about she had cancer?"

"Sylvia, she saved herself in the nick of time because I was about to kick her ass into the ground. Nobody asked her to tell us how she and Marvin got together and how they kissed in Times Square and all whatever else she did. Yick! Sickening. I just know Marvin got rid of her tail for sleeping with his cousin Harold. She was Marvin's ex-wife, and I was going to see that she stayed that way." They laughed again.

"I can't believe Kenny came back into my life."

"Me either," Rachel quipped. Sylvia gave her a harsh look. "But me and Kenny are cool now," Rachel quickly added, making the peace sign with her two fingers. "I really love the brother because he's a changed brother who makes my sistah happy."

"Who would have known that a pity party and quick stop at a grocery store was going to change my life forever?" Sylvia continued, ignoring Rachel's antics. "I love me some Kenny Richmond."

"Well, I'm sure it helped that the brother was still fine after all them years you all were apart, and he had a little bank roll to entice you."

"Got that right. But look at you, Miss Rachel. Snagged your man at our first support group meeting. Telling that raggedy story of yours hooked and reeled your man in like a school of tuna caught in a fishing net. You were good—no, brilliant."

"Yes, I was, but you know I was telling the truth about getting rid of my ex. That was the past. Now we're married, our husbands are business partners, and we all have babies—me, you, Mona, and Claudette."

The conversation was interrupted by the sound of the doorbell.

"That ain't nobody but that crazy Mona," Rachel said, "ringing the bell like she don't have good sense."

Sylvia laughed. "Let that child in. I'm going to the room and get Kenny Jr. and Serena."

Rachel pulled the door open and smiled with glee. Mona and Claudette stood at the door, the biggest grins on their faces. "Girl, look at you," Rachel said to Mona as she admired her dreadless hair. "No baby fat on you, and you look fabulous. Hi Michael Jr."

*Kiss, kiss.* "And so do you, Mrs. Fortune Five Hundred," Mona said in return, then turned to her son. "Tell Auntie Rachel hi."

"Hi Aunie Rachel," Michael Jr. said.

"And look at you, Ms. Claudette and little Miss Reagan," Rachel continued. "You're looking good in those matching kente outfits. Trying to get Reagan hooked on ethnic clothing since you couldn't do it with Reebe," she quipped to Claudette.

"Shut up and let us in," Claudette said, giving Rachel air kisses on both cheeks.

"Hi, Auntie Rachel," Reagan said without coaxing.

"Hey, sweetie. Your mommy got your hair all fixed up pretty, and you're so beautiful. I bet you hear that all the time."

"Yes," Reagan replied.

"Y'all come on in. Sylvia," Rachel shouted, "it's Mrs. Bourgeoisie and her hairdresser, packing two more children."

"Look who's talking, Claudette," Mona said as they made their way into the living room. "Got some nerve to call anybody bourgeoisie. These Fortune 500 wives don't do nothing but sit on their butts all day watching stories, buying up stuff on the shopping network, and got their maids cleaning the mansions their husbands bought them. Poor children are going to grow up spoiled."

"Just like, Ickelmay Uniorjay," Sylvia said as she entered the room with Kenny Jr. and Serena. Everyone laughed.

"Well, it looks like someone is having a birthday in here," Claudette said.

"Yeah, enough balloons to make you feel like you're right at the fair." Mona giggled. "Kenny Jr. sure is loved."

"Nothing too good for my baby boy. Outside, we've got clowns, face painting, you name it. But you know how it is since you all have children. So how are my girls doing? Group hug."

They drew to each other as if the air was sucked from

the middle. Their lives had become entangled—a single common denominator had brought them together. Not so long ago, each had been divorced, distraught, and then desperate to repair their torn lives that needed mending in the worst kind of way.

"Hey, that felt great," Rachel said softly, not wanting to break from the warmth of their nestling together.

"Yeah, it did," Claudette rang in. "Sylvia, I didn't know you could sling some pig Latin."

"Hey, I still got it," Sylvia said. High-fives went around the room.

"Well, how do you like my hair?" Mona chimed in. "Claudette wasn't down with cutting my dreads, 'cuz she says she's never cutting hers."

"I think your bobbed look is simply elegant, Mona," Sylvia said. "Turn around and let me look at you." Mona did a twirl in the middle of the floor. Michael Jr. giggled. "Can't tell that a baby's been in that belly. You're still lean and mean and still got those boobs to go with your bob."

"Yeah, baby," Mona said. "Michael loves up on these twins every chance he gets."

Everyone laughed including the children, although they didn't know why the adults were laughing so hard.

"Mommy, your turn," Kenny Jr. coaxed Sylvia. Everyone laughed again.

"Naw. I didn't lose all my baby fat, but Kenny Sr. loves me just the way I am."

"Just stay away from the ice cream bowl," Rachel said to Sylvia who gave Rachel the eye.

"Like I said," Mona added, "you and Rachel need to get up off them things you sit on all day long and do a good days work. That'll keep you fit, although I don't think Rachel ever gains an ounce of anything."

"No not an ounce," Rachel said as she took her turn to twirl around. "My husband loves his chocolate diva and we do more than I can say out loud to keep physically fit."

Serena clapped her hands.

"That's right, clap for Mommy, Serena." Everyone laughed.

"Well, I guess it's my turn," Claudette mumbled. "But instead of twirling around, I've got something I want to tell you." She winked at Mona and flung one of her braids off of her shoulder. "I've stopped smoking, for three whole months."

"Oh my God," Sylvia and Rachel said in unison and cupped their hands to their mouths. "That's so wonderful, Claudette; I'm so happy for you," Sylvia said, her eyes widened in shock.

"Yes," Rachel echoed.

"Now Reagan can have a smoke-free environment to live in," Mona added.

"What about the rest of my family?" Claudette questioned.

"And of course, the rest of Claudette's clan, although

they're used to it because they've been inundated with secondhand smoke for years."

"We're happy for you, Claudette," Sylvia said again.

"Mommy, Mommy," Kenny Jr. whined.

"What is it, sweetie?" Sylvia asked.

"What about my birthday party?"

"Of course, baby. Today is your day. As soon as the other children get here, we will go outside and have some fun."

"Yeah," Kenny Jr. shouted.

Sylvia looked at Kenny Jr. as he ran off to join Serena, Reagan, and Michael Jr. "My handsome guy will be three years old on Monday."

"He looks, just like Kenny Sr.," Mona said. "He's so handsome."

"I think all the kids look like their fathers," Sylvia said. "Serena looks like Marvin and Michael Jr. looks like Michael."

"Except Reagan," Claudette butted in. "She looks so much like her mother, Ashley. But she's got William's hair. I'm so glad Ashley let me adopt her. It would hurt to know that Reagan was with Ashley's family and they didn't treat her well."

"To think you and Ashley didn't get along in the beginning," Rachel put in.

"Well, it's good that she has a good friend in me. Ashley's been asking about you guys. She was right there in the beginning when we formed our support group. It hasn't been that long ago that we were all in need of some healing because our men had left us. It hurts because Ashley didn't have to kill William to get away from him."

"It's unfortunate," Sylvia said. "The signs were probably there, but we failed to see them."

"I don't know what signs were there that we didn't see," Mona chided. "I didn't think Ashley had it in her to kill a big ole Mandingo like William."

Rachel laughed, and Claudette stared back. "It's not funny."

"Come on, Claudette," Rachel said. "Don't be so sensitive."

Claudette rolled her eyes, then looked at her friends. "You need to go to the prison to see her. And don't sit and look at me like you're stupid and didn't comprehend a word I said, because you're guilty."

"We got it, Claudette!" Mona said. "Now let's get little Kenny's party started. Put on some music so I can dance."

# CHAPTER THREE

Kenny Richmond slipped through a side doorway off the garage and into the hallway that joined the kitchen and a set of back stairs that led to the second floor. He walked with a cell phone up to his ear and a briefcase in the other hand. Loud music met his ears and he frowned, telling the caller to wait a minute while he investigated. He had expected to walk into a house full of children who had come bearing gifts for his little boy's birthday, not all of his wife's girlfriends getting their party on. But what was a party, even a kid's party, without Sylvia's girls?

"Look, man," Kenny said to the caller, "I'll get back with you on that stock. I feel pretty good about it. Talk with you later."

Kenny closed his cell and thought about where he wanted to take Thomas and Richmond Tecktronics, Inc. His partnership with Marvin was a match made in heaven, and between the two of them, they had amassed a small fortune. It had grown from a medium-sized business to a Fortune 500 company and from five to over one hundred employees.

When Marvin Thomas founded the company some nine or so years ago, he was involved in the sale of high-tech computer programs. Now they were a multi-million-dollar company with their own technicians, some of them imported straight from Silicon Valley, who designed sophisticated computer programs and systems, video games, and educational resources. They were also sellers of quality computer systems, personal and portable, with a highly skilled sales force that were spread out globally and had infiltrated a network of large conglomerates to become a viable competitor in the marketplace. Kenny liked that Marvin gave him the space and latitude to handle things in his own way. After all, they were both laughing, running, and grinning all the way to the bank.

Making money and closing high-stakes deals had become Kenny's mission, along with keeping the woman who gave his life new meaning happy. For the moment, he'd push his wheeling and dealing to the side so he could enjoy his son's birthday party. Kenny adored little Kenny and counted him among the greatest gifts his wife, Sylvia, had given him.

He ran up the stairs and dropped the briefcase in his office that looked like an electronics showroom. Scattered around the wall were small shelves that held video games that he and others had invented, MP3 players, DVD players, wireless notebooks, and other handheld electronic devices. Home speaker systems were strategically placed in several locations. Kenny's desk was made of a high-resin, clear acrylic and held a PC system with all the bells and whistles a three-gigabyte computer could hold.

With reckless abandon, Kenny plowed through a stack of papers that were on his desk, hoping to find a list of figures he'd jotted down for a proposal he was working on. Not finding what he was looking for, Kenny walked the few feet to the door that led into the hallway connecting the master bedroom and his office. On each side of the hallway were his-and-her walk-in closets.

The master bedroom was painted a matte gold with an off-white ceiling tray in the center of the room that boasted a large crystal chandelier. Occupying one of the walls was a bronze and gold fireplace that extended from the floor to the middle of the wall. A brass mirror with floral etchings running along its base hung overhead. A king-size cherrywood sleigh bed sat in the middle of the room accompanied by two nightstands on either side, a large chest of drawers, and a three-drawer armoire that housed a flat-screen television. A small, round cherrywood table accompanied by two high-back chairs sat under a beveled glass window that provided a view of the orchard behind their yard. A sliding door led from their room onto the second-story balcony.

Kenny's walk-in closet was almost as large as Sylvia's.

His designer suits hung on the top rack along one wall, while his casual leisure suits took up space on the bottom. Long and short-sleeved shirts, polo shirts for playing golf, and easy lying-around shirts littered the opposite wall above his slacks, the expensive and not so expensive, which hung underneath. The middle wall showcased Kenny's collection of shoes. In the center of the room was a red plush chair that sat next to a built-in set of drawers that held all of Kenny's sweaters.

He settled on a yellow polo shirt that accentuated the color of his dark skin and a pair of brown slacks. Next he went into the spacious octagon-shaped bathroom with mirrors on three quarters of the walls. A Roman tub sat elegantly against a sea of floral and candle embellishments that were Sylvia's handiwork, underneath a window that was shaped like a half-circle. Kenny brushed his teeth and smiled when he looked in the mirror. "Man, you've come a long way." Last he splashed on some Karl Lagerfeld, his wife's favorite cologne ever since the day he walked back into her life.

After a last glance in the stand-alone mirror that sat to one side in the bedroom, Kenny dashed down the stairs and out into the three-car garage. Off to the side was an orange, kid-sized Hummer that was so true to life it came with its own motor. Kenny Jr. had been talking about it for days, ever since Michael Jr. said his dad was getting him one for his birthday. Kenny lifted the garage door and moved the car outside to the front lawn and around the side near the clown setup. There was no need to put a bow on it. Just seeing it would make Kenny Jr. go wild.

Kenny ducked back through the garage and into the house to surprise his son. As he approached the living room from the dining room, he heard the women talking and stood behind the door listening to their antics while he laughed to himself.

"Rachel, stop acting like you were born with a silver spoon in your mouth," Mona quipped. "You may be sitting on your 'a' double 's' now, but I'm sure you remember how good BellSouth was to you before… when you couldn't keep a husband."

"Mona, no need for you to talk, sitting up in that mansion of yours with Dr. Michael Broussard and all that he lavishes upon you."

"That's right, but even though my husband is who he is, I still have my catering business and my elite clientele has grown with it. I'm not satisfied with just being Michael Broussard's wife and concubine, I'm also an icon, and together we are a force to be reckoned with. In fact, I will be catering a big event next weekend that will encompass some of the oldest money in Atlanta. It's a fundraising dinner for Democratic presidential candidate Barack Obama, but I tell you that deals will be made in back rooms to the tune of several million dollars."

Rachel sighed. "Well, that's your life. I can't help that Sylvia and I are the wives of the two most important people in Atlanta and we've got it like this. And we don't care anything about your big party. Don't look at me like that, Mona. You started it."

"Hold up; enough of this," Sylvia chimed as Mona zoned in for the attack. "This is Kenny Jr.'s birthday party. We're going to open up presents in a few minutes. I'm trying to wait for Kenny Sr."

Kenny pushed open the dining room door as if on cue. "Surprise, everybody. Where's the birthday boy?"

"Daddy, Daddy," Kenny Jr. shouted upon hearing his father's voice. Kenny Jr. ran to his dad, who picked him up.

"Happy birthday, son. Daddy and Mommy have a special birthday treat for you."

"Yeah!" Kenny Jr. shouted.

"Were you listening to our conversation?" Sylvia said accusingly, her hands on her hips.

"Well, I wouldn't mind securing a spot on the guest list for that party Mona was talking about," Kenny said, giving Mona a wink. "Sounds like a place I'd like to be. Well, I see that the gang is all here. Mona, Claudette, Rachel, ladies."

"Hey, Kenny," they all said in unison.

"You all were having some kind of heavy conversation up in here. I was waiting for my wife to say how much she loved her husband and wanted to be alone with him." He laughed.

"Ooooooooooh," Mona crowed.

"I like that in a man," Claudette said, getting tickled as she watched Kenny undress Sylvia with his eyes.

With a quick stroke, Sylvia raised her hand and moved it forward as if she was getting ready to throw something. "No, Kenny, we aren't going to start that up again." She gave him a sly wink. "How many times do I have to tell you people that it's my baby's birthday? Next time, no adults will be allowed to stay." The ladies laughed, then calmed down.

"You're right, Sylvia," Rachel said finally. "Let's celebrate."

Kenny put Kenny Jr. down on the floor.

"Okay, kids," Sylvia said, "We're going outside. Some of the other kids are just now arriving. We're going to sing 'Happy Birthday' to Kenny Jr."

Everyone filed out of the house and into the yard that was decorated with red, yellow, and blue balloons. Little stations were set up for face painting, tattoos, and a space for the kids to sit and listen to clown jokes. The clown was six feet tall, and his face was painted white with red freckles. His hair was strawberry red, and a large red button nose sat in the middle of his face. He wore a clown outfit similar to Ronald McDonald's. A large sheet cake that was made in the likeness of Superman, Kenny Jr.'s favorite superhero, sat alone on a table. Hot dogs, potato chips, and punch sat at another station waiting to be served.

Kenny Jr. didn't even see the clown; he ran straight

to the orange Hummer and got in. Sylvia raised her hand over her mouth, looked at Kenny Sr., and grinned. He did it again. Kenny Sr. never failed to make his son happy.

Other parents and their children made a ring around Kenny Jr. as he sat in his Hummer. Little Kenny waved to everyone until Sylvia finally coaxed him out of the car. Again, Sylvia threw her hands up in the air and moved her arms like a maestro directing an orchestra. "One, two, and three. Happy birthday to you, happy birthday to you, happy birthday Kenny Jr., happy birthday to you."

Serena, Reagan, and Michael Jr. sang along with the adults and other children. "Let's open your gifts, Kenny," Sylvia said.

"Yeah," little Kenny shouted again. Sylvia gave him a large red and yellow bag with a giraffe on it from Serena. Little Kenny reached inside and pulled out a toy fire truck. Kenny was so excited. Aunt Rachel had also stuffed several cute shirt-and-pants sets in the bag. Then Kenny tore the birthday paper with all the balloons on it from the next gift, from Michael Jr. It was a model Hummer that Kenny Sr. was going to have to help Kenny Jr. assemble. Next was Reagan's gift. Kenny Jr.'s eyes got wide as he examined the X-Box video games. Reagan smiled.

After all the gifts were opened, the children ate and got their faces painted and listened to the clown who made them laugh the rest of the afternoon. Kenny went to Sylvia and kissed her. "Good job, Mrs. Richmond."

"Good job yourself, Mr. Richmond. You never cease to amaze me. When did you get that car for little Kenny?"

"When you weren't looking." They laughed and Kenny kissed Sylvia on the lips while he squeezed one of her healthy buttocks. "I love you, Mrs. Richmond. And I always will."

"Through the storm and the rain," Sylvia said, "I'll be by your side."

# CHAPTER FOUR

⚖ **M**arvin Thomas sat in his office ruminating on the advice he had received from his friend and attorney, Cecil Coleman. The weight of the world had fallen heavy on his shoulders, and even with the best advice, he wasn't sure what to do. Just this morning, he noticed gray strands running through his head faster than the speed of light.

He was at the beginning of a fight for his life, his livelihood, and his family. Hanging on the walls in his office were commendations and awards that he and TTTS, now Thomas and Richmond Tecktronics, Inc., had garnered over the years for being a reputable and new-age company. They were in competition with some of the largest white-owned companies in the U.S. and abroad, and they had been able to stand their ground.

Now someone wanted to eliminate the competition, them, namely; Thomas and Richmond. It would take everything they owned to fight the merger that was sure to take place, displacing him and Kenny in the end. Marvin had yet to tell Kenny about the warning signs and the flagrant attempts to manipulate them into giving in. Kenny would not understand—he had invested a lot in the company, and to hear him tell it, this was the happiest Kenny had ever been.

With elbows on the edge of his desk, Marvin leaned his face into his extended hands and cried like a baby. He'd always been strong and was always in the gap where others were concerned, holding up the torch and fighting their battles to the end. Although he was divorced from his ex-wife, Denise, when she needed him—when she needed someone to help her get through her bout of cancer—he was there. Now, he had to make a grave decision: fight the big boys or sell out.

Hurriedly, Marvin grabbed a tissue from the silver container that sat on the edge of his black executive desk, next to the picture of his family and a Newton's cradle—five steel balls suspended by wire that swing back and forth whenever you knock one into another. Soon after Marvin and Rachel got married three and a half years ago, Rachel had redecorated his office, making it look more professional. Black lacquered furniture with stainless steel accessories turned an ordinary office into an extraordinary one. A flat-screen television hung on the wall opposite his desk where he tuned in daily to CNN for the latest news and to gaze at the television ads they'd prepared that celebrated Thomas and Richmond Tecktronics' success. Black and gray carpet with a splash of red color running through it gave the room an executive look. With the tissue, Marvin wiped the tears from his face upon hearing Kenny's voice that preceded his entrance into the office.

Kenny bounced into Marvin's office with his cell phone still attached to his ear. "I'll meet you for lunch. I've got a hunch that I'll have that information by then. See ya."

Kenny closed his cell phone and glanced in Marvin's direction. Marvin leaned back in his chair. He was in no mood for talking—not even to Kenny.

"Hey, man, I was going to ask what the good word was," Kenny began, "but the look on your face suggests otherwise. What put that sour look on your face? Rachel's cooking?" Kenny laughed.

Marvin eased up in his seat without cracking a smile. "Streets aren't always paved with gold. Things aren't always the way they seem to be. One minute they're this way, the next another."

"So what are you trying to say, brother? You and Rachel are cool, right?"

"Yeah, me and Rachel are just fine. I love her just as much as you love Sylvia. I probably love Rachel more than you love Sylvia." Marvin swallowed, and let out a nervous laugh, remembering a romantic moment he recently shared with Rachel.

Kenny took a seat, concern written on his face. "I take it this has nothing to do with our wives."

"Right. I've been doing some thinking," Marvin said.

The tension in Kenny's face eased a little. "I've been doing some thinking myself. I've got a few ideas I'd like to pass by you—some long-range goals, our next steps, and how do we get there."

"Funny, I've been thinking along the same lines."

"Whew. You had me worried for a minute, Marvin. I'll have to learn to recognize your deep-in-thought look so that I don't trip next time."

"You know, Thomas and Richmond Tecktronics, Inc., has been an industry leader for the last three years. Can you believe we're moving and shaking with the Sonys and Toshibas, well, maybe not that big, but you know what I mean?"

"Umm-hmm," Kenny said, his voice barely audible.

"Anyway, we've developed software just like the Japanese. We've got video games that people all over the world are playing. Damn kids know how to manipulate those games backwards and forwards, but half of that population doesn't have a clue what the fifty states are or the names of our Supreme Court justices. They act as if the world was invented after the last commercial break, and we're the ones responsible for it. Richmond, can you name five Supreme Court justices?"

"'Uncle Tom' Clarence Thomas, David Souter, Scalia, Kennedy, and Ginsburg."

Shock registered on Marvin's face. "Damn, boy, you're good. I'm thoroughly impressed. You better keep those in your hip pocket because we may need all nine of them one day."

Kenny cocked his head and looked straight into Marvin's eyes. "It's me, Marvin. You need to shoot straight and stop talking like a white boy. What in the hell is up with you? No more beating around the bush or playing like you're the host of some reality TV show. I'm better than a fifth-grader. So if you've got something to tell me, spit it out."

"Nothing, it's nothing, man. I had a long talk with a friend of mine yesterday, and it made me take a long, hard look at my life. I'm good. Needed you to make me come to my senses with your assurances that things were moving in the right direction. How was Kenny Jr.'s birthday party?"

"Marvin, if there's something you need to tell me, now is better than later. I'd hate to learn something the hard way when it could have been resolved on the front end. By the way, Kenny Jr. enjoyed himself. Sylvia outdid herself with his party. She had clowns and all sorts of stuff to entertain the kids. I got little Kenny the Hummer he wanted. He probably won't play with the rest of his toys until it rains." The two men enjoyed a laugh.

"Thanks, Kenny. No need to worry. Everything is alright, man. I know your day is full, unless you came down here to talk to me about something specific."

"No, I was just checking on you—touching base. After you didn't stop by little Kenny's party, I thought I'd pay my partner a visit. If you're alright, I'm alright. I'll get back with you about my long-range plans."

"When my cousin Harold and I were partners, I trusted him with my life. I feel the same about you, Richmond. I'm proud of our partnership, if I hadn't told you that before. I love you, man."

Marvin watched as Kenny stood on his feet and came around to where he sat. It was easy to see that his tone and metaphor-laden conversation troubled Kenny. It was almost as if Marvin could hear Kenny's brain sizing up the last fifteen minutes, analyzing and reanalyzing what had been said or possibly implied. Although it might not be fair, he was going to wait until the last minute to let Kenny in on the time bomb that was ticking and on target to rock the fabric of his life as well as the lives of his family and friends.

"Love you, too, man," Marvin heard Kenny say. They shared a brother's handshake, and Kenny departed.

As soon as the door closed behind Kenny, Marvin picked up the phone. He pretended to dial some numbers, then looked at the phone and began to talk. "Baby, I love you and Serena. My whole world revolves around you and everything that I've ever done was to give you and Serena the life you so deserve. I don't know how to put this other than to just say it." There was a long pause. "Rachel, I'm deep in debt. I've made some financial decisions that have caused me some anguish. Now, I might lose the company because a larger firm is trying to buy me out and take over the company I've built from the ground up. I may lose everything...the house, the cars. I don't know what to do, Rachel. Help me."

Marvin placed the receiver on its base. The television commercial made it seem easy as actors portrayed parents who had to talk to their teens about drugs and went through a ritual of a practice run before the real meeting. The practice run was tense for Marvin, but he wasn't sure that he would be able to go through with the real thing.

His company's climb to the top made him blind to the economic crisis that loomed across the nation, even while politicians gearing up for the next presidential election were making light of it everywhere they went as they crossed the country talking to everyday folks. His mind way out in space, Marvin shook the clouds from his thoughts and turned on the TV. He gasped as he saw that another giant in the banking industry was about to fall.

# CHAPTER FIVE

Rachel flitted from room to room with her maid, Isabel, at her side, carrying two large books that contained swatches for her new project. It had been only three years since she and Marvin had moved into the three-acre estate that boasted a four-car garage; five bedrooms and five baths; a large solarium; and a chef's kitchen complete with orange-and-charcoal granite countertops, copper pots and pans extending from the ceiling, and a chef's butcher block fitted with an oven/grill and a sink large enough to hold a side of beef. Marvin enjoyed this item in the kitchen more than Rachel, and often was the head chef at many of the dinner parties they hosted at their home. But Rachel was set on giving the room and others in the house a face lift with the latest in drapery fashion.

"Isabel, what do you think about this fabric for the kitchen?" Rachel asked as she fingered it and glanced up at the window and around the room.

"That's nice, Mrs. Thomas."

"Are you saying that just to agree with me or because you really agree with me?"

"Because I agree with you, Mrs. Thomas. It is really beautiful."

"Well, I don't like it. It's too dark for this room. We need something light in the kitchen that will pick up the colors of the countertops but not make everything dark. You understand, Isabel?"

"Yes, Mrs. Thomas, I understand."

"Oh, Isabel, you're not much help. Roland should be here any minute. He'll have all the rooms picked out in no time."

Isabel rolled her eyes. "Yes, Mrs. Thomas."

Rachel moved to the dining room. This room was one of her favorites. It had an Asian theme, which included two large Oriental vases that stood three feet tall, a large Oriental watercolor painting that lay against a pale yellow wall with eggshell-colored crown molding that snaked around three walls, and a black lacquered dining room set that sat six but could be extended for eight. A six-by-four-foot Oriental rug sat underneath the dining room table.

Rachel fingered a pale, champagne-colored fabric with Japanese motifs embroidered in dark brown that she imagined would look elegant on the ten-foot window that looked out into a meadow filled with pine and dogwood trees. She nodded her head in approval. "I like this fabric for this room, Isabel."

"Yes, Mrs. Thomas."

There was a loud knock at the door, and Isabel made

a beeline for it. Rachel temporarily put the swatch books down on the dining room table and anticipated Roland's entrance.

"Girlfriend," Roland said upon entering and threw Rachel two air kisses. Dressed in navy pleated silk slacks, a white long-sleeved shirt opened down to the top of his breasts, and a burgundy linen vest, Roland swiped his hand in hello to Isabel, who wasn't interested in any kind of kiss from him whether it was real or one blown in the air. His makeup was flawless, setting off his manufactured cat eyes, and his hair was cut in a precision short Afro so tight that it looked tailor made.

"Water, Mr. Roland?" Isabel asked.

"No sweetie, make it stronger than that. I need me a nice glass of chardonnay. You do have some, Miz Rachel? I need a drink before I get to messin' up in here with you. I love working for you, Miz Girlfriend, but you always seem to make my pressure rise."

"Roland, you're a trip, but you're right about me working your bony ass today. I need new drapes for five rooms, and I want to know what you think of my choices."

"So you're getting ready to spend some real money today, Miz Rachel? You know that will make me very happy."

"Yeah, Roland. I need a change."

"I guess you and your man got it like that. 'Cuz these drapes that have already got these rooms looking fabulous got a lot of good years left on them. But I ain't mad, girlfriend. I'm trying to refurbish my condo. Where is that drink?"

"Here you are, Mr. Roland," Isabel said as she extended the glass of wine to him.

"Cheers, baby!"

"Cheers," Rachel said, hoisting one of the books up in the air. "I'll have my glass of wine later. I want to be fully cognizant of every decision we make." Isabel frowned with disgust and left the room.

Roland poured the sweet liquid down his throat. "Alright, Miz Girlfriend, let's get this party started."

Rachel and Roland spent the next three-and-a-half hours fussing over fabric, taking measurements, and making suggestions until choices were finally made and Roland had written up the order. He followed Rachel to the kitchen so she could put her copy of the order in the secretary drawer. "I'll call you tomorrow, girlfriend, and let you know what kind of damage you've done—and it's extensive enough, in fact, to call for disaster relief."

"You let me worry about that. I just want to know how fast you can get my order to me."

Rachel and Roland turned in unison at the sound of keys hitting the kitchen counter. Rachel smiled when she saw Marvin, and Roland grinned harder.

"Hey, honey, how was your day?" Rachel asked.

"What's going on, Rachel? What's this I hear about disaster relief?"

"Marvin, this is Roland." Roland smiled and gave Marvin a friendly wave. "He's the interior decorator I hired to do our drapes when we first moved in."

"Is something wrong with them?" Marvin asked.

Roland moved his head like a ping-pong ball as the conversation bounced between Marvin and Rachel.

"What's wrong, Marvin? Did something happen at work today?"

"What is he doing here?" Marvin asked, pointing to Roland, who made a poker face.

"Honey, I wanted to put new drapes in some of the rooms. I thought it would give the house a nice face lift for the fall."

"We don't need new drapes, Rachel. You're spending money as if it grew on trees. Do you have a clue what's going on outside of these walls? There's an economic crisis that's going to hurt all of us."

"Get a grip, Marvin. You haven't indicated to me that we had anything to worry about."

"Look, Miz Rachel," Roland cut in. "This is my cue to leave. You call me later and let me know what you want me to do. Girl, that's some sweet tea," he whispered to Rachel. "Fine as wine."

"Roland, let's go," Marvin said, showing him the door. "My wife and I need to talk. Don't get your hopes up."

"Good day, folks." Roland left in a hurry.

"Why were you so rude to Roland, Marvin? That isn't like you. He was a guest in our home and here at my request."

"Rachel, were you going to make a decision like this without consulting with me?"

"Honey, you need to relax and calm down. Whatever has irritated you should not be taken out on me. Yes, I was going to tell you all about what I was doing, but my God, I was only getting estimates."

"If I hadn't walked in on your little workshop, those drapes would've been hung up without my knowledge until the bill arrived. Look, I'm sorry, baby, for reacting that way, but I need you to be a little more frugal with your spending."

"What is it, Marvin? Are we in some kind of trouble?"

"No, nothing like that. I'm just afraid that with the housing market stiffening up as it is, there is going to be some real repercussions that will eventually affect how we spend money. Mark my words."

"Okay, baby, but I'm concerned about your well-being. Your outburst scared me."

"It won't happen again."

# CHAPTER SIX

Rain fell from the sky as if an airplane had burst the interior lining of a cumulous cloud, sending liquid spewing out every which way upon the city of Atlanta. The rain, along with the wind, knocked on windows, beat the sidings of well-constructed buildings, and scared the wits out of Sylvia as she rustled Kenny Jr. and his toys inside the house.

"I hope your daddy gets home soon." Sylvia sighed as she watched little Kenny rearrange his toy cars in the play parking garage. She walked a couple of feet to the couch, found the remote, and turned on the television to see what the newscasters were saying about the sudden downpour.

The phone rang. Startled, Sylvia jumped. "I hope nothing's wrong with Kenny Sr.," she said out loud before finally picking up the phone. She glanced at the caller ID, sighed, and answered.

"Hey, Rachel. How about this rain?"

"Yeah, girl. It just came out of nowhere."

"Well, I hope Kenny gets home soon. It's seven o'clock

and he should've been here. This weather reminds me of the day that tornado sneaked into Atlanta and caught us unaware."

"I don't think it's as bad as that, Sylvia, but I know what you mean. Speaking of Kenny, though, have you talked with him anytime today?"

"Early this morning, why?"

"I'm not really sure, Sylvia. Marvin came home tonight acting real strange. He claimed that nothing was wrong, but I've never seen him pull a temper tantrum before. Darn near kicked Roland out."

"That's it. Marvin caught you spending his hard-earned money. I told you that you didn't need to be getting any drapes when the ones you have will be good for the next two decades."

"I needed a change, and we can afford it."

"Rachel, you've got to be prudent. Yes, you've got money, you're sitting on a two-or-three-acre lot, got a loving husband and a beautiful child, but sometimes you've got to take time to find out what their day is like and what they might have gone through. If you look at the news channel every once in a while, you'll hear that the economy isn't faring so well, and that could have an effect on everyone."

"So what's Kenny saying, Miss Know-it-all?"

"Kenny has grown another appendage on his body. I can't get that cell phone away from his ear. He lives and breathes that thing. Says he's making deals to help boost the company's profit margin."

"Well, if you hear anything, let me know. I'm worried about Marvin. Can't put my finger on it, but something's going on with him."

"I hear Kenny now. I'll let you know if I find out anything."

"Thanks, Sylvia."

"Love ya, Rachel." And the line was dead.

"Hey, baby," Sylvia said, getting up to give her man a kiss hello. Kenny stopped long enough to give her a peck on the lips as he continued to talk to the anonymous voice coming through his cell phone. Sylvia's left brow furrowed as she wrapped her arms around her waist. This practice was going to stop as of today.

"Daddy, Daddy," Kenny Jr. shouted. Kenny Sr. lifted him up by one arm and placed a kiss on his forehead.

"Run on," Kenny Sr. said, letting Kenny Jr. slide back down to the floor. He looked up into Sylvia's agitated face and ended his phone call. "Baby, what's for dinner?"

"That will be the last time you walk into this house with a phone in your ear after being gone all day."

Kenny frowned.

"Leave the office," Sylvia continued, "at the office. It's family time now, and don't forget it."

"Okay, Mrs. Richmond, what got you all up in an uproar?"

"First, it's seven o'clock, and you should have been home. Second, it's raining hard enough for Noah to bring out the ark for a second ride, but we would have missed the boat if they were going two by two. Well, me and Kenny Jr. would have been on it, but your tail would be left out somewhere, floating around trying to find safety."

"Okay, Sylvia, what's this really about? I had a hard day at the office. It must be the weather because Marvin was acting strange today, too. Talking in riddles. It was crazy. Have you talked to Rachel? Is something going on with them?"

"Now that you mention it, I just hung up with Rachel as you were coming in. Funny, she was asking if you had shared anything with me about something happening at the office today."

"Why would Rachel ask you that?"

"Same reason you asked if I talked to her. She claims Marvin came home in an irritable mood. Said she's never seen him act that way before. He even threw Roland out of the house."

"Marvin needed to throw him out of the house. Roland equals money. Rachel has some expensive tastes, and while the company is doing great, that doesn't mean spend every dad-burn penny you've got. That's why I like my sensible woman. She likes nice but doesn't take it to the extreme. Come here and give your man a kiss."

"I don't want a kiss if it's going to be a repeat of what you walked in the house with. That was a waste of time."

Kenny drew Sylvia to him. "I'm going to show you

what a real kiss feels like." He squeezed her hard and placed a passionate kiss on her lips. "Kenny Junior, close your eyes." Kenny Jr. did as he was told.

"Remember when we first got back together after not seeing each other after all those years?"

"Yes," Sylvia said, her eyes closed, feeling the moment.

"The passion and desire..."

"I think that was all you, Kenny." Sylvia opened her eyes and stared at him.

"Maybe it was, but girl, I've got the hots for you, now," Kenny whispered in her ear. "Show your man that you love him." Kenny placed a long hard, hot kiss on Sylvia lips, and she returned it in kind. "Maybe it's time for little Kenny to go to bed." Kenny opened his eyes and looked at Kenny Jr. "Look at him, Sylvia. He still has his eyes closed."

They both broke out in a laugh, and so did Kenny Jr. Kenny Sr. scooped little Kenny up in his arms. "Time for bed, man. I'll give him his bath and you need to be waiting for me in the bedroom when I'm finished," Kenny whispered again to Sylvia.

"What about dinner?"

"I like leftovers, but right now I'm ready for dessert—creamy chocolate mousse."

"One dessert coming right up."

"Sylvia, there's something going on with Marvin. I feel it in my gut. I don't know what it is, but reflecting back on a couple of things he was saying, it requires some investigation."

"Well, take that phone out of your ear long enough to find out. Rachel thanks you in advance. Now, hurry up with Kenny Jr. and don't keep me waiting."

Kenny stuck out his tongue, made circles with it, and licked his lips. "Bring your A game, girl, 'cuz you're going to be singing like that rain outside."

"Bring it on!"

# CHAPTER SEVEN

Mona, dressed in a sleek, black St. John pantsuit, black patent leather stilettos, and large, round, black earrings that matched her bobbed hair, stalked the aisles of the supermarket for the ingredients that were going to make her She Crab Soup supreme. Fresh crabs were flown in from Maryland, and the petite sirloins had just arrived from Nebraska in vacuum-packed crates kept cool by dry ice.

Mona had looked forward to catering this event because the movers and shakers were giants in business and politics, and this was an opportunity of a lifetime, an opportunity that might make her part of the White House team who planned elegant and elaborate meals for the president and first lady, heads of state, foreign diplomats, kings and queens from nations all over the world. It excited her to no end that the invitation to the fundraiser came with a price tag of $1,500 a plate; she was already calculating her share.

She moved swiftly down the aisle that housed the seasonings and picked up a can of cayenne pepper and a bottle of dry sherry. Now, her She Crab Soup would zing with a taste the diners would never forget. Reaching up again, she grabbed a few more seasonings that she would surely need at a later date.

Finished, she wheeled her cart down the aisle in a hurry to get out of the store. Without looking left or right, Mona plowed straight ahead and suddenly hit a customer.

"Damn, lady, where did you get your driver's license? Mona?" Kenny asked as she peeled her hands from her face.

"Kenny, are you alright? So sorry, brother, I hope I didn't hurt you."

Kenny sighed and then they both laughed. "Girl, you better have insurance 'cause I'm going to sue you."

"I had lots on my mind. Trying to get ready for this fund-raising dinner I'm catering for Barack Obama. What are you doing in the store?"

"Sylvia asked me to stop by on my way home and get some tomato paste for the spaghetti sauce she's making. But look here, Mona. This might be my lucky day. I was serious when I said I'd like to be on the guest list for that event you're catering."

"Kenny, I have nothing to do with the guest list. And if you were on it, you'd have to come up with fifteen-hundred dollars to get in."

"Sh—," Kenny began and retracted his thought. He stood in the aisle a moment in deep contemplation.

"What if I pretend that I'm one of your workers for the evening? I can serve drinks or something else that's easy."

"This is important to you, huh?"

"It would mean the world, Mona. And, I won't sue your tail for causing me bodily harm with that grocery cart."

"Well, I haven't turned in my final list of employees to the host yet. I have until day after tomorrow." Mona screwed her face up and looked up at the ceiling in thought. "Okay, I've thought about it. If it's that important to you, I'll put you on the list. But your tail is going to work, and you will not ruin my reputation by pulling some crazy shenanigans while you're there. Is that clear?"

"Clear as a whistle. As always, it's a pleasure doing business with you, Mona."

"Just remember what I said or there will be hell to pay."

"Got ya. Give Michael my best." Kenny blew Mona a kiss.

"Will do."

Kenny strolled out of the supermarket on a high. Whatever was eating at Marvin could wait. He was going to be in the big leagues—with some heavy hitters, and he needed to get home and do some strategizing with his broker to make the best of an unusual opportunity.

# CHAPTER EIGHT

Marvin scribbled something on a piece of paper and set it aside. He blew air from his nostrils, then picked up the intercom.

"Yvonne, please come in the office and bring your steno pad."

"Yes, Mr. Thomas."

Yvonne had been with Thomas and Richmond Tecktronics, Inc. for ten years and had begun her career as a receptionist and now was the administrative assistant to the boss. She was short and way overweight unable to get rid of the extra pounds even after trying fad diet after fad diet. But she was proficient in her work, and Marvin rewarded her accordingly. Yvonne walked into Marvin's office with pen and pad, took a seat at one of the chairs facing his desk, adjusted her glasses, and waited for him to begin.

"Thursday, October 2, 2008," Marvin began. "Leave the name of the addressee blank...no, put Mr. Harold Thomas—look up the address for me."

"Okay, Mr. Thomas."

"The body of the letter is as follows:

"Dear Harold: It's with much regret that I find myself writing this letter to you. Although our estrangement has been of a mutual nature, I find myself missing the person who was not only my partner and cousin but a friend whose friendship I truly once cherished. Circumstances beyond my control have brought me to this moment.

"I have urgent business issues that I would like to seek your advice about, circumstances which I do not wish to discuss in this letter. It would be much appreciated if you could give me a call at your earliest convenience at 404-551-5555, day or night.

"Thank you in advance. I hope all is well with you. Sincerely, Marvin."

Yvonne stopped writing and looked at her boss over the top of her glasses. "Is there any way I can be of assistance to you, Mr. Thomas? I've been with you almost from the beginning, and I owe you a debt of gratitude for all you've done for me."

Marvin looked at Yvonne as if looking at her for the first time. She was an attractive woman, and if she lost about eighty pounds, she'd probably turn a lot of heads. "No, Yvonne. Sometimes you've got to handle some things by yourself. One more letter.

"Office of the Attorney General—look up the address." Yvonne looked up from her pad and acknowledged his directive.

"Dear Sir, Thomas and Richmond Tecktronics, Inc. has experienced considerable growth and profits during its ten-year tenure. Our products have served the public well and as a minority company, we have competed with some of the top producers of electronic products. We have a little over one hundred employees whose loyalty and commitment to the company's goals are second to none.

"Read that back to me, Yvonne." Yvonne read the first paragraph and waited for Marvin to continue.

"In our rise to our present status, we've made some good and bad business decisions—more good than bad. However, some bad investments have now caught up with us, and I'm appealing to your office to give us some latitude as we attempt to pay the federal government the 1.5 million dollars we owe in back taxes due to company losses we've experienced. Sir, I ask your assistance in allowing Thomas and Richmond Tecktronics an extension in paying the taxes it owes. This appeal, this request, is made with urgency as the company is also in the throes of a possible takeover."

As if a lightning bolt had hit it, Yvonne's writing hand began to shake and the pen fell to the floor. "Excuse me, Sir," she said, her voice nervous. She leaned over her chair and picked up the pencil.

"Are you alright, Yvonne?"

"Yes, sir." Yvonne looked thoughtfully at Marvin. "Mr. Thomas, are we in trouble?"

Marvin looked thoughtfully at Yvonne. He hated the desperate look on her face—the pleading and concern that begged for an answer. "We're almost finished. Read back the last sentence."

Yvonne's lips began to tremble. She adjusted her glasses and with the tip of her pen glided over her shorthand and began to read. "I'm also in the throes of a possible takeover." She refused to look up at Marvin.

"Alright. Beginning with takeover...let's say and depending upon the outcome, the company may be subject to new leadership. *New paragraph*.

"Thomas and Richmond Tecktronics is the company I built from the ground up. I'd like to preserve the legacy for my children. With your assistance, I've pledged to myself that I'll do whatever it takes to keep the company afloat. *New paragraph*.

"Thank you for your time and consideration, and I look forward to your favorable response. Sincerely, Marvin Thomas, CEO, Thomas and Richmond Tecktronics."

"Okay, Yvonne, if you can have those letters transcribed and on my desk in the next hour, I'd appreciate it."

"Yes, sir." Yvonne rose from her chair and turned around to face Marvin. She withdrew her glasses from her face. "Mr. Thomas, if this situation is going to affect my livelihood and position in this organization, would you be so kind as to let me know in time?"

Marvin wrung his hands together. Thoughts ran through his head as he looked at Yvonne who was anticipating his answer. She seemed so sincere. He wondered if she had ever been with a man. In all the time that she had been employed with the company, there was never any mention of a husband, let alone a man. A dedicated employee, you could count the amount of sick days she had taken in the last ten years on one hand.

"Yes, Yvonne, I wouldn't leave you in limbo. Every employee at Thomas and Richmond Tecktronics deserves to know in advance about their uncertain future. I just don't know how to go about telling them— I'm hoping that it will not come to that."

"What about Mr. Richmond? He doesn't seem to have the same…same concerns as you. Every time he comes into the office, he's always so chipper."

"Mr. Richmond isn't aware of the financial trouble we're in."

"But I thought you were partners?"

"We are partners, Yvonne, however as the CEO, I chose not to disclose all company matters to Mr. Richmond, although he's entitled to every bit of information I know. His expertise is in sales, and he pretty much leaves the rest of the company worries to me.

"I hope I was able to satisfy your question. I'd appreciate receiving those letters in the next hour."

"Yes, Mr. Richmond. Thank you."

When the door had closed behind Yvonne, Marvin picked up the phone and made several calls before finally dialing Cecil Coleman's office. He needed another meeting to sort things out because he was running out of time.

# CHAPTER NINE

"**G**irl, shopping does me a world of good," Rachel said, as she and Sylvia continued to browse the racks at Neiman Marcus."

"Me, too. Remind me to pick up a white formal shirt for Kenny. He's got a job with Mona, pretending to be a waiter at her catering affair tomorrow night so he can court one of the bigwigs with some proposal he's got."

"Does he know who's going to be there?"

"Besides Barack Obama? Hell if I know. Kenny's such a go-getter. He'd make a proposal to Mickey Mouse if he knew that there was a possibility that the big fake mouse would make a deal." The girls laughed.

"Marvin certainly needed someone like Kenny to help grow the company. Together our men have conquered the world. By the way, did you ask Kenny if he had noticed anything strange going on with Marvin?"

"Yeah, Kenny said he went to his office yesterday to touch base with him and he was saying off-the-wall things—talking in riddles. Kenny wasn't sure what to make of it."

"He seemed to be in a much better mood this morning. Well, I'm going to shop for myself to my heart's content."

"You still upset because Marvin told you to cancel the drapes?"

"Girl, Roland was some kind of mad. Called Marvin some kind of every name in the book and then some." The ladies laughed. "Oh, Sylvia, this pair of Cole Haan shoes is calling my name."

"I think you're right, Rachel. What's the asking price?"

"They say if you have to ask the price, you don't need to be in the store."

"And I say, Marvin is going to whoop your ass. No drapes, no shoes." Sylvia laughed at herself.

"Girl, please. This pair of shoes is going with this diva housewife." Rachel stopped and looked at the stake on the display that announced the price. She hit her chest with the palm of her hand. "Whew, a whopping three hundred and forty dollars. But girl, I've got to have them. I sure hope I put my Neiman's card in my purse."

"Yeah," Sylvia said, trying to suppress a giggle as Rachel clawed around in her purse for her wallet, "they don't take that other plastic stuff unless it's American Express."

"Here it is!" Rachel shouted in triumph.

"Hurry up and purchase your shoes, Miz Thang. I need to go to Macy's and look for a few things."

"Don't rush me, Sylvia. This is the fun part of shopping."

"Okay, Sis. Take your time. I'm going to mosey on over to Macy's. You know where to find me."

"In the kids department. It's not like Kenny Jr. needs another thing in his wardrobe."

"No, he doesn't, but I saw a pretty dress last week that I want to pick up for Serena."

"Are you trying to say that I don't buy my baby anything?"

Sylvia was holding her sides. Rachel was so comical to watch. "No, big baby. Serena's my godchild, and if I want to bless her with a new dress, that's what I'm going to do."

"Okay, you crazy girl. I'll see you in a moment."

Instead of the one pair of shoes, Rachel made it two. The second pair was on sale for one hundred and ninety-nine dollars—a steal. It felt good to be able to buy anything she wanted without worry. She just couldn't understand Marvin's sudden outburst about the drapes.

"That will be five hundred, seventy-six dollars and seventy-three cents," the sales clerk said.

Rachel gave the woman her Neiman's card with confidence and smiled when she was handed her bagged purchases. Looking around for something else to buy but not finding it, Rachel abandoned her search and headed for Macy's.

Swinging her package, Rachel spotted Sylvia. "Look at you with your arms full. Thought you weren't getting anything for Kenny Jr."

"Okay, heifer. I've got a dress in my hand for your

child, and you know better than to think that I wasn't going to get something for my own. Couldn't pass on these bargains. So shut up, and let's shop."

Rachel stuck out her lip. "Ouch. I deserved that, but I'm down with getting our shopping on."

"Let's do it," Sylvia said with a smile and shook her head at her best friend. "You make shopping fun."

Exhausted after two hours of serious shopping, Sylvia and Rachel headed to the check-out counter. Sylvia placed her items on the counter and whistled when the cashier gave her the total—buyer's remorse already settling in. She gathered up her purchases and waited for Rachel to check out.

"I'm hungry," Rachel said, turning slightly toward Sylvia as the cashier scanned her items.

"I'm a little famished myself. Let's go to the Cheese-cake Factory."

"Sounds good."

"Ma'am," the sales clerk said, "your total is four hundred and fifty-nine dollars. Will you be paying with your Macy's card?"

"No, Visa," Rachel replied. She pulled her credit card from her wallet and passed it to the clerk.

The clerk ran the card through the reader and looked up at Rachel. "Ma'am, your card is declined."

"What?" Rachel's eyes danced in her head. "Couldn't be. Swipe it again."

The sales clerk crunched her face and twisted her lips. "Whatever."

"Whatever," Rachel repeated. She felt her pressure rise and the onset of a headache.

The sales clerk took the card and swiped it again. "Declined," the clerk said in a nasty tone.

For a brief moment Rachel thought about taking off her shoe and knocking the smirk off the clerk's face. Before she could commit to anything, Sylvia stepped forward and offered to pay.

"No, no," Rachel said, shaking her head and waving her hand. "I have another card; I'll try it."

Rachel passed the piece of plastic to the clerk who took it reluctantly. Agitated, the clerk swiped the card so fast, Rachel could have sworn she stripped the strip off the back of the card.

"Declined," the clerk said with a smirk of satisfaction.

"Keep it," Rachel said. Her head ached and the veins in her temples began to flair.

"I'll put it on my card," Sylvia offered, patting Rachel on the shoulder.

"No, let's go." Tears formed in Rachel's eyes. She clung to her Neiman's bag and stormed out of Macy's.

Sylvia was at her side. "Hey, sweetie, it's going to be alright."

"That was so damn humiliating, Sylvia. Did you see how that nasty wench looked at me—like I was some kind of ghetto momma on welfare trying to charge a whole lot of stuff with no money? I just don't understand what's going on, but I've got to get to the bottom of this."

"Yeah, the sales clerk's customer service needed an attitude check. But, you're certainly no ghetto momma because the only plastic a ghetto momma is going to have is her driver's license. I want you to know, though, that there are a lot of good ghetto mommas out there that can't help the circumstance they find themselves in."

"Well, I'm not a ghetto momma." Rachel pulled her cell phone out of her purse and dialed Marvin's office.

"Yvonne, is Marvin there? I need to speak with him right away."

"Hold on a moment, Mrs. Thomas, and let me check. He has a meeting scheduled across town, and he may have left already."

"Thank you, Yvonne."

Seconds passed. "Mrs. Thomas, Mr. Thomas is not available. He must have already left for his afternoon appointment."

Rachel sighed. "Thanks, Yvonne. I'll try to reach him on his cell." She hung up and called Marvin's cell, but the call went straight to voice mail.

"Let's get lunch, my treat," Sylvia offered.

Rachel threw her arms in the air and let out a long sigh. "I'm not feeling lunch, Sylvia. I need to know what's going on with my cards."

"Calm down, sweetie. It's probably a fluke. Let's get lunch and we'll sort this out later."

"Maybe you're right," Rachel sighed again. "But let's

stop by the bank on the way. I want to have some cash on me."

"You got it."

Wide eyes stared, then shifted as the door that adjoined Yvonne's office to her boss' opened. Marvin walked the few paces to Yvonne's desk and sat on the edge of it.

"Thanks, Yvonne. I wasn't in the mood to talk to Mrs. Thomas at that moment. Did she say what she wanted?"

"No, sir. She said it was urgent, though."

"I'm sure it was," Marvin said under his breath. "Yvonne, how would you like to join me for lunch?"

"Well," Yvonne hesitated, her eyes shifting from her boss to the computer screen careful to avoid his eyes. "Don't you have an appointment with Attorney Coleman this afternoon?"

"That's true, but my appointment isn't until two-thirty. I think I'd like to take my loyal and trusted employee to lunch just before I go to meet Mr. Coleman. I owe you more than a quick lunch during Secretaries Week. Yvonne...you've been a rock, and whatever may happen to Thomas and Richmond or me, I'm going to make sure you're taken care of."

Batting her eyes, a broad smile crept across Yvonne's face. She adjusted her glasses and squeezed her lips together. "Thank you, Mr. Thomas. I appreciate your kind words and vote of confidence. I'll get my purse."

Marvin smiled at Yvonne's innocence and rubbed his chin. He slid from her desk and retrieved his coat from his office.

# CHAPTER TEN

The nerve of the city was busy transacting its business and reporting world news. Visitors from all over the world converged on Atlanta daily—Atlanta being the hub for international travel and to everywhere else in the nation. Colorful artwork graced the sides of buildings in the old part of Atlanta's downtown district while street salesmen capitalized on the historic moment in political history by selling Obama T-shirts.

Shifting lanes, Sylvia drove from Buckhead heading for the Cheesecake Factory. Rachel sulked and sat slouched down in the passenger seat of the car, although if it hadn't been for the seat buckle that caressed her breasts and held her in place, she might have slid to the floor. The awkward silence made Sylvia long for the comfort of Kenny's arms because Rachel's funk was beginning to depress her.

"There's a Bank of America," Rachel shouted, pointing to the building across the street.

Sylvia sighed. She was in the right lane of a divided and crowded four-lane street without the possibility of turning around. Five blocks down at the light, Sylvia made a right turn, made a U-turn, and then made another left turn at the light and headed back to the bank. Rachel had sat in silence while Sylvia negotiated the turns but nearly jumped out of the car when Sylvia approached the bank. It wouldn't have been a big deal to Sylvia if the person she was trying to cheer up wasn't acting if she was the one who had made her life miserable.

Sylvia watched as Rachel walked to the teller machine, slapped her debit card in, punched in some numbers, tapping her toes on the pavement as she waited for the money to be dispersed. All of a sudden a version of an Alvin Ailey dance performance commenced as Rachel's hands began to reach for the sky and back down again. She stomped her feet, slapped the side of the teller machine, then took her Coach bag by the handle and rammed the machine with all her might.

It was a sight. Sylvia laughed and laughed because Rachel looked so comical—like a wannabe bank robber who forgot to go inside the bank to steal money from the real tellers instead of an unmanned steel vault that was built like Ft. Knox.

But someone inside didn't think it was so comical. Sylvia sat up in her seat when four city cops surrounded Rachel with their guns drawn. With an outstretched hand, one of the cops reached out for Rachel, but she grabbed her face, covered her ears and began to wail.

Sylvia jumped from her car and ran to help Rachel.

However, the toting cops aimed their guns at her and asked her to halt. Hands flew straight into the air.

"Sir, Mrs. Thomas is my friend." Pointing to her car, Sylvia began, "I was sitting in my car waiting for her to get some money out of the teller machine. She must have gotten some bad news because right after she read the slip of paper the machine spit out, she has not been the same. Maybe I can talk to her."

"Well, go ahead," one of the police officers barked.

Shame tossed to the wind, Rachel sat on her knees on the ground, her face a giant puffy ball drenched with water. She started screaming again, uttering words that were incomprehensible.

"Rachel, sweetie," Sylvia began, "what's wrong?"

"There's no money in my damn bank account; that's what's wrong," she hollered between sobs. "It's got to be Marvin; who else? Sylvia, do you think he disappeared from the face of the earth with our g—damn money?"

"Calm down, honey."

"What kind of friend are you? The only thing you know to say is calm down, Rachel. That's not going to bring my money back. I don't want to calm down!" Rachel shouted.

"If you don't calm down," Sylvia said with fire in her eyes, "I'm going to do what these police officers are itching to do—that is smack you upside your head. I've put my neck out for you. Next time I'll just sit in the car and watch them beat your little ass."

The cops put their guns away and tried to hide their

snickering. It was apparent that the woman who was now sitting on the ground with her feet stretched out in front of her was too pitiful to attempt a bank robbery.

"Ma'am, you need to take your friend home where she can get some rest and maybe some help," the police officer said. Two of the other officers lifted Rachel from the ground.

Sylvia reached in her purse for a Kleenex. "Why did you have to embarrass us like that?" Sylvia asked as she handed a tissue to Rachel so she could wipe the snot from her nose. Rachel said nothing. "Let's go before they have us on the local news."

Rachel looked up at Sylvia with a tear-stained face. "Sorry," she mouthed. They walked back to the car, got in and sped away.

In a soft voice, Rachel asked, "Why is this happening to me, Sylvia? I'm a good wife and mother. I do my civic duties in my community. I go to church—well, every now and then."

"That's the problem," Sylvia said.

"What?" Rachel yelled.

"Calm...chill out."

"Too late."

"Look, Rachel. I don't know what's going on with your finances, and I'm sure there is a reasonable explanation for all of this. When you see Marvin tonight, he'll clear it all up."

"I hope so," Rachel pouted. "So...you were trying to

say a minute ago that I've been AWOL—absent without leave from my Father's house?"

"Sounds like you already know the answer." Sylvia patted Rachel on the arm. "It's going to be alright. Look how far we've come."

"You're right, Sylvia. I know I looked like Boo Foo the Fool today. Oh God, I hope no one saw me. I don't want to go down in the Lord's book of shame."

"You already have, sister. Expect the Lifetime Movie Network to offer you a movie deal any day now."

"Thanks for being there for me once again. If I were you, I would have left me as soon as the cops drew their guns."

"I'm sure you would have," Sylvia laughed, "but I'm better than that, and you know it."

"Would you have really kicked my behind?"

"So you were cognizant of what was going on. I'll tell you this one thing, Rachel Thomas, you were already tap dancing on my last nerve, and if you had dared to say one more thing, I was going to beat you down to the white meat."

"Violent, sister." Rachel shook her head. "Scared of you."

"You ought to be. And if I were you, you don't want to try me anymore today."

Rachel poked her mouth out and turned toward Sylvia. "One more question."

"What, Rachel? You're a lot of work, girl."

"All I was going to ask was if the offer for lunch is still on. Don't have any money on me, but a nice meal with my best girlfriend is probably what the doctor would order."

"Yeah, girl." Sylvia smiled. "Why don't we go to Steak and Ale for old times' sakes?"

"Let's do it for the Ex-Files. It's hard to believe we used to meet there as pitiful and lonely divorced souls looking for a way out of the gloom…"

"But we had a good time and now we're happier than we've ever been. I see a place to park. Hold on, girl, I'm going to do a quick 'U' and get that spot that has my name on it."

Rachel held onto the door handle to keep from sliding. "Steak and Ale, here we come."

# CHAPTER ELEVEN

Corporate types and other professionals crowded the restaurant for lunch. Chatter about the day's events could be heard from a table nearby and a celebratory roast for a pregnant woman surrounded by what looked like ten of her office mates bearing gifts took place at another.

"It will be a fifteen-minute wait," the hostess said to Sylvia and Rachel who stood along with several others who seemed anxious to have lunch.

"I wished we had gotten here at eleven-thirty," Rachel said. "We would have missed the lunch crowd."

"Well, it was a little hard to do that when you were out on the street auditioning for a part in *Bonnie and Clyde*."

"That was not funny, Sylvia. I lost my head for a moment, but I'm fine now. I just need to find my husband so I can tell him what happened. I'll call him when we leave the restaurant."

"Richmond," the hostess called out. "Follow me."

"That didn't take long at all." Sylvia grinned. "I'm going to get the biggest steak they have."

"I don't eat red meat, but I'm going to eat like it's my last day on earth."

"Be careful what you ask for."

The hostess seated them and passed out menus. "Your waiter will be with you in a moment."

"Choices, choices, choices," Rachel uttered, glancing through the menu for something that was going to satisfy and give her a moment of contentment, which she hadn't been able to achieve for most of the day.

"Well, I'm going to have a ribeye with a fully loaded baked potato and a scrumptious salad," Sylvia said, satisfied with her decision, closing the menu.

"I guess I'll settle on a grilled chicken salad. It won't damage your pocketbook or my gorgeous figure."

"You can have whatever you want, Rachel. What are girls for if we can't treat our sisters like queens every once in a while?"

"That's what I like about you big sister, Sylvia. You know, Kenny is a blessed human being. To have a second chance with such a generous, forgiving, understanding woman like yourself means the world. You know I'm talking about myself, too."

Sylvia smiled. "Ditto. Even with all of your drama, I couldn't have a better friend."

"Ladies, my name is Consuelo, and I'll be your server this afternoon. What would you like to drink?"

"I'm not driving," Rachel said without hesitation. "I'll have a glass of Beringer."

"So I'm stuck with drinking sweet tea?" Sylvia laughed. "Sweet tea for me." Sylvia twirled her index finger.

"I'll be right back," Consuelo said, and moved away from the table.

"Sitting in here reminds me of my working days when we'd come down here and celebrate someone's birthday," Rachel said.

"Missing the camaraderie of your BellSouth buddies? Every now and then, I think about putting my professional hat back on."

"Really? I thought you were enjoying being the stay-at-home mom and giving Kenny Jr. your undivided attention."

"I didn't say I didn't enjoy it, but I don't feel as fulfilled as I thought I would. I have given this a lot of thought. I'm going to open up my own event planning agency."

"Wow, Sylvia, that's exciting. I didn't know. I know that when Serena starts kindergarten, I'll probably go back to work."

"No more kids?"

"If I don't get a handle on what's happening with my finances, I'm not going to have any more anything."

"Hey, turn around and look over in the corner," Sylvia said, as Rachel strained to look in the direction Sylvia indicated. "Isn't that Marvin with...what's her name...?"

"You mean Yvonne?"

The color began to drain from Rachel's face. Her

teeth began to scrape together as her eyes began to take on a new shape while her cheeks sat perched next to her nose.

"What's wrong, Rachel?" Concern was written all over Sylvia's face. She couldn't take another one of Rachel's outbursts if that was what her sudden metamorphosis was leading up to. "Tell me what's wrong."

"You remember when I called Marvin's office to ask him about the credit cards?"

"Yes."

"Well, Yvonne answered the phone and said Marvin wasn't available and that he was on his way to an appointment. That couldn't have been more than thirty minutes ago. While I was at the bank making a fool out of my damn self, my husband has been sitting at a restaurant wining and dining his secretary. It seems his credit cards aren't having the same trouble as mine."

"You aren't going to go over there and confront him I hope?"

"Very good suggestion, Sylvia. Hell yeah, I'm going over there and confront him."

"Your Beringer and sweet tea," Consuelo said, setting the beverages down on the table. "Are you ready to order?"

"Consuelo, why don't you give us another fifteen minutes? When the time is up, we'll decide if we want to eat or not." Rachel blew air from her nose.

Hands knotted in a ball, Sylvia lightly rapped the

table. "Don't make a fool out of yourself, friend. It may be nothing at all. Yvonne may be an innocent pawn in all of this."

"Look at them chatting like they're the only ones in the room. That heifer doesn't even have her glasses on, and I know she can't see without them. I thought I'd conquered my jealousies as it concerned Denise, but what in the hell does Marvin see in that one?"

"Rachel," Sylvia said slowly, "bosses take their secretaries to lunch all the time."

"Not when you know your credit cards aren't worth two cents. I'm getting up and going over there, and don't try and stop me, Sylvia."

"Oh, hell. I'm going to the bathroom. I can't be a witness to this display of domestic violence. You're taking it to a new level, Rachel."

"Suit yourself." Rachel got up from her seat and marched to Marvin's table.

# CHAPTER TWELVE

$\triangle$ ylvia ducked into the restroom, hoping time would be on her side. By the time she reappeared, all of Rachel's steam and thunder would be gone and they could enjoy the lunch she so wanted to eat.

She exited the stall, and while she washed her hands, two women entered the restroom.

"That sister was laying that brother out," the girl with the red lipstick and long ponytail said.

"She should have knocked him upside his head. Did you see the sister cringe in her seat when the brother's girlfriend or wife got all up in his face?" the girl with the braids asked.

"Yeah, and I don't get it 'cuz she was fat and didn't look as good as the sister with the rap," Ponytail responded.

"Girl, I wish I would catch my old man up in some restaurant with some sloppy-looking wench when he got all of this," the girl in braids said.

Sylvia came from her corner after pretending to check her makeup. It was time to save Rachel from herself because if Sylvia didn't, she might have to resurrect the Ex-Files.

Shaking her head, Sylvia gathered her composure and exited the restroom. It was obvious that Rachel was still the live entertainment. Heads were turned in her direction as she waved her arms up and down, demanding an answer to this and an answer to that.

"Marvin, I'm not going to stand here much longer," Rachel shouted. "I don't understand how you can treat yourself and this woman to lunch when all over town my credit cards are getting no respect."

"I'm not going to talk to you about our business in front of the whole business community, and I certainly don't have anything to say to you until you calm down."

"Calm down? Is that all you people can say to me? You, Sylvia—calm down, calm down. My life is in crisis. How in the hell am I going to calm down?"

Yvonne fumbled in her purse for her glasses, put them on and got up to leave.

"Where do you think you're going, Yvonne? You lied to me. You told me Marvin was at a meeting, but you never figured you were going to bump into me... did you?"

Marvin stood up. "Rachel, shut up. I am on the way to a meeting in a few minutes. I just returned to the office after Yvonne hung up with you. She told you the truth, and I will not have you disrespecting her like that. Yvonne has regarded you as a friend and always talks highly of you, and in a matter of a minute, you've changed every good thought she's ever had about you."

"It's okay, Mr. Thomas." Tears rolled down Yvonne's face. She pushed past Rachel and fled to the bathroom.

"Hmph," Rachel said. "So if you got the message, why didn't you call?"

"Rachel, let's go. You've shown your tail for the last time today," Sylvia cut in. "Hi, Marvin." Sylvia sighed.

"Hey, Sylvia," Marvin said, his head bent down.

"Folks, you are going to have to take this outside the restaurant," the manager said, coming from out of nowhere. "You're disturbing the other patrons."

"I'm out of here," Marvin said, leaving several bills on the table. "I'll talk with you this evening, Mrs. Thomas." He pushed past Sylvia and Rachel and walked out of the restaurant.

"I don't know what's going on with you and Marvin," Sylvia said, "but you both need a therapist, and you need help real soon— more sooner than later."

"I can't believe he dissed me in front of everybody. My own husband—the man I would give my life for," Rachel said.

"Just think about how you've acted in the last hour or two," Sylvia retorted. "Maybe that'll give you a clue. I'm taking you home because I've had enough for today."

"Suit yourself."


"Hey, Mona, this is Kenny. Looking forward to tomorrow night. Sometime during the dinner, I need to have Michael introduce me to some of the bigwigs."

"He'll have to play it by ear, Kenny. My husband isn't going to compromise his chance to possibly become the next surgeon general—that is if Barack Obama becomes president."

"Get out of here. I know the good Dr. Michael Broussard is well known amongst Atlanta's social circles, but being considered for the spot of surgeon general is something to be proud of."

"Yes, my baby's got it going on. I'm so proud of him."

"Mona, I would have never said this to you, but you and Michael are a dynamic couple. I've even watched you evolve as a person—especially after you got all that cynicism out of you. You were a witch way back when."

"Watch it, Kenny Richmond, because I can have your name removed from that list you were so bound and determined to be on. But I deserved that—I wasn't too kind to you when you and Sylvia first got back together. Remember, that was the night I met Michael. He was so handsome."

"Yeah, I remember. It was the night that Sylvia and I knew that it was the beginning of the rest of our lives."

"Wow, Mr. Richmond, that was pretty poetic."

"Okay, Mona, just checking in with you. I'll be on my best behavior. I'm just trying to use every tool I've got to move Thomas and Richmond Tecktronics forward."

"Well, I'd like to help. We're all family now; we're in this together."

"Thanks, Mona. That feels good."

"I meant it, Kenny. You and Sylvia are close to my heart. See you tomorrow."

"Alright."

Kenny put the phone on its base and nodded his head. He smiled at the small walk down memory lane. Mona hated his guts then, but now she was a lioness with grace and beauty. He could have never conceived that a support group started by Sylvia for the lost and lonely would knit together a wonderful relationship between all the members. It was as if their destiny had been ordained by God and that the sun and the moon were put in the heavens exclusively for them—to light their pathway as love and prosperity rained down on them.

He swiveled around in the chair that sat beneath his desk and turned toward the picture of he and Sylvia on their wedding day. Picking up the photo, he kissed Sylvia. "I love you, girl." He remembered the day he whisked her off to a jewelry store in Buckhead so that he could place the engagement ring he had bought earlier on her finger. He remembered Jamaica and how blue the water was all around them on the island resort— the day they said "I do" with family and friends…good friends—Rachel and Marvin, Mona and Michael, and Claudette and Tyrone. And Sylvia was so beautiful— like a sea goddess dressed in an off-white and gold nearly sheer silk dress that was sleeveless and had a elegant handmade gold leaf braid that extended from the bodice and wrapped around her neck. He remembered the baby's breath that flowed through her upswept hair.

He also remembered attending the weddings of each of those friends—Rachel and Marvin, Mona and Michael, and the restatement of Claudette and Tyrone's vows. He put the picture down and suddenly longed to be home with his wife.

He had buzzed Marvin several times this afternoon, but since there was no answer assumed Marvin had given Yvonne the rest of the day off and took one, too. Kenny was concerned about Marvin's sudden mood change. It made him a little jittery. But promises of tomorrow night made Kenny put thoughts of Marvin's recent attitude on the back burner. He had put together some proposals that he hoped would net him either some new clients and/or investors.

Kenny made one last call, shut down his computer, picked up his briefcase and headed home. Outside of the building, a flower peddler was trying to get rid of his last two bouquets. Money in hand, Kenny bought both of them and made the man's day.

# CHAPTER THIRTEEN

"Exhale," Marvin said to himself as he sat in the underground parking garage. Images of his fight with Rachel invaded his thoughts—images he tried to shake but couldn't no matter how hard he tried. Some of her ranting and raving was his doing or undoing depended upon whose view it was, but her very immature and embarrassing public display in the restaurant was more than he could handle.

He should have told her about the credit cards—the what and the why. Admitting failure before it was time was not his style, either, and whatever lengths and hoops he had to go through to save Thomas and Richmond and his family's well-being was the risk he had to take.

The call from Cecil Coleman held a promise—a promise that he could fight the giants with a slingshot—the giants who threatened to make what was his theirs. If Cecil couldn't help, there had to be somebody who could.

Looking at his watch, Marvin exited the car and went into the building and caught the elevator to the first floor. It seemed as if it were just yesterday that he had passed this way—through the double glass doors that opened up into the foyer with the terrarium. Gretchen, the receptionist, looked up and greeted Marvin with a very sultry smile.

"Good afternoon, Mr. Thomas. If you'll have a seat, I'll let Mr. Coleman know that you're here."

"Thank you," Marvin said, changing his mind about flirting back. Gretchen's hair was pulled back into a bun that was piled high on her head, which made her look sexy. Gone were the horn-rimmed glasses and in their place, ocean-blue eyes that seemed to bore through Marvin's soul. It would have been a mistake to flirt. He could see Gretchen climbing over the desk that separated them, skirt and all. He shook the thought from his mind.

Several minutes went by before Gretchen called Marvin to her desk. "Mr. Coleman will see you now. Go down the hall to the elevators, which will be on your right. Take the elevator to the twenty-ninth floor. When you exit, make a sharp left turn, and Mr. Coleman's office will be right there."

"Thank you, Gretchen," Marvin said with a smile. "I know how to get there." She smiled back and Marvin was on his way.

The ride up was not as impressive a view as it had been the first time he had come to Lancaster, Bosche, and Coleman at Law. The urgency of the matter that brought him there was at the forefront of his thoughts.

He exited the elevator and approached Cecil's door that stood ajar.

Hesitantly, Marvin pushed the door open. Cecil Coleman's back was to him, giving instructions to someone Marvin didn't see. Marvin looked around and finally noticed the door that sat on the other side of the conference table.

"Hey, buddy," Cecil said, getting up from his chair to give Marvin a handshake. "Last-minute instructions to my secretary," he said, as if he could read Marvin's mind.

"I was wondering if you had a secretary. Didn't see a little cutie like the receptionist downstairs. She's flirted with me each time I've come."

"Who, Gretchen?"

"Yeah. Last week she had on those ugly glasses and her blonde hair was all over the place. Today, she looks totally different—almost as if she was expecting someone."

Cecil laughed. "It might have been you, partner. Anyway, I do have a secretary who shares an office with two others in the next room. Richard Bosche's office is on the other side. But let's talk about you."

"I want to save Thomas and Richmond Tecktronics. That's why I'm here. I've got to know that you're going to fight for us…and we're going to win."

"Have you shared this with Richmond? It would be a catastrophe to have this blow up in your face and you haven't let your partner in on what's going on."

"I plan to do it this weekend. I'm hoping you will have something concrete to tell me so that when I tell Kenny, I can assure him that our lives won't be interrupted and this was but a minor annoyance that's about to go away."

"It's not going away, Marvin. I've spoken with the bidders who want to make a tender offer on the down-low for your stake in the company." Cecil eyed Marvin, who sat with his head bent down and rolling his thumbs. "You do understand what that means?"

"I'm a businessman." Marvin looked up into Cecil's face. "They want to buy my fifty-two shares—my voting rights."

"Yes, and they are prepared to make it a hostile take-over if you don't acquiesce. These guys have long money, and I'm afraid you won't stand a chance."

"What about a leveraged buyout?" Marvin said frantically. "I'm in debt, and don't have the money to fight these guys."

"Who are you going to get within the company to tender the offer? Richmond, the partner you're getting ready to blindside with this horrific information? I say he's your best bet and the only way to possibly beat the hostile bidders to the punch, but I doubt that Kenny Richmond will have the capital himself since you say the company is in a financial stew."

"Hell, I've got to tell him. I've got to tell him tonight, tomorrow. I don't know if I can do it, though."

"Marvin, you don't have any time to waste. These people want an answer by tomorrow. After that, it could get very ugly. You don't have much of a choice in the matter.

"Whether you sell or they fight you for control of the company, they will have voting control, and with that they can complete the merger to gain the company's assets. Richmond will stand to lose out, too."

Marvin rubbed his head with his hand and stood up. He looked up at Cecil thoughtfully, then rubbed his moustache. Marvin continued to stand as if his shoes were cemented in place, stuck his forefinger out like he was going to say something, then changed his mind. Hot air blew from Marvin's lips. "I'll get back with you."

"Make it soon. Real soon. Sorry I couldn't be of any more assistance, but in light of your financial situation, there's not a lot I can do."

"You'll get paid."

"Come on, Marvin. I'm not talking about me. Look, I'll take this as pro-bono work because I've not done much but make contact with the bidders and listened to both sides."

"I can pay my way, Cecil. Send me the bill. I'll give you my answer by tomorrow morning."

Without a good-bye, Marvin hurried from Cecil's office. Inside the elevator, Marvin banged his fists on the steel doors. "No one's taking my company from me, not even Kenny Richmond. No one."

# CHAPTER FOURTEEN

**M**arvin rushed to his Lexus and barreled out of the parking garage. He drove blindly through the streets of Atlanta in search of a place to massage his throbbing head. It had been several years since he had a drink, which was by choice and not because he couldn't hold his liquor, but he felt it was the right thing to do since he was re-orchestrating his life so that it would be in line with his spirituality. All things had a time and a place, and now was the time he needed to console himself with the spirits—the liquid kind.

Racing through a yellow light, Marvin slowed down and pulled into a vacant parking space. He sat a moment, gathering the thoughts that seemed to cloud his senses. No one could touch him in the bowels of downtown Atlanta. Everyone here had their own agenda and private thoughts, although his were a recipe for disaster. After a minute, he opened the car door and ambled toward the nearest bar.

Small amounts of sunlight filtered in the bar, but not enough to illuminate the corner Marvin chose to sit in.

He hopped onto a bar stool and nodded to the bartender. "Jack and Seven," Marvin said.

"Coming right up, partner," the bartender said.

The bartender moved away from the counter and pulled a bottle of Jack Daniel's from the shelf. Rows of gin, scotch, and whiskey in every brand and label littered the wall. After mixing the drink, he handed it to Marvin and slapped him on the arm.

Bottoms up. Marvin sent the liquid racing down his throat and let out a throaty catcall as it burned on its way to the bottom. He licked his lips, then placed the near empty glass to his mouth again, allowing the residue to drip to his tongue. He lowered the glass. "Another," he said, waving his glass at the bartender.

At the end of the third round, the bartender refused to serve Marvin another drink. Marvin begged with his eyes, convinced that he couldn't go on without the help of Jack Daniel's. A long-legged sister dressed in a red, just-above-the knee knit dress topped off with a short, black jacket with a large button holding it closed eased up onto the bar stool beside him, her chocolate-coated skin reminding him a lot of Rachel. She sported a close-cropped Afro that defined her face.

"Hey, sweetie," the chocolate diva said to Marvin. "How about a drink?"

"For you or for me?" Marvin laughed.

"For me, silly." The lady tapped Marvin's arm. "You are too cute. Married I see, but that don't mean a thing. What's your name?"

"Marvin," he slurred. He took another look at the woman sitting next to him, admiring her long, shapely legs that ran down to the four-inch, black, patent-leather stilettos that graced her feet. *Thoroughbred*, he thought to himself.

"Okay, Marvin. Don't look as if you can hold your liquor. You don't mind if I have a Scotch on the rocks, do you?"

"Have whatever you like," Marvin said, his head swaying from side to side in slow motion as he tried to keep the chocolate diva in his blurred vision.

"Well, thank you, Marvin. That's mighty kind of you."

"My pleasure, Miz...ah..."

"My name is Peaches, and this is my seat on Thursdays and any other day I choose to come in here. Right, Earl?"

The bartender nodded in agreement.

"So what are you drowning your sorrows about?" Peaches asked.

It came out so quickly, as if he had rehearsed it over and over again just for this moment. "They're trying to take my company away from me."

"Who's trying to take away your company?" Peaches wanted to know.

"They are...I don't know their names. They want my fifty-two shares, and I'm not going to give it to them. They'll have to kill me first—over my dead body."

"Slow your roll," the bartender said. "Here's another Jack and Seven. You need it."

"Damn right," Marvin said, slurred. "I've built my

company from the ground up. I've invested more than ten years to get to where I am today—a Fortune Five Hundred company."

Peaches listened intently as the stranger named Marvin became more appealing to her, even in his drunken state. "So, you're the owner of..."

"Thomas and Richmond Tecktronics, Inc."

"I've heard of you," Peaches blurted out. "You make computer software and, of course, computers. I think you have the contract at the company where I work.

"Look," Peaches said, threading her arm through Marvin's. "When you finish your drink, why don't we take a ride? I'll drive because you're not in any frame of mind to do so."

"Peaches, you've got yourself a deal. I'm not ready to go home anyway. My wife showed her ass today, and I don't feel like talking to her right now."

"Well, we won't talk about your wife. Wives and boy-friends are not up for discussion."

"Peaches," the bartender began.

"Earl, don't worry about me. Marvin needs some company and eventually someone to take him home. Give me your keys, Marvin."

Earl shrugged his shoulders and walked over to the customers he had neglected. He knew that Peaches was like poison when she got under someone's skin, and there was no readily available antidote. Peaches helped Marvin to his feet and marched him out through the front door of the bar. Looking on, Earl felt sorry for Marvin and wished there was someone he could alert about his present state, but if Marvin had come there in the first place to drink away his worries, he didn't want anyone to know.

# CHAPTER FIFTEEN

Rachel paced the floor of her twenty-five-room house as a migraine knocked on the side of her head. The last time she checked the clock, it was seven-thirty, and there had been no sign of Marvin. Serena was knocked out in her bedroom, and now that Rachel was alone, all of her fears came rushing back to her.

Playing back the previous hours left Rachel exhausted. Earlier, Sylvia had dropped her off just like she was a stinking, rotten sack of potatoes. Rachel knew she acted like a fool, but it seemed out of nowhere life was trying to throw her a dirty boomerang. All she wanted was answers. If there was trouble brewing in her marriage, why hadn't Marvin been man enough to tell her?

There was no use calling Marvin's cell again. He refused to talk to her, and maybe rightfully so, but she deserved an explanation. What if Marvin went back to Denise for consolation? No, he wouldn't do that. Denise had a life of her own now.

"Damn, my head is killing me," Rachel said out loud. She went into the kitchen and pulled a glass out of the cabinet and filled it with water. Next, she got her headache medicine, took it and gulped the water down behind it. She eased into a chair at the kitchen table.

Everything in the room was still, the stillness magnifying the emptiness in the house. Rachel jumped up from the chair and grabbed the phone off the wall and dialed a number. One, two, three rings, and then an answer.

"Hello," the voice said.

Frozen at the sound of the voice, Rachel held the phone without speaking.

"Hello," the voice said again.

"Denise?" Rachel asked, as if she was surprised that the person she dialed would be at the other end of the line.

"Rachel? What's wrong? Is it Marvin?"

"Well, yes and no. It's nothing. You just came across my mind."

"I'm surprised to hear your voice. It's been such a long time. How are Marvin and Serena doing?"

Rachel felt foolish. If Marvin was with Denise, for sure she wouldn't ask how he was doing. "Everybody's doing fine."

"So what's up? You seem to be upset about something. I hear it in your voice."

"Well, Denise, I guess I was thinking about the family and how Marvin and Harold have been estranged for so long. I was by myself thinking how wonderful it would be for the two of them to work things out."

"You know, Rachel, I was thinking the same thing, too. I might as well tell you. Harold and I are going to get married."

"What? When? Congratulations."

"Thank you. We've decided to get married in December. Danica is almost five, and since I spend so much time with Harold, we thought it was the right thing to do. I really do love him, and Danica loves her father. To have both parents in the home and not having to divide her time at one place or the other was best for Danica, and, of course, for me and Harold."

"Marvin will be elated to hear it. Look, keep me abreast of what's going on. We'd like to be there to celebrate with you."

"Would you pass it on to the girls?" Denise asked.

"I sure will. Although we don't need a reason to get together, this will definitely be another one of our success stories."

"Yeah, even though I didn't go to many meetings, I considered myself one of the Ex-Files members, too."

"I'm happy for you and Harold, Denise. I truly am."

"I am, too. And Rachel, I'm glad you found the man of your dreams, even if he is my ex-husband. I was stupid and foolish back then, but the cancer and my will to live for my daughter put a lot of things in perspective for me. I was crazy to have an affair with my husband's cousin and then get pregnant on top of it, but I've moved on since my divorce, and I know now that Harold and I are meant to be. We took our time to become friends, and we found love waiting around the corner. All that is left is for Marvin and Harold to be reunited."

"Beautiful," Rachel choked. "I'll be sure to tell the ladies and Marvin. It was good talking to you."

"You, too, Rachel. Take care."

Rachel hung up the phone and began to cry. For once, her life had been perfect—the perfect husband, the perfect family, the perfect friends, the perfect home— she couldn't ask for more. She turned off the lights in the rooms downstairs and climbed the stairs to her bedroom.

Time had flown, and it was now nine o'clock. No phone calls or sign of Marvin. She walked to the bed and sat on the edge, looking at the phone and willing it to ring. Ten minutes passed by, and she lay on top of the bed with all of her clothes on in total darkness, crying for Marvin to come home.


"Where am I?" The buzz that had overtaken Marvin's senses was beginning to come down. He squinted and looked around at the room that seemed foreign to him. Pictures of people he didn't know were lined up on an off-white dresser with a large mirror hanging over it. Large hats in a variety of colors were slung on a rack in one of the corners. The light was low, and when he looked into the mirror, he gasped in horror.

His eyes widened as the image in the mirror reflected a terrible truth. He was naked to the waist, and when he looked down at the rest of his body, his worst fears became reality. He was completely naked—in his birthday suit. He scrambled from the bed and looked around for his clothes. Whatever had taken place in that room, he was not conscious of it. He had to get home to Rachel and Serena.

All of sudden he remembered he had been drinking in a bar because he was despondent about the possibility of losing all that he owned. Where was he? Oh God. There was no way he could be with the woman he met at the bar.

Alone in the room, Marvin searched for his clothes. Not finding them, he went into the bathroom to see if they were there. No luck. Just as he stepped from the bathroom, the door to the bedroom opened. Marvin covered himself with his hands as Peaches, dressed only in a see-through shirt, entered the room with a tray of crackers, cheese, and a glass of wine.

"Well, we've come back to life, and I've brought you a little something to reward you for a job well done. I don't cook, otherwise I would have made it a lot nicer."

"I don't know what you're talking about, ah..."

"Peaches. You've forgotten my name. Well, you were hollering it over and over again just a while ago."

Peaches set the tray down at the end of the bed. "Let me look at you again. No point in covering up because I've seen all that you've got. Baby, you're a stallion. I'd let you ride me every day of the week."

Marvin stood transfixed in the middle of the room. Over-powering perfume filled the air, and he wrinkled his nose in disgust. "Look...look, Peaches, if it's money you want, you can have what I've got. I've got to get home to my wife and child."

"That's not what you were saying earlier. Remember, wives and boyfriends are off limits. Why don't you come over here and stoke my fire some more? Your head is staring straight at me, which could only mean you want more."

Embarrassed, Marvin covered himself with his arms as best he could, turning from her burning gaze. "Please give me my clothes. I need to get home."

"I love a man who begs," Peaches said, twisting her lips. She picked up the glass of wine from the tray and sipped it slowly.

"Listen, Peaches, I have a hundred dollars in my pants pocket. You can have it, just let me have my clothes."

"I'm not your whore, Marvin. Anyway, I've already helped myself to your money." Peaches put the glass down, slipped off the shirt, and walked over to where Marvin stood. She removed his arms from across his genitals and fondled him.

Marvin tried to move back, the perfume making him gag. Peaches grabbed him around his neck and pushed her naked body into his. She grabbed his buttocks and kissed his lips. "The only way you'll get your clothes back," she said seductively, "is after I feel you pulsating inside me, and my river has overflowed."

"Bitch, I'm not doing anything to you. I have a wife whom I love and adore, and if I'm going to give anything to anybody, it's going to be to her. Now get your damn hands off me and get my clothes and my keys. And if you don't in the next three seconds, I'm going to press rape charges against you. Now move."

"You weren't that good anyway." Peaches took the glass she had been drinking from and threw it against the bathroom door. It fell on the tile in the bathroom and shattered to pieces.

"Well, I don't remember a thing, and I don't want to."

"I wonder what your adorable wife would say when I call and tell her you went down on me like a hungry dog?"

Marvin grabbed Peaches by the shoulders and shook her as hard as he could. "You do that, you dirty bitch, and I'll have you brought up on charges so fast you would have thought you were inside a dryer on spin dry. Now get my clothes before I kick your ass."

Peaches waltzed into the living room and came back with Marvin's clothes. "You want to suck my tit—"

"Hell no." Marvin dressed as fast as he could, not bothering to button his shirt or put on his tie. He checked to see if he had his wallet and its contents. The money was gone and so was one of his credit cards, but she'd find out soon enough that it wasn't any good in Atlanta or anywhere else.

About to flee from the hell hole, Marvin realized he didn't have his keys. He headed back into the bedroom where Peaches was standing naked just beyond the door with his keys in her hand.

"Looking for these, lover boy?"

"Just give them to me and we can call it even."

"Give them to you just like that. Why don't you reconsider, Marvin, and stay a little while longer? I forgive you for the vile things you said about me. I'll make it worth your while. You've got me all worked up; you can't just leave me so unsatisfied. You said yourself that the missus was pretty mad at you and probably hasn't missed you at all."

"My keys, Peaches."

"So you're going to leave me all hot and wanting you?"

"Use your hands."

Peaches stared at Marvin and smiled. "You did like it." She threw the keys at him and slammed the bedroom door.

"Bitch."

# CHAPTER SIXTEEN

"Hey, Claudette. I need to be out of the shop by eleven," Mona said. "I've got to pick up my dress for this evening and check on the dinner preparations. I've been doing nothing but food prep for the last couple of days."

"What's on the menu?" Claudette asked, placing the towel around Mona's shoulders. "Sneak me a doggie bag if you can."

"The main meal will be a choice of pan-blackened salmon or petite sirloin served with a salad of mint, romaine lettuce with blood-orange vinaigrette, glazed parsnips, and young carrots; grilled asparagus with a Bearnaise sauce; roasted potatoes; and a nice champagne. The choice of soups for the evening will be She Crab Soup and a celery broth. Jumbo cocktail shrimp with a sweet cocktail sauce on the side will serve as the appetizer. For dessert, they will have a choice of lemon custard cake, coconut ice cream with blackberry-ginger sauce, or a vanilla buttercream cake with strawberries. It will be fancy and first class, after all, they are paying fifteen hundred dollars for the meal."

"Oh, I wish I could be there to see you work it. I know you're good, Mona girl. Get up and let's go to the shampoo bowl."

"Initially, Michael didn't want me to cater the event, but I had to remind the brother that this is what I do. And you know that I do it with class and style. After all, that's how I met him." The ladies laughed. "Are you happy, Claudette?"

"Happy as a pearl in an oyster shell. Like you, I'm doing what I do best, fixing nappy folks' hair. I know you all think I'm a magician, but for some folks you can only do the best you can. Now, I'll have their hair looking good, but can't do nothing with the rest of their body."

"Just make me look pretty," Mona pleaded.

Claudette shampooed Mona's hair, giving her a deep massage with her fingernails. Mona continued to "ooh" and "ahh" even as Claudette rinsed her hair with warm water. Thoughts of good times roamed through both of their heads, and before long, Mona's hair was being blow-dried and curled.

"Mona, remember when I told you and the girls that you need to go see Ashley?"

"Yeah, I remember, and we're going to do it."

"I'm going to schedule a date and call everybody so that we can do it together. You all have neglected her, and she is one of us. It's like you all have kicked her to the curb. Everybody's gotten married and gotten their lives back on track. You, Sylvia, and Rachel are living in your fine homes, but you've forgotten what came before. Please, we've got to do this. I may need you to encourage Sylvia and Rachel to get on the bandwagon."

"This is important to you, huh?"

"It should be important to you. Mona, Ashley is special to me. Not just because she let me adopt Reagan; she and I bonded, and I understood what she was going through."

"How do Kwame and Reebe feel about you spending all your time with Reagan?"

"You know Reebe has always been her own person, doing her own thing. Kwame doesn't really care. He and Reagan get along fine. Sometimes I think T is a little overprotective of Reagan."

"Just like you, mother hen?"

"I treat all my children the same. I'm just trying to be careful that I don't make the same mistakes with Reagan that I did with Kwame."

"Claudette, you have to be careful because kids become jealous when they see you giving a little more to another child than what they got."

"Mona, if my kids think that, they're crazy. I've done everything in the world for Reebe and Kwame."

"Couldn't stop Kwame from burning your shop down."

"It was an accident, Mona, and don't forget it."

"Ouch, you didn't have to pull my hair. You can forget about the tip I was going to give you."

"It doesn't matter, just never let me hear you say again that I haven't done for Reebe and Kwame. They are my first loves, and I'd do anything for them."

Mona peered at her watch. "It's getting close to eleven. I hope you're almost through."

Claudette pulled the flat iron through Mona's hair without another word.

Marvin brought his feet to the floor and sat up on the worn, brown leather couch in his home office. Sleep eluded him, and his back ached as a result. He placed his elbows on his knees and cupped his face in his hands.

Visions of a naked Peaches danced in his head like an erotic slideshow. He shook his head to erase the memory, but it was stuck there like a tick on its victim. The screen in his head replayed his sin over and over until Marvin could take no more. He grabbed his head, then jumped from the couch and began walking in circles. He wanted to believe that his flesh had not touched that of Peaches—that he had not destroyed the sanctity of his marriage. But when he let his mind wander for only a moment, the blood rushed to his organ in total surrender.

He went to the bathroom next to his office and showered. Hot, steaming water rushed over him as he scrubbed the stench from his body. Tears mixed with the rushing water and fell to the shower floor. The more Marvin lathered, the harder he scrubbed, but it didn't erase the vision or the nasty feeling that seemed to take hold of him. He tried telling himself that it was a night he didn't remember, couldn't remember—that he'd been blinded by alcohol and fear. When he turned the shower off, he didn't feel any better.

It was still quiet in the house. He listened for any movement from Rachel or Serena but heard none. It was ten forty-five in the morning.

What was he going to do for clothes? Marvin had the shower placed next to his office because he often worked late nights in his office, but he didn't keep any clothes there. He spied a pair of jeans and a T-shirt he'd worn on the weekend thrown over the back of the couch he'd slept on. He put them on; his clothes from yesterday would be history. He'd find the nearest garbage dump and get rid of them and all other reminders of a day he longed to forget. For now, he folded them and placed them under a cushion on the couch.

He looked around the room, then walked into the interior of the house, where all else was quiet. Marvin grabbed his keys and went into the garage. He had a decision to make today—one that didn't come easy— but he knew what it would be, what it had to be. He hit the remote, got in the car, and drove away.

Rachel watched from her bedroom window, their bedroom, as Marvin headed down the street. She grabbed her chest with her hand and prayed to God for an answer. This couldn't possibly be a sign that her marriage was over. She and Marvin loved each other and their daughter, Serena.

Rachel wasn't sure what time he had come home, but he must have looked in. When she woke up, she found a comforter covering her body—clothes and all. That was a sign that he cared.

Serena began to whine, and she knew her day was about to begin. Before going to check on Serena, Rachel got on her knees. "Lord, tell me what I've done wrong and how I can make things right with my husband. I don't know what's going on, but if I have in any way caused this situation to come upon us, please forgive me, Lord. I'm so sorry.

"My husband is a good man, and I love him. I know I've done some stupid things, Lord, things I need to be punished for, but I also know I've done nothing to cause my husband to push me aside. Please help me fix it."

"Mommy, why are you crying?" Serena asked, patting Rachel on the shoulder.

Rachel picked Serena up and sat her in her lap. "I love you, baby. I love you, Serena. Mommy feels bad right now, but I'll feel better in a minute. We're going to get your bath and something to eat, and you and Mommy are going to read some stories."

"Yeah," Serena said. She jumped from Rachel's lap and danced in her nightgown.

"Give Mommy a kiss, Serena." Serena placed a kiss on Rachel's lips. Rachel took Serena in her arms and placed kisses all over her. "Mommy loves you, and don't you forget it."

"I love you, too, Mommy."

# CHAPTER SEVENTEEN

Horn-rimmed glasses sat on the edge of Yvonne's nose. She didn't look up when Marvin walked in, although he stopped to look at her. When she didn't respond, Marvin walked into his office and closed the door.

Several minutes later, the door to Marvin's office opened. "Yvonne, would you please hold the letter that was addressed to Harold Thomas. I'm having second thoughts about sending it out."

Yvonne looked up with panic in her eyes. "I...I sent it out yesterday right after you signed it, Mr. Thomas."

"Ohhhhhhhh," Marvin sighed. "Well, it's gone. Don't worry about it."

"I'm sorry, Mr. Thomas. I was just following orders."

"You did right, Yvonne." Marvin started to retreat to his office but turned around to face Yvonne. "I'm sorry for yesterday, Yvonne. Mrs. Thomas learned some bad news, and I guess she lost it. I do apologize for her antics and for you having to endure what should have been a discussion between her and me at home."

"It's alright, Mr. Thomas. I know that it wasn't your fault. I'm fine. Oh by the way, someone named Peaches called. She left her number and said it was urgent. Here's the number."

Marvin took the piece of paper with Peaches' number on it. Saliva caught at the back of his throat, and he turned quickly and retreated into his office before Yvonne could see him sweat.

Flopping down in his chair, Marvin stared at the number. Why was this bitch calling him? She'd gotten what she wanted from him, and he had nothing left to give. Yesterday was a mistake, and he hoped he didn't have to pay for it for the rest of his life.

Marvin fingered the paper again and picked up the phone. He dialed the number Yvonne had written down and waited for the phone to ring. A female voice answered on the first ring.

"May I speak to Peaches?" Marvin asked, trying to be pleasant.

"Well, I wasn't sure that you would return my call. I'm pleasantly surprised."

"Isn't that what you asked my secretary to tell me to do?"

"Right, Marvin. I'm sitting at my desk with my legs open and touching myself—like you did yesterday."

"I'm not up to playing games with you, so tell me what this is all about."

"Now, Marvin, there's no need for you to be nasty to me. See, I tried to use your credit card this morning, and it was declined. I'm not mad, but I should be."

"Serves you right. The Bible says that you're not to steal."

"And the Bible also says that you should not commit adultery."

"Peaches, I didn't commit any such act. You probably forced yourself on me against my will, because I have no recollection of having done any such thing."

"I do. I even have a picture to prove that you were in my room in all of your glory."

Panic seized Marvin. He began to pant and grabbed his chest. "Peaches, I haven't done anything to you. I gave you money—"

"And a no-good credit card. I'd hate to have to tell the missus what a bad boy you've been."

"My threat stands about reporting you to the police for rape."

"Have you done it? Who's going to believe you the day after tomorrow or next week? I know that much because I work for attorneys who handle corporate sexual abuse cases."

"What do you want from me, Peaches?"

"You're a big businessman. I want fifty thousand dollars to leave you alone and keep the picture out of the tabloids."

"You wouldn't!"

"Try me."

"Peaches, I don't have fifty thousand dollars. That's the reason I was in the bar in the first place. That's the reason my credit card is no good. I'm going to lose my business."

"Don't lie to me. You were wearing expensive clothes and I checked out your neighborhood."

"You bitch. If anything happens to my family, I'm going to—"

"You're going to what? From what you just said, you can't do diddley. I want fifty thousand dollars, and I'll give you thirty days to get it to me. After that, your wife, your partner, the whole business community will know what kind of snake in the grass you really are, Marvin Thomas. You don't want to disappoint me. Get my money."

The line went dead, and Marvin slammed the phone down. He picked up the phone again and dialed.

"Hello, Gretchen, may I speak to Cecil Coleman, please?"

"Sure, Mr. Thomas. I hope you're having a great day."

"It could be better, Gretchen."

"Well, hold on a moment. I will get Attorney Coleman for you."

Marvin hung on the phone, bouncing the words in his head that he planned to deliver to Cecil. His thoughts kept passing back and forth like a ping-pong ball—he would say this, no, he would say this instead. But it was inevitable what he had to do.

"Marvin, my man. What's the good word?"

"Sell. I've thought it over, and I'm going to sell my

fifty-two shares of stock in the company. Just let me know what else I need to do. I've got to step out now; you can reach me later."

"You sure, man?"

"Cecil, I'm more than sure."

"Alright. I'll contact the bidders and let them know your decision. You'll probably need to have a board meeting to advise your shareholders. I'll be in touch."

"Okay." Marvin hung up the phone. He had to make another call, but he needed a moment to get his composure. Tears blinded his eyes, but he refused to make a sound. The decision had been made, and all that he had worked for was now in someone else's hands. He picked up the phone and dialed.

"Marvin?"

"Hey, Rachel. We need to talk."

# CHAPTER EIGHTEEN

"Baby, you look absolutely fabulous," Michael said to Mona, who was busy admiring herself in the mirror. "Why don't we skip tonight's affair and let me entertain my wife in ways she can only imagine."

Mona stopped cold and turned toward Michael with a sultry look on her face. "Baby, if I weren't getting paid big bucks for this evening, I'd readily take you up on it. How about a rain check?"

"You promise to look that gorgeous when the night is over?"

"Michael, baby, sweetheart, you know that I look gorgeous in whatever I wear, even if it's nothing at all. But this isn't what I'm wearing tonight. I'm taking the dress I'm wearing with me so that it won't get wrinkled before the event gets underway."

"You're right about looking gorgeous in anything, baby. Why don't you give me a kiss so I can have something to remind me of what I'm to expect later?"

"You didn't hear a word I said. Be glad I don't have my lipstick on already."

"Mona, you take the fun out of seduction."

Mona stopped what she was doing and walked over to Michael. She rubbed his bald head, then grabbed him around the neck and threw her lips on his, tasting and nibbling. He joined in, wanting to pick her up, lay her on their king-size bed, and make passionate love to her. Fearful of a scolding, he embraced and kissed her tenderly, backing away from her as the heat between them became too much to bear.

"Baby, maybe you better scoot because you're making it impossible for me to focus on what I'm supposed to be doing."

"You're supposed to be getting ready. I put your tux in the hall closet. I'm going to take Michael Jr. to Sylvia's so he can play with little Kenny."

"Is Kenny still serious about approaching Vincent Kinyard with his proposal? This guy owns property from Maine to Mexico—big luxury condos and resorts on every island in the Caribbean and elsewhere."

"Oh God, yes! Kenny would do anything for this opportunity. I'm going to have a good time watching him serve my guests."

"What do you mean, serve your guests? Mona, you're not putting Kenny to work? How humiliating for a man of his caliber to have to resort to such?"

"Michael, listen to yourself. Is that how you feel about me...that what I'm doing is beneath you or Kenny?"

"No, baby, I didn't quite mean it like that."

"That's what it sounded like to me. I know I'm not deaf."

"What I meant was—"

"Careful now, or I won't need a rain check."

"Mona, please. All I meant was, if Kenny was going to make this proposal, it would look rather odd for him to be serving the folks he's trying to do business with."

"How else was he going to get into the event? He didn't receive an invitation. But I see what you mean, sweetie. You do make a lot of sense."

"I understand what you were trying to do, sweetheart, and I love you all the more for it."

"Okay, we're good. I'm going to put my lipstick on and get Michael Jr. so that I can take him over to Sylvia's. I need to be at the country club by two to make sure all is in order. I've got my best chefs on the job."

"With you at the helm, I know this affair is going to be exceptionally wonderful. Why don't I take Michael Jr. to Sylvia's?" Michael's eyes radiated as he watched Mona in a moment of innocence. "Cat got your tongue?"

"You are so good to me, Michael Broussard."

"Thoughtful." Michael smiled.

"Thank you for taking Michael Jr. to Sylvia's for me. I love you, baby, and don't you ever forget it."

"I'm the one who's blessed," Michael said. "I've been blessed since the day I met you."

"Thank God for second chances." Mona kissed Michael, picked up her garment bag with her dress, and headed out of the room. "Thank you for coming into my life."

Morning had come and gone, and the afternoon was drifting by. Rachel moved back from the large beveled window that looked out over the expanse of yard and the street beyond it. Nothing seemed to stir or move except for an occasional squirrel that barreled down from one of the tall pine trees and onto another.

Rachel and Marvin's marriage was in trouble. He was avoiding her but had made it plain that they needed to talk. She needed to talk to someone, though, but Sylvia was out of the question. Rachel had probably alienated herself from the best friend she had—the one person she trusted to be there for her whenever she needed someone.

*Click, click, click, click, click.* Rachel jumped and straightened her face at the sound of tiny feet running over the stone tiles, followed by Isabel. She managed a smile as Serena stood tall in her play heels.

"Look at me, Mommy. I'm as tall as you."

"You are so beautiful, Serena. Isn't she, Isabel?"

"Absolutely adorable," Isabel said, giving Serena a wink. "Mrs. Thomas, do you mind if I take Serena to get some ice cream? I promised her if she ate all of her fruit and vegetables, that I would treat her to some ice cream if it's alright with you."

"Yeah, ice cream," Serena shouted.

"Serena would enjoy that, Isabel. Let me get my purse and treat you both. Take your time."

"Thanks, Mrs. Thomas. I'll take good care of Serena."

Rachel went to the kitchen and got her purse. She handed Isabel a ten-dollar bill. Thank God she kept readily available cash for rainy days, although she never expected a downpour like she experienced yesterday. She hurried back to the foyer and gave Isabel the money.

"Give Mommy a kiss, Serena. You do what Isabel tells you to."

"Okay, Mommy." She kissed Rachel, waved good-bye, and headed out the door with Isabel.

Rachel watched from the window as Isabel backed her car out of the driveway, then drove away. Loneliness began to set in, and she moved away from the window and walked into the kitchen. She looked at the phone on the kitchen wall and turned away. Before other thoughts could trickle in, she grabbed the receiver and dialed Sylvia.

"Hey, Sylvia," Rachel said as soon as she heard Sylvia's voice.

"Hey, Rachel, how are you doing today? You and Marvin get it straight?"

"Yeah, he's calmed down. He was a little upset with me, but we kissed and made up."

"That's good, girl. You might want to look into taking some anger management courses. You can't allow yourself to explode like that, especially in public."

"I know. I've kicked myself in the behind for being such an a-hole. Some screw has to be loose up there."

"Don't say that too loud. People have been saying

that for years. Look, hold on a sec; I'm trying to help Kenny get together for tonight."

"Okay."

Rachel held on for two minutes. Why did she lie to Sylvia? She was miserable, and she needed to tell somebody.

"Hey, Rachel. Sorry to keep you hanging. Let me call you back later. Kenny is going to the fundraiser Mona is catering. My baby is trying to lay a business proposition on one of the bigwigs, and he's using Mona as a way to gain access. That man of mine stops at nothing to make a buck."

"Alright. I'll be here."

"You okay?"

"Yeah, I'm still embarrassed about yesterday. Just making sure my best friend didn't kick me to the curb."

"Never, girl. You're a piece of work, but I love you anyhow."

"Sylvia?"

"What is it, Rachel?"

"Marvin didn't come home until early this morning and he slept in his office. When he got up this morning, he left without saying good-bye. When he did call, the only thing he said was that we needed to talk, and then hung up. Sylvia, I know that I was out of order, but my God, I couldn't have been that bad. I can't believe this is happening."

"Oh, sweetie, I'm so sorry." Sylvia sighed. "Look, if

you feel like driving and you still haven't heard from Marvin in a few hours, you and Serena come on over. I'm watching little Michael for Mona. The boys enjoy each other's company."

"I don't know if I'll feel up to it."

"Let me get Kenny squared away, and I'll call you in a few hours. It's going to be alright, Rachel. Haven't we come through some things together? We're tough as nails, and whatever is eating at Marvin will pass. You know you've got a good man who loves you to death. Be patient and give him a chance to explain."

"You make it sound so simple, Sylvia. I feel a little bit better. I'll call you in a few hours."

"Okay, sweetie. Gotta run. My big baby is calling me."

Rachel hung up the phone and got up and went to her room. Why hadn't Marvin called her again, and what was going on with him? They could talk about anything, even the silliest stuff that didn't make any sense at all. Their lives were an open book with one another—no secrets.

There wasn't anything she could do. She lay on the bed and pulled the covers up over her. When she woke up, darkness had fallen.

It was too quiet. She jumped up and ran downstairs and found Serena and Isabel watching television.

"You're still here, Isabel. I'm so sorry. It's way past time for you to go home."

"I couldn't wake you, Mrs. Thomas, and I didn't want

to leave Serena. You've been doing a lot of lying around lately. Are you pregnant?"

"Heaven forbid. No, I'm not sure why I'm so tired."

"Well, Mr. Thomas called again."

Rachel's eyes widened. "He did? Why didn't you wake me up?"

"I tried, but you wouldn't budge. He told me to let you sleep and that he was working late."

"Oh, I see. Well, thank you for taking Serena for some ice cream. I'll take care of you for those extra hours you had to stay."

"Don't worry about it, Mrs. Thomas. If I didn't love Serena so, I would have poured cold water on you to make you wake up."

"That wouldn't have been a good thing. Thanks again. Drive safely."

"Good night, Isabel," Serena said, taking her eyes away from *SpongeBob SquarePants* for only a second.

"Good night, Serena...Mrs. Thomas."

"Good night, Isabel."

Rachel couldn't wait for Isabel to leave. She made sure Serena was alright, then went into the kitchen and picked up the phone. Nerves were getting the best of her, but she wasn't going to wait any longer for Marvin to call back. Isabel said he'd phoned, so she was only returning the call.

Chills went up her spine. What if Marvin didn't want to talk to her? Rejection was one thing she was not ready for, but he was her husband, and she had to hear his voice.

She dialed and it rang. A lump formed in her throat. She hit the off button but hit redial almost immediately. It rang again, and finally a voice, his voice, Marvin's voice answered.

"Marvin, baby, what's wrong? Please tell me what's wrong so that I can fix it."

"You can't fix it, Rachel. You can't and I can't."

Panic rose in her throat. Her head began to throb, but she willed herself to stay calm. "What are you talking about, Marvin? I love you. Make me understand. I'm so sorry about yesterday. If I could take it back, I would. I was just flustered because everywhere I turned, the word 'rejected' was staring me in the face, and I just lost it."

"Rightfully so. I haven't been forthcoming with you."

"Marvin, you're scaring me. Baby, please don't tell me our marriage is over."

"I'm not sure that I can explain it to you."

"I can take it. I can take it. I'll do whatever I need to do to make things right. I'm sorry about not telling you about the drapes, I'm sorry."

"Rachel, be quiet. It's not about you—not directly."

"Then what is it about, Marvin? You're scaring me."

"Rachel, the company has been deep in debt for the last six months. I made some very large equipment purchases to better compete with the Sonys and Toshibas."

"They're giants, Marvin. They've been around for years and years."

"I know. How well do I know. I was borrowing from Peter to pay Paul. I even used all of our savings to get the company out of arrears. I owe back taxes, and that's why the credit cards were frozen. I had to put a halt to your spending because I was not man enough to tell my wife what was going on."

"Does Kenny know?"

"No, but I have to tell him soon. See, out of nowhere, this company approached me about buying me out."

"You mean like a takeover?"

"Yeah. It's like they could smell that I was in trouble. I went to a friend of mine who is an attorney to seek his advice. The advice wasn't good."

"What do you mean, it wasn't good?"

"He said because I didn't have the capital to fight with, my only recourse would be to sell my shares in the company."

Silence. "You own the majority shares, Marvin. Please tell me you didn't—"

"Didn't sell my fifty-two shares of stock? Yeah, I sold them, which means Thomas and Richmond Tecktronics, Inc. is no more."

"Oh, my God." Rachel began to hyperventilate. "Oh, my God. What's going to happen to all the people who work for you? Oh, my God."

"I don't know, Rachel!"

Marvin began to cry. Rachel could tell that he had laid the phone down. Tears streamed down her face, while her hands trembled. "Marvin, if you can hear me, talk to me."

All she heard were muffled cries, and then he was back on the phone.

"Rachel, I can't deal with this. I don't even know how I'm going to tell Kenny."

"You are a strong man, Marvin. I'll be with you when you tell him, if you want. Kenny is resilient; he bounces back like a rubber ball. He's at Mona's function now trying to strike a deal."

"I don't know if I can tell him. I'm a coward, Rachel."

"No, you aren't. Stop saying that. I remember how you went to bat for Claudette, Ashley...Oh, my God, Ashley. I've got to go see her. But you've been the foundation for everyone else, Marvin. How can you neglect yourself?"

"How? I've let you and Serena down, and you had no idea. What kind of man does that to a family he loves?"

"You're getting downright depressing. Now shape up. All is not lost."

"I sold my fifty-two shares, Rachel. The business is gone. I have nothing left. I was calling to say good-bye."

"What are you talking about, Marvin Thomas? Don't you cop out on me and Serena. I believed in you, dedicated my life to you. Don't do this to me, man. Don't talk about turning tail and leaving us to fend for ourselves."

"You'll be alright, Rachel. Gotta hang up now."

"No, Marvinnnnnnnnnn!! No, no, no, no, no. Marvinnnnnnnnn!"

She heard the dial tone. "Marvinnnnnnnnnnnnn!"

# CHAPTER NINETEEN

**M**ona pushed open the double doors to the dining area at the country club. The room was elegant beyond her expectations. Mesmerized, Mona could only stand and stare at the well-dressed tables that were skirted with pintucked gold silk tablecloths. Floral centerpieces of hydrangeas, white lilies, and white roses adorned each table surrounded by the best china and flatware. Crystal flutes and water glasses made the tables sparkle. Place cards that corresponded with a list the hostesses would be given had been meticulously set in front of each dinner plate. Balancing the table and adding to the floral delight were tall vermeil candelabras. Mona would wait until fifteen minutes before the guests were to arrive to light them.

She hurried to the kitchen to see if all was in order. The chefs were busy with last-minute preparations, barking orders that made Mona smile. She inspected the food, dipping her finger in the orange vinaigrette to make sure the taste was just as she intended. She had come much earlier in the day with a crew to set up and bring many of the items she had prepared. Pulling off the affair was no small feat, but her catering business was now listed with the premier services and on the Who's Who of Catering.

Mona's staff would arrive within the hour, so she sauntered off to a private room that was set aside so that she could refresh herself and change her clothes. She shook her head as she thought about Kenny and how he was going to pull off his proposition. If anyone could do it, Kenny could. Michael had given him a rundown of who the players would be, and if she knew Kenny, he was going to use the information to his advantage.

Before the hour was up, Mona had reset her face, sprayed her body with a small amount of Pleasures Delight, and gone to the closet to pull her dress from the garment bag. It was a beautiful cobalt, V-neck, satin sheath dress by Nicole Miller that grabbed every curve on her body with perfection, amplifying her generous serving of breasts, although not distastefully. She shook her hair and the layers fell in place on command. The guests would be left wondering if she was the meal of the day.

Happy with the way she looked, Mona took off to the dining room to greet her servers. They would all be wearing sleek black-and-white uniforms. She made an exception for Kenny.

They all gathered around when Mona entered the

room. Instructions were given down to the minute detail. Any onlooker might have thought that tonight's affair was a state dinner at the White House in honor of the Royal Highnesses the Prince of Wales and the Duchess of Cornwall or the former president of South Africa, Nelson Mandela. The players were big and would be writing hefty checks in support of the Democratic candidate running for the White House.

Kenny smiled in amazement at the way Mona orchestrated her workers with such finesse. He needed someone like her on his team, who would help skyrocket his and Marvin's company up the leader board. Strange things were going on with Marvin, but Kenny would deal with that later. Tonight, an opportunity was ripe for the taking, and all his efforts would be concentrated on spearing his victims and drawing them in.

The countdown had begun. Mona lit the candelabras, and the room sparkled. Everyone was in place and ready to make their boss proud. Several doors opened and voices could be heard.

"One, two, three, four—it's on," Mona announced. "Take a deep breath, and let's do it."

The guests filed in one by one, directed to their seats by the hostesses. There were businessmen and women from every persuasion—doctors, lawyers, bankers, educators, financial analysts, judges, clergy, the mayor, and city councilmen along with their spouses or significant others. They smelled like money, looked like money, wore gowns and tuxedos that cost a lot of money, and walked like they had money up their behinds. But when the good Dr. Michael Broussard spotted his wife, his jaw dropped, all semblance of the upstanding doctor shed for a moment.

"I want you, Mona Broussard," he mouthed, tossing her an air kiss that she accepted with pleasure.

"I want you, too," Mona mouthed back. She smiled as her husband entered the room and was escorted to his seat. He was the best thing that had happened to her in a long time.

Eight persons were to be seated at each of seventy-five tables. Pleasant conversation filtered throughout the room until the mayor, who escorted his wife, moved to the front to sit at the head table.

"Excuse me, everyone," the mayor shouted, silence finally enveloping the room, except for the light dinner music that played in the background. "Our guest of honor will be here in a moment. I understand that he has just entered the grounds, and once he has joined us, we will begin with dinner and end the evening with words from our guests and dusting off of the old checkbooks." There was laughter from the guests. "Enjoy your meal."

Mona smiled and looked back at her servers who hugged a breezeway that led from the kitchen into the banquet room. She decided to give Kenny a break so that he would be in the ready position when the opportune moment came.

All of sudden there was a ruckus, and all heads turned toward the entryway. Several men dressed in black suits, each with ear-pieces locked around their ear lobes, entered the room followed by a tall, thin, handsome black gentleman wearing a tuxedo and a great big smile.

Mona clasped a hand over her mouth, as did the other members of her staff, when they saw Senator Barack Obama walk into the room. There were hushed murmurs, hand claps, then a standing ovation. Senator Obama held both hands in the air and waved his welcome.

After Senator Obama, the mayor, and other city officials were seated at the head table, the mayor announced that dinner was served. Mona's staff worked the room like a precision drill team. Knives and forks clinked together, while daintily held wineglasses were high in the air. Mona was pleased because all seemed pleased. As soon as the dinner plates were emptied, the servers quickly removed and replaced them with the dessert of each diner's choice, which all seemed to enjoy.

Mona watched as Michael walked to where she and Kenny stood. A worried look came across her face, but she eased up when Michael took Kenny aside.

"Kenny, when I give you the signal, that will be the time to approach Kinyard. I've put a pitch in for you, so you go in there and give it your best shot."

Mona smiled at her man. Kenny shook Michael's hand. "Thanks, Michael. I owe you big for this, man."

"Don't forget what you just said when you and Marvin take top spot in the electronics world. And, my wife is a witness."

"Got that right, babe," Mona said, giving Michael an air kiss.

"Okay, I'm going back to my table by my lonesome. I think the mayor is getting ready to say something."

"Okay, Michael. I'll be looking for the signal." Kenny smiled.

Everyone watched as the mayor rose to his feet. He asked the guests if they enjoyed their meal, and everyone clapped. He acknowledged Mona and her staff for the fine meal and shared that she was the wife of the well-respected Dr. Michael Broussard of Emory Crawford Long Hospital. Everyone clapped again.

There were a battery of speeches and campaign rhetoric extolling Senator Obama's outlook for the country and his hope-fully successful bid for the White House. Finally, Senator Obama rose to the microphone and thanked all of the guests for their support. He talked about change being good for the city of Atlanta, the state of Georgia, and the country. Then he asked for their monetary support so that he could take his message all over the country.

Another standing ovation and thunderous applause filled the room. When it subsided, peppier music was piped in. Throughout the room, conversations could be heard about the Democratic candidate and his message of change as they wrote checks for five hundred, one thousand, and five thousand dollars. Evidently people were ready for change in the country, and they were willing to help it happen by investing in the country's future.

Kenny suddenly moved from his perch. He strode toward Michael and a group of men and women with a purpose and a portfolio in hand. He extended his hand to each person as Michael made the introductions. The wives left the group, while Michael, Vincent Kinyard, and a Mr. David Eason remained at the table.

After sitting down, Kenny laid out his plan of equipping Mr. Kinyard's hotels and resorts with state-of-the-art computer equipment. He described the new iPod technology—a touch of the finger was all they needed in their stress-free world. Kenny felt confident that his proposal was well received. He waited while the two men considered the idea, and finally Vincent Kinyard spoke and did all of the talking.

"Impressive, Mr...."

"Mr. Richmond," Kenny said enthusiastically.

"Yes, Mr. Richmond. I agree that what you have is state of the art. I'd like to know a little more about distribution, service, and volume discounting. But I do like the product, even without looking at the specs."

"This portfolio is yours to keep and peruse. It has all the specs for the products that I just spoke to you about. We have our own design team, and marketing and development departments. I call them our dream team. If there is something else you'd like to see, I would be more than happy to share it with my developmental group."

"The name of the company is Thomas and Richmond Tecktronics, Inc.?" Mr. Kinyard asked.

"Yes," Kenny said.

"Your partner is Marvin Thomas?" Mr. Kinyard continued.

A puzzled look crossed Kenny's face. Even Michael saw the distress in Kenny's facial expression. "Is something wrong, Mr. Kinyard? We are a reputable Fortune 500 company."

"Mr. Richmond, without going into a lot of details because it's apparent you are unaware of the state of your company..."

"What do you mean by '*the state of your company*'?"

"Just today, Mr. Thomas sold us fifty-two shares of his stock in the company, which means I now run it. Of course, the paperwork has yet to be completed, and—"

Kenny jumped up from the table. "You're a liar."

"Okay," Michael broke in. "That won't be necessary."

"But did you hear what the man said?" Kenny asked. Looking at the two men, Kenny pointed his finger. "I don't know who you are or what you're talking about, but you've got it all wrong, especially if you're talking about running Thomas and Richmond after all the time, money, and energy I've invested into this company."

"Please don't be concerned about your place in the company, Mr. Richmond; it's safe. We definitely need someone like you on the team. You have insight and forward thinking when it comes to building a company and watching it grow."

Kenny withdrew his proposal from in front of Mr. Kinyard. Just as he was about to say what was on his mind, a hand tapped him on the shoulder.

"Hello, gentlemen," Senator Obama said. "I need your help to make my vision of a better nation for the American people a reality."

"Yes," the gentlemen said almost in chorus.

Senator Obama shook each hand and said, "Don't forget to vote on November fourth—earlier would be preferable." Waving his hand, he turned and left with the Secret Service tagging alongside him.

"Mr. Richmond," Mr. Eason said, speaking for the first time, "we can work this out. I like your drive and energy. You've got great ideas. We can work together."

"I don't like you very much at this moment."

Kenny took his proposal and left the three gentlemen at the table. Chatting with her team, Mona stopped when she saw Kenny approach. She wanted to hear the good news, but instead Kenny whizzed past her and out the door without a word.

She ran into the dining room and searched for Michael. He saw Mona's frantic look and headed her way.

"What happened?" Mona asked as she caught up with Michael. "Kenny walked out without saying a word."

"Sounds like Marvin sold his shares in the company. And he owned the majority stock." Michael pursed his lips. "I don't think Marvin told Kenny."

"Oh, hell."

"It's worse than that, baby. Far worse."

Marvin sat in his closed office and tapped the letter opener on his desk. He looked at the clock; it was now 9:00 P.M. Rachel's voice floated back to him, calling his name over and over. She was beautiful—the love of his life. The only thing he wanted of her was to bear his child, which she did without thought, and together they became parents of the most beautiful little girl he had ever seen. Yes, Serena was his heart.

But he had turned out to be a big disappointment. All that he worked for had vanished into thin air—no, he'd given it away like there was no tomorrow. Now he had nothing, and he couldn't go home to his family empty-handed.

He laid the letter opener down and picked up the bottle of Tylenol he kept in his desk. Arthritis was creeping up on him, and the capsules kept the ache in his joints to a minimum. He opened the bottle and poured the contents on his desk. Without water, he took five pills and swallowed them whole and then took a few more and waited for something to happen.

# CHAPTER TWENTY

Kenny tore off the jacket to his tux and jumped in his car. He pulled his cell from his pocket and dialed the Thomas residence.

"Hello," Rachel said.

"Rachel, this is Kenny. Let me speak to Marvin."

"He's not here, Kenny."

"It's nine o'clock. Where in the hell is he?"

"I don't know, Kenny. I haven't seen him all day. I'm really worried about him. The last time I spoke with him, he was talking crazy."

"I wonder why? I'll talk to you later."

Kenny hung up the phone and dialed Marvin's cell. No answer. He called the office. No answer. Kenny beat the steering wheel with his hand and drove blindly through downtown Atlanta. Before he knew it, he'd driven to his place of business and parked in the space marked KENNY RICHMOND. He stared at the sign for several minutes, then opened the car door and got out. Drenched in anger, Kenny hadn't even noticed Marvin's car parked a few feet away.

He hurled expletives at Marvin, but only the trees and shrubs were witnesses to the outburst. Kenny walked to the entrance with his hands in his pockets, unable to open the door when he reached it. Tears began to form in his eyes, and before long they came down in buckets, barreling down his face at record speed. He could not comprehend that what he believed might have been his fortune had turned out to be his misfortune. And for some unknown reason, it seemed God allowed it to be revealed the way it was because the man Kenny trusted was a coward and didn't have the balls to tell him the truth. The more he thought about it, the madder Kenny got.

Kenny used his key and entered the building. He walked, then picked up his stride, continuing to hurl curses and punch his fist in the air as if he was gearing up for a heavyweight fight. It was dark in the outer office of Marvin's suite, but upon entering, Kenny saw that a faint light oozed from beneath the closed door.

"Marvin, are you in there?" Kenny shouted to the rafters. Silence ensued. Kenny banged on the door to Marvin's office, but there was no response. Twisting the handle on the door, Kenny barged in and found Marvin sitting with his head on his desk.

"Damn you, Marvin. When were you going to tell me? Huh?" Kenny hit the wall. "What do I look like to you—some kind of fool that would not have understood? Nigger, answer me. Don't lie there and pretend that you don't hear me. I've given my all to help you make this company what it is, and when the going gets rough, you just give it all away—everything you've worked hard all your life for like it was pennies you were throwing in a fountain. What's wrong with you? Answer me!"

Marvin didn't budge. Kenny moved in front of Marvin and noticed the overturned bottle for the first time. "Oh, hell. You are a damn coward."

Kenny shook Marvin, but still no response. He reached in his pocket and pulled out his cell and dialed 9-1-1. "Hurry, please," Kenny barked, after giving the dispatcher the address and information.

"Sir, please check his pulse."

Anger ate at Kenny, inside and out. His first thought was to let Marvin do what he'd set out to do—kill himself—because if he came to, Kenny was going to kill him for sure. He reached over and pulled up Marvin's arm and placed two fingers over his wrist. The pulse was faint, but there was one. "There's a slight pulse," Kenny said to the dispatcher.

"An ambulance should be there any minute."

"Alright."

Kenny pulled up one of the chairs that sat opposite Marvin's desk and slumped into it. He picked up Marvin's hand, searching again for the pulse that was barely there. "Don't you die on me. Don't you dare die on me until I've had my say. Cheated me out of my company, now you're trying to cheat me out of having the last word. No, sucker, you better hope you live. Your tail is going to straighten this mess out. I'm not going to work for some Joe Blow that don't give a crap about Thomas and Richmond Tecktronics the way we do. Hell no. Ain't going to happen in this lifetime."

Sirens screamed outside. "I'll be back, Marvin. I've got to let the paramedics in so they can take you to get that poison out of your stomach. After that, you're mine, buddy. You're all mine."

Kenny placed Marvin's arm back on the desk and walked to the door with his head down. He looked back at Marvin and turned to walk out the door. "Oops, excuse—Rachel?"

Rachel looked at Kenny and then into Marvin's office. She pushed past Kenny and rushed to where Marvin lay slumped on the desk.

"Oh, my God, Marvin...baby. What have you done?" Rachel first lifted his head and then his hands and checked for signs of life. "Help! Somebody help me."

Rachel grabbed the phone and picked up the receiver. Kenny went to Rachel and put the receiver down.

"I've already called for the ambulance. They should be here in a minute."

Rachel glared at Kenny as tears ran down her face. "What did you do to Marvin? Were you even going to call and tell me my husband had tried to take his life?"

"How long were you standing outside the door?"

"I just arrived. I don't know why I didn't come right away after I had talked with him earlier. But after you called, I knew I needed to check on him."

"Marvin sold me out."

"He's in trouble, Kenny. You're his partner, and you should have known. This is the man who gave you access to *his* company, the man who allowed you to prosper." Rachel pointed her finger at Kenny. "Yeah, Marvin had his faults, but you're equally responsible. So don't go putting the blame solely on Marvin. Now get out of my way and let the paramedics in so they can take care of my husband."

Kenny could hear Rachel's sobbing as he made his way down the hall. How had all that Marvin had done suddenly become his fault, Kenny wondered. Maybe Rachel was right. Maybe he was responsible for some of what happened, but he had only a day or two before begged Marvin to tell him what was going on because he sensed that something wasn't right. He should have insisted, but his ego was riding high about the big opportunity that turned out to be a bullet in his head. He heard the paramedics knocking and he ran to let them in.

# CHAPTER TWENTY-ONE

Twenty-one pills had been pumped from Marvin's body. They stood vigil by his bedside, lips sealed as each family represented said a silent prayer and tried to understand the rhyme or reason behind Marvin's attempt to end his life. It was a scene reminiscent of their earlier days together, their old group reunited by the bond that connected them. Before, they were simply individuals trying to massage their broken hearts, to move forward with their lives after divorce had rendered them confused, lonely, and in need of closure. However, each had managed to find their pot of gold at the end of the rainbow as their lives prospered and new life and new love sprung forth.

Sylvia and Kenny, Mona and Michael, Claudette and Tyrone, and Rachel prayed that Marvin would be alright. The doctor's prognosis was good—Marvin would be released sometime tomorrow with a clean bill of health. Well, maybe a clean bill as far as his physical health was concerned, but his mental state was still in question. That was the battle that loomed over Rachel and her extended family.

Kenny inched closer to Rachel, who clutched the side of the bed where Marvin lay resting. "Some pretty strong words passed between us today." Kenny reached out and put his arm around Rachel's shoulders. She didn't move. "Didn't mean to say all those things, you know. I was just hurt because I had asked Marvin only a couple of days ago to let me know what was going on with him when I sensed that something had him preoccupied."

"I'm not mad at you, Kenny," Rachel finally said, putting her arm around Kenny for support. "I was mad at him, too, but I didn't want him to die. When you called earlier, I knew why. Wasn't sure how you found out, but I knew why."

"We've got to help him get well, Rachel. That's my brother lying there." Kenny squeezed her arm. "I promise that I'm going to do whatever I can to help save the company because it was Marvin's life."

"We've got to save Marvin Thomas first or there won't be a Thomas and Richmond." Rachel snuggled tightly into the crook of Kenny's arm. It felt safe, if only for a moment.

As if an alarm clock had gone off, Marvin woke up, lifted his head slightly, and looked around the room. Though dazed, he could make out the faces of his wife, Rachel, and his business partner, Kenny. Focusing, he saw Sylvia, Tyrone, Claudette, and Mona and Michael gazing at him like he was just born—a brand-new baby—and they were checking to see who he looked like and if he had all of his fingers and toes. But Marvin wanted the images to go away because now he re-membered what he had done only hours earlier, what he'd done to become trapped in a hospital bed. He had hoped to never wake up.

"Marvin," Rachel whispered. "Baby, I'm here. I'm here for you. I'm not going to leave your side."

Marvin smiled and blinked in understanding. The others moved closer to the bed, taking turns stroking his arm, placing a kiss on his forehead, or squeezing his hand in reassurance. Marvin tried to close his eyes, but Kenny took up the lens. He wondered if Kenny was aware of what he'd done…what he hadn't been man enough to tell him. Finally, his eyelids gave way.

Everyone's chattering was getting on his nerves. Why couldn't they just go away and leave him alone? Because they loved him.

"Marvin," Rachel cooed. "The doctor said you're going to be alright. You'll even get to go home in the morning. I'm going to take good care of you."

Tears formed in the corners of Marvin's eyes. He didn't deserve Rachel. She didn't deserve what he'd put her through. He felt her breath on his face as she leaned over and kissed him on the cheek. His eyelids fluttered. "Okay, baby."

Everyone cheered. "Thank you, Lord," Sylvia cried. "God, You are so good."

"All the time," Claudette chimed in.

"Yes, He is," Mona said, not wanting to be left out.

"Why don't we all leave and let Rachel and Marvin have some time together?" Sylvia suggested.

"That's a great idea, baby," Kenny said, grabbing Sylvia and leading the way.

"Thank you all for being the best friends in the whole world," Rachel said. "We couldn't have made it without you. And Claudette, let's set aside a day to go and see Ashley. She deserves our love, too."

Claudette smiled. "You're right, she does."

# CHAPTER TWENTY-TWO

"Hey, baby, some night, huh?" Sylvia asked as she pulled off her coat and hung it up in the guest closet.

"Yeah, quite an ordeal," Kenny responded, as he dragged behind Sylvia and headed straight for the bar. He shook his head. "I can't believe this night." He turned and looked at Sylvia.

"What is it, babe? What's on your mind? I noticed that you and Rachel were in deep conversation."

Kenny picked up a glass from the bar and filled it with Hennessy. "Let me take you back to what happened at dinner tonight." He looked around. "Where's Kenny, Jr.?"

"I called Maya, and she came and got little Kenny and Michael Jr. She's going to keep them overnight. Little Kenny will get a chance to play with his nephew. I can't believe my daughter and I have children that are practically the same age."

"Well, I appreciate you giving me a son in your old age." Kenny laughed for the first time in a while. Then his face took on a serious look. "I learned something tonight, baby, that is going to affect us, possibly in a negative way."

Sylvia walked over to where Kenny was standing and put her arm around his waist. "Does...does it have anything to do with Marvin and why he tried to commit suicide tonight?"

"It has a whole lot to do with Marvin. He sold his shares in the company—all fifty-two of them."

Sylvia's mouth gaped open. "What? Are you sure, Kenny? Why would he do something like that without telling you?"

"Exactly what I wanted to know. Except that when I went looking for him so he could offer an explanation, I found him stretched out on his desk with a stomach full of pills. I was so damn mad, Sylvia, I wanted to shake him awake and kick his ass. Unfortunately, the pills beat me to it."

"You know, this may explain why Rachel was having trouble with her credit cards the other day. We had gone shopping, and everywhere she tried to use her credit card, it was declined. Even at the bank. It made Rachel go ballistic."

"And you're just now telling me?"

"You were so excited about going to the dinner Mona catered. You talked about nothing else, so I didn't burden you with the day I had spent with Rachel. Oh, my God, she was a monster, and it didn't help that we ended up at Steak and Ale, and there was Marvin sitting with his secretary eating a steak when Rachel had been humiliated all over town."

"He was with Yvonne?" Kenny frowned. "That's strange. I've never known Marvin to ever take Yvonne out to lunch."

"I think it was innocent enough. But Rachel turned that restaurant out, shouting and screaming at Marvin like he was the creature from the Black Lagoon. It was downright embarrassing. I'm not going to show my face in there for the next three years."

"Rachel knew what Marvin had done."

"How do you know that, Kenny? She couldn't have known it while we were out shopping."

"I'm not sure when Rachel found out about what Marvin had done. When we were standing at his bedside, Rachel told me she knew. She showed up at the office after I had called their house looking for him. I was angry and I guess she knew that I must have learned what Marvin did and figured that was why I was trying to locate him. I said some terrible things to him, although he didn't hear me...but I believe Rachel did. She had some pretty choice words for me, too, and she was apologizing to me at the hospital because she understood better than either me or Marvin how I was feeling."

"What are we going to do, Kenny? Does this mean... does this mean you are without a job?"

"Not exactly. Last night at the dinner, the men I made my proposal to just happened to be the ones who purchased the stock from Marvin."

Sylvia slumped down in a seat nearby. "Shut the hell

up. So, what you're telling me is that you and Marvin don't own Thomas and Richmond Tecktronics?"

"You've concluded correctly, but they did tell me that my proposal was great and that I had no fear of losing my position with the company. Bastards! Who are they to tell me that my position is safe when I'm in partnership with the owner of this company?"

"I can't believe Marvin did this to you, to us. After all that you've invested in this company, surely Marvin owed you more than a cheap cop-out. Don't get me wrong, I'm glad he's going to be alright, but it makes me so pissing mad that he didn't think enough of you to at least give you a heads-up."

"Imagine how I feel. You know, babe, now that I've had some time to let this episode digest, I'm going to give Marvin a couple of days, then go and have a talk with him. He didn't even try to fight, didn't ask anyone to help him, but now that I know what's been eating at him, I'm going to make a few suggestions. We're not going to give up that easy."

"That's my man—a fighter."

"I didn't give up on you, did I?"

"Kenny Richmond, you're just a lucky man. If I hadn't been in that grocery store that Sunday, you would still be just an ex in my book."

"Girl, don't go playing like that. This was our destiny; can't deny it. So why don't we go on up to bed. I'll get out of this monkey suit and you go and put on one of those fire and desire numbers that always has me lusting for your flesh."

"Boy, it's two in the morning. I'm tired after all the excitement."

"Daddy needs some TLC, sugar, and I promise if you make my dreams come true, I'll make yours come true beyond your wildest imagination."

"Sugar, I've got a wild imagination, so you've got to bring it or stay at home. Although, I'm tired, you've got my adrenaline flowing."

"Girl please, you know you're my freak of the week and then some. If we had a chandelier in the bedroom, you'd be swinging from it."

"Naw," Sylvia said seductively. She took her index finger and curled it, beckoning for Kenny to come closer. Before Kenny realized what was happening, Sylvia unhooked her belt, slipped it from her slacks, and smacked his behind like she was controlling a lion with a whip. She walked backward up the stairs, unbuttoning her silk blouse as she inched her way upward. She threw out her belt again, but this time Kenny grabbed it and pulled himself up to where she had fallen back on the step. He held the belt solidly in one hand while he straddled her and placed wet kisses all over her mouth and neck. He stopped long enough to unbutton his shirt and slide out of it; his slacks were next to go. He let out a roar and tilted his head back, coming back down for the kill.

Sylvia lay trapped in the middle of the step like a helpless damsel in distress with one leg stretched straight out, the other bent at the knee. Kenny's hot breath licked at her making her weak from the heat. Not putting up a fight, she let the lion lick her neck, tracing his tongue down to her breasts until he finally dropped the belt and ripped the blouse from her body. He roared again, which made Sylvia giggle, but she gave up the ghost when he devoured her whole, pawing and licking, her kicking and screaming until her legs trembled in surrender.

Out of breath, the lion lay upon the lioness satisfied that she was satisfied. He placed another kiss on her lips, then he raised his head and said, "I'm the king of the jungle."

"Yes, you are, baby," the lioness said in a soft whisper, her body limp with perspiration. "You're the king of my jungle."

"Now if I can only save our kingdom from falling down."

"You've marked your territory; nobody can take it from you."

Kenny smothered Sylvia with kisses. She wrapped her arms around him. "Today is a brand-new day," Kenny whispered, his breath still hot on Sylvia's face. "I won't let those men take the company from us."

"I know you won't, baby, 'cuz you're the king of the jungle."

Their bedroom felt like a dark cloud without rain. Seeing Marvin stretched out on the hospital bed had left Mona with a sick feeling in the pit of her stomach. Marvin was the champion in their group. He made sense when everyone else didn't. She couldn't believe that of all people, he would resort to ending his life when the chips were down.

Mona glanced back at Michael, whose silence meant he was hurt too. He looked up when he saw Mona looking, then went to her and wrapped his arms around her neck.

"What a damn shame. Mona, this was supposed to be your night, but Marvin had to upstage you by trying to kill himself."

"A damn shame indeed. I can't forget the look on poor Kenny's face when he practically ran from the country club after talking with those men. How could Marvin be so selfish? Was he even thinking about the lives he was going to affect by giving away the company? Poor Rachel."

"And Kenny had his stuff together, too. It was a pitiful sight to have to witness. When Kinyard said that he had bought Marvin's shares in the company, I swear Kenny turned deep purple. He was like a hot pot with no handles. You couldn't touch him, he was so mad. If Barack Obama hadn't been there, I believe Kenny would have kicked someone's ass tonight, especially when Kinyard told him that his job was safe."

"Marvin looked pitiful. As much as I want to hate him, he's still a good man. He's got some serious issues that he and Rachel are going to have to work through. Glad I'm not in their shoes. In fact, let's stop talking about them and let me give you that rain-check I promised."

"Ohhhhhh, that's what I'm talking about, baby."

"Michael, it's funny how talking about the depressed makes you horny."

"Baby, in my profession, that's called passive aggression. I say, bring it on."

Mona began to laugh.

"What's wrong with you?" Michael asked.

"Baby, you should see yourself trying to get out of your clothes. You've got your shirt hanging on by one sleeve, and you've got one leg in and one leg out of your boxers all at the same time." Mona giggled again.

"Ready to box?" Michael looked at Mona with lust in his married soul. "Come on, girl, I'm not going to be able to wait too much longer."

"I'm ready, Dr. Broussard."

Michael rushed to where Mona stood in her lacy, slate-blue bra and panties and wrapped his arms around her and hypnotized her with a passionate kiss. He stopped and looked at her, then politely lifted her from the floor and carried her into the bathroom. He lifted her into the shower, getting in behind her, and turned the water on. The steam cloud provided the perfect curtain as the water beat down on them and cleansed their souls.

Claudette took off her coat and slipped onto the couch. Tyrone followed, putting his arm around her. They sat in the dimly lit family room without uttering a word. Ten minutes passed.

"Baby, would you like for me to make you some tea?" Tyrone asked. "It might soothe your soul."

"Back in the day, I would have lit up a cigarette. Something about the nicotine eases the pain. There was so much pain in that room tonight, Tyrone; I just couldn't take it. Seeing Rachel all bottled up in her sadness..."

"At least Marvin's going to be alright. It seems like the whole room was mad at him. Whatever was on Marvin's mind that made him do what he did had to be pretty awful. He's a good man, though. He's done so much for everyone in our group, especially us."

"I know," Claudette said. "I was thinking that very thing, but it still made me mad to think that Marvin would cop out like that. We don't know the full story, but when they're up to sharing, we'll be there for them."

"Want that tea?"

"No, sweetie. I want you to stay close to me. I thank God every day that you and I were able to have another chance at our marriage. Funny how it came to be," Claudette said in a faraway voice. "If Kwame hadn't thrown that cigarette into the wastebasket, our lives might have taken a different path. God has a way of getting our attention."

"Why don't we get up and go to bed, Claudette? It's two in the morning. We'll be more comfortable."

"I want to stay here. Don't ask me why. I'd like it a lot if you snuggled up with me on the couch, Mr. Beasley."

Tyrone smiled. He lifted Claudette's braids from her face and watched as sleep overtook her. "Good night, Mrs. Beasley. Everything is going to be alright."

# CHAPTER TWENTY-THREE

The sudden realization that someone was in the room made Rachel sit up in the recliner that she had used as a bed. She brushed back her hair with her hands, then wiped her mouth as the image of a man in a white coat taking Marvin's vitals filled her vision. Marvin was sitting up and looked well rested.

"Didn't mean to wake you, Mrs. Thomas," said Dr. Campbell, a short man with graying temples. "Marvin here is going to be alright. I'll complete his discharge papers, and you'll be free to take him home."

"Thank you, Dr. Campbell. Thanks for all you've done to save my husband."

"That's my job, ma'am. He's going to need some TLC, and I'm going to leave that part to you."

Marvin didn't say a word, but Rachel noticed that he managed a half smile. "I can handle that part."

Dr. Campbell turned to Marvin and patted him on the arm. "You can go ahead and get dressed. Your discharge papers should be ready in a few minutes. I'm going to give you a referral to our staff psychologist, and I've recommended at least three sessions to begin. I advise you to take it easy for a few days before trying to go back to work. In fact, I'm scheduling your first appointment with the psychologist for Monday. Do you have any questions?"

Marvin looked from Dr. Campbell to Rachel. He let out a heavy sigh. "No...no, I don't think so."

"Well, if you do, your wife has my number, and you can call me anytime. And I do mean anytime."

"Thanks, Dr. Campbell." Marvin reached up and shook his outstretched hand.

Dr. Campbell left the room and quiet ensued. The quiet was so constricting that Rachel almost gagged. She stood up to move close to Marvin, but he put out his hand for her to stop.

"I can get dressed by myself," he said.

He slid off the side of the bed, pulling the hospital-issued robe around him, and moved to the chair that sat near the foot where his clothes were neatly folded. With hands clasped together, Rachel watched from where she stood, wanting to assist Marvin any way she could. His silence said something else—that he didn't want to talk about it, that he wanted to be alone, that maybe he wished he had died.

Tears appeared from nowhere and ran down her face. The feelings of rejection and helplessness were more than she could bear. Marvin seemed weak, sitting on the side of the bed to put his clothes on—his back to her. Rachel squeezed her lips together, willing the pain to stay inside and not erupt as it threatened to do. She had to be strong no matter what because God hadn't spared Marvin's life for her to leave him.

Rachel sat in the chair and waited for Dr. Campbell to return and for Marvin to acknowledge her. She was his wife, for heaven's sake, and she was already aware of what had brought him here.

The door to the room opened and Dr. Campbell walked in. It was obvious that he felt the tension as he looked from Marvin to Rachel, Marvin sitting on the side of the bed and Rachel sitting in the recliner.

"Is there something I can do?" Dr. Campbell asked, his tone gentle and considerate.

Marvin shook his head no. Rachel got up and shook the doctor's hand and took the papers he came to deliver.

Dr. Campbell looked in her eyes. "If you need me for anything, call me." He patted Marvin on the shoulder and left the room.

"It's time to go," Rachel said, making an attempt to push past the awkwardness.

Marvin stood up and came around the side of the bed. He looked at Rachel, and the tears began to flow from his eyes.

"It's alright, baby. I'm going to take care of you."

Marvin offered a faint smile and wiped his face. Then the door flew open one more time. "Wheelchair for the patient," the attendant said, oblivious to the emotions that were running high. "I'm NASCAR bound, so you can have a fast ride or a slow one."

"Slow ride," Marvin said. Rachel looked straight ahead. They would have plenty of time to talk later.

# CHAPTER TWENTY-FOUR

Ashley Jordan Lewis enjoyed the few hours she was able to leave her jail cell. While many of the women hung out in the yard and smoked cigarettes or played checkers, she found comfort in the gym or the library. In fact, she liked the library so much, she was allowed to work there for three to four hours a day.

Reading was never her passion, but she found it stimulating, and soon became absorbed in suspense and mystery novels. She was also allowed to use the computer, cataloging books and checking to see what new releases were on the market. When no one was looking, she'd browse the internet to catch up on the latest news.

Today was no different than any other day—the same powdered eggs and bacon for breakfast. Ashley usually sat alone in the chow hall, not comfortable around the hardened female inmates that were her neighbors of sorts. She didn't even give a thought to the fact that her very own crime, labeled heinous and calculating, put her in the same category as the ones she feared. No, poisoning her husband to death was just not the

same as pulling a trigger twenty-one times, one bullet
for each year a woman on her cell block was married
to an over-the-top abusive cop husband. Nor was it the
same as the brutal ax murders of six men by a woman
who picked up men on Interstate 75, had sex with
them, and then put them out of their misery because
they reminded her of her insane father who molested
her as a child. No, the murder of her husband, William,
was quick, easy, painless, and almost uneventful. He
never knew what had happened, but that's what he got
for threatening her.

Ashley put her empty tray away and headed for the
library. Going to the library was like stepping into the
sunshine or going on a small journey far away from
Atlanta. She would get so absorbed in a book that she
would allow herself to be transported to that particular
place in time, becoming the characters she read about
without acting out the scenes in the real. The library was
virtually empty when she arrived, and that made her
happy because she would have more time to herself.

She placed the few books that had been returned back
on their shelves, stopping long enough to flip through
the first few pages of each one to see if it might be a
book she wanted to read. When the books had been
shelved, she went to the media lab, which was where
she was assigned, and sat down at a computer.

Skipping the library sites where she generally did her
searches, Ashley went straight to the internet, which

was already logged on through the system. World and local happenings dominated the home page of the internet server. Suddenly she jumped back and cupped her mouth with her hand at the picture that flicked on the screen.

"Oh, my God," Ashley said out loud. She looked around to see if anyone heard her, and when she was sure that no one had, she clicked the picture of Marvin Thomas. The headline was set in a bold, large font. The story read: *Marvin Thomas, CEO of Thomas and Richmond Tecktronics, Inc., was found last evening slumped over his desk from an overdose of pain killers. He was found by his partner, Kenny Richmond, who called 911. Mr. Thomas was rushed to Mercy Hospital and treated. At press time, Mr. Thomas was said to be in fair condition.*

Ashley scratched her head and pulled her fingers through her blonde hair as she read the article over and over again. The article never stated why Marvin tried to take his life, but Ashley was dumbfounded and couldn't believe that this was the same Marvin Thomas who was so positive about life and willing to help everyone who needed it. Thinking about Marvin made her think about the rest of the group, the Ex-Files, whom she hadn't seen in several years except for Claudette who visited her on the regular. Claudette was her unsung Shero, having adopted her daughter—the daughter she conceived with her now dead husband and whom she'd feared would be rejected by her parents because of their hate for William because he was black. She owed Claudette a lot.

Sunlight replaced the darkness that had engulfed the house only hours earlier, its brilliance so radiant that even the drapes that were wrapped around the double window, hanging by an antique rod, looked like an opening to a faraway place in a fairy tale. In fact, the light was so bright, Rachel shot up in the bed with a sudden realization that she had overslept. The digital numbers on the clock radio that sat on the nightstand read 11:25. Panic gripped her as she turned her head to look at the place where her husband was sleeping, only to find it empty.

Rachel jumped to the floor, sliding her feet into her slippers. The quiet in the house turned her panic to fear as she realized she hadn't heard the ramblings of Serena, who would have been climbing all over her, begging to watch television or requesting a bowl of cereal.

Not bothering to wash her face, Rachel reached for her silk robe that hung on the back of the bathroom door. She rushed from the room calling Serena's name, and when there was no answer, she took the stairs two at a time, stopping at the bottom. The sound of laughter met her ears.

Creeping as if she was on the verge of surprising an intruder, Rachel tip-toed toward the sound of Serena's voice coupled with that of her father. Rachel clasped her hands to her heart, the tension melting as she watched father and daughter entertain each other.

"Hey," Marvin whispered when he realized Rachel was standing at the entrance to the family room.

"Hey yourself. Why didn't you wake me and shouldn't you be resting?" Rachel asked Marvin all in one breath. Serena ran to her and begged to be picked up, while Marvin remained propped up on one of the decorator pillows that dotted the couch.

"I'm fine, Rachel, really. No need to fuss over me. I think I'm going to drive to the office today."

"Why? Today is Sunday. There's nothing at the job that can't wait until tomorrow if you choose to go there. Just take it easy, baby. You don't know how much I worried about you."

Marvin stood up and looked into Rachel's worried eyes. "Baby, I can't say enough how sorry I am to have put you through this. At that moment, I just wanted to die—get away from the world."

"Marvin, don't talk like that."

He kissed her forehead, and ran his hands through her hair. "You may never understand what I was going through or how I felt, Rachel. When you came into that restaurant the other day ranting and raving it was the last straw. I'm not blaming my actions on you, but it was almost confirmation for what I thought I needed to do—leave this world behind."

"Why didn't you trust me enough to share?"

Marvin shrugged his shoulders. "You're not listening. Rachel, you are so emotional. You don't take time to think things through and to ask yourself the what, the why, and the how. You just go off, and when you went off without me being able to give you an explanation, I knew that I had done the right thing in not confiding in you."

"But you confided in Yvonne. She's not family."

"I didn't totally confide in her. She was privy to a couple of letters I wrote that caused her to worry about her future. In the event that I wouldn't be around to treat her to one more Secretaries Day luncheon, I elected to do it then. She didn't have to say anything, and it made me feel at ease, that is, until you walked in."

"Wow" was all Rachel could say. "That hit below the belt."

"Didn't mean to, but that's the way it is. Look, how about I take my two favorite girls to dinner after I come back from the office?"

"Ummm," Rachel sighed. "If I can't talk you out of staying home, Serena and I are going to accompany you to work."

"No, I need to go by myself." Marvin kissed Rachel's forehead again. "I need to sit and think about what I'm going to do."

"I thought you decided to sell the company?"

Marvin held up his hand. "I don't want to talk to you

or anyone else about that at this moment. Baby, give me my space so I can work this out in my head."

Rachel backed away with her arms at her side. She felt as though her feelings had just been run over by a steamroller; stomped on and mashed down to the core. Moisture formed in her eyes and threatened to expose her, but she kept the tears at bay, at least until she was alone.

All of a sudden her temples were pounding and her head felt like it was on fire. A fierce headache threatened to take her out, making her recoil and move swiftly toward the drawer that housed her migraine medicine. If she had to fight, she would.

Rachel grabbed Serena by the hand and moved toward the kitchen, not bothering to look back at Marvin, who was looking at her. She felt his stare; it was like a leech, holding on for dear life while sucking the blood out of her. It was better to let him go so he could sort out the complexities his life had become, because if she didn't, next time the call might come from the coroner's office. But she would be here if he needed her.

Silence grabbed the air, choking out all sounds of life. And then there it was, a slight squeak and a sudden thud. Maybe Marvin didn't plan to shut the door so hard, but then there was silence again.

# CHAPTER TWENTY-FIVE

Rachel wasn't sure how long she had sat in the family room, but it was obvious she'd been there awhile. Thoughts of her outburst at the restaurant began to haunt her as guilt was getting the best of her. She wiped her mouth and blinked to clear her vision, relieved to see that Serena was still watching her *Dora the Explorer* video.

Yawning, Rachel got up from the couch and stretched her arms realizing that she was still in her gown and robe. She glanced at the clock on the wall and couldn't believe it was almost one o'clock.

She waited until Serena's video was over and turned off the television. "Come on, Serena. Mommy's got to get out of her night clothes. I might as well wash some clothes while I'm at it and give Isabel a break."

Rachel showered and put on a pair of jeans and a loose-fitting, pink paisley top, something easy to work in. She brought the clothes basket to the wash room, stopping in each bathroom to grab dirty washcloths and towels. With Serena at her side, she went down to Marvin's bathroom and gathered up his dirty linen and was about to go back upstairs when Serena called out to her.

"Mommy, Mommy, look."

"What you got there?" Rachel asked, kneeling down to see what Serena kept tugging on that was stuck underneath the cushions on the couch in Marvin's office. Rachel pulled up the leather cushion and threw it to the side, then stared at the couch with a puzzled look on her face.

*Why would Marvin put his suit underneath the cushions?* Rachel wondered. Knowing that the answer wasn't going to just materialize, she seized the jacket and pants and had just begun to probe when an overpowering smell made her head hurt. *Sniff, sniff.* She withdrew her nose quickly, the fragrance pulsating inside. It didn't take a fool to know that the strong, sweet odor was that of some woman's expensive perfume.

In horror, Rachel threw the suit on the floor and stomped on it. "Did you think I wasn't going to find out, Marvin?" Rachel screamed out loud. "Did you think you could hide your whore from me and I wouldn't know? It was just an innocent lunch you said. You lying bastard." She threw up her fists and screamed.

Serena began to cry, pulling at a crazed Rachel's leg. "Let go, Serena. Let go of Mommy."

Rachel moved Serena to the side and went around to Marvin's desk. She went through his drawers, tossing things aside but not finding anything at all suspicious.

With all her might, she shoved everything on top of the desk to the floor. Serena, scared of her mother's bizarre behavior that she didn't understand, began to wail.

When Rachel was done, she sat in the middle of the floor, while Serena stood over her.

"Mom...my, Mom...my, ahhh, ahhh, ahhh, Maaaa...my."

Rachel grabbed Serena and sat her on her lap. "Mommy's sorry, baby. I don't know what's going on; Mommy doesn't know what to do." *Huhhhh, huhhh, huhhh, huhhh,* Rachel sighed as her chest heaved in and out. "Rock-a-bye baby in the tree top," Rachel sang.

Serena calmed down, her face wet with tears. She cried some more, but soon fell asleep in her mother's arms.

When Marvin returned home, the house felt tight as if it was held together by a giant rubber band, stretched to capacity and ready to burst any minute like a time bomb. This house that had held so much love for him now seemed to condemn him for being a failure to all that depended on him.

There was no welcome mat standing at the door to greet him, but he was cool with that. Rachel was probably sulking somewhere in the house because he had spoken the truth about her behavior. There was no doubt in his mind that he loved her, but he needed space so that he could work out all the problems that had complicated his life, that had him making rash decisions, that had him bouncing off the walls, that made him want to take his own life and to hell with everyone else.

Voices floated up from somewhere below. Marvin stopped and leaned over, to listen. It had to come from the television in his office since it was the only room downstairs besides the exercise room that had a TV in it. He started down the stairs just as the phone rang. Three rings, and he picked it up.

"Hello, Thomas residence."

"Hey, Marv, this is Harold. How you doing, man? Got your letter yesterday."

Marvin let go of a sigh, grateful that Harold wasn't calling to discuss his brush with death, something he wasn't ready to discuss in detail with anyone. "I'm glad you called, and...glad you got the letter."

"It seemed urgent, so I thought I'd better call right away."

"Without beating around the bush, I should tell you the company is in serious trouble, but I don't want to talk about it now. What is your schedule like tomorrow? Can you come to Atlanta?"

"Yeah, Marv. Whatever you need. What time you want to meet?"

"Let's say ten-thirty. I've got to get in touch with Kenny Richmond; he needs to be there. At that time, I'll explain all."

"I'll be there, Marv."

"Harold, thanks, man. I hope we can bury our differences and move forward. I would like that very much, cuz."

There was a short pause. "I've waited for this day for awhile. While you're on the phone, I want you to know that Denise and I are getting married." Another pause. Harold continued when Marvin didn't respond. "I'll understand if you want to change your mind about meeting me. I just wanted to be up front since we're moving forward with our lives."

"I'll admit it took me back for a second, but I'm happy for you and Denise. I'm glad that you all have been able to work through the custody issue, although I never expected this outcome."

"It's been hard on Danica. She loves both me and Denise. Shuttling back and forth between the two houses was taking a toll on all of us, and then Denise seemed to be hanging around whenever Danica was at my house. It was an easy conclusion, although we didn't reach it overnight."

Marvin laughed. "Congratulations, cuz. I wish you all the best. See you at ten-thirty tomorrow morning."

"Gotcha. Give my best to Rachel."

"Will do."

Marvin hung up the phone and realized that he had not seen hide nor hair of Rachel. Maybe she was still upset with him for leaving the house. He hadn't even gone to the office; he couldn't face the place where he almost ended his life. He had driven to the bar where he had met Peaches, hoping that by chance she would be there so that he could talk some sense into her. He had nothing to give her, and he couldn't risk his wife finding out about a tryst in which he hadn't even been a willing participant.

Marvin walked downstairs, the voices on the television getting louder. Where were Rachel and Serena? Puzzled, he turned at the end of the hallway and walked in his home office and froze. Shock turned to anger as his eyes scanned the disheveled room—files, important papers and documents, pictures, a desk lamp as well as his flat-screen monitor lay strewn on the floor. And then he saw it, understood the source of contention. *What in the hell had Rachel been looking for in his office?*

"So your lying ass decided to come home," Rachel said, coming out of his bathroom, startling him.

"What in the hell is this and what were you looking for in my office? Where is Serena, Rachel?"

She picked up his suit and shoved it in his face. "Smell it. Smells like you've been with a Harlem whore. You said you were just taking her to lunch because you felt bad for her because she was worried about her job. You sleep with her, too?"

Marvin snatched the suit out of Rachel's hands and threw it on the couch. He threw up his hands, his palms in Rachel's face. "Are you finished, Rachel? I was not with Yvonne, for your information. Or anyone else for that matter," he lied. "This is exactly what I mean when I say you fly off the handle without getting the facts first."

"So what are the facts, Marvin? Huh? Tell me why

your suit is drenched in a woman's perfume. Is that why you left the house and didn't want me to tag along? Huh? And don't lie to me. I've heard enough lies to last an eternity."

"Honestly, I don't know how the perfume got on it." Marvin looked away in thought. "I was so upset after leaving Cecil's office."

"Who in the hell is Cecil? I don't know any Cecil. Don't make up things to confuse me."

"Cecil is my attorney, Rachel," Marvin said harshly. "He's an old friend who handles corporate takeovers. I went to see him about what I was going to do. That's when I told him to sell my shares. I knew it was the biggest mistake of my life, but I didn't know what else to do. So I...I went to a bar and got drunk."

"Do you really expect me to believe that since you don't drink?"

"Rachel, I'm about tired of you. I'm trying to explain this the best way I can. Now, if you'd shut up a minute, I'm going to try to finish this."

Rachel turned and walked toward the bathroom, stopped, turned around, and stood in front of Marvin with her hand on her hip. "I'm listening."

She excited him. Marvin loved Rachel more than she could imagine. Even in her anger, she was beautiful. Her figure was still together, and if he weren't so mad at her, he'd scoop her up and make love to her right on the couch. In fact, it wasn't a bad idea.

"I'm listening," Rachel said again.

"You're beautiful."

"And you're a heathen."

Marvin laughed. "Rachel, I got sloppy drunk that night. I'm sure I passed out right at the bar. I swear a few hours later I woke up in my car, not knowing where I was and wishing I was at home with you and Serena. Hell, I'd just sold the company without telling Kenny, without telling anyone what I was doing. I sacrificed my family and the livelihood of all my employees."

Marvin reached for Rachel and took her arms and placed them around his waist. He circled her neck with his arms and laid his head on her shoulder. "It had nothing to do with you, baby. I just lost the faith."

Rachel held him tight until she finally pulled away. "Marvin, baby, you have to promise me that you won't keep anything else from me. I'm stronger than you think. We went through some tough moments before we got married, but since then, our lives have been heaven sent. I want what we have now forever, Marvin. You owe me that. I wouldn't mind having another child with you, if that's what you want, but talk to me. I'm not a stranger."

Marvin hugged her tight, then pulled back so he could see her face. He brushed back her hair with his hands. "You're right, baby. You are my soulmate, and I want what we have, too. I love you, Rachel, and I always will. I just have to find a way to get out of the mess I'm in."

Her lips met his, and they enjoyed an intimate kiss. Marvin looked at the couch, but felt it wasn't the right moment to make love to his wife. He kissed her again, just glad to be able to hold her in his arms and gather strength from her. Relaxed, Rachel let her emotions flow as she joined him in another passionate kiss.

"Mommy, Daddy, why are you kissing?"

Marvin and Rachel turned around and laughed at Serena, who had finally awaken and had come to find her mommy.

"Why don't I run and get some Chinese takeout, unless you want to go with me?" Marvin asked.

"We'll wait until you come back," Rachel said. "I love you, Marvin."

"I love you, Daddy."

"I love you both."

# CHAPTER TWENTY-SIX

"Hey, Claudette, this is Sylvia."

"Good morning, Mrs. Richmond," Claudette teased.

"Girl, cut that out. You know my first name; use it."

They both laughed. "What time are we rolling out to see Ashley?" Sylvia asked.

"I'm waiting for Mona to pick me up now. She had to wait for her nanny to get to the house to watch Michael Jr. Reagan is in preschool, and Reebe is going to pick her up for me."

"So, you're not taking Reagan to see her mother?"

"Sylvia, I'm Reagan's mother. Remember, I adopted her."

"Ouch. I didn't mean any harm by that, Claudette. It's just that Ashley is the child's biological mother, and I just thought that…"

"That's what you get for thinking. No, I thought this should be a time that just us girls meet with Ashley. It's going to be a shock for her to see you for the first time in how long?"

"I know, Claudette. I feel ashamed. If that's how you want me to feel, you've succeeded in making me feel that way."

"Look, Mona is blowing her horn. We'll see you in a half-hour, Sylvia. What about Rachel? Did she change her mind?"

"Rachel is next on my list. She seemed distant and non-talkative. Go, we'll talk when I see you."

"Okay, girl. Be ready."


Ashley lay daydreaming on her small cot in her three-by-five cell. She looked forward to her visit with Claudette. Claudette would fill her in on all the goings-on in and around Atlanta, especially about the group she adored but that had now estranged themselves from her. It had not been her intention to kill William at first. He kept boxing her in until she couldn't take it any longer. She would have remarried him in a heart-beat if his love for her would have been real, but all he really wanted was the unborn baby she was carrying, because his mistress lost hers. Ashley hoped Claudette would bring Reagan even though it was a school day.

"Lewis," the guard called, "your visitors are here."

"Visitors? I'm expecting only one visitor," Ashley responded.

"Well, tell that to the bunch who's waiting in the room to see you."

Shock registered on her face and surprise in her eyes when Ashley walked into the reception room bound in ankle and wrist cuffs and saw Claudette accompanied by Mona and Sylvia. Speechless, she looked from one to the other, wondering what had prompted this sudden visit. It must have had something to do with Marvin, she thought, but Rachel was missing. They hadn't set foot in the prison in over two years.

"Oh, oh, my God," Ashley said, putting her hands to her mouth upon seeing her old friends. Claudette stood back and smiled.

"Hey, Ashley," Sylvia said, walking toward her with her arms outstretched. Sylvia hugged her while Ashley gave Sylvia a kiss on the cheek. "It's so good to see you. I know it's been a while, and I feel terrible for not coming. But I'm here now to try and make it up to you."

Ashley managed a smile.

"Yeah," Mona interrupted, giving Ashley a hug and a cheek-to-cheek kiss. "I feel bad, too. Claudette practically threatened us..." Sylvia gave Mona a swift kick in the leg. "Ouch."

Claudette laughed. "Hey, girl, how you doing?" Ashley and Claudette exchanged hugs and kisses. "You look good in those blonde cornrows."

Ashley smiled. "How am I doing? Well, I think I've read every book in the library, the food is still horrible, haven't made many friends but I don't want to—I'd say I'm doing quite well."

That seemed to put everyone at ease. They laughed. "Well, as I was saying," Mona continued, ignoring Claudette and Sylvia's stares, "we just knew we were past due and needed to give you some love."

"Thanks, Mona," Ashley said, a little overcome with emotion. "I really do appreciate you all coming to see me."

"I like your jewelry, Ash." It took Mona to bring attention to the obvious.

"If I could," Ashley began, "I'd give these bracelets to you, Mona. But you wouldn't want them—too constricting." No one laughed. Ashley turned toward Claudette. "I see Reagan isn't with you."

"No," Claudette began. "We wanted this day to be time spent with you and us."

Ashley smiled. "It was just that I was hoping to see her smiling face. Give her a kiss for me."

"I will," Claudette said.

"Well, tell me how you all have been. By the way, where is Rachel?" Ashley passed her eyes over Claudette, Sylvia, and Mona, wondering who would be the first to break the news about Marvin.

"Rachel is a little under the weather," Sylvia said, not wanting to get into any discussion about Marvin.

"Oh, I'm disappointed that she's not here. Give her my love."

Everyone sat at the table wondering who was going to speak first, wondering what they were going to say. *Thump, thump, thump* went Sylvia's fingers as she drummed them on the table.

"Okay, ladies, you've got to lighten up," Ashley said, standing up to stretch. "I'm the one behind bars. You look like you're going to the guillotine. You should see yourselves; you're depressing to look at."

"You are so funny, Ashley," Sylvia said. "Yeah, what's wrong with y'all?"

"Girl, please," Mona cut in. "I know Miss Saddity from the City ain't trying to act like she's not having trouble finding things to say. Look, we love you, Ashley. You're our girl, even though you're locked up in this joint. Couldn't your father pull some strings or call in some favors for you?"

"This sounds like the old group," Ashley admitted. "Mona, if it was that simple, I would have been out of here a long time ago. But I killed a man. They said it was premeditated murder, cold and calculated. Even if Daddy could pull some strings, William's sisters were going to see to it that this rich white girl wasn't getting out no time soon."

"Whoa," Mona said. "Now that's deep."

"Why don't we change the subject?" Claudette begged. "Ashley wants to know what you two have been up to."

"You know what I'd like to know?" Ashley asked.

"What, girl?" Sylvia asked with a smile on her face.

"What happened to Marvin? Since you turkeys got here, I've been waiting to see who was going to tell me first—that is, since Rachel isn't here to tell me herself."

There was a moment of silence, then a sigh from one of the ladies, then quiet again. "Marvin is under a lot of stress, Ash," Sylvia began.

"Give me the abbreviated version; I read the news," Ashley said with humor written on her face.

"I guess she told you, Sylvia," Mona quipped, then let out a holler.

"Alright, alright, alright," Sylvia said. "To tell you the truth, we don't know the whole story either. Kenny told me that Marvin sold his shares in the company—all fifty-two of them, which means Marvin no longer owns the company and Kenny may not have a job. You know my baby was some kind of freaking mad."

"Now you're talking," Ashley said.

"You think this is funny?" Sylvia jumped up from her seat. "I'm not telling you this to provide you some kind of entertainment you've been missing. Girl, this translates to my livelihood, my family's livelihood. Kenny worked too hard for this company to see it all go down the drain." Sylvia stopped. The tears began to flow, and she covered her eyes and let it go. What she was feeling had finally come out. She was afraid.

"Enough of this," Claudette said.

"Do they have some tissue in here?" Mona asked. "Sylvia's got bubbles coming out of her nose."

All of sudden, Sylvia began to laugh. "It takes Mona to take a serious moment and twist it around into being something funny." Everybody laughed.

"Whew," Ashley said. "I hoped that got me off the hook."

"No," Sylvia said. "Come here, girl." Sylvia hugged

Ashley. "We miss you. It was starting to feel like the Ex-Files up in here. In a weird sort of way, our group is still together. We formed a bond that is too deep to tear apart. Look, we're still here supporting one another, and Ash, we're going to do better about coming to visit you, but we do hope you get out soon."

"It's going to take a miracle and a whole lot of prayer," Ashley said. "I know what they mean about people getting converted when they go to prison. Of course, I'll never be a Muslim." Everybody laughed. "But I do have a connection to a higher being. I ask God every day to forgive me for what I did. If I had never gone back to William, I wouldn't be in this predicament."

"Girl, you should have listened to me," Mona said. "I tried to tell you over and over that that man didn't mean you no good. You just had to give him some, and it was all over then."

"You're right, Mona. I should have listened, but I wanted revenge. I wanted to show his mistress that I still had power over my husband whether he was an ex or not."

"Well, the unthinkable happened," Claudette said. "I just wish Ash had let me get a piece of that Mandingo before she put him out of his misery."

"Oh, Lawd." Mona laughed. "Yeah, remember the day William had your big booty up in the air and put you off his property because you wouldn't leave? Lawd, I wish I could have been there to witness that. I can't believe that was over three years ago."

"It wasn't funny then, but it is kind of funny now," Claudette put in. "That wouldn't have happened if Ashley hadna popped his big head and told him to move out of the way because she was going with me to the doctor."

"The things we can laugh at now," Sylvia said. "Ash, what do you need besides your girls checking on you every once in awhile?"

"Nothing. Just don't forget me. This is like therapy. Even though all you hussies got married, you should keep up your meetings and maybe rename the group."

The ladies chatted for the next hour and a half, telling Ashley all about the children, especially Kenny Jr.'s birthday party. Their lives had gone on, but there was a vacant spot that would never be filled until Ashley could make it back to the other side.

"Well, sweetheart," Claudette began, "we're going to have to head on back. We enjoyed it, and I'll see you in a couple of weeks...with Reagan."

"Yeah, girl, it was so good to see you," Mona said. "Now, I feel as if my guilt has rolled away."

"I love you, Ash," Sylvia said. "You know that you've always been in my heart, and I think about you all the time. I was delinquent in visiting you, but no more. Give me a hug."

"Group hug," Ashley shouted. Mona and Claudette moved in to join Ashley and Sylvia. "Feels like old times."

# CHAPTER TWENTY-SEVEN

Cars littered the parking lot as would be the custom on a Monday morning or any other day of the work week. Marvin looked at them and then at the building that housed the enterprise that he had built from the ground up. It had made him a rich man, but he had never believed, even in his wildest dreams, that all of this could come crashing down around him.

He looked at the cars again—inanimate objects made of steel. They couldn't feel or defend themselves. They were at the mercy of man's manipulations. But for the one hundred or so employees that owned those cars, man's manipulations, were about to wreak havoc on their lives as there was a strong possibility they might have to feel the sting of a pink slip.

Marvin shook his head to try to rid it of the psychological traffic that had dominated his brain since he'd sold his shares. He wasn't sure when it had happened. Maybe it was when he'd realized that he was still alive and had to face the next day, but something inside was begging and shouting at him not to give up. He thought about Rachel and how all of this had affected their lives, which had been so wonderful and almost perfect up to now.

Yvonne was busy preparing budget information for the accounting department when Marvin walked into the office. Startled, she looked at Marvin like she had seen a ghost. The whole world had seen the article in the paper about her boss' attempted suicide, and for Yvonne to see him standing there in the flesh like nothing had happened caught her off guard. She hadn't expected to see him, but there he was dressed in a light-weight brown blazer and jeans; another day at the office.

"Uh, uh, uh, good morning, Mr. Thomas."

"Good morning, Yvonne."

"Coffee?" she asked, her eyes magnified ten times through the lens of her glasses.

"Yes, that would be great. And would you please phone Mr. Richmond and ask him to come to my office?"

"Yes, sir. Right away."

"Great." Marvin half smiled and walked into his office, closing the door behind him.

He touched his desk and ran his fingers along the perimeter, stopping to recall the moment he had decided to end it all. Nothing had changed—the chair looked the same, the papers he left in his basket were still there. So this is what it would have looked like if he had transitioned to the other side and his spirit had a chance to take a peek—business as usual.

Marvin was still in a trance-like state when he heard the knock at the door. He willed his legs to move to the other side of the desk before he asked the visitor to come in.

"Mr. Thomas," Yvonne began, pushing the door open, "you have several messages from Miz Peaches." Marvin shot up in his seat, maybe a little too fast, but he recovered before Yvonne was even aware. "And...Mr. Harold called to say that he might be a few minutes late?"

"Yes, Yvonne. Mr. Thomas is expected at ten-thirty. Have you spoken with Mr. Richmond yet?"

"Oh, yes. He'll be here in fifteen minutes."

"Thank you, Yvonne. Please close the door behind you."

Fifteen minutes wasn't enough time to call Peaches. He pulled his coffee cup close to him, picked it up, and took a sip. He sighed, took a last look at the clock, then dialed Peaches' number almost as if he had committed it to memory. He waited.

"Hey, handsome," she said. "Getting in a little late this morning. I like ten o'clock scholars." No "This is Peaches" or "Hello, Mr. Thomas." She'd gone over the line. What if he had had Yvonne dial the number?

"What do you want, Peaches? You need to stop calling my office and stop calling me handsome. I might have had my secretary place the call."

"Well, I know better than that. I see you fidgeting in your seat now. Getting all worked up just from the sound of my voice," Peaches whispered. "Because you've got me all worked up. I'm squeezing my knees together, trying to keep from screaming out loud about how hot you've made me down there. It would be nice to feel you between my legs, putting me out of my misery."

Marvin put his hand over his crotch. "There's nothing you can do for me except go somewhere and fall off the face of the earth."

"Let's not be bitter. Now if you had a little, Peaches, you wouldn't need to have gone through all the trouble you did Friday night. I do read the papers. And if I didn't know better, I'd have thought you were trying to kill yourself so you could get out of paying me my fifty thousand dollars."

"Peaches, I don't have fifty thousand dollars. How can I make you understand that?"

"You're right. You can't make me understand. Lover boy, you're just going to have to work something out. I don't have any suggestions, but I'm sure you'll come up with something if you don't intend for your wife to find out about you and me."

"Bitch," Marvin growled through his teeth.

"Now, now, name calling doesn't become you. Yeah, I'm a bitch. I'm *your* bitch, and I'm ready to rock your world anytime and any place."

"I don't want you to rock anything. I want you to go away and leave me and my family alone. I already have the woman I need."

"Well, okay then. Just know you have twenty-seven days left before I make good on my promise, Mr. Marvin Thomas. See, I've already left a message for Mr. Kenny Richmond to give me a call. You wouldn't—"

There was a knock at the door. "It's Kenny," the voice from behind the door said.

"I've got to go." Marvin hung up the phone and tried to compose himself. "Come in."

Kenny eased through the doorway dressed in a tweed blazer, black slacks, and a black shirt that was open at the collar. He glanced at Marvin, not quite sure what to expect. Marvin watched Kenny examine him like he was a bizarre new project that he'd like to observe, take apart, and dissect, in order to truly understand its inner workings. Kenny was unusually quiet this morning, not the overly exuberant partner that usually came into his office talking loud and shooting the breeze.

"Marvin," Kenny said at last. He reached between the two chairs that sat in front of Marvin's desk, across the desk, and gave Marvin the brother handshake. "You doing alright, man?"

"Yeah, yeah. I'm alright, now. Have a seat." Marvin lifted one of the chrome steel balls on the Newton's cradle that sat on his desk. He let the ball go and watched as it hit the next ball, the lot swinging back and forth, clicking and clacking, until it stopped. That exercise offered Marvin a temporary distraction from the obvious concern that was written all over Kenny's face.

With elbows on his desk and his chin resting on the heels of his hands, Marvin looked straight into Kenny's face. "Kenny, I've invited my cousin, Harold, to meet with us. I asked him here because he was with me when I started this company, and I'm going to need his expertise to help guide me, no us, through some things. I will be frank about what's ahead of us, and after my ordeal this weekend, I've made some other decisions that I want to share with you. But before Harold arrives, I want to apologize to you for not believing in myself enough to come to you when I realized that we were in trouble. I value you as a partner, a friend, and I appreciate all that you've done to thrust Thomas and Richmond Tecktronics to the status it has enjoyed."

"Well, thanks, Marvin. That's good to hear. Yes, I was disturbed, actually angry, when I heard about you selling your shares in the company. It hurt more because I thought we were partners and trusted each other."

"We do, Kenny. It's on me. In fact, I'm ashamed of how I handled the whole thing. It's turned my house upside down. I can't eat or sleep." Marvin leaned back in his chair. "I've got the livelihood of our employees at stake, also."

"By the way, how is Rachel? The girls are going to see Ashley today, and Sylvia says she called Rachel to see if she wanted to go, but she was acting real strange, and of course, bugged out. I really didn't expect to see you here this morning. I know the both of you have been under a strain."

"Rachel is taking this a lot harder than all of us. She's fragile, not always trusting, but I love her. We'll get over it." The intercom buzzed. "Excuse me; it's Yvonne on the intercom."

"Yes, Yvonne?"

"Mr. Harold Thomas is here, sir."

Marvin looked at his watch. "Send him in."

# CHAPTER TWENTY-EIGHT

Kenny stood as a man who favored Marvin walked through the door in a blue suit with soft green pinstripes running through it, his hand extended. Today, Harold walked proud, Marvin thought, almost as if the rift between them had never been. It had been more than three years since Marvin last saw him—the day Denise had her breast removed, and Harold had brought Danica to see her. Marvin wondered how his and Denise's lives would have turned out if he had not caught her and Harold in bed together. He dismissed the thought from his mind. Denise was his ex, and Rachel was now his wife.

"Kenny, Harold Thomas," Marvin said. Kenny and Harold shook hands like old friends. "Harold, Kenny Richmond."

Marvin stood and stretched out his hand to greet his cousin. Several seconds passed when they realized that their hands were still locked together—a moment of solidarity and the past forgiven. Kenny offered Harold the seat he was sitting in, and they both sat down and crossed their legs.

Marvin sighed. "Gentlemen, Thomas and Richmond Tecktronics is in a financial rat hole. Unfortunately, I've gotten us to this point by making some very bad investments that I had not thoroughly investigated."

Kenny's expression changed several times. His eyebrows twitched, as he braced his elbow on the arm of the chair while balancing his chin on his knuckles. Marvin watched him in his peripheral vision, trying to gauge his mood and get a sense of what he was thinking.

"As you both know, the market is in a vulnerable state, and if the failure of our large banking systems and the impact that it's having on the New York Stock Exchange continues, we are doomed. There will be no money to borrow.

"I guess you can say that we're there, and I've used a lot of my own money to oversee some of our operations. It was over-whelming, and I started letting some of my personal business slide to try and save the company. As much as I hate to admit it, I panicked, and made a terrible decision without telling my partner." Marvin stopped and looked straight at Kenny, then away. "Then like a fool, I tried to end it all as if the problem would go away. If something had happened to me, it would have been a bigger mess for my family, and of course, the company.

"I've called you both together because I've made another decision for which I need your blessing. Partner, I know that this is something that we should have discussed, but I want to present it this way. And once you hear what I've got to say, you'll understand why Harold is here."

Both Kenny and Harold sat up tall in their chairs, waiting for Marvin to drop the ball. Tension was in the air, and only Marvin could relieve it or make it worse.

Marvin sat in silence for a few minutes. He wasn't sure why it was taking so long to say what he had to say. He knew he was taking the right step, but he wanted to be sure Kenny would be right in step with him.

"Gentlemen, I've changed my mind about selling my shares. I plan to fight for the company, and I hope you're in there with me, Kenny. I will need Harold to help reorganize."

The tension melted off Kenny like ice cream that had been sitting outside the freezer too long. He jumped up from his seat and clasped the sides of his head with his hands, then threw them up in the air. "That's what I'm talking about. Let's save the company."

Kenny began walking in circles. "I'm all the way in there with you, Marvin. You had me scared for a moment, but I'm ready to rumble. Thank you, Lord."

Marvin smiled as did Harold. "We're in for the fight of our lives—an all-out war," Marvin said. "I made a verbal acknowledgment that I was selling my shares, but I haven't signed anything, nor were you privy to what I did beforehand. Since these guys didn't have any shares of our stock prior to their request to acquire mine, we may have a good chance to recover. But I'm sure it will become a hostile takeover bid. I'm not sure who they've retained to represent them, but I have one of the best corporate attorneys on retainer. He's a friend of mine by the name of Cecil."

"Cecil Coleman of Lancaster, Bosche, and Coleman?" Kenny asked.

"Yes, you know him?" Marvin asked.

"Damn, this is a small world," Kenny said. "Cecil married a second cousin of mine. We weren't close—didn't run in the same circles. This is kind of funny. I never thought I would ever need him for anything. You know...Cecil thought he was better than us poor relatives."

Harold spoke up for the first time. "Richmond this is your time to show him what you're made of, and I'll be behind both of you."

"Good," Marvin said. "I've got to call Cecil to let him know about my change in plans. I want you both to be a witness to the phone call. Hold on a moment, Yvonne is buzzing me." Marvin picked up the phone. "What is it, Yvonne? Can't it wait?"

"Well, it's that woman, Peaches, again. She insists on speaking to you, now."

"Pass the call." There was a short pause. "Excuse me, guys, I've got to take this call."

"Hey, lover boy, your wife has a lovely voice. Don't worry; I didn't say anything...this time."

"Alright. Thank you very much. I'll talk with you later." Marvin slammed the phone down.

"Are you alright, Marvin?" Harold asked, knowing his cousin better than anyone.

Marvin sat back in his chair and contemplated the question and how he was going to respond. He locked his fingers and joined his thumbs together and held them up to his face. He dropped his hands, then looked from Kenny to Harold.

"No, I'm not alright. I have one other thing that I need to share with you, and it's not to go beyond this room."

"What is it?" Kenny asked with a puzzled look on his face.

"You may not want to know, but I've got to tell someone. I'm being blackmailed."

"Blackmailed? By whom?" Harold asked, now standing. "Does it have to do with the takeover?"

"Indirectly," Marvin said matter-of-factly. "Where do I begin? It was the night I called Cecil and told him to sell my shares. I couldn't believe that I had done it. Rachel and I had had an awful fight that day. Anyway, after I left the office, I went to a bar downtown to get drunk."

"But I thought you stopped drinking," Kenny said.

"I did, but I needed something or someone to talk to…to understand what I'd been up against. The stress was killing me. While I was at the bar, this woman comes up to me, and I bought her a drink. She was nice looking, friendly. But you won't believe what happened.

"I must have passed out because I don't have any recollection of anything that happened. Gentlemen, I woke up in this room...a room that was not familiar to me. And...and I was naked."

"Oh, hell," Kenny shouted. "Oh, Marv, please don't tell me..."

"Don't tell you that I slept with her?"

Harold's eyes were wide with shock. "Marvin, you didn't?"

"I don't know what I did because as I said I have no recollection. But she has pictures, and she is black-mailing me to the tune of fifty thousand dollars, which she's given me twenty-seven days to pay. If not, she will tell Rachel and the whole world. She's already left a message for Kenny to call her."

"I did have a phone message that was vague," Kenny said.

"Look, do you want us to get rid of her?" Harold asked. Kenny looked at Harold and then at Marvin, surprised.

"Do you mean, 'exterminate'?" Kenny asked.

"Well, not kill her or mutilate her body," Harold said.

"Yes," Marvin said without emotion. "I need to come up with a plan because I don't believe she'll go away even if I paid her the fifty thousand dollars. Yeah, we need to put our heads together and come up with some-thing."

"Three heads?" Kenny asked.

"Don't be a chicken butt," Marvin said, laughing at Kenny. "We're not going to kill her, just give her some of her own medicine."

"Oh," Kenny said, not sure what he was agreeing to.

"Let's call Cecil," Marvin said. "I'm ready to get this war started so we can move on to other things. We must keep the bit about this woman, Peaches, between us— absolutely no wives. I've had calls from the press because of my attempted suicide, and I'm sure there will be many more calls with this takeover, but I'll handle it. If you guys will assist me with the behind-the-scenes work, I'd appreciate it."

"Let's call Cecil," Harold reminded him. "I'm ready to help you move forward."

Marvin placed the call and waited for Cecil to come on the line. "Hey, Cecil, this is Marvin Thomas."

"Marvin, my man, how are you doing? I read the papers and…"

"Cecil, I've got you on speaker. My partner, Kenny Richmond, and my cousin, Harold Thomas, are here with me."

"Did you say Kenny Richmond?"

"Yeah, Cecil, this is Kenny, your wife's cousin."

"So you're the Richmond in Thomas and Richmond. I thought your name sounded familiar."

"Look, Cecil," Marvin interrupted, "the reason for this phone call is to tell you that I'm not selling my shares. I rescind my offer. I'm prepared to fight if I have to."

"What?" Cecil screamed into the phone. "That's suicide, Thomas. No pun intended, but you're messing with some pretty powerful guys, and they're not going to take this lightly."

"You're the big corporate attorney who's got accolades on the wall for your business savvy. Now, if you're not up to the job, we can get someone else with a fancy law degree. Just know that we're ready to fight. Are you on the team or not?"

# CHAPTER TWENTY-NINE

Sylvia jumped when she heard the door slam that led to the garage. Alarmed, she stopped what she was doing to see what the commotion was all about.

"Hey, baby," she said as Kenny brushed past her with briefcase in hand.

"Hey," was the reply.

"Unh, unh. What's up with you, Kenny? We aren't going to have no mess in this house."

"Nothing, baby. Just a long, hard day."

Sylvia followed Kenny into the kitchen. "Kenny, the way your eyes are darting around, you look like you're burning up with fever. Boy, you ain't acting right."

"Where's my son?" Kenny asked as he turned away from Sylvia's glaring eyes.

"He's asleep. Now stop the charade and tell me what's going on."

Kenny opened the refrigerator and took out a bottle of water. He unscrewed the cap and took a few gulps, closing his eyes as he did. He could feel her presence and her anger as she waited for an answer. For a moment he thought it quite comical the way she was playing it up.

"How was your trip to see Ashley?" Kenny asked.

"Don't change the subject, Kenny. What's up with you? What happened at work today? You did go to work today."

"Sylvia, what's with the twenty questions?"

"It wasn't twenty but I can make it twenty, smart mouth." Sylvia snatched the bottle of water from Kenny's hand and slammed it down on the granite counter while spilling some of the contents on the floor. "I'll give you ten seconds to move those lips and tell me what's going on or I'm going to call the insane asylum and tell them to pick your butt up. You're not going to have me walking around like Rachel's doing now."

Kenny sighed. "Come here, girl, and let me hold you."

"Not until you tell me something."

"I met with Marvin and his cousin Harold today."

"Yeah, and...?"

"I've got some good news, I think."

"What do you mean, you think?"

"Sylvia, baby, just let me get it out, would you?" Kenny paused and looked at Sylvia. She was so beautiful, healthy hips and all. "Sexy" was the word that came to mind, especially the way she looked with her hands on her hips like she was mad at somebody. "Marvin had a change of heart and wants to fight to keep the company. He wants to rescind his offer to sell his shares."

"Well, isn't that a good thing, baby? Isn't that a move in the right direction?"

"You would think so. But I have a feeling it's going to cost us more than we've got. I got the feeling from Marvin's lawyer, who just happens to be married to my cousin, Trina, that we're not big enough to play hardball with these people. I met a couple of the guys Friday night at the dinner Mona catered. They smelled like mean old money, and my gut feeling is that they're not going down without a fight."

"So if this was the news, why were you acting so weird?"

"You're still asking questions, Sylvia? Wasn't that enough?"

"Look, I'm just like two bookends. I know everything there is to know about you—how you think, what triggers this emotion or that emotion..."

"Since you think you know me, what does this mean?" Kenny looked Sylvia up and down, his eyes full of lust and desire.

"Kenny Richmond, it just means you've got an itch that you want to scratch and you want some of this. You can have anything you want, baby, once you tell me what's up."

Kenny stood in front of Sylvia, pulled her hands off her hips, and held them behind her. He aligned his body with hers, the granite countertop supporting his back as he leaned further into her. Kenny blew his breath in her face and teased her with his tongue, then kissed her passionately as he stroked her back. He moved his hands from Sylvia's back down to the mounds of her buttocks, squeezing them and pushing himself into her. Then abruptly she pushed him away.

"Nice try, baby," Sylvia said. "You got me going, but as I said, not before you tell me what's going on."

"Lord, have mercy, girl. I can't believe you're going to make me stop with my…"

"Uhh, I'm waiting."

"Get a chair, girl. You're not going to believe what I'm about to tell you."

"Now we're getting somewhere," Sylvia said. "And don't you leave out a single detail."

# CHAPTER THIRTY

Thoughts ran deep as Ashley recounted her visit with Claudette, Sylvia, and Mona a few days ago. Although puzzled by their sudden appearance, she was happy that they had come. Often she thought about them and how they had been supportive after her divorce from William and had given her the courage to stand up to him.

Last evening, she received another strange call. Her father wanted to come see her. Ashley could count the months on one hand—five months to be exact—since either her father or mother had come to see her. Yes, they were grateful that William was no longer in her life, but they were upset at the scandal it had caused. The headline popped in her head: ASHLEY JORDAN-LEWIS, DAUGHTER OF FAMED ATTORNEY ROBERT JORDAN, ARRESTED FOR THE MURDER OF HER HUSBAND, WILLIAM LEWIS.

Her parents weren't sorry about William's demise. They hadn't liked him in the first place because he was black, regardless of his middle-class upbringing and being in the top ten of his class at Georgetown. She loved William, but his love had turned sour, and their marriage had ended in divorce.

She washed her face, tuning out the part of the story that had landed her behind bars. She told herself that she looked forward to seeing her father, although he probably was there to see a client.

"Lewis," the guard called, clicking her nightstick up against the bars. "You have a visitor."

Ashley gathered herself as she was and followed the guard to the reception area where she'd recently been with the girls. As she walked through the doors, she saw her father. He seemed as if he had aged—his hair was a little whiter and his jaws sagged. He wore a navy blue suit, probably from his favorite designer, Versace.

His smile was endearing. "Hi, sweetie, how are you?"

"As well as can be expected in this hellhole," Ashley replied.

Her father looked away. Ashley thought she saw sadness in his eyes. "Sit down, Dad. I'm fine."

Conversation was somewhat strained. As if the moment of guilt had passed, Mr. Jordan began to ramble about how her mother was doing and the rest of the family, although Ashley wasn't the slightest bit interested. They hadn't bothered to come see her, and out of sight, out of mind.

"Well, are you handling any big cases?" Ashley asked when it appeared her father was more relaxed.

"Yeah, I'm working on several cases, but I've got this

case that is going to be a humdinger. I'm representing this big firm who is in a takeover bid with this minority, black-owned electronics company that doesn't stand a chance in hell. The owner sold his shares, and then, as if he had some kind of epiphany after he tried to kill himself, turned around and said he's not going to sell."

Ashley sat straight up in her seat, a visual of a headline that she'd read over the weekend crowding her brain. He just couldn't be talking about Marvin. She set the thought aside as she listened to her father going on about his case.

"The guy is loony tunes, if you ask me."

"What's the name of the company?" Ashley asked.

Her father looked at her with interest. "It's Thomas and Richmond Tecktronics. Why do you ask?"

"Boredom," she said, her heart palpitating twenty beats a minute. "I like to keep up on current events."

# CHAPTER THIRTY-ONE

S everal days had passed since Sylvia and the girls had gone to see Ashley. She was feeling a little guilty that she hadn't encouraged Rachel to come along. It would have been great if Rachel could have been with them.

Now new fears enveloped Sylvia; as it seemed that at every turn a new crisis was erupting. Ever since Kenny had opened Pandora's box and had sworn her to secrecy, she had a burning desire to see Rachel. She didn't know what she was going to say, but she knew what she wasn't going to say—what she couldn't talk about—because she knew the risk she would be taking letting others know that Kenny had breached Marvin's confidence.

While the housekeeper watched Kenny Jr., Sylvia went to the kitchen and grabbed the phone, dialing before she lost her nerve. She paced the floor, working up enough courage to say the right thing when Rachel answered. "One, two, three," Sylvia counted. And then there was Rachel's voice.

"Hey, Sylvia," Rachel said in a low voice.

"Hey, girl. I've missed you. How've you been doing?"

"Oh, alright. You know Marvin's gone back to work. Didn't take any time off to recuperate. Has Kenny said anything to you about how Marvin's been acting?"

"What do you mean?" Sylvia said too fast. "Kenny hasn't said anything to me."

"Are you alright, Sylvia? You seem uptight."

"I don't mean to be. Would you like to have some company? I won't bring Kenny Jr."

"If you promise not to come over and act like I'm a germ you don't want to catch. Marvin is trying to work through his ordeal. I believe he's changed his mind about the company. It's going to be hard for a while, but we're going to make it. I might have to go back to work, though."

"You're going to be fine. I prayed for you last night. Oh, Mona, Claudette and I went to see Ashley the other day. She looks good and said to tell you hello."

"Next time, I'll go with you. Well, come on over, friend. I could use one. And I've missed you, too."

"I'll be over in a second," Sylvia said, her eyes growing moist.

"Okay, I'll be here when you get here."

After securing Kenny Jr. with the next-door neighbor, Sylvia headed to Rachel's. Sylvia parked her Lexus in the driveway and slowly got out. She could have walked if she wanted to, but she had a strong feeling that she might need to leave in haste. Sylvia had no idea for what reason, but she thought driving would provide the fastest getaway.

Upon closing the car door, Sylvia walked toward the back of the house, snapping her head left and right like a thief in the night making sure of her surroundings. It was almost as if she expected to be jumped any minute by a would-be carjacker or a rapist, but this was not that kind of neighborhood. Sylvia was afraid of what she would find inside with Rachel's nerves so raw and on edge, especially with all that she had been through with Marvin.

She looked up when she heard the door open as she prepared to ring the bell.

"What took you so long?" Rachel asked. "It's not like you live on the other side of town. Come on in."

Sylvia hugged Rachel, who seemingly held on for dear life. It was Sylvia who pulled away first. "Let's go inside."

It felt like she was in a mausoleum—stuffy, boxed in, and unable to move. Sylvia moved further into the house and noticed that papers were everywhere, and Serena's toys were strewn about on the floor of the family room, although she wasn't to be seen. Rachel lay on the couch, her legs hanging over the arm, while Sylvia took a seat in the nearest chair. "Where is Isabel?" Sylvia asked.

"I had to let her go."

Sylvia's eyes widened. "Oh, I'm sorry, Rachel."

"No need to be. Nothing stays the same, girl. You think you're on top of the world and are going to stay there forever. Then things happen, things you never expect, things that aren't shared and life suddenly goes down the drain. I feel like the Dow Jones, spiraling down, down, down out of control. I would have never thought this could happen to us, Sylvia. I can't believe that my wonderful, beautiful, unafraid, God-fearing husband just tried to commit suicide. How could that be?"

Sylvia got up, held Rachel's legs up, and sat down on the couch next to her. Sylvia put her arms around Rachel, then pulled her close, kissing the top of her head. "Baby, it's going to be alright. Just think back on all the things you went through with your ex, Reuben, and Marvin's ex, Denise, and you still weathered the storm. You're a tough little cookie. You didn't take any of that crap lying down. I think you would have kicked Denise's butt that night at the Ex-Files meeting if she hadn't pulled that wig off her head, declaring that she had the big C."

"That was then, Sylvia. This is now. Marvin had me acting a fool on the streets of Atlanta because I couldn't use my credit cards and I didn't know why. The man I trusted with all my dreams and my future let me down. I just can't believe it!" Rachel wailed.

"Sweetie, that's why you can't give everything away. You've got to keep some things for yourself—like putting money away for a rainy day. You hope that you never have to use it, but if a rainy day should come, and sometimes it comes in torrents, you have something to fall back on. I believe with all my heart that Marvin didn't intend for this to happen, and that it just happened. I know he loves you and Serena with all of his heart because that's the kind of man he is..." Sylvia stopped, conflicted by the information she was sworn to keep secret. It would hurt Rachel to her heart if she ever found out about Marvin's infidelity, even though he claimed to have no recollection of it.

"What's wrong, Sylvia?" Rachel asked, suddenly sitting up straight. "Why did you pause?"

"Oh, I guess I'm just overwhelmed. It suddenly dawned on me that if this is touching you, we could be next—cause and effect."

"Huh?"

Sylvia spoke as if she was auditioning for a part in a movie about the economy gone bad. "Me, Kenny, Kenny Jr. are tied into the future you just described. My husband being partners with your husband means that Kenny is also in jeopardy of losing his job, maybe losing our home, and so many other things."

"Sylvia, I understand." Rachel hesitated. "Ahh," she sighed.

Sylvia rubbed Rachel's back. "You alright?"

"No, Sylvia, I'm not alright." Rachel held her face in her hands and began to cry. "Sylvia, there's more."

"What is it, Rachel? Things are looking up, aren't they,

especially since Marvin wants to fight for the company?"

Through wet tears, Rachel sang. "Serena found one of Marvin's suits hidden underneath the cushions in the couch in his office downstairs. Sylvia, it reeked of perfume, and when I confronted him about it, he tells me some story about going to this bar and getting drunk when he doesn't even drink. Then he had the nerve to tell me he woke up and he was in his car. No further explanation. I want to believe him, but would you believe a story like that?"

"You have to trust Marvin," Sylvia said, knowing good and well that Marvin had had sex with some cheap whore he'd met at the bar, and that he'd woken up in her apartment and not in his car like he'd told Rachel. Keeping a blank face was difficult, and she felt that Rachel had a right to know the truth. But then there was her husband whom she loved and trusted, and to betray his confidence would be the worst kind of evil. Sylvia would do her best to listen and be a good friend.

"I want to believe him so bad, Sylvia, but my heart tells me he's lying. First, the credit cards and now this. I don't know how much more of this I can take."

"Let's not rush to judgment. I'll be there to hold your hand through it all. Why don't you and Marvin consider coming to my church one Sunday and talking to Pastor Goodwin?"

"Sylvia, I don't want anyone else in my business. It's bad enough that all my close friends know what's going on in my household, but I don't need some preacher asking me all kinds of questions so he can use it as text for his next sermon."

"Now, that's not fair. Pastor Goodwin is a good man. He's a 'practice what he preaches' man, with ethical and moral values. Anything you tell him will be kept in strict confidence. Remember Margo Myles, who came and spoke to our group? She is Pastor Goodwin's sister."

"What you said didn't convince me of anything. Pastor Goodwin doesn't have the power to restore everything back to the way it was a week ago. He's got to call on God, too. I have, and God didn't answer. So please don't tell me what God can do because he passed over 5555 Riverdale Court like it didn't even exist."

"Maybe because God knows that you have a hardened heart and wasn't ready to receive."

"You can leave now and go back to your home that God didn't curse." Rachel pushed Sylvia aside, got up, and walked out of the room.

Stunned, Sylvia got up from her seat and stood in the middle of the floor, waiting for Rachel to return. When she didn't, she called out to her. "Rachel!" There was no answer. "Rachel, let's not end this way."

A voice floated back to her from the distance. "Lock the door on your way out."

# CHAPTER THIRTY-TWO

Cecil Coleman stood on one side of the long conference table with his hands in his pockets. He was dressed in his best Armani suit—a brown silk fabric with a hint of black fibers throughout—accentuated by a long-sleeved black shirt and a multi earth-toned tie. He faced a three-man team that consisted of Attorney Robert Jordan, Vincent Kinyard, and David Eason of Regal Resorts, Inc., who came armed to do battle for what they believed to be theirs.

Cecil watched as the men gauged his importance and assessed his wealth. They surveyed his office, taking snapshots with their eyes while storing the information in their mental chips for later evaluation. Finally sitting down, Cecil brought the meeting to order.

"Gentlemen," Cecil began, "I don't think I need to go into a long, drawn-out speech about why my client has had a change of heart about selling his shares of stock in Thomas and Richmond Tecktronics, Inc. The facts are what they are. This company is the product of a lifelong dream of Mr. Thomas, who has aspired to become an entrepreneur, businessman, and image-maker ever since he could read. This company comes at the price of the blood, sweat and tears of Mr. Thomas' parents, who labored long and hard to give him and his siblings the opportunity of a good education in order that he could realize this dream. Yes, Mr. Thomas may have abruptly agreed to sell his shares of stock—mind you, the decision was made under duress and without consultation with his partner—but he is now of reasonable mind and is unwilling to go through with the sale."

Attorney Jordan cocked his head and looked into Cecil's face, while he drummed on the top of his briefcase. "Mr. Coleman, while my client may sympathize with Mr. Thomas'...shall I say...a humble rise to business ownership as you so eloquently put it, the fact remains that there was an implied contract per your verbal communication that Mr. Thomas wished to sell his fifty-two shares in Thomas and Richmond Tecktronics, Inc., which he now intends to breach. We do not intend to negotiate or renegotiate; we've come to finalize what we started, and if your plan is to renege as you seem to indicate, then we are prepared to fight."

Cecil sat with his fingers clasped together, the two index fingers joined at the tips to make a V. He brought them to his mouth and blew into it, contemplating his next move as he readied for battle.

"Mr. Jordan, while Mr. Thomas was grateful initially for your clients' desire to purchase the stock of Thomas and Richmond, I must ask, if it's not unreasonable to do so, what interest do they have in a venture that is not remotely associated with their business?" Cecil pointed in the direction of Kinyard and Eason. "Maybe Mr. Kinyard or Mr. Eason can enlighten me. Normally, a company looking to merge with another does so to expand their present holdings, so I fail to find the association."

*Uhh, uhh.* Kinyard coughed and tried unsuccessfully to rid himself of the frog that found its way into his throat. He pushed back in his chair and crossed his leg, leaning back like an old-school power player, locking eyes with Cecil's. But he found he was no match for Cecil and let his head drop before he spoke.

"Mr. Coleman," Kinyard began, pursing his lips, "it appears you're a well-educated businessman and know that in order to possibly move up to an office on the thirtieth floor from the twenty-ninth floor, you're going to have to make a bigger name for yourself by winning the big headline cases. For me, it's diversifying my assets by building a conglomerate that will house an array of products that will not only be profitable but complement each other for more than a season. My resorts are one thing, but upon acquiring Thomas and Richmond Tecktronics, we plan to expand on what is already there and move the market into international waters and cyberspace."

"First, Mr. Kinyard, I'm not amused by what you

believe my aspirations are or your advice on how to acquire them if I was so inclined. I'm not the subject of this inquiry, so let me remind you to stay on the topic of this discussion."

"Spare me, Mr. Coleman; it is quite obvious that you have a thirst for power," Kinyard said.

Cecil looked from Jordan to Kinyard. He wasn't going to let this old battle-ax rattle his chain with his racial undercurrents. Whatever he was, Cecil had worked hard for it just like anyone else in his position. The man was intimidated by him, and he was going to keep him on guard. The more Cecil talked with this asshole, the more resolved he became to fight for Marvin and win. He smiled.

"Maybe we got off on the wrong foot," Cecil said. "My client rescinds his offer. Mr. Thomas' partner, Mr. Kenny Richmond, who was unaware of what was taking place, is supporting Thomas' decision not to sell his shares. Thomas and Richmond Tecktronics will have an emergency meeting of their board of directors this week to discuss the proposed buyout and Thomas' decision not to sell, and until after that time I have nothing else to share. This meeting is adjourned."

Cecil stood and didn't allow the discussion to continue. Jordan, Kinyard, and Eason sat still in their seats, not sure what had just happened. They were dismissed. When they didn't move, Cecil stood by Jordan.

"You can call me next week if you want to continue talks. Have a good day."

The three gentlemen got up from their seats and left without a word. *Slam* went the door after the last of the three men had exited the room. Served them right for coming up in his office with a haughty attitude like he didn't know what he was talking about. Pissed, Cecil crossed the length of the room, went to the bar, and poured a glass of scotch. He walked to the window and looked out. He raised his glass high and shouted, "To the HNIC at Lancaster, Bosche, and Coleman at Law."

# CHAPTER THIRTY-THREE

Kenny huffed as he shuffled into the house and made his way into the kitchen. He dropped his keys on the countertop and drew in a deep breath. Sweat covered his face—a product of the weather and the tension that had taken residence in his body.

Opening the refrigerator, Kenny took out a bottle of water and closed the door. He uncapped it, and threw his head back and let the cool water quench his thirst. As he turned around, Sylvia, who had entered the kitchen, startled him. He jumped, spilling water over both of them.

With a worried look on her face, Sylvia brushed Kenny's face with her hand and pecked him on the lips.

"Hey, babe," Kenny said.

"Hey, sweetie." Sylvia wrapped her arms around Kenny. "Day wasn't so good?"

"Sylvia, I'm worried about Marvin and the company. I wish he had come to me earlier. If he had, we wouldn't need an attorney to bargain with the devil to get our company back. You won't believe who the attorney is."

"Who?"

"My cousin Trina's husband, Cecil Coleman. You may not remember Trina; I haven't seen her in over ten years and she and Cecil weren't invited to our wedding. I think I glimpsed her at one of our family reunions. Trina is the granddaughter of my mother's oldest sister. There's no love lost between my mother and Aunt Lovey."

"Oh, I remember Aunt Lovey. When we were together all those years ago, you took me to some family get-together, and she and your mother got into it about something your cousin Mabel said to your mother."

"Yep, that's Aunt Lovey and my momma. Mabel is Trina's mother. They haven't spoken in years either. Anyway, Trina is a prosecuting attorney here in Atlanta the last I heard and Cecil is a high-profile attorney who handles mergers and takeovers. I guess that's why Marvin hired him. They always thought they were better than the rest of us."

"Well, I love you, baby."

"I know you do," Kenny said as he placed a kiss on Sylvia's lips. "What worries me, Sylvia, is this extortion attempt by this woman who claims to have had sex with Marvin. I'm so glad I told you. I definitely need to talk to someone about it. Anyway, I don't really believe she had sex with my buddy."

"Huh?"

"Baby, I believe this woman set Marvin up, although

there is no doubt about him being in that room with her. He was too drunk to do anything and remembers nothing. I'm going to the bar where he met this woman and try to get some answers."

"Baby, do you have to be the one to do the investigating? Please don't go meddling in something you can't handle."

"Sweetie, this affects us, too. Marvin's cousin, Harold, will be with me."

"That's reassuring."

"I know, Sylvia, but we've got to get something on this woman and shake her down. We are going to be in financial ruin if we don't...let me back up, in even worse financial ruin if Cecil can't fix the situation with Marvin's shares. But we've got to get this woman. I hate parasites like her, and I'm going to squish the life out of that bug if I get my hands on her."

Kenny stopped talking when he realized that Sylvia was staring at him with her arms folded across her chest. He arched an eye-brow as if to say, *and what?*

"Do you know how you sound, Kenny? You sound like a man who's out to kill someone...like you're out to prove something. This all sounds dangerous, and I'm not sure that my husband should be the one on the case." There was no smile on Sylvia's concerned face.

"Babe, no one is talking about killing anyone, but I've got to do this. I'll be careful. I'm going to change my clothes and take a run through the neighborhood so I can let off a little steam." Kenny kissed Sylvia on the cheek and walked out of the room.

Kenny traded his sports jacket and slacks for a pair of white-and-blue Nike running shorts, a T-shirt with a picture of Barack Obama on the front and the words OBAMA '08 printed at the bottom, and a pair of running shoes. Sitting on the red plush chair in his huge walk-in closet, he quickly laced his shoes and pulled a sweatband from one of the drawers in the closet.

With the last lace tied, Kenny closed his eyes and rubbed his forehead. The Marvin debacle was taking a toll on him, and he wanted it to all go away. He gave a deep sigh and hoisted himself up from the chair and headed downstairs. He took the stairs two at a time until he hit the bottom.

"Sylvia, I'm out. I'll see you in a little bit."

"Okay, baby," Sylvia shouted.

The ground felt good to Kenny's feet. He tore around the side of the house and headed for the street. He turned around and saw Sylvia staring at him as she stood on the porch. He waved and then disappeared down the street.

Kenny broke into a slow jog. As he passed the houses that lined his street, he looked at each one with interest as if noticing it for the first time. Each structure had its own unique architecture and the landscaped yards were replicas from *Better Homes and Gardens* magazine. It was obvious money flowed throughout this gated community and on the surface it appeared recession proof.

There were a good number of affluent African-American families in the neighborhood. Several football players on the Atlanta Falcons football team lived there, and the Thomases, Marvin and Rachel, lived several blocks from the Richmonds. All in all, it was a nice, quiet place to live and had been cited as such in the local newspaper.

Sweat formed on Kenny's head, his headband catching the water that dared to drip down his face. In the zone, Kenny picked up his pace. He felt on top of the world. It had been several weeks since he had put on his running shoes, but he was back in the groove and made a promise to himself that he would get up early and run each morning.

Kenny made a right turn and dashed across the street to take the trail that bordered the neighborhood and the golf course that sat on the premises. There were others out on the trail, enjoying the coolness of the early evening. Kenny looked at his watch. He had only been running for fifteen minutes.

After thirty minutes into his run, he spotted a black female wearing a pair of short shorts and a midriff top running in his direction. She was still a short distance away, but he could tell that she was in fine physical shape. The legs were as shapely as the body they held up. She was probably one of the NFL wives. He hadn't seen any of them out on the trail before.

As he neared the woman, Kenny averted his eyes and lowered his head to avoid eye contact. Just as he thought he passed the woman, he stopped at the sound of his name.

"Kenny, is that you?"

Kenny jerked his body around and stared at the woman who'd called his name with familiarity. "Trina?"

"Oh, my God, it is you!" Trina exclaimed. "What are you doing out here?"

"I live here," Kenny said. Trina looked surprised, and Kenny enjoyed every minute of her discovery.

"Shut up. Cecil told me you work for this big electronics firm that he's representing, but he never mentioned that you lived in our neighborhood."

"That's probably because he never asked. He probably thought it could never be possible, but it is the reality. I live on Riverdale Court."

"Tell me it's not that big two-story brick giant with the double columns out front and the lions guarding the stairs that I've admired ever since they built it."

"That was a wild guess, but that's our house."

"Shut up. What does your wife do?"

"Her name is Sylvia, and she looks after our son, Kenny Jr."

"Excuse me, cousin. Give me a hug."

"I'm not sure you want a hug from me," Kenny said. "I'm wet."

"Well, so am I," Trina said. "We're family." She patted Kenny on the back in a fake hug, and he returned the favor. "Wait until I tell Mama that you live in the same neighborhood."

"How is cousin Mabel?" Kenny asked.

Trina waved her hand. "You know how Mama is. She's stubborn as a goat. I bet she and cousin Trudy haven't spoken in years."

"They haven't, last I heard," Kenny replied.

"Well, how's your mama doing? I can't remember the last time I saw Trudy."

"Getting old and mean. But I love her to death."

"I'm going to tell Cecil that we must get together sometimes—we should have you over for drinks and refreshments. We live on Lake Front Drive just in front of the lake."

"I'll tell my wife to expect the invitation."

"Good. So how's business? Cecil didn't go into the case with me, but he said it was going to be an uphill battle."

"I have faith," Kenny said, not sure where he pulled it from. Time and time again, Pastor Goodwin said to worry was a sin, and if you pray and have faith, God would see you through. He wasn't so sure he believed that at this moment, but faith was the only thing he had to hold on to. Regardless of how he felt, he wasn't going to tell Trina a thing. It was none of her business, and it pissed him off that Cecil had discussed their case with her.

"Well, I'm going to run on home. Give my regards to your wife." Trina blew him a kiss.

"It was good to see you again, Trina. I look forward to receiving the invitation."

They ran off in opposite directions. The last thing Kenny expected was to run into his cousin and have a moment of lust over her sexy body. He laughed at the thought, but took a last look at her departing hourglass figure. Trina had to be hugging thirty-nine or coming up on forty, but she did look good even if she was his cousin. In a much better mood, Kenny decided to do another mile, then run home to Sylvia.

# CHAPTER THIRTY-FOUR

**K**enny couldn't wait to tell Sylvia that he had run into his cousin, Trina, and that she'd invited them over. Sylvia listened to Kenny with amusement as he excitedly talked about Trina as if she were some kind of new superhero.

"You should have seen her, Sylvia. Trina acted as if we were kissing cousins and it had been only days instead of years since we last spoke to each other. She's a piece of work."

"Sounds like you enjoyed it, especially telling her that we lived in the same neighborhood."

"Baby, I almost peed on myself trying to hold in the laughter when she found out which house we lived in. All of a sudden, I was the golden child—her cousin who was big time."

"Just don't let it go to your big head because our ordeal is not over. I hope and pray that we won't have to be the first or the last house to put up a FOR SALE sign because we can't pay the mortgage."

"I know, baby, but for once it felt good to not have Trina looking down at me because she thought she was so much better. I know who I am and where I come from, but I feel blessed that God gave me a dynamite job, a fantastic and beautiful wife and child, and the means to afford some niceties that I can give my family."

"You're a good man, Kenny. I just don't want you to let what God blessed us with go to your head."

"Okay. Where's all this coming from?"

"I'm sorry, baby. It's just that my visit with Rachel earlier today didn't go well. I think she's depressed, and I suggested she see Pastor Goodwin. From there, it got out of hand, and she basically told me to leave. She's worried about how they're going to manage if things don't turn around for Marvin."

"Rightfully so."

"But she thinks we're sitting over here unscathed when that's not true. This situation affects all of us. I've been praying for her and everyone at the company. Truthfully, I'm scared, too."

"Come here, baby." Kenny took Sylvia in his arms and hugged her tight. They rocked each other without a word for the next five minutes. "I'm going to do everything in my power to keep you safe from harm, but it's going to take a whole lot of prayer and faith."

"That's my man. I love you, Kenny."

"I love you, too, Sylvia."

The moment was interrupted by the ringing phone.

Reluctantly, Kenny removed his arms from around Sylvia and picked up the phone, but not before he gave her a quick peck on the lips. "Hello?"

"Kenny, this is Harold."

"What's going on, man?"

"Look, I'm still in town and got to thinking about what Marvin wants us to do about that woman. If you can get away, how about we hit that bar where Marvin said he met her? We can at least talk to the bartender, or if we get lucky, we can talk to her."

Kenny looked at his watch, then back at Sylvia who was still standing in the place he left her, her hips tilted in a sexy pose while she monitored his conversation. "Yeah, that'll be alright. I've got to shower and change. Just got back from a five-mile jog."

"Alright, see you in, say, an hour at the office?"

"Sounds like a plan." Kenny hung up the phone and faced Sylvia, whose face was contorted with eyes that pierced straight through him.

"And where do you think you're going, Mr. Richmond?" Sylvia asked, her hands still on her hips.

"Remember the little thing that I told you I need to take care of? Well, Harold thinks now is a good time to put our plan into action."

"And just what is your plan? You don't know the first thing about interrogating anybody. What if this person you're going to question has a gun and turns it on you? Have you thought about that? How are you going to defend yourself? Lord, Lord, I don't know about the people in my life."

"If you don't want me to go, I'll call Harold and tell him so."

"This isn't a joke, Kenny. I'm concerned about your safety because you for sure aren't."

"Calm down, Sylvia. We're only going to talk to the bartender, and I promise that we'll be cautious about our approach to this thing." Kenny jumped in front of Sylvia and pretended he was a detective searching for clues. "Just think of us as Starsky and Hutch, Shaft and Rambo."

Sylvia began to laugh. "Boy, go take your shower and get out of here. You look more like Abbott and Costello—the blind leading the blind." Sylvia laughed some more.

"It ain't that funny, baby."

Kenny showered and jumped into the clothes he'd worn earlier in the day. He reached for his cologne but thought better of it, given Sylvia's mood at the moment. One last look in the mirror, and he was ready to go. Snatching his jacket from the hanger, Kenny practically ran down the stairs where he was met by his inquisitive wife.

"You rather like this detective stuff, huh?" Sylvia asked, kissing Kenny hard on the mouth.

"What was that for, babe? I'm not going to be long."

"Just wanted you to remember who you belonged to. Don't want you to fall off in some bar and end up like Marvin—in somebody's bedroom with the jewels that belong to me dangling in front of someone else."

Kenny laughed. "Now, Sylvia, you didn't have to go there. You know your man got exactly what he wants right here in this house standing right in front of him. I know where my jewels belong, and if you have some doubt about it, I'll take the time right now to show you."

"I have no doubt that you know, but it wouldn't hurt to get a sneak preview of the coming attraction."

"Baby, be waiting for me when I get back. I'm going to wear your jewel case out. *Rrrrah, rrrah.*"

"Bye, sweetie, and be careful."

"I will." And Kenny was out the door, his adrenaline running high because of the task he was about to undertake. He jumped in his car and plowed out of the garage, ready for his date with destiny.

The darkness had overtaken the city, and the night life had emerged from nowhere. Lamplights illuminated the city just as the moon illuminated the sky. There was a certain eeriness about the night—like they were bad boys, hiding in the shadows of dirty deeds or the thought of one.

Like scenes out of a movie thriller, several images played out in Kenny's mind as he drove to meet Harold. There was the bartender jacking him up against the wall and as soon as the image faded, a shapely brown-skinned female was up in his face, pouring her breasts into his chest, while she strangled him with her tongue, torturing him over and over with her kisses.

Kenny shook his head to wipe the images from his

brain. The red light ahead made him get a grip and pull himself back to reality. Maybe Sylvia was right about his not being ready for this challenge. Hell, he had played more women than he could count in his heyday, but maybe that was the problem. He was no longer that Kenny Richmond.

At the next light, he made a right turn and saw the large sign that announced Thomas and Richmond Tecktronics, Inc. He turned in the lot and drove to the executive parking lot where he saw Harold's black Hummer glistening under the lamp light. This assignment was for the good of the order, and he was ready to get it on.

Kenny jumped from his car and slid into the passenger side of Harold's vehicle. They were two men on a mission and all systems were go. Taillights followed by back-up lights signaled that the mission had begun. Harold backed up, spun the Hummer in a ninety-degree angle, and sped out of the parking lot into the night.

# CHAPTER THIRTY-FIVE

Shadows were painted on the walls of the family room as Marvin entered the dark house, looking for his wife and daughter. He could hear Larry King's interview with John McCain, the senator answering questions about his choice of a female running mate. It certainly had sparked the almost lethargic Republican race for the White House, but Marvin wasn't interested in any of it at the moment.

He entered the room and found Rachel staring at the television while Serena was sound asleep in her arms. Rachel looked up and gave him a half smile, then drifted back to the television interview.

"How was your day? And why are you in the dark?" Marvin asked as he walked over to the lamp that sat on the end table and turned it on.

"Probably not as good as yours. And to answer your second question, because it's peaceful."

"Well, my day was spent with our finance department looking over our financial statements and strategizing as to how we can bring the company back from the brink. I've arranged an emergency meeting with the board of directors to brief them on all that transpired just before...I offered my stock for sale and my brief brush with death. Hopefully, they will accept the plan of action that the accountants and I have come up with."

"Sounds like you've been busy. I had a visit from Sylvia."

"Good. I'm glad that you weren't alone all day."

"It wasn't a good visit, Marvin. I'm tired of people acting as if they're immune from our situation and we are the ones who need prayer and salvation."

"What did Sylvia say?"

"It's not what she said so much as how she said it, with that 'I'm above all of that because me and my God have it going on' attitude."

"Okay, Rachel. Tell me exactly what she said. Certainly, she didn't come up in here with that kind of attitude...like she's untouchable."

"She suggested that I see her pastor like he can save the damn world."

"Ahh." Marvin yawned. "I see what this is about."

"No, no, you don't see. You weren't here. Maybe I shared too much...maybe I gave her the indication that I needed help."

Marvin's studied Rachel. A severe frown reshaped his face. "So just what did you tell Sylvia? Did you tell her something that would prompt her to suggest a visit to Pastor Goodwin? Did you tell Sylvia about the suit you found and what you suspect? Huh?"

Rachel shifted in her seat and woke Serena up. Serena wiped her mouth with her hand and was still in a daze when she realized Marvin was in the room. Immediately, she jumped from her mother's lap and threw herself at her dad.

"Daddy, you're home. Daddy, I want some chicken nuggets from McDonald's."

Marvin patted Serena's head. "Hi, sweetie, give Daddy a kiss." Serena kissed him and he kissed her in return. "You sure you want McDonald's?"

"Yes, Daddy! Yeah! Mommy, we're going to McDonald's."

"We'll finish this later," Marvin said to Rachel. "Maybe you should take Sylvia's advice. It wouldn't hurt for me to see him myself." He picked Serena up, grabbed his keys, and headed out the door.

Harold pulled the Hummer to the curb in a vacant spot three doors from the bar. A red light blinked on and off outlining the words EARL'S TAVERN. Harold cut off the motor and sat still for a few moments, working up the nerve to begin the interrogation. A frown was etched on Kenny's face as he flexed his muscles and emitted a small sigh. With arched eyebrows he looked at Harold and waited for the signal, and when Harold nodded his head to the left, they both exited the vehicle.

Darkness enveloped them as the front door of the bar closed behind them. The place was small and dinky.

Just inside the tiny foyer was a long bar with maybe fifteen stools that were almost all filled with what might have been Wednesday night regulars. Smoke swirled in the air and laughter along with it as the bartender, who was now looking the duo over, finished a jaw-dropping funny joke.

Kenny made a connection with his eyes and then walked to one of the four tables that sat off to one side in a semi-circle around a small stage. The smell of chicken being fried met their nose, and Kenny motioned the lone waitress to the table.

"What's on the menu?" Kenny asked the petite wait-ress, dressed in a white top and black slacks with her hair piled high on top of her head.

"Chicken dinners," she said. *Pop, pop.* She folded her gum over in her mouth and cracked it again. "Do you want the chicken or not?"

"Harold, what do you want?"

"I'm hungry; I'll have a chicken dinner and a beer," Harold said.

"A beer for me, too," Kenny said. The waitress started to walk away and Kenny called her back before she was out of earshot. "Excuse me..."

*Pop, pop.* "Yes?" the girl asked.

"What is your name?" Kenny asked.

"Who wants to know?" the waitress said with a scowl. *Pop, pop.*

"Never mind. Who's in charge of this joint?" Kenny asked.

The waitress' mouth stood still, and she stared at Kenny then at Harold. "I don't know why you're asking me all these questions. If it's food and drink you want, I can handle that."

"Tika, let me handle these gentlemen." Tika walked away. "I'm Earl," a large man said, peering down at Harold and Kenny. He was dressed in a long-sleeved, white collared shirt and black Wrangler jeans. "I'm in charge of this joint. What can I do for you gentlemen?"

"Have a seat," Harold said, speaking for the first time. "We have some business we need to talk to you about."

"I'll sit if I think we have something to talk about," Earl said, keeping an eye on the two.

"We're harmless," Kenny began. "We're here to try to get some answers for a friend of ours."

"What you talking about?" Earl asked, eying Kenny with suspicion.

"A good friend of ours came into your bar last week," Harold said.

Cutting Harold off, Earl sat down. "Y'all five-o or some kind of detectives?"

"No, man. Relax," Harold said. "This doesn't concern you, but maybe you can help us. See, my friend came in here last Thursday and met a woman. I believe my friend got drunk and then left with this woman."

Harold and Kenny watched Earl closely. "Ummph," Earl said, nodding his head as if he remembered something.

"Earl, I need a drink," one of the patrons called from the bar.

"Yeah, Earl, my glass is empty," someone else hollered.

"I'll be back, gentlemen," Earl said. "I believe I do remember the night."

"Bingo," Kenny said, after Earl got up and went back behind the bar. "I hope he'll be straight up with us."

"If we're straight up with him," Harold said, "I don't think we'll have any problems getting information."

A plate of fried chicken, macaroni and cheese, collards, and cornbread was set on the table. No smile or "Enjoy your food," came from the waitress. There was no *pop, pop* to break the silence either, just the glare of her accusing eyes was all they got. Then she broke the silence. "Earl will bring your beers to the table." And she was gone.

Three minutes later, three beers hit the table—one for Kenny, one for Harold and one for Earl.

"Alright, you were saying that your friend came in last Thursday and got a little loaded and left with a woman. Are you sure it was this bar? You know men and women come in here all the time and pair up with one another."

"No disrespect, Earl," Kenny cut in, "but our friend was no regular here. In fact, he's a local businessman who just...well, let's say he had a lot on his mind that night. We believe that the woman he left with took advantage of him and is now trying to blackmail him for money he doesn't have."

"What is this woman's name?" Earl asked.

"Why don't you tell us, Earl?" Harold jumped in. "A few moments ago you acted as if you remembered the incident well. We're just trying to help our friend get out of the trouble he may have brought on himself."

"What do you want with her?" Earl asked, being protective of the woman he had yet to name.

"Nothing," Harold said. "We'd like to ask her a few questions."

Earl was silent for a moment, debating whether or not he was going to give up the name. He looked from Harold to Kenny. They didn't look like thugs; they were dressed like businessmen and seemed to be genuine in their concern. He sipped his beer and put it down, making one more go-around in his head. "Peaches is her name. She goes by the name of Peaches."

"Where can we find this Peaches?" Harold asked.

"If you hang out long enough, you'll run into her here."

"How well do you know this Peaches?" Kenny asked. "Does she have friends? Where does she work?"

Earl wasn't going to hand Peaches over like that. "Look, she's just a regular here. I don't get all into my customers' business. I provide them with what they want to drink, a little laughter, and a place to hang out for a while before they go to their lonely existences.

Yeah, I do know that most of the patrons here don't have nobody—this is their refuge and circle of friends."

"So is this Peaches one of the lonely ones or does she just prey on the lost souls who just happen to journey in here on a whim?" Kenny asked.

"Can't answer that for you," Earl said. "Gotta get that from the horse's mouth. Well, I've got to get back to my regulars. They miss me when I stray too far away from the bar. I hope you fellas get the answers you're looking for."

"Thanks, Earl," Harold said, finishing off the last of his macaroni and cheese. "We appreciate you taking the time to talk with us."

"No problem."

Earl strolled back to the bar. Whispered conversation passed from one patron to the next as they prodded Earl for details on his encounter with the two foreigners. Harold and Kenny watched them all with interest, wondering if any one of them would give them a lead to Ms. Peaches.

"What do you think?" Kenny asked Harold.

"Well, he didn't say much of anything...nothing for us to go on but a name, something we already knew. Hell, Peaches is probably not even her real name, but I guess it's a start. I think we should sit awhile, and see if she sets foot in here tonight."

"I might have to get myself a chicken plate because my wife has probably cleaned up the kitchen and gotten ready for bed. She's worried about me being out here... afraid something might happen that I can't handle."

"Well, Kenny, I was a little worried myself, although I think we're okay. Earl seems nice enough, and he didn't have to give us the woman's name."

"Yeah, I think you're right. Let me get that waitress' attention. I wonder what Earl pays her an hour? Her service isn't worth two cents."

Harold laughed. "You're right, man. In this dump, you get what you pay for."

The hour was going on nine. A few women straggled in and sat at the bar, but none seemed interested in either Harold or Kenny. About nine fifteen, a small band made up of a guitarist, a saxophonist, and a soloist came on stage. They were straight from the sixties, wearing red shiny suits with red shoes to match. Two of the men wore Jheri curls, and the singer was bald.

The microphone screeched as well as the guitar as they tuned their instruments and tweaked the amplifiers. Before long, old school music floated in the air and two couples took to the small dance floor. Harold and Kenny watched while bobbing their heads to the music.

Realizing he'd lost track of time, Kenny looked at his watch. "Man, I've got to get home. It's ten-thirty. If this Peaches was coming tonight, she probably would have been here already."

"Don't turn your head," Harold said suddenly. "I

think our Miz Peaches has just arrived. She's talking to Earl and he's giving me the look. Yep, she's heading in our direction with a drink in her hand. Let's play ball."

"Hello," said the medium brown-skinned woman with the short Afro and painted lips. Kenny slowly turned around at the sound of the voice. The long-legged woman wore a tight-fitted denim outfit, and he let his gaze travel up her body.

Harold got up and motioned for the woman to sit. "My name is Harold and this is Kenny. And what is your name?"

"Ummmm, Peaches," she said at last, taking a sip of her drink and offering a smile.

"A Georgia peach," Kenny said, entangling her in his web.

"Never saw the two of you in here before."

"New in town," Kenny said. He saw Peaches' eyes perk up when he said it.

"You here on business?" Peaches asked, stroking the side of her glass for effect.

"Yeah," Harold said. "It's been awhile since I've been to Atlanta. Where is the real nightlife?"

"Would you like me to show you?" Peaches asked excitedly. "I know exactly where we can go and have a good time."

"What do you think, partner?" Harold asked.

"I'm ready," Kenny said. "We couldn't go wrong with a beautiful woman by our side."

"Well, let's go," Peaches said. She looked up and Earl was waving for her to come to the bar. "Talk to you later, Earl. I've got some important business to take care of."

Harold and Kenny looked in Earl's direction and nodded their heads. He didn't return the gesture. He watched as the door closed behind the trio and didn't let go until he heard his name.

"Earl, I need a beer!"

# CHAPTER THIRTY-SIX

Peaches chatted incessantly as she left the bar, sandwiched between two gorgeous men. Her eyes lit up the midnight sky when they slowed and stopped in front of the black Hummer. She was appraising and examining, making mental notes as she prepared cue cards for her next score.

Before Harold was able to open the door good, Peaches had already made a home in the front passenger seat of the car. Nods of approval passed between Harold and Kenny, and the plan was underway.

"Where to, pretty lady?" Harold asked, looking Peaches up and down.

Peaches feigned innocence as she instructed him to go down Peachtree heading toward Buckhead. "There's a little club called Sambuca that's got some wonderful food and great live music. I'm not sure if there's entertainment on Wednesdays, but I think you'll like it anyway." Fanning as if she was hot, Peaches unzipped her jean jacket to the crest of her breasts, liking the fact that Harold kept sneaking a peek.

"You married?" Kenny asked.

"No, and I'm available. I've got a better idea," Peaches said abruptly, as if the thought had just occurred to her. "If you gentlemen want to play instead of going to the club, we can go to my place and hang out. I don't have anything to drink at the house, so if you don't mind stopping to get something, that would be great. I really don't mind doubling my pleasure."

Harold looked in the rearview mirror.

"What do you have in mind, Peaches?" Kenny asked. "I like to know what I'm getting into."

"Baby, you look way too smart for me to have to spell it out to you, but I will if you want me to."

"How about you spelling it out?" Kenny continued.

"Have you ever experienced a threesome?" Peaches asked.

There was no answer. Finally, Harold spoke. "I'm not into any kinky mess like that."

"Where are you brothers from? That's the way we roll in the ATL. I promise you a night you won't soon forget. I'll take you first," Peaches said to Kenny, twisting her body around in the seat until her face was between the two bucket seats in the front. She flashed a winning smile. "And I'll save you for last," she told Harold, pivoting her body around and leaning over just enough to touch his arm with her breasts.

"What do you say, partner?" Harold asked, looking in the rearview at Kenny.

"I say we pull into that vacant lot over there, so Peaches can give us a preview."

Harold did as Kenny suggested. "Why are we stopping?" Peaches wanted to know. "I'm not some whore you picked up from the street corner."

Kenny unbuckled his seat belt and moved in between Harold's and Peaches' seats. "Well, if you're no whore, tell me who you really are, and don't take all night."

"What is this? Let me out right now." Peaches unsnapped her seatbelt and pulled at the door handle, but the door was locked. "I don't know who you bastards are, but you better let me out of here. And you're going to be sorry you set eyes on me after I report you to the police."

Kenny grabbed her arm. "Bitch, you're not going to tell nobody nothing."

"Who are you two freaks?" Peaches shouted. "Let me the hell out!"

"Does the name Marvin Thomas ring a bell with you?" Kenny taunted her.

Peaches searched Kenny's face. She looked away and sought an explanation from Harold. "What do you want from me?"

"We want you to leave Marvin the hell alone. That means you are not to call him, disturb his family, and..." Harold began.

"And you can forget about the fifty thousand dollars," Kenny finished.

Peaches drew her hand back as if she was going to hit somebody.

"Now I wouldn't do that, pretty lady," Kenny said. "It's two of us against one, and you're no match for the both of us. I say you get back on your broomstick and ride the hell out of my friend's life. Tonight, you've received a warning. And you better consider yourself fortunate because if either of us had our way, you would... oh, never mind."

"What we're saying," Harold said, cutting in on Kenny, "if we hear that you've in any way threatened Marvin or his family or that you insist on this extortion scheme of yours, we will see to it that you won't bother them again. Your time is up, cuz; you've done played this game with the wrong person and for the last time. What you say, Kenny, 'bout we turn around and dump this baggage and then head for club Sambuca?"

"Sounds like a plan, my man." Kenny sat back in his seat and buckled his seat belt. A smile crossed his face that he couldn't erase. Harold jerked the Hummer from its resting place, and they headed back toward town.

Silence engulfed the car as the city raced by. Peaches fidgeted in her seat until she finally reached in her purse and pulled out her cell. Harold reached over and snatched it from her hand. "You'll get it back at the end of your ride." Peaches sat back in her seat with her mouth turned down.

As Harold neared Earl's Tavern, Peaches sat up.

Harold stopped a block short of the place and unlocked the door. "You're free to get out of the car now," Harold said to Peaches.

A mean frown had replaced Peaches' pleasant features. Her eyes looked like little slits on her chocolate brown face. "My cell phone," she said as she slid from the seat. "What you two fools don't know is that you've messed with the wrong person. And I will get my fifty thousand dollars."

"I strongly suggest that you don't go through with your threat." Harold hurled the phone out of the open door and heard it hit the concrete. "Sorry about that," Harold said, and sped off with the door still open.

Harold stopped a few blocks ahead and gave Kenny time to jump to the front and close the car door. They gave each other high-fives.

"Miz Peaches is going to think twice about messing with Marvin after this night," Harold said.

"Oh yes she will. A threesome, Harold?" Kenny laughed.

"I wanted to see if she could work it. Just kidding."

# CHAPTER THIRTY-SEVEN

Peaches was steaming mad as she stomped back to Earl's. Marvin and his goons had not seen the last of her. If they wanted to play hardball, she was going to throw them a curve that they hadn't anticipated. She wasn't scared of them, and they weren't going to come between her and her next payday. How could she have been so stupid? Maybe that was what Earl had been trying to tell her.

Fuming, she walked into the bar and saw Earl staring at her. She sat at an empty table and let out a sigh. "Earl," she shouted, waving her finger to come over, "I need to talk to you a moment."

Earl came from around the counter and sat at the table with Peaches. "What's up, Peaches? You're back early."

"Who were those two goons that were in here?"

"You mean the two goons you left with? They were too much for you, huh?"

"Shut up, Earl. I don't need that. They might have hurt me."

"Did they put their hands on you? All they said was that they wanted to talk to you."

"So why in the hell didn't you tell me that?"

"Because you were too anxious to get out of here to hear what I had to say. I tried to warn you, but no, Peaches was strapped to her next victims."

"Well, I'm the victim here." Peaches pounded the table and puffed up her cheeks. She had been outdone, and she wasn't going to let Kenny and Harold get away with it. Marvin was going to know who was in charge after she paid him a visit—better yet, paid his wife a visit. "Hmmmm," Peaches said out loud.

"What you thinking?" Earl asked. "You best be careful before some of your mess backfires on you."

"Don't you worry about me, Earl. I'm going to be alright. Someone else needs to worry about what might happen to them if they…"

"If they what? Peaches, I'm warning you. Your games are going to be the death of you. I don't know what all you're into, and I don't want to know, but I can give it a strong guess. I do care about you. You've been a regular here for a long time, and I'd like to see you stay one."

"Earl, have I ever told you about the night I accidently killed my first husband?"

Earl stared at Peaches. "No, I don't think you've ever told me that story."

"You probably wouldn't have stomach enough to sit through the gory details, but I tell you this, it wasn't pretty. And if you mess with Peaches, no matter who you are, you're liable to encounter the same fate as my ex."

Peaches kept talking in a trance-like state. "His name was Nate...short for Nathaniel. Mr. Nathaniel Franklin. He was a fine, deep dark chocolate brother. He lifted weights and his body was made of steel. Lawd, Earl, that man could turn me out. The sex was better than anything I've ever experienced in this life. It was an out-of-body experience. Earl, that man would make me have multiple orgasms—one, two, three, four in a row. I was afraid that when I woke up from what felt like a dream, my body would be in little pieces because the power of those orgasms made me convulse to death. I mean, a magnitude of six on the Richter scale. Anyway, I couldn't get enough."

"Why are you telling me this?" Earl wanted to know. "I'm not interested in your sexual exploits, whether it's with your husband, ex-husband, or whomever."

"I'm getting to it, Earl. Don't interrupt me."

Earl rolled his eyes but settled in for the story.

"Earl, the man was mean. Couldn't hold his liquor worth a darn. He was a hard-working man, though, and always brought Peaches his paycheck. Yes, he was a fine hunk of a man," Peaches said, caught up in the memory.

"Peaches, what is the point of this conversation?" Earl asked.

"Don't rush me. I've got to take my time if I'm going to tell it right."

"Well, I've got other customers to tend to, so if you—"

"Alright, alright. We were married for three years, and it was rocky at best. Earl, I won't ever forget the night it happened. We had had a terrible argument about some guy he thought I had been with. Some of his buddies had seen me dancing with this guy over at this place called the Lyons Den. Yeah, I was talking to him. He came to my table, wanted to dance, and I couldn't resist the opportunity to rub shoulders with a good-looking man who smelled like hot apple pie with vanilla ice cream on top. Hell, Nate hadn't taken me anywhere exciting after we got married. All he liked to do was screw.

"Earl, it got ugly. I was standing in the kitchen when he came home from work late one night after drinking with his buddies and began to yell at me at the top of his lungs. Called me a tramp and every other four-letter word he could think of. Then he reared back and sucker-punched me full force in the face, and I landed on my butt across the room. It didn't take much because I was a size four back then, and if the wind hit me just right it would have done the same thing. But Nate had no business putting his hand on me. My momma didn't raise none of her girls for some man to abuse.

"He was still cussing and swinging—knocked over a couple of my nice crystal pieces. I realized that I wasn't going to get any peace unless this man was quiet. I never thought I'd use it, but before I realized what I was doing, I pulled out the gun I had hidden in one of the drawers in the kitchen and brought it forward and pointed it toward his head. Surprise was written on his face, but that man just didn't believe I would use it.

"I hollered back just as loud as he hollered, telling him to back away and get up out of the house because I was going to blow his brains out. Do you know what the stupid fool did, Earl? He said the only thing I was good for was lying on my back and the only gun I was going to get off was his, and that I better put the gun down and get busy taking care of his needs."

Earl breathed deeply, not sure he wanted to hear the rest of the story, but he waited for Peaches to continue.

"He tried to take the gun from me and I let my trigger-happy finger do the talking—six rapid shots. *Whomp.* His body fell to the floor like a sack of granddaddies."

Peaches searched Earl's face to see if he was still with her on her walk down memory lane. Earl's face betrayed him. He'd been listening to the banter of his customers' sordid lives for years, but tonight was the first time that he'd heard the true confession of a killer, and for the first time he knew how a priest must feel bearing the crosses of the sinners who dared lay their dirty souls at their feet. "What did you do?"

"I called the police." All of a sudden Peaches became animated. She stood up and illustrated her point. "The police arrived in twelve minutes flat. I poured my soul out to the first officer on the scene, holding onto him for dear life. I explained how Nate had come home in a drunken stupor and put his hands on me, accusing me of adultery. I told them how he went to the kitchen and got the gun and pulled it on me, but he stumbled and I grabbed the gun as we fought and it went off."

"But you just told me that you got the gun and pulled it on Nate."

"Yes, Earl, I did, but I couldn't tell the police that, now could I?"

Earl shook his head and started to rise from his seat. Peaches reached out for his hand. "Sit, Earl. Sit with me a minute. Remember, I shot the man six times. Don't you want to hear how I explained it?" Earl's face was blank, and Peaches went back to her story.

"I told the officer that Nate tried to get up after the gun went off and the bullet hit him and he fell. I was scared, and I just kept squeezing the trigger. My whole body was shaking and pouring with sweat when they arrived, and they became very protective of me considering the ordeal I had just gone through."

"Did you have to stand trial?"

"I did and did a little time, but after Nate's friends finished testifying about him drinking at the bar on the night he was killed and what he said he was going to do to me, it was an open and shut case. In the end, I was free of that bondage and vowed that I would never let a man treat me the way Nate had."

"Instead, you would take out your pain on other men?" Earl asked sincerely.

Peaches looked Earl squarely in the eyes. "It's not that I don't like men, Earl, because I do in the worst way, but I have to deal with them on my terms. I will not be taken advantage of nor will I allow any man to use me for his gratification, sexual or otherwise, unless I authorize it. Whenever I'm with a man, I've got to be the one in control."

"So you're not capable of love."

Peaches contemplated Earl's question. "I'm not sure what love is." Peaches looked away and then back. "Not a lot of love ran in my family when I was growing up." She bit her lip.

"Peaches, I don't know what you're up to or why those gentlemen are inquiring about their friend who was in here last week, but I'm warning you to be careful. You may have had the upper hand before, but you can't always win and be in control. You may have just met your match, and if you're not careful, the consequences may not be so pretty. I hope you will be smart from here on out."

Peaches was not amused. "I'm glad I wasn't paying for this session. So do me a favor, Earl, and do what you do best. Get me a drink."

# CHAPTER THIRTY-EIGHT

"Still awake?" Kenny sat down on the side of the bed where Sylvia sat reading a book.

The frown on her face said it all. Sylvia looked up, rolled her eyes, and went back to reading her book. "It's after midnight and you reek of smoke. Please take a shower and then I may consider having a conversation with you."

"Don't be like that, babe. Harold and I had some good results tonight, but we had to play the waiting game in order to score. We were able to talk to the bartender who gave us a name, but the big prize was reeling in the big fish—the one and only Peaches."

"So what did the two of you do that took all night to achieve?"

"We threatened her. And I'm more than sure that she set Marvin up. She came on to us like magnets, practically throwing herself at us."

"And I bet you ate it all up. I can practically see the adrenaline flowing through your body. Your temples are jumping up and down with excitement."

"Sylvia, you're exaggerating. I can't believe you're acting this way." Kenny stood up. "I'm trying to save the company and our asses."

"I realize that, Kenny. But I was worried about you. Did you ever think to give me a call to put my mind at rest? I couldn't have screamed any louder about my concern for you being out there trying to do some under-cover work. A phone call, Kenny, one lousy phone call would have put me at ease. Now I'm tied up in knots, and this book hasn't helped any of the uneasiness I've been feeling."

Kenny sat back down and rubbed Sylvia's arm. She dropped the book and extended her hands, palms out. "I'm glad you're okay, but go take a shower and scrub the Peaches off you."

The biggest smile looped around Kenny's face. "Can I interest you in some strawberries, Mrs. Richmond? If the answer is yes, I'll add whipped cream, but that's for me."

A faint smile crossed Sylvia's face. "Strawberries? Why are you still standing there?"

Kenny pecked Sylvia on the lips. "I'll be back in a few."

Sylvia buried her face in her book. She was never worried about where her husband's heart was, only that the man she adored and loved with all her heart was in one piece. "Oh, baby," Sylvia yelled loud enough for Kenny to hear, "Marvin called and said there is an emer-gency board of directors meeting tomorrow morning at ten."

Kenny stuck his head out of the bathroom. "Thanks, babe, and think strawberries."

Dressed in an oversized T-shirt, Peaches brushed her teeth, then placed a silk cap on her head. Exiting the bathroom, she dragged her feet to the closet to prepare for the next day. The large walk-in closet was filled with business suits, pant suits, snazzy dresses, sleazy dresses, you name it. Peaches dragged the hangers to the left as she examined each article of clothing until she stopped at a little tiger-print number—a snazzy Lycra dress that might have been mistaken for a blouse with a V-cut neckline. She pulled it off the rack and examined it, licked her lips, turned it around, held it high while cupping her chin with her other hand, then nodded her head in approval. She held the dress up to her chest, her eyes dazed. "You and me are going to make a fuss tomorrow. We'll see what Mr. Marvin Thomas has to say when I walk up in that company of his and expose his dirty little secret. Mess with me if he wants to because fifty thousand dollars will become a million dollars."

Peaches laid the dress across the lone chair that sat in her bedroom. She allowed her mind to wander to the night she'd brought Marvin to her apartment. He was a handsome man, but drunk as a skunk and in no way cognizant of the things Peaches had planned for him—things that would cause him to pay dearly. She sat on the edge of the bed and brought her hands to her face and blew into them. There was a moment of regret—Earl's admonishments jarring her conscience—but visions of her run-in with Harold and Kenny interrupted the moment.

She got up and opened the drawer of the nightstand that sat next to her bed and pulled out the semi-automatic weapon that lay hidden beneath a mound of papers. Fingering the pistol, she closed her eyes and recalled Harold and Kenny's threats and how Harold threw her cell phone out of the truck and to the ground. She put the pistol back in the drawer and got into bed. Tomorrow was a new day, and by day's end, everyone was going to give her the respect that she deserved.

# CHAPTER THIRTY-NINE

A wave of anxiety engulfed the board room when Marvin walked in, followed by Yvonne. A hushed silence fell over the thirteen members of the board of directors, including the company's attorney, Reggie Smith, whom Marvin had kept in the dark; the chief accountant for the firm, Wayne Shields; and his partner, Kenny Richmond. Marvin looked around the room, gauging each member's mood. He took his place at the head of the conference room table that sat twenty-five comfortably, while Yvonne passed out folders that contained information about the day's meeting to each member present. Kenny came over and sat next to Marvin.

"Good morning, everyone," Marvin said. Each member scrambled for his or her seat and waited for roll call. Immediately after roll call, Marvin went into action.

"As you are all aware by now, Thomas and Richmond Tecktronics is in dire financial trouble. A handout is in your packet that details the company's budget and receipts as of the end of August 2008." Marvin sighed. "Unbeknownst to you, Regal Resorts, Inc., tried to buy out Thomas and Richmond. Unfortunately, under duress and without consulting with this body, I offered my fifty-two shares of stock for sale to Regal Resorts, a painful mistake that has cost me sleepless nights and as you know, almost my life. Many of you may think that I'm not capable of running the company, and I do understand if you should feel that way. But my brief encounter with death was unfortunately what I needed, although I would not recommend it as a suitable route to reclaiming one's sanity."

A faint smile appeared on Marvin's face at his attempt at humor, however, the stoic looks on the faces of the board members said they weren't amused. He looked away and continued.

"Our accounting department has retained an outside firm to complete an in-depth audit and they'll be prepared to give us a report by the end of next week." He looked up and stared into the eyes of Reggie Smith. "I have also spoken with an attorney, Cecil Coleman of Lancaster, Bosche, and Coleman, an old friend of mine who has a lot of experience with mergers and buyouts, and who's agreed to work with me...with us to regain my shares of the company. Although the agreement between myself and Regal Resorts, Inc., was verbal only, Regal Resorts contends that it was an implied contract. I've called this meeting today to share this information with you and to seek your approval to proceed with fighting the buyout and adopting the strenuous budget that Wayne, along with Mr. Richmond and myself, has worked out. Any comments? Discussion?"

All thirteen hands flew into the air. Marvin leaned back in his seat and waited for the first question. He knew there would be concerns and questions, but now he was afraid of the questions that were about to be asked.

"Certainly you knew long before your...brush with... you know...that the company was in dire straits," Gwen Robinson, one of two women on the board, stated. "Why are you just now sharing this with us? We believed in this company, enough to invest our money in it, to not have been made aware of the situation we now find ourselves in. Maybe you aren't fit to run the company. Please tell us why you're just now sharing this information with us, Mr. Thomas."

A smug look was painted on the face of every member of the board. From the nods that went around the table, it was clear Gwen had spoken up and asked the questions they all wanted to ask. Marvin rubbed his hands together and contemplated his answer.

"Miz Robinson, your question deserves the best answer I can give. In an attempt to expand the company's holdings nationally as well as globally, I took a lot of risks that did not pan out right away. And then there were the sudden failures of Lehman Brothers and J. P. Morgan. This meant that the ability to borrow money had ground to a halt, and I had hoped that the crisis was only a temporary one. I used my own money to subsidize some of the deficits that Wayne alerted me to. But when the crisis ballooned to where I could no longer remedy the problem on my own, I panicked.

"I know that this won't be any consolation to you, but my family has suffered. I'm behind on my mortgage—received the final overdue payment notice yesterday."

The group registered surprise and shock on their faces. Even Kenny snapped his neck as he abruptly turned his head to look into the face of his friend who was in greater turmoil than he had imagined. Suddenly, Sylvia's comments about not getting a big head and her wake-up-and-look-at-the-whole-picture sermon registered in living color.

"I can go on," Marvin said, "but it's too heartbreaking for me to say out loud."

"So why didn't you tell your partner, Mr. Richmond?" someone else inquired.

"What guarantees do you have that this plan of yours will work?" asked another.

"How much will it cost us to fight the merger that was your doing?" Gwen asked, realizing she had forgotten this very important question.

"And if we agree to support your plan that you contend will work, what guarantees do we, the investors, have that you won't sell us out again?" asked yet another.

Why, why, why and how, how, how? The questions kept coming, and Marvin felt like an avalanche of hostile fire was falling on top of him. That is, until Kenny spoke up.

"Let's have some order," Kenny began, rapping the table with a gavel. "Mr. Thomas has presented us with a feasible budget plan, thanks to Mr. Wayne Shields, who has spent a lot of time working on this plan. Mr. Thomas and I have worked diligently with Mr. Shields, cutting costs where necessary with our employees being our first priority. The budget will be very tight, and we will have to suspend some of our operations for a few months until we can get back on the leader board. We have imposed tighter controls, and I want to be on record as being the first person to stand behind Mr. Thomas' plan that I deem to be workable as long as we are diligent and adhere to it."

"That's plausible, Mr. Richmond," Gwen began, grandstanding for the captive audience. "I'm not sure that you realize that you are partly responsible for this as well. I've served on many boards of companies, and I have yet to see one where a partner is totally unaware of the economic welfare of its business. You could very well be cited for negligence."

Steam was forming in Kenny's nostrils, but he was not going to let this barracuda see him sweat. He had just about enough of Gwen Robinson's rebukes. Gritting his teeth, Kenny spoke up.

"Miz Robinson, that is a fair statement." Kenny looked into the faces of the board members without looking at Gwen. "My area of expertise has been in sales—getting the large and small ticket items into markets tapped and untapped. I've relied heavily on the market forecasts of our company analysts and their ability to provide me with the temperature of the buying markets, the cash flow of our customers, and our ability to supply. I'm not in any way minimizing my responsibility in the situation Thomas and Richmond presently finds itself, but I did rely on that information being shared with me, or what you call full disclosure." Kenny felt Marvin staring at him but went on with his speech. "I'm neglectful because I didn't get involved enough in that aspect of the business, but Mr. Thomas and I have agreed that we will work in tandem to bring this company back from the brink."

Marvin spoke up. "In the midst of this gloomy forecast, I do have some good news. I received a letter this morning from a charitable organization acting on behalf of an anonymous investor, who is interested in purchasing five hundred thousand dollars of our educational software for one of their charities if we agree to donate one dollar for each software package that is purchased. This investor read about our charitable efforts toward several schools in the New Orleans area who were still behind in reopening their doors in the aftermath of Hurricane Katrina. This is good news."

Silence, then handclaps filled the room. Marvin looked at Kenny and smiled. "Yvonne, please go to my office and retrieve the letter and make copies for each of our board members."

"Yes, sir." Yvonne left the room.

A stocky, middle-aged man with graying temples and hazel eyes that accentuated his medium-brown skin cleared his throat. "I'd like to make a motion that we approve Mr. Thomas' new budget plan that will be microscope-monitored by the audit team; authorize Mr. Cecil Coleman to move ahead in his attempt to secure and salvage Mr. Thomas' fifty-two shares of stock that he had verbally promised to Regal Resorts, Inc.; and that we support him and Mr. Richmond in their efforts to get the company back on track. We do not support a buyout."

"I second the motion," another member said.

"Let's take a vote," the chairman of the board said. "All who are in favor of the budget plan; retaining Attorney Cecil Coleman to secure and salvage Mr. Thomas' fifty-two shares of stock from Regal Resorts; support Messrs. Thomas and Richmond in their effort to get the company through this crisis; and do not support a buyout of this company; say 'Aye.'"

"Aye," said twelve members of the board.

"Against?" the chairman asked.

"Nay," Gwen Robinson said.

"The 'Ayes' have it," the chairman said. "Mr. Thomas

and Mr. Richmond, we will await the report from the auditors and expect to receive detailed updates on Attorney Cecil Coleman's efforts in gaining control of your company stock and the cost of this effort. Our vote today indicates that we have faith in your abilities to pull this company from the brink. Please don't disappoint."

"Thank you, Mr. Chairman, for your vote of confidence. I, as well as Mr. Richmond, will do everything in our power to preserve the integrity of Thomas and Richmond Tecktronics, Inc." Marvin breathed a sigh of relief.

# CHAPTER FORTY

Yvonne walked briskly back to the office to retrieve the letter her boss wanted her to copy for the board members. It was obvious the board was torn over their support of Marvin, and she was anxious to do whatever she could to make them believe that her boss was on the up and up, even if all she could do was copy a piece of paper and get it back to her boss in record time. She was well aware that this was attached to her livelihood, although Marvin had promised to help her salvage her job should things take a downhill turn. Her step quickened as she neared the door to her office.

Upon opening the door, Yvonne immediately went into Marvin's office and scoured his desk for the letter. An infectious smile enveloped her face when she located it. In her excitement, she accidently hit the Newton's Cradle, and the metal balls began to knock into one another. Yvonne viewed it as a good sign. She felt it in her bones; all was going to be well.

Yvonne stepped around Marvin's desk and headed to the copier with her head lowered as she examined the letter. A loud gasp flew from her mouth as she tried to pass from Marvin's office into hers. A woman dressed in a tight-fitting leopard dress that plunged at the neckline, definitely inappropriate for the time of day, stood in the doorway with her arms extended along the door frame. Large hoop earrings adorned her ear lobes, and her black pointed-toe stilettos squeezed her feet. She scowled at Yvonne, and Yvonne gave her the once-over.

"May I help you?" Yvonne asked, looking over the top of her glasses, trying not to judge.

"It depends. Is Mr. Marvin Thomas in? I need to see him right away."

"Your name, please?"

"It's not important who I am. What's important is that I speak to him right away. And it's in his best interest that it be right away."

Yvonne assessed the woman standing before her. She looked like a common street tramp, and there was no way Yvonne was going to interrupt her boss for that kind of person no matter how urgent the demand. "Mr. Thomas is in a meeting right now and can't be disturbed."

"Well, you need to disturb him if you don't want me to cause a ruckus."

"I can't disturb him if I don't know who you are and why you need to see him so urgently."

Disgust was written on the woman's face. She turned

up her lips and sucked her teeth. "Tell Mr. Thomas that Peaches needs to speak to him right away. Hurry up; I don't have all day."

Peaches! So this was the woman who had been calling her boss demanding to speak to him. Whatever business this Peaches had with Marvin must be serious, Yvonne determined. "You'll have to wait a minute. I have to make copies of this document and get it to some important people."

"Well, hurry up. This best not be a stalling tactic."

Yvonne kept her eye on Peaches as she quickly made twenty copies of the letter. Finished, she called Terri, the main receptionist, and asked her to come to her office. When Terri arrived she looked from Yvonne to Peaches, rolling her eyes over Peaches and wrinkling her nose.

With her hands on her hips, Peaches' eyes bored through Terri's. "You got a problem?"

Ignoring Peaches, Terri turned toward Yvonne. "What do you need, Yvonne?"

"I need you to stay with Miz...Peaches until I return from the conference room. I need to get these papers down there now."

"Hold up," Peaches shouted. "I don't know what you two non-professional, so-called secretaries are trying to pull. I don't need a babysitter; I need to speak to Marvin Thomas, now. I've tried to be patient, but my patience has about run its course. Yvonne, or whatever your name is, I've already warned you about what I'd do if you failed to do as I ask."

"Let me tell you one thing, Peaches, or whatever *your* name is," Yvonne retorted. "You don't scare me."

Shock draped Terri's face. "You alright, Yvonne? I've never seen you upset before."

"Just watch Miz Peaches until I come back," Yvonne said.

"I'm going with you," Peaches said, and headed out of the door right behind Yvonne.

Yvonne stopped in her tracks and faced Peaches. "No, you aren't. You will go back inside my office and wait with Terri until I return."

"Yvonne, what's taking you—" Marvin began, but stopped when Peaches stepped in front of Yvonne.

"I need to speak to you now," Peaches demanded of Marvin.

"I can't talk to you right now. I'm in a very important meeting. Thanks, Yvonne." Marvin took the copies of the letters and left Yvonne and Peaches with puzzled looks on their faces.

Peaches shrugged her shoulders and followed Marvin down the hall. "You best stop and listen to what I have to say," she said to Marvin, her voice carrying down the hall. Marvin stopped, turned around abruptly, and glared at Peaches.

"Bitch, you better get out of my face and off these premises before I have you put off," Marvin hissed.

"Let me share something with you, Marvin. The next time you send your goons to do your dirty work, let them know I have something for them. I don't scare easy, and I don't plan to go away. I want my fifty thousand dollars or there will be hell to pay."

"Your threats don't mean anything to me, Peaches. And after talking with my partner, I've decided that I will not give in to your extortion attempt."

"What the hell are you talking about? You will pay the money you owe me. Don't get it twisted, remember I have incriminating evidence on your ass."

"I don't owe you a damn thing, Peaches. Now get the hell out of here."

"Marvin, what's taking you so long?" Kenny asked, walking toward Marvin. "The board is getting restless." He stopped in his tracks when he saw Peaches. "What is she doing here, Marvin?"

"She's on her way out," Marvin said. He turned and walked away.

"Do I need to remind you of our conversation last night?" Kenny hissed at Peaches.

"Like I told Marvin, you don't scare me. You'll have to kill me before I'll go away. Just make sure your friend has my fifty thousand dollars."

Kenny looked up and down the corridor. He grabbed Peaches' arm and shoved her toward the exit, her heels digging into the carpet. "You don't scare me either, and you can kiss that fifty thousand dollars good-bye.

You aren't worth the two dollars it cost to print the money. Now get out of here before I break your arm."

With her free hand, Peaches dug her nails into Kenny's hand that encircled her arm. Unfazed, Kenny held on and shoved her out the door. Peaches stopped, turned around, and faced Kenny from the other side of the glass, glared at him, then flipped him the bird. He smirked and managed a half smile as he watched her walk away. Serious consideration had to be given to the Peaches situation because she was a ticking time bomb that needed to be defused.

# CHAPTER FORTY-ONE

Rachel's swatch book that contained the samples of fabric she had chosen for the new drapes throughout her house was nestled among Serena's toys. She picked up the book and flipped through the pages, remembering the day she and Roland were making measurements and finalizing her choices. It was one of the last days that Rachel remembered having a smile on her face—her mood had been great and family life as she had come to know it was at its best.

She continued to finger through the pages of the book, and let go a smile. Somewhere in the middle of the night, hope had reached out to her, and for the first time since Marvin's ordeal, she believed that she, Marvin, and Serena were going to make it as a family.

Rachel got up and picked up the ringing phone that sat on the coffee table. "Hello."

"Hey, babe," Marvin said. Rachel perked up. There was a smile in Marvin's voice.

"Hey, babe," Rachel answered. "How's your day going?"

"Better than I could have imagined. The board has

agreed to the plan that our accounting department has developed along with my and Kenny's blessing."

"That's great, Marvin." Rachel hesitated. "But what about your stock?"

"Baby, the board agreed to retain Cecil Coleman's firm to try to secure the stock. I just got off the phone with Cecil, and he's elated. We're going to win this, Rachel. It is going to be a fight to the finish, but I'm in for the long haul. You didn't marry a quitter. I owe you and Serena the life you so deserve."

Rachel held the phone away from her face while tears of joy ran down it. Hope was on the way.

"Rachel, are you there?" Marvin's voice floated through the receiver.

"Yeah, baby, I'm here." She sniffed. "I'm so happy for you...for us...for the company. I love you, Marvin."

"I love you, too, Rachel. Don't go and make drapery orders yet."

Rachel's mouth fell open. How did he know that she had been looking at the swatches? "No, baby, I'm not even thinking about drapes or remodeling." She stifled a giggle.

"It will be awhile, but we're going to make it. How about I take my two favorite ladies out tonight?"

"Can we afford it, Marvin?" Rachel teased.

"Naw. I'll borrow the money from Kenny. I'm kidding. I think I can squeak out a meal at our favorite family restaurant—TGI Friday's."

"What time are you coming home? I want to be ready. I'm sitting around here in a beat-up T-shirt, baggy pants, and a pair of old flip-flops."

"Put on something pretty for me, and be waiting at the door at five. Kiss, kiss. Love you."

"Love you, too. Kiss, kiss." Rachel hung up the phone and sat down and finished thumbing through the swatch book.

Rachel pulled her head out of the book at the sound of the doorbell. She cocked her head at the sound of whimpering as Serena walked in the room straight from her early afternoon nap. *Kiss, kiss.* "How's Mommy's baby?" Rachel asked Serena. Before Serena could answer, the doorbell sounded again. *Who could this be,* Rachel wondered.

"Mommy," Serena whined.

"Mommy will be right back, Serena. Play with your doll baby while Mommy see who's at the door. Then we're going to go upstairs and get ready because Daddy is going to take us out to dinner."

"Okay," Serena continued to whine.

Rachel looked back at Serena and, happy that she was alright, went to the door. She couldn't make out who was behind the door through the frosted glass, but it appeared to be a restless person because they rang the doorbell again.

"I'm coming," Rachel spouted off.

Reaching the door, Rachel opened it and gazed at

the medium-height woman with a short Afro, wearing a skin-tight leopard outfit, sunglasses that covered her face, and large hoop earrings. The woman stared with her nose in the air, then made a vertical assessment of Rachel, taking stops along the way. She scrunched her nose when she made it to Rachel's feet, adorned in simple flip-flops. But Rachel made an assessment of her own and did not hide the fact that whoever was gracing her steps was wasting her time.

"Yes?" Rachel finally asked with a severe frown on her face.

"Uhh...are you Mrs. Thomas or the hired help?"

Rachel's eye began to twitch. "And who wants to know?"

"Don't worry about it. I have a delivery for Mrs. Marvin Thomas."

Rachel's eyes went directly to the manila envelope the woman held in her hand. The woman took a long last look at Rachel and handed her the envelope. "You'll understand the message," the woman said, and turned and walked away.

"Huhhh," Rachel sighed. She watched as the woman walked down the street. *Where did she come from? Where was her car?*

Closing the door, Rachel went inside, holding onto the envelope. Her mind lingered as she thought about the mysterious woman who had just graced her doorstep. *What was so important that she had to make a special delivery, the contents of which were sealed in a manila envelope?* Rachel wondered. She checked her watch; she had an hour before Marvin would be home. Curiosity got the best of her, and she went into the kitchen to get the letter opener.

Rachel sliced opened the envelope and pulled out the piece of paper. The paper was folded in half, and when she opened it a look of horror crossed Rachel's face. Her hands began to shake.

"Oh, my God. What is this? What is this?" she screamed. The paper dropped to the floor, and a flood of tears broke loose from Rachel's eyes. "Marvin Thomas, you've got some explaining to do. I don't believe this. Lord, why me?"

Like a scene out of a shoot 'em up, Rachel's body slumped to the floor. She sobbed uncontrollably and beat the floor with her fists. "This is the last time I will be humiliated by you, Marvin. The last time."

# CHAPTER FORTY-TWO

It was getting dark earlier. In another month, Daylight Saving Time would be over. Jumping in his Lexus, Marvin was happy that he decided to leave the office early. He was even happier that Rachel received his news in good spirit. They were going to make it; he could feel it in his bones.

All the good news from the day made him speed up. Eating a meal out with his girls was the way to end a fabulous day. He glanced at the clock in the car. He promised to pick Rachel up at five and he had ten minutes to get home on time.

Everything seemed alive as he drove through his lovely neighborhood—almost as if he was looking at it from a different perspective. What a difference a day made. He pulled in the driveway and almost honked the horn, but he decided against it. Instead of parking in the garage, he parked in front of it and ran in to get the girls.

"Hey, baby," Marvin yelled upon entering the foyer. "Are you ready? I can't wait."

Marvin stopped when he realized he hadn't received a response. He moved into the hallway and ran down the steps and into his office. Not a soul was there. Taking the stairs two at a time, he climbed back up and quickly ran up the stairs to the bedrooms.

"Rachel, Serena? Where are you? You're not playing hide and seek on me, are you?" Puzzled, Marvin walked into each of the four bedrooms and then the recreation room, opening and slamming doors. "If you didn't want to go out, you should have said so, Rachel."

Irritated, Marvin ran down the stairs and into the family room. The television was off, and there was no movement. Then he spotted her sitting in the dark on the couch.

"Rachel." No response. Marvin moved in front of her. Rachel's arms crossed her bosom, and he noted that she had been crying. "Rachel, what's wrong? Where's Serena?"

There was no movement from Rachel. She continued to sit and stare ahead.

"Okay, Rachel. Enough of this. Tell me what's going on."

"I'll tell you what's going on. I'm leaving you, Marvin."

"What in the hell are you talking about, woman? You, me, and Serena are supposed to be going out to dinner to celebrate. What could have happened in the last hour?"

"A lot has happened, Marvin. Seems I don't know you at all. You're certainly not the man I believed you were. Maybe I understand now why your ex, Denise, got with your cousin, Harold."

Marvin moved the coffee table and lunged at Rachel, pulling her up from the couch. "I don't know what's gotten into you, but you're going to start talking now. I've apologized for the things that have happened in the last few weeks, but I'm sick and tired of your antics. I don't deserve this. You may mock me, but I meant what I said. Now I'm beginning to wonder if I said them to the wrong woman."

*Slap.* Marvin pushed Rachel back down on the couch and brushed his bruised face with his hand. "Don't you ever raise a hand to me again."

"You won't have to worry about it, because Serena and I are gone."

"Oh, hell no you aren't. You can get out, but Serena stays here."

"That's all you ever wanted anyway was a baby. Mad that Denise didn't give you one, but now that I've given you the one thing that you wanted, I'm dismissed."

"You dismissed yourself, Rachel. Don't you dare undermine my love for you. I was the one staple in your life. Your girls even said that you couldn't keep a man."

"Well, Mr. Marvin Thomas, you're just one of the statistics. I don't want a cheat or a liar." Tears rolled down Rachel's cheeks. She picked up the manila envelope that sat on the coffee table and threw it at Marvin.

"What's this?" Marvin asked with a puzzled look on his face.

"Why don't you look in it and see?"

Marvin opened the envelope and pulled out the piece

of paper. He unfolded it and gasped. "Where in the hell did you get this from?"

"Straight from the whore's hand. The bitch had the nerve to come to our door and hand it to me, special delivery. Ain't that nothing?"

Fire was in Marvin's eyes. "Rachel, I'm telling you, this is a set-up."

"Are you going to say that you weren't there? Tell me you don't remember anything...that you got drunk and...I can't stand you, Marvin. I hate you."

"Rachel, I was there but don't know how I got there. Baby, you've got to believe me. I love only you, and I haven't looked at another woman or even wanted to be with another woman."

"Well, how do you explain this, Marvin? Huh? You must think I'm the biggest fool that walked the planet. Tell me, how did you just happen to be in some woman's room with all of your damn clothes off, doing who knows what to her?"

"Baby, I know what this looks like, but I promise you there is another answer. She's trying to extort fifty thousand dollars from me. If I was having an affair with someone, do you think they'd go to this extreme?"

Rachel's eyes widened. "You're holding the answer. Figure it out!"

"Jesus!" Marvin shook his head.

"No need of calling on Jesus. He had nothing to do with this."

"I'm tired of fighting with you. You can choose to believe me or not. She came to the office today in retaliation for Kenny and Harold roughing her up."

"You've got them involved in your mess? Jesus, Marvin. What's gotten into you? No wonder the company is doing belly flops. You are out of control. So you got Kenny and Harold to do your dirty work. Shameful."

"I didn't do anything to that woman. Dinner's off. I'm going to my office."

"Walk out like you always do; I'm walking out for good."

"Get to steppin' if that's what you want to do. But leave my daughter here."

Marvin turned and looked at Rachel. He loved her, but he wasn't going to put up with any more of her abuse, no matter how guilty he looked. Enough was enough. She would be the one to make amends. He walked out of the room and went up the stairs to find Serena.

# CHAPTER FORTY-THREE

Rachel watched Marvin retreat up the stairs. She wished she'd kept Serena downstairs with her. She must have fallen asleep if Marvin hadn't seen her when he first came in the house. There would be no way she could get Serena out of the house now. The master had gone to claim his prize—his daughter. She couldn't compete.

Uncertainty about what she was going to do set in. There was no way that she could stay in the house...at least not for the moment. Rachel went to the phone. She needed Sylvia, but their last visit together filled her with regret. If she couldn't call Sylvia, she had to call someone.

With steady fingers, she punched preset button five.

"Hey, stranger, what's going on?"

"Hey, Mona."

"It must be serious if you're calling me instead of Sylvia."

"You've heard about our spat, I assume."

"Sylvia might have been a little tough on you, Rachel, but that's what tough love is all about. You both need to stop this mess and make up. I can't be there for you like Sylvia."

"Stop kidding around, Mona, because I need you. Can I come over?"

"Sure, Rachel. You bringing Serena?"

"No, she's with her daddy. I need to talk to someone bad...like, right now."

"Come on over. Michael is on call tonight. Won't be home until late."

"Thanks, Mona. I'll be there shortly."

"Girl, you know I've got your back." And the line went dead.

Mona immediately dialed a number.

"Hello?"

"Sylvia?"

"Hey, Mona. What's up?"

"Get your ass over here right away. Your girl Rachel is in a bad way. I don't know if I can handle it by myself."

"That's probably not a good idea, Mona. She hasn't spoken to me since the day we had that fight at her house."

"Well, I think you've got to be the bigger person and swallow your pride. I'm gonna need some help with the sister because she didn't sound too good."

"Got an idea. Why don't you call Claudette, too? That way Rachel won't be so angry at just seeing me, and you won't get blamed for going behind her back."

"Shoot, I will anyway. But that's a good idea, Sylvia. Kind of like the Ex-Files reborn."

"Yeah, but not for the reason Ex-Files was started. At least I hope not. I'll let you in on a little secret. I know Kenny is going to kill me, but I'm not sure what Rachel is coming to your house to share. So that you're armed, Marvin might have slept with another woman."

"Shut up, Sylvia! Marvin, our Marvin Thomas? Noo-ooooo. Girl, you're lying."

"Rachel told me herself. Now, his business partner, who just happens to be my husband, thinks it's a set-up. Even went out and did some investigative work."

"How did Kenny find out?"

"Marvin told him about it. Oh, I forgot. The woman is trying to extort fifty thousand dollars from Marvin to keep this a secret."

"Girl, how long have you been sitting on this piece of dynamite and not shared it with the rest of the girls? This is better than the soaps. Damn, Sylvia, I can't believe you didn't let that burden you were bearing all by yourself out of the bag."

"Kenny would have killed me, and he's still going to kill me because I know you can't keep a secret."

"Shouldn't have told me. I ain't made no promises to nobody."

"All I want to say, Mona, is let Rachel tell you first. I have a feeling she will."

"Okay, okay. I will. Look, let's give Rachel about a half-hour to get to my house. Why don't you come in about an hour?"

"Sounds good. Don't forget to call Claudette. And have some snacks waiting for us, especially something strong to drink."

Mona laughed. "Girl, I know what you mean. I'm going to get a shot of tequila now."

Mona and Sylvia laughed.

"See you in an hour," Sylvia said.

# CHAPTER FORTY-FOUR

**M**arvin looked in on Serena. As if on cue, Serena began to stir. She looked like an angel, lying in her bed so peacefully. Truth be told, she looked a lot like Rachel.

Serena's room was all dolled up in pink and purple. A mural that consisted of cute little fairies that floated across a beautiful landscape adorned the wall, and black princesses with magic wands, a take on the Disney Princess theme, bordered the room. One of Rachel's artist friends had been commissioned to do the work.

Serena's bed looked like a place for a sleeping beauty, surrounded by plush toys and her very own miniature kitchen. A fluffy, deep-pile, white throw rug with a school of fairies in a variety of colors woven into the fabric sat in the middle of the floor, while her pink and purple pillow and bedspread matched the gowns of the black beauties on the border.

"Mommy. Where's Mommy," Serena said, sitting up and wiping her eyes.

"Mommy's gone out for awhile," Marvin said, not sure whether Rachel had left the house or not. Marvin picked Serena up and held her in his arms. He kissed her cheek, and Serena laid her head on his shoulder. "Awful late for a nap. You're going to be up all night."

"Hungry, Daddy."

"Okay. Daddy will take you to get some chicken nuggets, your favorite." Marvin held Serena away from his shoulder and looked at his little girl. From that angle, she looked like a younger version of her mother. Marvin smiled.

"Yeah!" Serena said.

"Daddy's got to make a call first, and then we'll go."

Marvin took Serena to the family room so she could play with her toys. There was no sign of Rachel. He passed through the kitchen and out into the hallway that led to the garage. Her car was gone when he opened the door.

Upset, Marvin went back into the family room and picked up the phone. He dialed Kenny's cell phone and was pleased that he answered on the second ring.

"Hey, Marvin. What's up? Things went pretty well today," Kenny said with excitement.

"Yeah, but I've got a bigger problem," Marvin said.

"What is it?"

"Peaches has been to my house."

"What do you mean she's been to your house?"

"Just what I said. She handed Rachel an envelope that had a picture of me and Peaches in a compromising position. Now Rachel's gone."

"Damn. I thought Peaches got the message."

"Apparently, she didn't. I've got to take care of her. She's not going to destroy everything that I've worked so hard for. She thinks she's slick. I've never hurt a woman before, but this might be the first time."

"We've got to come up with something, quick. Our energies need to be channeled into fighting this merger, not this beast of a woman. What kind of woman would try to extort money that doesn't belong to her in the first place? She's not a half-bad-looking chick, and I'm sure there are some brothers out there who would love to handle her."

"It has something to do with control. I recognize that same spirit in Denise, although she played the game a little differently. Harold told me that he and Denise are getting married."

"Does that bother you, Marv?"

"When he first said it...yes. But when I think about how unfaithful Denise was, there is no way on earth I would take her back."

"Anyway, you have Rachel. Your good woman."

"I don't know, dawg. The events of the last few weeks have made us distant. And Peaches certainly isn't helping me to regain my wife's trust. Peaches doesn't even want me. It's all about the money."

"I'm on my way home. Sylvia is calling me on the other line. I'll think about things and give you a ring once I get home."

"Okay, Kenny. Look, thanks for being there."

# CHAPTER FORTY-FIVE

Mona flitted around the house like a chicken with its head cut off. Being armed with a bit of gossip always made her antsy. She wasn't sure what she would say to Rachel, but the fact of the matter was that she didn't know what Rachel wanted to talk to her about. It felt good know-ing that she was going to have backup. Claudette had agreed to come, although Mona wasn't forthcoming with any of the tidbits that Sylvia had shared with her. This had to be natural.

She jumped at the sound of the doorbell. Little Michael charged into the room pointing at the door.

"Doorbell, Mommy."

"I've got it. I think it's your Auntie Rachel." Mona moved gracefully toward the door in her long, red satin caftan. "Hey, Rachel," Mona said, stopping to give Rachel a kiss. Little Michael waved. "Let's go back in your playroom and play with your toys," Mona said to Michael.

"Hey, Mona," Rachel finally said. "Michael Jr. keeps you busy I see."

"That's not the half of it. And at night when his daddy comes home, he keeps me busy, too."

"Too much information, girl."

For the first time, Mona got a good look at Rachel. Rachel looked frazzled and not her usual coiffed self. Mona started to say something about the cheap flip-flops that dangled on her feet but changed her mind.

"You want some water or something stronger?"

"Probably the something stronger. A glass of chardonnay would be fine."

"One glass of chardonnay coming right up. So what brings you to my neck of the woods?"

"Mona, it's a long story. I would have never believed it myself it if didn't happen to me."

"Sounds serious," Mona said, concern written on her face. She went to the wet bar and poured Rachel a glass of wine. Rachel was quiet until Mona returned. Mona handed Rachel the glass and noticed that her lips were pinched. Rachel tried to relax. "What's wrong, Rachel?"

Rachel took a sip of the wine and put the glass down on the table that sat next to her chair.

"Things are pretty rocky at my house, Mona. It's more than Marvin's attempted suicide. When I look at your beautiful home with the twenty-foot vaulted ceilings, open-air living space, a lake next to your twenty-foot pool and tennis courts, I get a little jealous."

"You and Marvin have a beautiful home, too, Rachel. You need to stop looking at what me and the doctor have and appreciate that fine living you're doing across town. We're both extremely fortunate to have the husbands we ended up with. I count my blessings every day."

"Your husband isn't in a mess. My fine home...may not be my fine home in a month, maybe two."

"What you talking about, Rach?"

"We're about to lose everything. Marvin sold his majority shares in the company, and now we're fighting to get them back." Rachel lowered her head, then brought it back up and gazed into space. "This was not what I bargained for when I married Marvin."

"But you married him for better or worse, didn't you?"

"Yes, Mona." Rachel lowered her voice; she was becoming irritated. "I did, but the man I married was a go-getter, a strong mover and shaker, taking the fast track up the Fortune Five Hundred chain. He wasn't a quitter."

Mona moved over to Rachel and rubbed her back. "I didn't mean to upset you. Sometimes life throws us a curve ball, and it's all in how you handle the situation."

"That's true, but tonight I found out that my husband is not perfect." Rachel picked up her glass and took a sip. Mona sat down on the couch adjacent to Rachel.

"You want to talk about it?" Mona asked.

"His lover showed up at my door and handed me an envelope. Do you know what was inside the envelope, Mona? It was a picture of them naked, and she was on top of Marvin."

The house was still. Nothing ever kept Mona from running her mouth, but she found herself speechless. Sure, Sylvia had told her of the possible infidelity, but to hear the graphic description of what caused Rachel's pain made her ache.

Mona swallowed hard. "I'm so sorry, Rachel. What did Marvin say? Surely, he had an explanation...a good one."

"What was he going to say? His naked ass was in the picture. And I saw her in the flesh. He had to be mighty desperate to put his...his thing in her nasty stuff."

"Oh, Rachel. Marvin doesn't deserve you. I can't believe that he would do this to you."

"He claims that the woman is trying to blackmail him for fifty thousand dollars. I don't believe that crap for one minute. She wants my husband, and she's going to go to whatever lengths necessary to see that she gets him."

"Well, you need to fight for your man."

"For what? How long would this have gone on if she hadn't shown up at the house with the picture? I've got to get tested. She probably has AIDS."

"Calm down, Rachel. We got to make sense of all of this. The Marvin I know loves you, heart and soul. I know pictures don't lie, but there has to be some explanation."

"This doesn't even call for an expert opinion, Mona. As you said, the picture doesn't lie. What if that had been Michael in the picture instead of Marvin?"

"You know, Mona. I would be kicking ass first and taking names later."

"See. What happened to a reasonable explanation?"

*Whew.* This was more than Mona bargained for. Rachel needed some real help, and none that she could provide. She needed a professional.

At the sound of the doorbell, Rachel straightened up. "Are you expecting company?"

"I don't know who this could be." Mona said, ignoring Rachel's direct question. Mona went to the door. "Oh what a surprise. Rachel, it's Claudette." Rachel frowned.

"I was in the neighborhood," Claudette began. "I remembered you said that Michael was working late tonight, and I decided to stop for a minute to see what you were up to. Time for you to come into the shop and get your head done."

"Hey, Claudette," Rachel said, her voice cool.

"How have you been? Missed you the other week when we went to see Ashley."

"Could be better, Claudette. How's Ashley?" Rachel asked.

"She's doing quite well considering she's sitting in jail on a murder conviction. Served that asshole right. Ashley should have clubbed him to death."

"Okay, Claudette," Mona said, taking a peek at Rachel. "What would you like to drink?"

"Just water," Claudette said. "Trying to lose weight now that I've quit smoking."

"Scared of you, girl," Mona said. "I'll be back in a sec with your bottle of water."

"I need to see Ash," Rachel finally said. "She made the hard choice by killing William. I don't know if I could do time."

"I won't say that Ashley was justified in killing William," Claudette began, "but sometimes when you've been abused by a man long enough, you do crazy things for survival. Like your last ex-husband, what's his name?"

"Reuben."

"See, if I was with Reuben and he did all the stuff he'd done to you, girl, he'd be in worse shape than what you left him in. I'm a non-violent person, swear to God I am, but put your hands on me, you're a goner. T never put his hands on me but that one time, and I kinda asked for it."

"What about the time Ashley's husband had your butt up in the air and threw you in your car?" Mona said as she returned to the room with Claudette's bottled water. Mona looked at Rachel.

"Ooooooooooooooh, ooh, ooh, ooh," Rachel laughed.

"Hee, hee, hee, hee, heeeeeeeeeeeeeeeeeeeeeee," Mona followed in laughter. "That was a good one."

"You got me," Claudette said. "Maybe I'm all talk now, but if I was in a real situation like Ashley, I might have reason to hurt somebody."

"You're all talk, Claudette," Mona said, getting in a last laugh.

"This isn't about me," Claudette stammered, looking from Mona to Rachel.

The doorbell sounded again. "Saved by the bell," Mona said, moving quickly toward the door. "Guys, it's Sylvia. I can't believe that everyone stopped by on the same night."

"Hi, everyone," Sylvia said, giving Mona a kiss.

"Tight jeans look good on you, Sylvia," Mona said. "Got to let the brothers know that the booty is alive and well."

"Quit, Mona, while you're ahead," Sylvia scoffed. Sylvia reached over and gave Claudette a hug. She hesitated at Rachel's turned back and found a seat. "I just love your house, Mona. It's so mod, colorful and beautiful."

"What is this, Mona?" Rachel asked all of a sudden. "Looks like the Ex-Files reloaded."

"I'm going to get ready and go. I suddenly feel tired."

The girls stared at Rachel. "You're not going anywhere, Rachel," Mona said sternly. "You are our sister, and you're in trouble. We're here for you as always. I wasn't sure what prompted you to come to my house on a weekday, Rachel, but I knew I would need reinforcements. And now we're all here. You can either share your story or I will fill everyone in."

Rachel looked around the room. Only love for her looked back. She wanted to reach out to Sylvia and tell her she was sorry, but her pride kept her from doing so. It was easy to share her sob story with Mona because she didn't judge, although the more she thought about it, the more she realized that neither did Claudette or Sylvia—even Ashley. She felt embarrassed, and it kept her silent for longer than she intended.

"Let's take a time-out," Mona said. "What can I get you to drink, Sylvia?"

"I'll start with a chardonnay," Sylvia said.

Mona smiled. "Same thing Rachel's drinking. You two always did think alike."

Rachel knew what Mona was trying to do—melt the ice between her and Sylvia. Sylvia was only trying to be helpful, trying to be her friend.

"Sylvia," Rachel spoke up. Three pairs of eyes focused on Rachel. "I'm sorry about the other day. I was under a lot of stress and I didn't handle things well." Rachel looked at Mona. "I hope you'll forgive me, Sylvia. I've missed you terribly."

Sylvia went to Rachel and squeezed her tight. "I've never stopped loving you, friend. Just gave you your space because I knew you needed it. And I promise to be more sensitive."

"No, you didn't say anything wrong or out of order," Rachel pleaded. "It was me. I called you over to the house and rejected the very advice I was seeking. I realize that advice is not always going to be what you want to hear, although I don't always take and run with every piece of advice given to me."

"That's for sure," Mona said. "Now if you had made up earlier, all you would have had to do was go around the corner for advice. But this is good. I think we need to get together more often."

Sylvia clung to Rachel. "I say we plan another trip to the spa. How about it, Rachel?"

Rachel smiled. "I'd like that. And this time we should go on a day when Claudette can go."

"All of their open days are my work days," Claudette began, "but I'll work something out. Maybe a Tuesday during the day would work."

"Sounds like a plan," Mona chimed in. "I love it when things come together."

Rachel looked into Sylvia's eyes. "Tonight feels like the first time the Ex-Files met and we were sharing our stories."

Sylvia smiled. "Look how far we've come."

"We've got miles to go," Rachel said, staring into space.

"Look, I've thrown a little something together to coat your palates, and when we're finished we're going to listen to Rachel and then pray."

Astonished, Sylvia looked at Mona. She didn't believe the word "pray" had come from Mona's mouth.

"I don't know why you hussies are looking at me like that. I pray all the time. Me and the Lord are tight. Our relationship is better than most. Oh yeah. My God is an awesome God. He just answered my prayer."

"You don't cease to amaze me, Mona," Sylvia said. "Prayer definitely is in order."

"When we do, let's offer up a prayer for Ashley," Rachel said. "I'd like to go with you next time."

"Ooh, there is a God," Claudette bellowed. "I feel him all over me. Y'all are making me want to shout up in here."

"You can shout if you want to," Mona said, giving Claudette the evil eye, "but if you break anything..."

"You've got to pay for it," Sylvia, Rachel, and Claudette said in unison. Everyone laughed.

Being surrounded by her sisters was the next best thing to survival for Rachel. She wasn't sure what was going to become of her and Marvin, but she knew that she'd be able to get through it with the group's support, especially with Sylvia's.

"Mona, can I stay with you tonight?"

# CHAPTER FORTY-SIX

**C**ecil Coleman picked a hair from his chin, then splashed on his favorite cologne. He put his hands on his hips and flashed a toothy grin.

"Look at that six-pack," Trina teased, easing herself into the large tiled bathroom with the Roman tub and separate shower. The smell of spice permeated the room from the scented candles that surrounded the tub. A long, gold-painted, wrought-iron, boat-shaped basket that held several green, orange, red, and gold macramé balls adorned one corner of the tub. Trina went to her husband and encircled his body with her arms, planting kisses across his back. "You smell good, too."

"All for you, Trina girl." Cecil turned so he could admire his wife. "Girl, you're supporting that itsy-bitsy push-up bra. Tryin' to tempt a brother when he's in a hurry. Please don't tell me you wear a thong to court."

"What they don't know won't hurt them."

"Baby, I do appreciate that you've kept that fine figure of yours in excellent shape over the years. Lionel

Richie might have sung it, but you're my brick house. Kiss me, girl." And their lips met in joyful harmony.

Cecil was the first to pull away. "I've got to go, baby."

"But today is Saturday. You've worked hard all week, and you need to take some time for yourself."

"Wish I could do that, Trina, but I'm working on this case for Marvin Thomas. His board of directors have given me the green light to fight for Marvin's shares. I don't know why I let him proceed with making that offer in the first place, especially since he was under duress, but I'm going to fight those white boys on this. It's going to get nasty."

"Guess who I ran into the other day jogging in the neighborhood?"

"Spare me the twenty guesses and just tell me."

"My cousin Kenny. You won't believe where he lives."

"I can take an educated guess," Cecil said, putting on his round-neck sleeveless undershirt. "In the neighborhood."

"And how about on Riverdale Court in the house that I've envied ever since they built it?"

"No kidding. I guess we'll have to find somewhere else to live. Too many black folks moving in. Before long, it will become a real ghetto full of wanna-be professionals."

"Listen to you, Cecil. You're not the only black person with money. Yes, we're doing alright for ourselves, but never forget where you came from."

Cecil stopped and looked at Trina. "Just kidding, baby." He paused, then continued, "The other day, those white boys looked at me as if I was some kind of token attorney. I've earned my way to the twenty-ninth floor, and no one is going to take that away from me. Every day that I go into the office, I stop and stare at my name written on the bronze plaque with the other partners. I've defended and fought against big and little companies on mergers, buyouts, takeovers, and I want what Cecil Coleman is due. Is there anything wrong with that?"

"No, Cecil. Not a thing. If we can go back to the present for a moment...I was thinking about inviting Kenny and his wife, Sylvia, over for a few refreshments, maybe next Friday if it's alright with you."

"Do what you want, Trina. Just let me know when and where."

Trina went to Cecil and wrapped her arms around his neck. "Cecil, you are one of the best corporate attorneys in the city of Atlanta, and in my estimation, in the country. You're one of the smartest men I know— black or white. You deserve everything that you've earned, and I'll always be by your side no matter what. I love you for who you are. Don't change, baby."

"Thanks, Trina. I love you, too." Cecil reached down and kissed his wife. "I've got to go. I've got some research that I need to do. I'm going to win this case, Trina. I'll be back in a little while."

Trina watched as the door closed behind Cecil. She was worried about him, but she knew he would be alright. Stress always came knocking at the door when he was involved in a big case. This one was no different.

It was eight o'clock and still too early in the morning to get her day started. The maid had come in and cleaned yesterday, and the house smelled fresh, like lilacs.

Trina lay down on the large sleigh bed she shared with her husband. She had cases she needed to go over, but today was going to be the day she did for herself. On days like this, she felt bouts of loneliness. After two miscarriages, she and Cecil remained childless, and there were many days of wondering what it would've been like to have a son or a daughter.

Sleep overtook Trina. Two hours passed before she was roused from her slumber. "Goodness, I've got to get up. I can't sleep the day away."

Trina put on a pink-and-white jogging suit and grabbed a bagel. Her thoughts went back to Cecil and his quip about moving from the neighborhood. It bothered her in a crazy sort of way.

Without giving it a second thought, Trina grabbed her purse and left the house. She drove to the end of Lake Front Drive and turned right. At the end of the street, the sign read RIVERDALE COURT. She made a right turn into the cul-de-sac and stopped in front of Kenny's house.

It would have been nice if she had called first, but

she didn't have his number. Curiosity brought her there because she wanted to know if Kenny was living better than she. Trina admired the house; it was huge and architecturally beautiful. The stone lions that guarded the house seemed tame. Before she lost her nerve, she walked the brick path and climbed the stairs to the porch.

Trina rang the bell and waited a few minutes before ringing it again. She pasted her ear to the door to hear if there were any signs of life. It was quite embarrassing when the door flew open and she almost fell in.

"Well, look who's here?" Kenny said sarcastically. "My cousin, Trina, decided to pay me a visit. Come on in."

"I was out in the neighborhood...and...here I am."

"Where is Cecil?" Kenny asked, looking past Trina. "Not ready to sit with the not-so-wealthy side of your family?"

"That's not fair, Kenny. In fact, he's gone into the office to work on the case for your firm. He puts his heart and soul into his work, and I'm sure he's going to win this case for you."

"Well, we're counting on him in the worst way. Come in. There's someone here I want you to meet."

Trina gazed at her surroundings as she followed Kenny into the house. The interior was just as gorgeous as the exterior. Money had been spent on decorators, she noted, because everything in the house was quality and immaculate.

They entered the family room, and Trina was in awe. The collection of art made her giddy, being a collector herself. Then she noticed the scatter of family photos that graced the mantel on the large fireplace and were placed throughout the room. She hoped she'd get a chance to look at them. The furniture in this room was more mod, but complemented the fine furniture that she'd seen in the rooms she passed on the way in.

"This is my wife, Sylvia," Kenny said, disturbing Trina's personal tour of the Richmond house.

"It's nice to finally meet you," Sylvia said, extending her hand.

"And this is my partner, Marvin Thomas," Kenny said. Marvin stood and shook Trina's hand. "Trina is my cousin and also Cecil Coleman's wife." Marvin seemed impressed. "Trina is also a prosecuting attorney in Atlanta."

"So you're the Marvin Thomas my husband is so hyped up to defend."

"Yeah, Cecil and I go way back. We did undergrad together and then he went on to law school, and I went on to get my master's degree in engineering. If I may say so, it's nice to meet you, also."

"The pleasure is all mine," Trina said. "As I told Kenny, I was just passing through."

"Would you like something to drink," Sylvia offered. "I've made mimosas."

"Sure, I'd like to have one," Trina said. "I didn't interrupt anything?" She noticed the looks of concern on everyone's faces.

Marvin spoke up. "This may be divine intervention. I have a situation that you might be able to help us with, Trina."

Trina saw the frown on Kenny's face. "What is it, Marvin?"

Marvin looked at Kenny and back at Trina. He waited until Sylvia handed the mimosa to Trina before he got started. "I'm being blackmailed to the tune of fifty thousand dollars by a woman I don't really know."

Marvin had piqued Trina's interest. "How did this woman come to blackmail you?"

"It's a long story," Marvin said.

Trina took a sip of her mimosa. "If I can have a refill on my mimosa when I've finished this one, you've got my attention."

"No problem," Sylvia said civilly.

Marvin shared the sordid story of how he met Peaches and how she took him to her room and stripped him down to make it look as if they had sex together, leaving out the more graphic details. "She took photos of us lying together in the nude," Marvin said, pausing a moment, looking away from the group. "My wife... my wife...let me back up. This morning, Peaches came to my house and handed my wife an envelope with a picture of Peaches and me in a compromising position. And my wife is very upset and has left the house."

"Do you have a copy of the picture?" Trina asked. She noticed that both Sylvia and Kenny seemed disgusted by the question. "It's not that I want to look at it, but it should be kept as evidence." She saw Sylvia and Kenny relax.

"Yes, it's at home, and I've put it away for the time being."

"Do not destroy it under any circumstances," Trina advised. "An analyst can determine whether the picture is posed or not."

"Really?" Kenny asked. "That's amazing."

Trina looked from Kenny back to Marvin. "Marvin, do you know the woman's full name?"

"Peaches is all I know."

"You need to find out what her full name is. Peaches may be just a nickname. If she's done this before, there may be something on her in the criminal justice system that we might be able to use as leverage to run her in. When does she want the fifty thousand dollars?"

Marvin sighed. "I have less than three weeks to come up with the money, which I refuse to pay. Peaches has been stalking me...calling on the job, showing up at the office. I can't take much more of this."

"I understand that your wife is upset, but if you believe that this is a set-up, you must convince her so that you can have a united front," Trina said. "I know I'm not in her shoes, and I understand where her mind is at this moment, so I hope that what you say is true. Infidelity is a cruel thing."

"I couldn't get through to her, especially with everything that has gone on with me lately. I don't even know where Rachel is. She hasn't called, not even to check on our child, but I believe she's alright."

"She's at Mona's," Sylvia said, holding her head down. "I saw her last night."

There was a bright light in Marvin's eyes. "How was she?"

"Not very good." Sylvia stood up and went to Marvin. "Give her some time, Marvin. You can let Serena stay with us if you like. I think that woman coming to the house and confronting her on the porch was a bit much."

Marvin bit his lip. "I'm going to kill Peaches. If I ever get my hands on her, I'm going to wring her neck. She's trying to destroy my family and everything I've worked for."

"Listen, Marvin," Trina snapped. "No one is going to kill Peaches, literally. We're going to do that in a court of law. Remember, you have some responsibility in this, too, because if you hadn't gone to that bar and drunk yourself into oblivion, none of this might have happened."

Marvin sat back in his seat. "Yeah, you're right. Kenny, what'd you say about making a visit to Earl's? The answers lie there."

Kenny looked at his wife and back at Marvin. "I'm with you, man. Let's go so we can get some answers."

Trina extended her glass. "May I have another mimosa?"

# CHAPTER FORTY-SEVEN

It was going to take more than a cup of coffee to keep his mind alert while sifting through prior case studies. Cecil sipped his coffee and pored over the briefs that had brought him fame and acclaim. There wasn't one precedent that looked like the Thomas and Richmond Tecktronics, Inc., case he was working on, but he knew that in the end this case would be a first and his victory.

He relaxed in his leather chair and contemplated the earlier conversation he'd had with Trina. *Was he becoming too arrogant? Did he think he was better than other black folks who had only done what he had done—worked hard to get where they were?* Cecil wanted to believe he wasn't that kind of human being, but if he searched his soul, there was a bit of a pompous attitude bottled deep inside.

He recalled how he'd looked at Marvin, who he'd felt was beneath him. But the truth of the matter was, Marvin had made his way all by himself and was doing just as well. And so what if cousin Kenny had made it; there was room enough for all of them. Blackness united.

Big business was ruthless. Cecil watched the failing economy along with everyone else. It wouldn't be long before everyone fell to their knees asking the Lord to bail them out. He smiled at the possibility of a black president running the country. Heaven help him.

In the middle of his thoughts the telephone rang. Strange to receive a call on a Saturday morning. Cecil answered the call on the fourth ring and was surprised to hear Robert Jordan's voice at the end of the line.

"Cecil, this is Robert Jordan. I had hoped to find you in your office."

"Now that you have disturbed me in my office on a Saturday, to what do I owe the pleasure or displeasure of this phone call?"

"Umph," Jordan moaned, loud enough for Cecil to hear. "Regal Resorts wants to meet next week at a place of our choosing to discuss litigation on the merger. I do hope we can keep it out of the courts, though. An expedient resolution to this matter would be most favorable."

"That's highly impossible since the board of directors at Thomas and Richmond Tecktronics do not agree to the buyout. Now, we can resolve this in a favorable manner if Regal agrees to back out of the deal."

"Let's meet next Wednesday at noon. I'll have my secretary follow up with the location."

"Let me check my calendar. It appears to be clear. I'll await the place."

"Cecil, you're wasting your time defending this corporation. Regal Resorts has more capital and is poised to fight to the death on this one."

"Jordan, bring it on. They haven't been up against me. I know your reputation, but I've got one, too."

"See you next week." *Click*.

Cecil picked up a piece of paper he had been doodling on. Robert Jordan had better watch out. Balling up the paper, Cecil took it and threw it at the window. "You want to play hard ball," Cecil said out loud, "come on. I'll be ready for you."

Sylvia left her guests and went upstairs to her bedroom. Glancing toward the door to make sure no one was listening, she dialed Mona's number.

"Mona, this is Sylvia. How's our girl doing?"

"Rachel had a sleepless night. She cried for a while until Michael gave her a sedative. I feel so bad for her, Sylvia. I don't know how long she plans to hole up over here, but she's gotta face Marvin sometime. And what about Serena?"

"Look, Marvin is over here talking to Kenny and Kenny's cousin who's an attorney in town. I think Marvin forgot I was in the room, and he spilled his guts about the night with that woman. I'm as convinced as Kenny that Marvin might very well have been set up."

"Well, that's no consolation to Rachel. She's got a picture of her husband butt naked with some slimy ho, and I tell you, Sylvia, if I had received a picture like that with Michael in it, I'd have to do the Lorena Bobbitt on him. Ain't gonna have no crap like that up in this camp."

"I know. Kenny would probably be dead already." Sylvia and Mona laughed. "I'm going to keep Serena until Rachel feels like coming home. Kenny and Marvin are going to do some more investigation into this Peaches woman."

"What you mean more investigating? Sylvia, you know more than you've been sharing. Girl, you know I like the juicy gossip. It makes the world go around. Maybe one day, I'll even write a book."

"Write a book? Girl, you keep stirring the pots, though, you're enough mystery and intrigue all by yourself."

"I think I hear Rachel going to the bathroom. I'll call you later. And you can come over if you want to."

"Mona, you just don't want to be with Rachel all by yourself. Handle it. Feed her. Fill her up with drink. Give her another sleeping pill. Now, that was easy, wasn't it?"

"Sylvia, I'm going to kill you. Bring your butt over here later on. I like that we got together last night."

"Alright. I'll bring Kenny Jr. over and I'll see if Marvin will let Serena come with me. After his and Rachel's fight yesterday, Marvin may be using Serena as leverage to get Rachel to come home."

"Well, I hope she gets her butt up from here and

goes on home soon. I can't handle nobody else's crisis right now."

"Shut up, Mona. You know we'd be there for you."

"Yeah, yeah. Ooh, I've got to go. Rachel's out of the bathroom, and I bet she's coming in here. Bye."

Sylvia sighed. Dealing with Mona was always an ordeal. She sat on the bed and thought about Marvin's insistence that he didn't know what happened in that room with Peaches. An idea popped into her head. *Oooooooooh yeah, she was going to become the next black Nancy Drew or Valerie Wilson Wesley's Tamara Hayle.*

Quickly, she redialed Mona's number and waited for her voice. "Hey, Mona, this is Sylvia again. Listen. I've got a plan that's going to take you, me, and Claudette to engineer."

"What you talking about, Sylvia? I ain't no spy."

"I'll call Claudette and have her meet me over at your house. We're going to get to the bottom of this Peaches and Marvin ordeal."

"Sister, you don't have a license to kill. Leave that to Double Oh-Seven. Now, I'm double-oh out."

"We're not Charlie's Angels either, but what if I tell you we're going to have fun while we're doing it? The three of us are going to Earl's Tavern, or whatever it's called, and hang out."

"Risky. Furthermore, I don't trust you. What about Rachel?"

"She's a risk. I'll tell you the plan when I get to your house. 'Bye."

# CHAPTER FORTY-EIGHT

Robert Jordan slammed on his brakes. He nearly missed seeing the *Stop* sign. The call to Cecil Coleman hadn't gone as planned, and he had to figure out another way to impress upon Coleman that he needed to leave the takeover case alone. It wasn't that Jordan couldn't win it, but Regal Resorts didn't want to waste a whole lot of money and energy on a black-owned company whose shares they could've snatched up just as easily another way. It happened to be an opportunity that fell into their laps, and upon further examination of the portfolio, they'd decided Thomas and Richmond Tecktronics was well worth keeping.

He was not in the mood to visit his daughter. She had asked him to come, but going to the prison to see Ashley bordered on tedium. How many more years would his family have to endure it? Although he loathed William, Ashley didn't have to kill him. Damn, they had just gotten divorced.

The visitors parking lot was sparse for a Saturday. Grudgingly, Jordan got out of his car and proceeded into the maximum-security facility. Because he was an attorney, he was able to bypass some of the red tape regular visitors had to go through just to see an inmate. He manufactured a smile upon seeing Ashley.

"Hey, Dad, glad you could come," Ashley said, taking a seat in the visitors room. "You look beat."

It always pained Jordan to see Ashley bound in hand-and-leg cuffs. She seemed to have accepted her fate and was living each day as it came. No makeup, no pretense, no office gossip or tales of a marriage that shouldn't have been. But he was going to do everything within his power to cheer his little girl up.

"Yeah, I'm working on a case that should be cut-and-dried, but I'm going to have to work harder to win this son-of-a-gun than I had previously thought," Jordan said.

"Is this the takeover case you told me about the last time you were here?"

"Yep, one and the same. I'm surprised you re-member."

Ashley dropped her head for a moment and brought it back up to gaze at her father. "Not a whole lot to keep your mind saturated. I'm so thankful that I get to help out in the library. I can still stay in touch with the outside world."

"Well, the outside world isn't doing so good." Jordan exhaled. "The economy is in crisis, and the handwriting is on the wall. There are going to be more takeovers and mergers. I'll admit that this Thomas guy has a good attorney working for him, but in the end he's looking at losing it all."

"Is there any way that Mr. Thomas can save his company?"

"Now, who are you rooting for? The idiot made an offer to sell his majority shares in his company to my client, who accepted. Sounds to me like Thomas is fresh out of luck."

"But maybe this guy has seller's remorse. It happens all the time. We do things without thinking them through first and act on it before we realize what we've done."

"You're talking about yourself now, Ashley. As much as I hated William, I hate even more having to see you behind bars. I'm glad he's not in your life anymore but at such a terrible cost. I guess that's the price of passion."

Ashley sat still as her father recounted the story of how she'd ended William's life. She didn't need another reminder of what happened; the fact that she was here, in the maximum security prison, was reminder enough. Her mind was on Marvin, though, and all he and Rachel stood to lose. Marvin had worked so hard to build his business and to make it what it was today. There had to be something she could do, but she wasn't sure what it was. She pulled herself out of her daydream at the sound of her father's voice.

"Where were you? Definitely not in the room with me after I drove all the way out here."

"Sorry, Dad," Ashley said. "Something you said put me deep in thought."

"Well, why was it that you had to see me today? As I've said, I'm pretty busy, and I've got some research to do on this case. It may take me all day."

"There's someone I need to help get out of a jam. It's going to require a large sum of money. Dad, this may seem unorthodox, but I need you to tap into one of the trusts that Granddaddy left me and send the amount to an address that I'll give you."

Robert Jordan looked at his daughter like she was insane. "You can't be serious, Ashley. Who is this person and how much money are you talking about?"

"Dad, I can't disclose the name of the person at the moment, but the sum is five hundred thousand dollars."

"Have you lost your mind, Ashley? Is that woman who adopted your baby trying to extort money from you? I can have a settlement worked out for her in no time."

"No, Dad. No one has asked me for money. This is something I've gotta to do."

"I'm getting ready to leave. I want you to think about what you've asked me to do. Your grandfather is probably rolling over in his grave now. He didn't leave you the trusts so that you can do frivolous things with them."

"But he did leave it to me to use at my own discretion."

"Well, I'm going to have a talk with the medical personnel to see if they've been neglectful of you and whether or not you need a psychiatric evaluation."

"Dad, you can leave now. My request was not far-fetched, and I'm very much in touch with my faculties." Ashley stood up and looked at her father. "I'd like to have my request taken care of within the next week and a half."

Robert Jordan stood and stared at his daughter. His anger was about to boil over. Ashley had gone against him all of her life, making one inexcusable mistake after another. Now that he had the upper hand and was executor of her estate since she was in prison, he was going to exercise his right. He took one last look at Ashley and walked out of the room.

# CHAPTER FORTY-NINE

ylvia and Claudette arrived at Mona's at the same time. Sylvia brought along Serena, accompanied by Kenny Jr. She couldn't wait to see Rachel's face.

"Hey, Sylvia." Claudette climbed the steps to the porch and greeted Sylvia with a hug and a kiss, and then stooped to kiss Serena and Kenny Jr. Sylvia gave Reagan a kiss, too.

"Hey, Claudette. Ready for some adventure?"

"I'm not sure since you didn't tell me anything. I called Mona, and she said you've got us going on some secret mission. I just want to come back in one piece so I can go home to Tyrone."

"You and Tyrone are doing so well."

"We're blessed, Sylvia. Our family is back on track and I'm getting my health together. It couldn't be better."

"Ring the doorbell, Kenny," Sylvia said.

"Okay, Mommy."

They waited on the porch. "Auntie Mona," the children sang when Mona opened the door. Serena, Kenny Jr., and Reagan hugged Mona's legs. She laughed.

"Michael Jr. is in his playroom. It's about time you heifers got here. It's hard having a conversation with a zombie."

"Move out of the way and let us in," Claudette ordered chuckling.

The crew tumbled inside—the children's laughter heard above everyone else. Sylvia began to tear up at the sight of Rachel's face; shock replacing calm as Rachel saw Serena enter the house. She jumped up from her seat and clasped the sides of her face with her hands.

"Baby, sweetie," Rachel gasped as Serena ran to her mother. Rachel picked Serena up and hugged her tight, while Serena slapped kisses all over Rachel's face. "Mommy missed you. How did you get here?" Rachel continued to shower Serena with hugs and kisses.

"Auntie Sylvia," was Serena's reply, pointing her little finger at Sylvia.

Rachel looked into the faces of Sylvia and Claudette. "What are you guys doing here? You were just here last night. I'm fine, really."

Sylvia walked over to Rachel and gave her a kiss on the cheek. "Rachel, sweetie. Sit down. We've got something to share with you."

"What is it, Sylvia? Don't keep me in the dark."

"Mona, why don't you send the kids to little Michael's room?" Sylvia suggested.

"Yeah, yeah, that's a good idea."

"What are you guys up to?" Rachel asked again. She looked from Sylvia to Claudette, who had yet to utter a word.

"I'm in the dark like you," Claudette finally chimed in. "I'm just following instructions as usual."

"Well, somebody needs to talk to me. My nerves are on edge, my marriage is going down the tubes, and you guys look like Abbott and Costello trying to fake the funk on somebody."

"Rachel, I called Mona and Claudette together because we're going to become detectives, like black Charlie's Angels," Sylvia began.

"Sylvia, please. Pray tell, what is Larry, Curly, and Moe going to do?" Rachel laughed.

"I thought we were Abbott and Costello?" Claudette said, wanting to get in her two cents.

"Let's get on with it, Sherlock," Mona said, re-entering the room. "I'm ready for the mission."

Rachel began to fidget in her seat. "What is it, Sylvia? Why are you being so secretive?"

Mona and Claudette took a seat and waited for Sylvia to begin.

"It's like this," Sylvia said. "Marvin was over at the house today." Rachel sighed and rolled her eyes. Sylvia ignored her. "Kenny's cousin, who's a prosecuting attorney in the DA's office downtown, happened to stop by. Out of the blue, Marvin told her all about Peaches."

"What? What in the hell did he do that for?" Rachel yelled, rising from her seat.

"Calm down, Rachel. After hearing Marvin's side of the story from his own mouth, I'm inclined to believe that this woman may have set him up. Kenny's cousin Trina was listening intently, and she advised Marvin to get some more information on this Peaches woman."

"Sylvia, his naked ass was underneath that cheap piece of...cheap piece of crap, who was also naked and doing you know what to Marvin. Do you have some theory other than what the photograph plainly showed that a jury would buy? Marvin is guilty as charged. Hell, I'm getting worked up all over again just thinking about it."

"Hear me out, Rachel," Sylvia begged. "Me, Claudette, and Mona are going out on a limb for you and Marvin because we love you."

"All of you are idiots. I'm the person in possession of the photograph that shows her husband with another woman doing the nasty in living color. What if it was one of your husbands instead of mine? Would you be so fast to forgive, or rush to judgment because you can't dispute the evidence? For all you know, Marvin could be putting on a performance for you stupid people in order for you to believe his story, which apparently you have."

"Hold on now, Rachel, there aren't any idiots up in my house. Further, Sylvia dragged me into this mess and told me I had to help her," Mona said. "But to be part of something mysterious is just up my alley."

"That's because your behind is nosey," Claudette said. "You know Mona can't help herself."

"Whatever," Rachel said. "You all are wasting your time."

"Let us be the judge of that," Sylvia said. "I heard Marvin speak passionately about what happened that night. All we're going to do is try to prove it...well, maybe get a little something, something on the woman so maybe someone else can prove it. But what we need from you right now is to watch the children while we're on our crusade."

"So what's the plan, Sylvia?" Mona wanted to know. "Are we going to be undercover?"

"We're going to Earl's Tavern, hang out, drum up some conversation with the regulars, and hopefully get the scoop on Peaches."

"Sounds mighty weak to me," Rachel said. "You amateurs don't know what in the hell you're doing, and you can get yourself hurt. The photo doesn't lie."

"There's a possibility it might," Sylvia said. "Trina said an expert might be able to determine whether the photo has been doctored or not."

"Ummph," Rachel sighed. "I know what I saw on that piece of paper."

"Stop being so negative, Rachel," Claudette cut in. "I know how you feel, but if there is an ounce of truth in Marvin's story, why don't you let your best friends help solve the mystery? The nerve of the woman to come to your house and deliver the photo so she can extort money. Smells like desperate to me. She ain't on the up and up. I'm with the girls; we're going to make Miz Peaches, whoever she is, regret that she ever stepped foot on your doorstep."

Rachel began to relax. "You think Marvin might be telling the truth?"

"Honestly, I do, Rachel," Sylvia said. "If he had something to hide, he wouldn't have been pleading and searching for answers. He loves you, Rach. That man loves you with everything he's got. Don't give up on your good man so fast. We haven't."

All eyes were on Rachel. She felt like the bare behind on the Pin the Tail on the Donkey game. "I'll think about it. I appreciate you guys for doing this for me and Marvin, but can I ask you one little bitty question?"

"What, Rachel?" Mona chimed. "I know you aren't complaining about the accommodations. I've given you plenty to eat, plenty to drink, you've used two boxes of tissue and two rolls of toilet paper."

"Mona, I don't know what I'm going to do with you." Rachel laughed. "If these guys hadn't come charging in here like they did tonight, I was ready to pay you a month's rent."

"You ain't got to change your mind about paying for room and board. My hand is out. But does that mean you're not staying long?" Mona laughed and the others followed. Rachel kept her mouth closed.

"Mona, girl, you don't have any sense," Claudette said. "So what did you want to ask us, Rachel?"

"So is that why y'all look like hoochies?"

# CHAPTER FIFTY

A light drizzle forced the sun to recede behind the clouds that had formed and were moving fast over the Atlanta area. The autumn had been unseasonably warm and every bit of rain that fell was more than welcomed.

Marvin and Kenny dashed to Marvin's Lexus and headed downtown. Both men were silent as they rode out of their quiet subdivision and into the throes of urban sprawl, stopping and starting every few minutes on the congested streets like they were waiting to get into a ball game. Their victory in the boardroom had been overshadowed by Marvin's demons, specifically the one named Peaches, and someway, somehow, the demon had to be eradicated.

"A penny for your thoughts," Kenny said, deep in his own.

"Ahhhhhh," Marvin sighed. "Just wondering how I got into all this mess. This wasn't supposed to happen to me, Kenny. I'm the one who saves everyone else."

"You're only human, bro. What you're going through could happen to anyone."

"But I'm to blame for the mess I'm in. I've always said that I wouldn't be the face of the successful white collar worker who made it big and ended up an Enron artifact."

Kenny managed a snicker. "Nicely said, my man. However, it's happened, and you and I must face it head on. But first we've got to get this thorn out of your side. And just so you know, I believe you, Marvin, when you say that you didn't submit to Peaches willingly."

Marvin was silent for a moment. "The bad thing is that I had not taken a drink in over two years because I wanted to live a different life as a father and a husband. I was brought up in the church, and I wanted to kind of go back to basics once Serena was born. Hell, I wasn't even a recovering alcoholic. And to think that in one night, one night, Kenny, I tried to drink for all the time I hadn't in the last two years, only to end up on the wrong side of right."

"No, man. You ended up in some woman's bed naked as a jay-bird. Got your freak on without really being there. What a waste."

"Kenny, man, this is not a laughing matter. Imagine my surprise when I woke up and realized I wasn't in my house, with my wife. Lord, I know how Adam must have felt in the Garden of Eden when God looked down at him in all his nakedness after he'd eaten the forbidden fruit. And all he could find to cover himself with was a big fat fig leaf." They laughed.

"How was she, Marvin?" Kenny joked.

"Shut the hell up, Kenny. I don't want to joke about anything as serious as this. The truth is, I didn't feel a thing because my blood alcohol level had to be over point ten. Let it go. We're almost there."

Kenny rode the rest of the way in silence. All of this talking about Marvin reminded him of someone he had hurt some twenty or more years ago. While he wouldn't acknowledge it out loud, Kenny knew he had been a whore in the worst kind of way. He'd love them and leave them and didn't give a crap about what they thought. The one person who had his heart knew of his wanton behavior, and he counted himself blessed that as a changed man, he'd found her again and was able to rekindle that love. He knew in his heart he didn't deserve Sylvia, but even a sinner deserves a second chance.

Marvin looked at Kenny. "We're here," Marvin said. I hope we get lucky today. The sooner Peaches is out of my life, the better for all of us."

"Let's do it," Kenny said, jumping from the truck. The thrill of the hunt excited Kenny, and he, like Marvin, hoped they could catch a big fish today.

Their eyes adjusted as they walked into the tavern. Not many patrons on a Saturday afternoon. A few stragglers sat at the bar, and Earl was in his usual place shooting the bull and entertaining the customers.

Earl wiped down the bar with swift circular motions, and placed clean glasses in a small rack to dry. He stopped short when he saw Marvin and Kenny approach. The friendly face of a few days ago was gone and replaced with a scowl—no welcome sign here.

"What do you two fellas want?" Earl asked in a gruff voice. "'Cuz if you didn't come in here to have a drink, you might want to see yourself back out the door."

The other patrons moved their heads like zombies in Earl's direction, trying to understand who had come in and interrupted their easygoing afternoon. They sat stiffly as if at any moment Earl would push a button and they would head into battle at the order of their commander-in-chief. In truth, none of them could hurt a fly because they spent their lonely days on a beat-up bar stool, glad to have Earl's company.

"We've come in peace," Marvin said, almost pleading with Earl. "We just want to ask you a few questions, if we may. It'll only take a few minutes, and we'll be out of your hair."

"No questions and no answers." Earl looked at Kenny and placed his finger in his face. "You told me that you and your partner weren't going to do anything to Peaches. You boys upset her, and Peaches doesn't take too kindly to being pushed around by no grown-ass man."

"Did she tell you," Marvin interjected, "that she stripped me of my clothes...and hers too and took a picture of us as if we were having sexual intercourse and is now blackmailing me to the tune of fifty thousand dollars?" Marvin saw the surprise in Earl's face. "She's harassed me, my family, and my employees and has threatened to go to the newspaper with this photo and who knows what else if I don't give in. I say that I'm within my rights."

"So why are you telling me?" Earl asked, visibly upset at Marvin's account of things.

"Because I'd hope you'd reason with me and see how I feel as a man...a man whose family has been threatened. I need to put a stop to it. All I need is a name—her real name."

"And what are you going to do with this information?" Earl asked.

Kenny took over. "Earl, we understand that this Peaches might be a regular here and perhaps a good customer, but we need something as leverage to get her to quit this vendetta that she's fabricated. If we had her whole name, maybe we can find something on her that we might be able to use."

Earl's eyes shifted between Kenny and Marvin. His hand shook slightly, grabbing the edge of the bar to calm the nervousness that had become transparent. "Peaches is all I know. She's never given another name, and I've never asked."

"As often as she comes in here, surely she's told you things about her," Kenny pushed.

"So, you're asking me to be disloyal to a loyal customer," Earl said, giving Kenny the evil eye. "That's like a psychiatrist violating a patient confidentiality clause."

"If that's what it is, I guess you're right," Kenny responded.

"Let me tell you something," Earl began. "I don't even like you. Peaches told me how nasty you were to her."

"Did she tell you how she propositioned us? Wanted to have a *ménage à trois*."

"A what?" Earl bunched up his face in confusion.

"A threesome." Kenny waved his hand in surrender. "We're not having any luck here, Marvin. Let's go home."

"I'm not ready to go yet, Kenny. Earl hasn't told us anything yet."

"Don't plan to tell you anything, either," Earl retorted. "And since you're not ordering a drink, it's time for you to leave. You're taking space from my paying patrons."

Marvin took a card from his pocket and handed it to Earl. "If you feel like talking, give me a call."

Disappointed, Marvin and Kenny walked out of the tavern.

"If you had let me handle it and hadn't been so combative, Earl might have said something," Marvin said to Kenny.

"He wasn't going to tell you nothing. We didn't get anything out of him the other night, and I doubt that he'll say anything later. You could have saved your business card."

"Look, that bartender knows something. I watched his body language. Did you see how his body tensed when you said you needed Peaches' real name so that you could possibly find out something on her? I swear that joker was shaking in his boots. You probably didn't notice because you were so busy trying to yank the truth out of him."

"That may be true, Marvin, but we're still at ground zero. Nada. Nothing. Our hands are still empty and that bitch, excuse my French, Peaches, is still out there on the loose trying to wreak havoc on you and the company. I say we ought to give her some back street whoop-ass."

"Kenny, I'm too grown for that crap, and so are you. We're CEOs of a big company. That's not how we do business. We hire someone to teach Peaches the facts of life. You can't play the big dog's game."

"Now, that's what I'm talking about. I'll give Peaches one thing, she's not a dumb broad. She comes with her guns loaded. Knows how to play the game, but she's not going to win this one."

"No, she's not," Marvin said matter-of-factly. "I'll call Harold. He's got a few numbers of people who can hook us up in his black book."

"Okay, dawg. I still say your detective skills are whacked."

"Okay, Mr. Kenny Richmond, I'm taking you home. I've had enough negative energy around me for one day."

# CHAPTER FIFTY-ONE

They were a motley crew dressed in a wide range of looks from skin-tight leggings and just-above-the-butt, revealing tops that could make a sleeping man aroused to Claudette's over-sized African-print ensemble that was large enough to stuff a whole circus into it. Hoochies. That was Rachel's word for her bizarre-looking friends who had it in their minds that they were going to save her marriage. None of them had been in a tavern ever, but in their minds' eyes, the way they were dressed was how folks looked who hung out in places like that.

"Glad I'm not going with you misfits," Rachel said, laughing as she watched Mona, Sylvia, and Claudette get into Sylvia's car. "Be careful in this rain."

"You know we're doing this for your ass," Mona said. "Don't you forget it when we nab that Peaches woman and beat her into oblivion with our bare hands."

Rachel couldn't stop laughing. "Mona, you know Sylvia's going to do all the work. You go on and keep the rest of those men gawking."

"So you're saying that Sylvia and I can't catch a man's

eye?" Claudette wanted to know. "Don't forget I stood up to Ashley's dead husband, God rest his soul. Peaches, or whatever her name is, don't want to mess with me."

"Y'all are so sensitive."

"I want you out of my house by the end of the day," Mona shouted. "I've got to get you back to your husband so he can take care of your spiteful little behind. Getting my hair wet on account of you."

"Okay, you guys get out of the rain and find Peaches. Thank you and I love you." Rachel threw the trio a kiss and waved as Sylvia pulled away from Mona's house and drove down the street.

Rachel felt blessed as she moved back into the house and walked into the room where the children were playing. Her friends believed what she wasn't ready to believe, and that was that her husband had not betrayed their love and the photo that found its way on her doorstep was only the illusion of a very sick woman.

Rachel squeezed her hands together and tried to focus on the positive. She and Marvin had a wonderful life and they were meant to be. Yes, she was blessed to have friends who'd go the limit to try to right a wrong because they believed in their hearts Marvin was telling the truth. She smiled.

"Do you know where you're going, Sylvia?" Mona asked. "Looks like you're taking the scenic route."

"Sit back and relax, Mona," Sylvia said. "I'll have you

there in no time. Kenny didn't believe me when I told him we were going down to the tavern to conduct our own investigation because we could get more information out of the bartender than he or Marvin could. He gave me directions anyway, and according to my navigation system, we're just about..."

"There it is," Claudette called out from the back seat. "Earl's Tavern is up there on the sign."

"See that open spot right there," Sylvia pointed, "I ordered it so we wouldn't have to be riding all over the world trying to find a parking spot."

"How did you do that?" Claudette asked.

"Claudette, sometimes I wonder about you. You fell for that garbage. Sylvia was just lucky, that's all. You didn't see her up here praying that she'd find an open spot. I was praying right along with her 'cause this place gives me the creeps. Can't stay down here long, plus I can't do no good shopping down in these parts."

Sylvia cracked up. "Mona, give it up. For once get shopping off the brain. We've got some business to take care of. I want you ladies to follow my lead."

"You know, Sylvia darling, I don't follow anybody anywhere."

"Mona, aren't you in my car? Like I said, give it up."

"Ooh, Sylvia told you, Mona," Claudette blared.

"Shut up, Claudette. Alright, Sylvia. Claudette and I are following your lead. You better not mess this up. And remember why we're doing it."

Sylvia threw her hands up. "Okay, enough. You're going to blow our cover before we even get out of the car. We're going to go in there and pretend like we're good friends just out on a Saturday for a good time. We'll each order a drink; it's on me."

"Now you're talking," Mona cut in. "I'm listening."

"We're going to sit close to where the bartender seems to be stationed so that we can hear his conversation. I'm not sure what I'm going to say yet, but it'll come at the right moment."

"You sure about this, Sylvia?" Claudette asked with sudden reservation. "Sounds kind of flaky to me."

Sylvia turned around and looked at Claudette. "Do you want answers to help Rachel?"

"Yes, I guess so. I mean you dragged me into this... whatever it is. So now that I'm here, I'm down with whatever."

"Whatever!" Sylvia huffed. "Let's go. The rain has let up a bit. We can run for it."

The ladies got out of the car and practically ran to Earl's. They opened the door and went inside. Once inside they stood a second to allow their eyes to adjust to the light, or lack of it. They saw the bar off to the left and the few tables that sat to the right and what looked like a tiny stage. Sylvia moved forward and the others followed. Earl's eyes lit up as the trio took seats in front of him.

"Would you ladies like to sit at one of the tables?"

Earl offered, pointing in the direction of the four empty tables.

"No, the bar will do," Mona said, rushing past Sylvia and extending her hand to Earl.

He seemed flattered, Sylvia noted, and the trio hopped up on the three stools close to the cash register.

"And what would you ladies be drinking?" Earl asked, his attention focused on Mona as he shook her outstretched hand. He patted it and seemed not to notice the five-carat diamond wedding ring that swallowed up her finger. His eyes drew scribbles all over the parts of her body that were visible from behind the bar, but he let his gaze rest just a little too long on Mona's mouth.

Mona blushed and covered her mouth. "I'll have a pomegranate martini," she said.

Sylvia gave her a look. "I'll have a glass of white wine," Sylvia said, continuing to roll her eyes at Mona. Earl turned to her and gave her a nice smile.

"I'll have a glass of water with lemon," Claudette interjected. Earl looked in her direction as if noticing her for the very first time.

"We'll get you some water from the kitchen," Earl said, whistling for one of the waitresses. "No disrespect."

"Yeah, whatever," Claudette mouthed, not too happy about the treatment she was receiving.

"I've never seen you ladies in here before," Earl began. "Are you from these parts?"

"Noooo," Sylvia jumped in. "My girls and I came to town to have a girl's day. We're just hanging out."

"You've come to the right place," Earl said, leaning on the counter and back into Mona's face.

Mona puckered up her lips and threw Earl a kiss. He smiled; Sylvia and Claudette frowned.

"I like plump and juicy sisters like you," the man who sat next to Claudette said to her. "You're pretty, too."

Claudette looked at the man in disgust. His breath reeked of beer and his fingernails were dirty. "Well, this plump and juicy sister has a man and is not interested in anyone else. I'm just hanging with my girls today. We're going to do the spa thing and—"

"You ought to let me go with you. I'd love to rub oil all over your body." The man grinned as he checked out her cleavage.

"Maybe you didn't get my meaning when I said I've already got a man who takes care of me right nice. I'm trying to be nice here."

"Lady, I don't want no trouble. You come up here sitting next to me and smelling all good. Can't fault a man for trying."

"I'm sorry, too," Claudette said. "Enjoy your afternoon." She turned her back on him and listened to Mona trying to play Earl with her phony voice.

"I bet you flirt with all the ladies who come in here," Mona said to Earl, not waiting for Sylvia's lead.

Earl picked up a toothpick from a little wooden box

that sat on the counter. He grinned. "Naw. Most of the women who come here have been coming so long they look like the next. Nothing as pretty as you has come through those doors in a long time."

"You're just bullcrapping me, Earl. A man as fine as you got to have a special someone."

Earl blushed and took the opportunity to take a towel that hung under the sink and wipe his brow. "Miss, I didn't get your name..."

"Mona."

"Mona, you just want to see me sweat. I know you've got a man because you're wearing that big ole rock on your hand."

Mona held her hand up so everyone could see. "You mean this ole thing? Me and my old man are no longer together." Sylvia and Claudette gawked at the same time, disbelief written on their faces. Sylvia kicked Mona; Mona laughed out loud. "I wear this thing just to remind myself what it was like."

"Umph," Sylvia said. "And she's going straight to hell."

A puzzled look crossed Earl's face. He looked from Mona to Sylvia. "Your friend thinks differently."

"Oh, don't mind Sylvia. She's had a hard time with men." Sylvia kicked Mona harder. "Ouch. I guess that wasn't everyone's business. Too much information."

"I'm getting ready to leave," Claudette announced, jumping from her stool. "This is not what I came here for. We were supposed to—"

Sylvia put her finger over Claudette's lips and gave her the evil eye. "I know this is unorthodox," Sylvia whispered to Claudette, "but Mona is just trying to loosen up the old goat for the kill."

"Sounds like she's propositioning him instead. I wish Michael Broussard could hear what his wife told that big ole oaf. It would serve her right if he gave her walking papers."

"Claudette, cool out. We're a team. Let's give this a few more minutes. Remember, we're doing this for Rachel."

"Yeah, whatever. I'd rather be home with T and Reagan."

"You will soon enough. Patience."

"My friends don't have any manners," Mona explained to Earl. She let out a fake laugh. "That's why you don't bring your girlfriends around when you're on the hunt for a new man. You're so cute."

"Okay, Mona," Sylvia whispered. "Cut the crap and remember the mission."

"Earl, how about another drink," Mona sang.

"Anything for you." Earl blew Mona a kiss.

Earl moved away from the counter to fix Mona another pomegranate martini. In a matter of a second, it felt as if a blizzard had blown in the place. A brown-skinned woman with a short Afro, wearing a low-cut red and gold jumper whizzed in, oblivious to all else in the room. Her large gold hoop earrings swung as if an invisible child was playing on them in a playground.

"Earl, Earl, I need to talk to you—now."

"What is it, Peaches?"

Sylvia, Mona, and Claudette sat still, afraid to move in their seats. Payday. It had come without any coercion. It appeared that the mission was just about to be accomplished without having to abort.

"I can't talk here."

Earl smiled at Mona. "I've got to finish fixing this lovely lady her martini."

For the first time, Peaches noticed Mona, Sylvia, and Claudette. She pushed her nose up in the air and rolled her eyes. Mona turned slightly toward Peaches and rolled her eyes in return.

"Well, hurry up," Peaches admonished. "Earl, you can do better than that," she whispered loudly. Mona cut her eyes at Peaches again. "Look, my blood pressure is up, Earl," Peaches continued. "The folks I told you about aren't cooperating. I'm at wits' end. They don't know who they're messing with."

Earl brought the martini to Mona and set it down in front of her. He grinned. "I hope you like it."

"If it's as good as the first one," Mona moaned, "I'm sure it will be."

"Excuse me," Peaches said, tapping Mona on the shoulder. "Earl and I were talking and you just interrupted."

"I'll chalk it up to the fact that your hearing must be

impaired," Mona snapped. "Earl asked me a question, and I was only being polite by answering it. It seems you're the one who owes me an apology, because you were the one who interrupted our conversation. I don't know you, but if I were you, I wouldn't put your hand on me again."

"Heifer, I ain't scared of you and you don't want to mess with me. Earl knows what happens to people who have crossed me."

"Look, miss," Sylvia butt in. "We don't want any trouble. We just came in here for some girlfriend time. I think it's time to go, Mona."

"I second that," Claudette said, drinking the last bit of her water. "Mona, you heard what Sylvia said."

"I'm cool, y'all," Mona said, waving her hand to stop the protest. "I'm not leaving my martini. We'll go in a few minutes."

"At least you've got some sensible friends," Peaches said.

"This ain't about them. It's about you disrespecting me. But you know what, I'm too classy and intelligent to fool up with you. Earl is yours."

"Hey," Earl said. "Now, Peaches is one of the regulars who come here. She and I don't have no kind of...you know...uh relationship."

Peaches relaxed and began to laugh. "And how come we don't, Earl? You afraid of this? Earl knows too much about me and, anyway, he don't have a pot to piss in.

What if I told you ladies that my man is getting ready to make Peaches a very happy woman."

Sylvia was the first to inquire. "How's that, Peaches? I need a man to make me happy."

Mona returned Sylvia's evil stare.

"For my birthday, my man is going to give me fifty thousand dollars to put down on this gorgeous house."

"Does he have a brother?" Sylvia asked. Mona sat sulking and sipping.

"No, there's only one of him; that's unfortunate for you. He's so handsome. Got cocoa-brown skin and dreamy, bedroom eyes that are hazel. He has a thick black moustache that's sprinkled with a little gray, and his body is to die for. He looks like he's lifted weights all his life...you know, the muscles are all in the right places. I'll let you in on a secret. He's married, but he promised that his divorce should be final in a few months. He already has a big gorgeous house, but there would be too many memories."

"No man is that fine," Mona said with a sour face.

"You haven't met my man," Peaches tossed back at Mona. "Anyway, you aren't his type."

"What's his name?" Claudette asked, putting in her two cents and taking the conversation away from Mona. "If he doesn't have any brothers, he's got to have some cousins, uncles, second cousins, or something."

Peaches laughed. "Can't divulge his name, but when I see him, I'll ask for you." Peaches turned toward

Earl. His eyes were penetrating. "Why are you looking at me like that, Earl? Something on your mind?"

"What was so important when you first ran in here?" Earl asked.

Peaches sighed. "Earl, I was over-reacting. Nothing. Everything is going to be alright. I feel it in my bones. Now give me a drink!"

"Your boyfriend and that goon from the other night came in here about an hour ago," Earl said. "They wanted information about you, but don't worry, I refused to give it to them."

"What did they want to know, Earl?" Peaches threw her arms on her hips and paced in a circle. A scowl snaked across her face in a complete metamorphosis.

"That house you're planning to buy may take a lot longer for you to get. You're playing a dangerous game, Peaches, and these guys aren't some two-bit players. They didn't come here to shuck and jive. They're out to get you."

"We'll see about that," Peaches said, more to herself than to Earl. "Wifey must have shown him the picture. He's scared," Peaches mumbled. "He's scared. Mess with me, I'll have some-thing for him."

The ladies sat paralyzed for a second time tonight. "Ready to go?" Sylvia asked.

"Yeah," Claudette almost screamed.

"Look, it was nice meeting you, Earl," Sylvia said. "I hope everything works out for you, Peaches."

"For damn sure, or else," Peaches said to no one.

# CHAPTER FIFTY-TWO

*Clickity, click. Clickity, click. Clickity, click.* Sylvia, Mona, and Claudette almost toppled over each other running from the tavern. The rain had stopped, but they couldn't wait to get into Sylvia's car.

"What are we going to do, Sylvia?" Claudette asked, shutting the door on her side of the car.

"Yeah," Mona chimed in. "You're the one heading up this mission—"

"You mean the mission you tried to take over?" Sylvia asked.

"Moving too slow for me." Mona huffed. "A big old tough man like Earl wasn't going to just up and tell you anything. You had to knead him, rub his temples, make him salivate before preparing him for the kill."

"Whatever, Mona. I was with you, but sometimes you take things to the extreme."

"Sylvia, you asked me to be part of this mission, and I delivered. He was into me. You see how he reacted when Peaches came rolling up in there. He was on the defensive, and if she had said anything out of order, he would've put her in her place."

"Peaches said she wasn't scared of you, Mona," Claudette added and then cracked up. "How did she say it, Sylvia?" Claudette and Sylvia mimicked Peaches.

"You heifers," Mona wailed.

"Remember, you're the heifer," Sylvia said, laughing. Claudette joined in. "Mona," Sylvia continued, "in spite of all that, you did a good job."

"Yeah, yeah. The question is what are we going to do with the information? I've got to get Rachel out of my house tonight."

"We're going to tell Rachel what we heard," Sylvia began, "as well as Marvin and Kenny. Earl was talking about them when he mentioned the two men that came into the bar."

"We figured that," Claudette said.

"Anyway," Sylvia continued, "Peaches is a dangerous woman. I'm not so sure it's a good idea for Rachel to go home. What if that crazy Peaches goes back to their house and threatens Rachel again?"

"I don't think she'd go there a second time," Mona said. "For all Peaches knows, Marvin may have set up surveillance, and while she's crazy, I don't think she's stupid. And I need Rachel to go home to her husband. She's high maintenance."

"Look at the pot calling the kettle black," Claudette roared. "But we've got to call everyone together tonight and decide what we're going to do with this information. Since we're going to your house, Mona, sounds like the place to be."

"Whatever." Mona sat in thought. "I wish I could have punched that ghetto mama right in the mouth. Talking to me like I was a nobody. If we weren't on a so-called 'mission,' she'd be missing a couple of front teeth and eating cement sandwiches. Then I'd take those big-behind earrings of hers and slip them over my hips and play hula hoop. Mess with me." Claudette and Sylvia laughed.

Sprawled out on the couch, Marvin jumped as his cell began to ring. He sat up and grabbed it off the coffee table, praying that it was Rachel. There had not been any contact between the two of them since she left the house. Now Serena's absence was taking loneliness to a whole new level, but Marvin was going to do everything in his power to settle the rift between him and Rachel. Sadness clouded his face when he saw that the number didn't belong to Rachel, but all the same he was happy to hear a friendly voice.

"Hey, man, what's up?"

"Marvin, my man. Tell me the good word. Checking to make sure that things are going in the right direction."

"Harold, I wish the good word was Peaches is out of our hair and the company is making a comeback. The good news is that the board of directors have decided to stand behind me in trying to secure my stock back from Regal Resorts and will work with the plan that we came up with."

"Well, that's good news, Marv. What are you fretting about?"

"Cecil Coleman thinks it's going to be a fight to the death, and it's going to cost all I've got to fight these mothers."

"Look, Marv, I know that things have been distant between us, but I'm doing good here in Birmingham, and if you need my assistance, I'm offering it. It's the least I can do."

Silence ensued, then shallow breathing. Marvin swallowed hard trying to completely put out of his mind the image of his ex-wife and his cousin, Harold, naked in his townhouse. Marvin had reminded himself frequently that he was over that period in his life, and his marriage to Rachel had been the beginning of his new life. It was like peeling off old layers of skin and uncovering the new.

"Marvin, are you still there?"

"Yeah, Harold. I...I was just thinking."

"Man, I'm sorry. I was not trying to awaken sleeping giants. I do want you to be comfortable about me and Denise being together and our impending marriage."

"I am. I am, Harold. Really, I am. Every now and then something triggers old memories, but I'm good. Back to the company...I appreciate your generosity, but I'm going to try to work things out on my own. But I'm glad to know that if I should need to call upon you, you're there."

"No doubt, cuz. No doubt. Now what's up with this Peaches woman?"

"She made a visit to my house and handed Rachel the picture of us in her apartment with me in my birthday suit."

"Oh, crap. How's the little lady taking it?"

"She walked. Didn't go far. She's at Mona's. Kenny and I went to Earl's this afternoon to see if we could get Earl to give us some information on Peaches. No luck. His mouth is permanently sewn shut where she's concerned. I wonder what Peaches has on him. I just feel this woman has a dark side that we need to uncover."

"She's still demanding the fifty thousand?"

"Yes. I guess giving that photograph to Rachel was to put the pressure on. But she's not getting one red cent."

"I can hire a private detective, if you want."

"That's not a bad idea, Harold. Maybe you can help. Hold on a second, my other line is beeping." Marvin clicked the call over. "Hello."

"Marvin, this is Mona. Look, I need you to come to the house as soon as you can get here."

"Something wrong with Rachel, Serena?"

"No. No. They're fine. Sylvia, Claudette, and I went to Earl's this afternoon. Guess who walked in?"

"Peaches?"

"The one and only. I don't know what you saw in that huzzy."

"C'mon, Mona. There's not one thing about that woman I like. In fact, I detest her."

"Umph. So how did you end up naked with her?"

"Okay, Mona. I'm through. I'm on another call."

"Wait, Marvin. I'm serious now. Just messing with you. We really need you and Kenny to come over so we can discuss what to do with the information we have. And...I think Rachel is ready to come home."

"You're not lying to me, are you?"

"No, brother. You've got that girl's nose wide open. She may have been mad at you, but she needs her Marvin."

"Do I need to call Kenny?"

"No, Sylvia is doing that. Just bring your ass on over now. See you in about a half hour."

"Okay." *Click.* "Harold, don't do anything about the private detective yet. It appears that we've got our own private detectives in the form of Rachel's girlfriends. Seems that they, too, went to Earl's but came away with much more than we did. Mona wants me to come over so they can discuss whatever it is they found out. I'll hit you up later with an update."

"Okay, Marv. I'm here if you need me."

"Thanks, man." The line was dead.

Marvin put on his shoes and grabbed a light coat from the guest closet in the hallway. He ran to the kitchen to look for his keys, shuffling mail and the newspaper. Still not finding them, he ran down to his office and found them on his desk. Like a kid on Christmas Day, he took the stairs two at a time and raced out of the house and into his car. He reached for his phone to call Kenny, but thought better of it. If Rachel was truly ready to come home, he wanted to be alone with her and Serena—a hopeful beginning on the path to healing their fractured marriage.

# CHAPTER FIFTY-THREE

Margaritas were flowing and loud laughter along with them. Mona was imitating Earl trying to come on to her. "He would have looked just like Shrek if he was green," Mona said. The girls went to howling.

"But you told him he was handsome," Claudette chimed in. "Didn't she, Sylvia?"

"You know you did, Mona," Sylvia confirmed. "Rachel, it was disgusting to watch. Mona even blew a kiss at those sloppy lips." Rachel shook her head and began to laugh. The others joined in, holding their sides from laughing too hard.

Marvin stood outside and rang the doorbell for the fourth time. He could hear the noise coming from inside and was concerned about what he was getting into. He buzzed a fifth time and was about to turn around when a friendly face appeared at the door.

"Marvin, come on in," Michael Broussard said.

"Man, how can you stand it up in here?"

"You know how Mona is when she gets it in her mind to entertain, regardless of the occasion."

"Well, I was told to get here right away. Is Kenny here?"

"Not yet," Michael said. "Come on in and take a load off. You might as well get a Margarita, too."

"No, I'm laying off the alcohol. That's what got me into the mess I'm in now."

"Okay, brother, but don't mind me if I have a stiff one. I'm going to need it to get through this evening."

"Knock yourself out," Marvin said, following Michael into the house.

The laughter ceased as Marvin edged his way into the room. His eyes immediately latched onto Rachel, but she turned away as soon as their eyes met.

"Hey, Marvin," Mona, Sylvia, and Claudette said in unison.

"Let me take your jacket," Mona said. "Take a seat. What you drinking?"

"Water," Marvin said, not taking his eyes away from Rachel.

He sat in one of Mona's colorful chaise longues. Inching his way to the edge closest to Rachel, Marvin whispered her name. But she refused to acknowledge him, keeping her face turned away. Marvin sat back.

"Rachel, can we go somewhere and talk?" he asked.

Rachel kept her back to him. "Not now, Marvin. I'm not ready."

Mona returned to the room with Marvin's water. "Okay, what's going on in here?" She handed the water to Marvin. "Do you see your wife sitting in the chair next to you?" Mona instigated.

"Yes, Mona," Marvin said without a smile. "I'm very well aware that Rachel is sitting there."

While looking at Marvin, Mona nodded her head toward Rachel and mouthed the words *Get over there*. Sylvia and Claudette walked out of the room so they wouldn't have to participate in Mona's manipulations. Rachel got up from her seat and walked out of the room with them.

"Boy, you're so slow," Mona lashed out at Marvin.

"Mona, I tried to talk to her, but she didn't want to. You said we were going to talk about what happened at Earl's. So let's get to it."

"We've got to wait for Kenny. Now I suggest you work a little harder on Rachel. You know how she falls apart when you flash those teeth at her."

Michael walked in the room just in time to save Marvin. He sipped his drink, and looked at his wife. "Marvin, don't mind Mona. She's a lot of hot air sometimes. Mona, leave my buddy alone, and go in that kitchen and convince Rachel that she needs to talk to Marvin."

"Oh, Michael, you just won't let me have any fun."

"If you're a good girl, you'll get paid handsomely later on. Deal?"

"Deal. I like them odds, baby." Mona walked over to Michael and gave him a kiss on the lips. "I'll be on my best behavior the rest of the evening." She walked over to Marvin and gave him a kiss on the temple. "Just messing with you, my brother. I'll go in and talk to Rach."

"Thanks, Mona."

"Ready for that drink, Marv?" Michael asked.

"I'm going to play it safe and drink my water. I was just about at the threshold though. But I've got to keep focused."

"Don't worry, man. It's going to be alright. I've heard what the girls did, and you'll be proud of them. If it means anything to you, Marvin, my money is on you. I've got your back."

"Thanks, Michael. That's encouraging. Now, if I can get my life back on track."

"You will. You will."

"Why didn't you heifers tell me that Marvin was coming over?" Rachel shouted. "First, you run out of here talking about getting information on Peaches to clear Marvin's name. Nothing is going to erase what I saw on that piece of paper. He was screwing that woman, and you can't tell me any different."

"Hold up, Miz Rachel," Mona broke in. "These heifers—Sylvia, Claudette, and myself are distraught that you would call us out of our name, especially when we went to great lengths to get information to clear your husband's name. Put our lives on the line."

"Nobody told you to do that."

"Okay, Rachel," Sylvia cut in. "You're right; no one told us to be stupid and help a friend, but we wanted to because we believe that there is something to prove and we don't want to see what was a good marriage go down the tubes. Besides, we got a bingo."

"Yeah," Claudette took over. "Your Peaches came into the bar while we were there. That sister is an angry black woman, and I can tell you first hand that she's not on the up and up. But we're going to save the conversation for when Kenny gets here."

"Kenny? What's Kenny coming here for?" Rachel asked.

"Because we got an earful this afternoon," Sylvia said. "Marvin and Kenny were down there earlier, and they are convinced that the bartender knows something, but they couldn't get him to spill anything. But our luscious diva, Miz Mona Broussard, got the ball rolling, and we are more than convinced that Marvin is an unlucky pawn in Peaches' game. We were almost in a barroom brawl, but we managed to keep our cover to get this information."

Rachel looked among each of her friends. "I know that you all love me to do this for me. Sometimes I'm selfish and a little stubborn—"

"That's an understatement," Mona mumbled.

"But your hearts are like pure gold," Rachel continued.

"Well, let me cut in on you, Miz Rachel," Mona said. "There's a man out there who's hungering to talk to you. He, too, went out on a limb to try to prove his innocence, regardless of what you saw in that picture." Mona put her hands on her hips. "Anyway, at least talk to him, Rachel, and see what he's got to say. You know your man has been through a lot."

"Hold it, Mona. I appreciate you all, but it's not that easy. Yeah, I love Marvin—haven't stopped loving him—but it's difficult..." Rachel shook her arms for emphasis. "It's difficult to erase the image I saw on that piece of paper. All kinds of things ran through my head besides why did he do it. Did he even have the decency to wear a condom or did he give me AIDS?"

Rachel grabbed her head. "It's like seeing Reuben with that teenage girl freebasing in my living room all over again. I thought it would be different when I married Marvin, and for the most part, it has been different. In fact, I believed we had a marriage made in heaven."

"You do, Rach," Sylvia cut in. "I can't pretend that I know how you feel. Sure we've all gone through some rough times in our lives, including ex-husbands who were unfaithful, but I believe that your and Marvin's marriage was made in heaven. I don't even blame you for the way you feel about Marvin, but what we're saying is that we don't want you to give up on him because we believe he allowed a situation to get out of hand, out of control, and then that picture just made things worse.

But Marvin wasn't a willing participant. And we're going to prove it."

Rachel stood as still as the woman who turned to a pillar of salt in the Old Testament. Her eyes searched Sylvia's, as she absorbed everything her friend had said. Lips turned up, her eyes began to tear, and Sylvia took Rachel in her arms and let her cry on her shoulder. Mona and Claudette fell in line.

There were faint sniffles, and silent tears streamed from the faces of all—their bodies draped over one another, resembling one of the rock clusters of Stonehenge. Seconds turned to minutes, and they jumped when the door leading into the kitchen opened.

Michael observed with interest what seemed like some ritual being performed. "Excuse me," he said slowly. "Am I interrupting anything? Mona?"

"Baby, we're done. Just having one of our sister moments."

"Well, Kenny is here accompanied by his cousin—some cute attorney."

"Oh, Trina," Sylvia said.

"We better get out there and protect our men," Mona said.

"I'm going to call T and tell him to come over since everyone is here," Claudette said softly. "He's still part of this group."

"Good idea, Claudette," Sylvia said, giving her a kiss. "Didn't mean to leave T out."

Everyone began to walk out of the room. Rachel grabbed Sylvia's arm. "Sylvia, thank you. Thank you, girl. I love you so much. You're the best friend that I have. I'm going to go out there and be brave. Just have my back if I get cold feet. I want to believe Marvin, I really do, but it's going to take time. But I'm willing to listen. Thanks, sis."

"You're welcome, sweetie. I love you, too." They hugged each other and went in to join the others.

# CHAPTER FIFTY-FOUR

The air was thick when Sylvia and Rachel entered the room. All eyes were cast in their direction and the only sounds were of the children playing in the distance. One pair of eyes remained fixed on Rachel as she quickly found a seat next to Mona. She allowed herself a hasty look in Marvin's direction, then offered up a promising smile that faded almost as soon as it had come.

Marvin smiled back, then turned his attention toward Sylvia, who stood up and began to speak.

"I'd like to thank everyone for coming." For a moment, she felt as if she was conducting an Ex-Files meeting. "We are assembled tonight on behalf of our sister and brother, Rachel and Marvin. They have been through a lot, and I believe each and every one who's assembled has in some way taken on the task of assisting our brother and sister in overcoming the obstacles they face."

Sylvia watched as Trina leaned over in Kenny's space and whispered something to him. Kenny smiled. Ignoring it, Sylvia continued.

"Today has been a fruitful day. As most of you know,

Marvin and Rachel have suffered an additional setback in their lives, and the culprit is a woman who, like the devil, is seeking to destroy their marriage."

Mona shifted in her seat and folded her arms across her chest. A look of boredom was etched on her face.

"Let me move on. Today, Mona, Claudette and I ventured to the bar that is at the core of this situation. Our plan—"

"Your plan," Mona corrected.

"My plan was to find a way, through conversation, to get the bartender—the owner of the establishment—to open up about Peaches, the woman in question."

"You don't have to be so mysterious," Mona said, jumping to her feet. "Everyone knows that Rachel is in possession of a picture of this Peaches woman and Marvin naked and in a compromising position—a big source of contention." Silence filled the room, and each person glanced around the room at the others.

"Hold on now, Mona," Marvin said angrily, jumping to his feet as well. "You don't have to be disrespectful."

"Yes, Mona," Claudette jumped in. "Try to exercise a little more sensitivity."

Seething, Rachel crossed one leg over the other and swung it back and forth, looking straight ahead but at no one in particular.

"Okay, okay, but you all know me," Mona pleaded. "Sylvia is taking her sweet time, as usual, to get to the point. Cut to the chase, sister," Mona said to Sylvia.

"Sit down, Mona," Michael cut in, surprising everyone in the room. "We know you're special, but let Sylvia finish."

"I don't believe my own husband put me in my place in front of all of my friends. That's alright. I'll fix him later." She sent a wicked wink in Michael's direction. "Go on, Sylvia."

"Now that you all have been entertained and I've gotten the floor back, I'll cut to the chase. Peaches rushed into the bar complaining to Earl, the bartender, about things not going well with her plans. She even talked about giving, quote"—Sylvia made air quotes with her fingers and wiggled them for illustration—"the picture, end quote, to you, Rachel, although she didn't call any names. When she realized we were sitting within earshot and had overheard some of her conversation with Earl, she told us that she had met this fine man who was married but going to leave his wife for her. She said he was going to set her up in a brand-new house. In fact, she and our diva, Mona, almost went to blows because the bartender had his eye on Mona, which meant he was distracted, irritating the hell out of Peaches."

"I should have put my foot up her behind right then and there," Mona interrupted. "Called me out of my name and put her hand on me." Mona shook her head. "Rachel, I must love you, girl, to take that kind of abuse. If Sylvia and Claudette weren't there holding me back and reminding me every five seconds what the mission was, I swear that ghetto sister would've been eating the floor."

Everyone laughed. Sylvia relaxed and held her sides, trying to contain her laughter. "Mona was a hot mess," Sylvia said. "And if she had gone to duke city, we probably wouldn't have heard the next part of the conversation Peaches had with Earl."

"What happened, baby?" Kenny asked.

"After Peaches talked about how her man was going to set her up, Earl told her that she might have to wait awhile on that. Told her that her 'boyfriend,' and I assume she was referring to Marvin, and the 'goon' from the other night..." Sylvia got tickled and couldn't stop laughing. Her eyes glassed over and tears ran down her face.

"You know that goon was you, Kenny," Mona said, getting joy out of watching Kenny twist his face. Mona joined Sylvia in laughter.

"I should've taken care of her when I had a chance. And I would have if Harold hadn't held me back," Kenny said.

"Kenny Richmond," Sylvia said and began to laugh. "You big gooooooooooon."

The whole room exploded in laughter. Even Trina, who was for the most part reserved, let go of a great big howl.

"Ooooh," Sylvia said, regaining her composure, "anyway, Earl told Peaches that you and Marvin were trying to get information on her. Peaches hit the ceiling. I wouldn't put it past her to be packing."

Trina stood up. "Thanks for letting me participate in your get-together. I already feel like family. As you know, I'm Kenny's cousin."

Sylvia lifted her eyebrows, but only Kenny saw her—a private joke between them.

"And after talking with Marvin and Kenny earlier today, I believe we really do have a case of extortion and bribery. With all that Sylvia has said, there's enough evidence to somewhat support my theory or at least to justify delving further to find a possible link to something larger. Only thing, it is just a theory unless we can come up with something concrete. If we can ever get the bartender to talk—at least tell us what he knows about Peaches or give us her full name, we may be able to look into her past and possibly stumble onto something that will support our cause. Nine times out of ten, women like this have preyed on other men. I see it all the time."

"I have a surprise," Sylvia said, taking back the spotlight. "I didn't tell the girls about this because I didn't want them to give it away."

"What are you talking about, Sylvia?" Mona asked.

Stooping down to the floor, Sylvia picked up her purse and fumbled around in it for a second. "Bingo." All eyes bulged from their sockets as they gazed at the small silver box Sylvia held out, suspended in air by a small leather strap.

"That's my girl," Kenny sang, getting up to kiss Sylvia. "Detective Richmond, is this what I think it is?"

"Mr. Richmond, I do believe you're hot. Yeah, I've got Peaches on tape. I didn't want to say anything until I was able to listen to it myself. Oh yeah, Peaches' voice is crystal clear."

Marvin stood up and clapped his hands. "Good work, Sylvia." Everyone clapped and Kenny gave her a big hug.

"I don't want to burst your bubble, Sylvia," Trina interrupted, "but the recording might not be admissible as evidence in a court of law since Peaches was unaware that you were recording her. But good work."

Everyone began to high-five each other. The smiles, laughter, and congratulations were contagious. Kenny and Michael surrounded Marvin and assured him they were one-hundred-percent behind him, while the girls huddled around Rachel. Abruptly the noise stopped like someone had turned down the volume on a good song.

"It's the doorbell," Mona said, racing to see who had the audacity to interrupt their celebration. "Claudette, it's Tyrone."

Claudette went to grinning.

"Hey, everybody," Tyrone said as he entered the room. "What did I miss?"

"Everything," they all said in unison.

"I'll get you something to drink, T," Mona said.

"We just heard what might be some good news for a change, and we're celebrating."

"Make mine a beer," Tyrone said. "Sorry I'm late."

"Hey, baby," Claudette cut in. "Glad you're here."

"Would have been here earlier if I had known, and you know I can't stay away from you. Where's Reagan?"

"She's playing with the children."

"Come here, girl," Tyrone said to Claudette.

Rachel watched as Tyrone took Claudette in his arms and kissed her right in front of everyone. They fit together like a jigsaw puzzle, so easy was their love.

Rachel looked away and searched out her husband, who was talking to Kenny and Michael. She walked the short distance and stood behind the men. To a bystander, she looked as if she were eavesdropping on a very hot conversation. Rachel tapped Marvin on the shoulder, and surprise registered on his face.

"Excuse me, gentlemen. I hope you won't mind if I pull my husband away so I can speak to him."

"No, no," Michael was the first to say.

Rachel turned around and saw Mona nudging the ladies. Marvin took Rachel's hand and together they walked into the library and closed the door.

"Baby," Marvin began.

Rachel put up her finger. "Shhh, let me talk. This is hard enough." She looked into Marvin's eyes, full of love for her. She looked down, then back up. "We have some wonderful friends out there who believe in us. At first, I wanted to come to you and say something—I'm not sure what, but something to appease the girls so they wouldn't be disappointed, especially after all the effort and trouble they'd gone to on our behalf. But tonight I've truly come to realize what a wonderful man I married.

"I would be lying if I said that all this Peaches mess didn't hurt. I'm still struggling with the hurt and humiliation. But I want to believe what the others believe...that you were a victim of circumstance." Rachel stopped and wiped away the tears that rolled down Marvin's face. "I love you, Marvin." Rachel broke down and couldn't continue.

Marvin folded her in his arms. "I love you so much, Rachel Thomas. Life is not worth living without you."

Rachel pulled away. She wiped her face and looked into Marvin's eyes. "This is the last time I'll ask, but I must. I'll accept whatever answer you give me."

Perplexed, Marvin kept quiet, preparing for Rachel's question.

"Did you sleep with Peaches?"

Hurt dotted Marvin's face. "No, Rachel. I barely remembered the woman's name, let alone how I ended up with her. I was stoned out of my mind because of what I was going through with the company. Things happened that I can't give an account for, except that when I woke up and realized I wasn't next to you I knew that I was in some kind of trouble. I have taken a vow to never take another drink."

Rachel managed a smile. "Don't say never. Remember, Harold and Denise are getting married, and we're definitely going to have to toast those nuptials."

"Glad to have you back, Rachel."

"I love you, Marvin. Just one thing. I want to stay another night at Mona's."

Hurt registered on Marvin's face once again.

"Just until tomorrow, baby. I want to enter the house alone—give myself an opportunity to come to grips with being home, but I'll be there when you come home."

"Don't open the door for no one."

"Not even Sylvia, Mona, or Claudette?"

"You know what I mean. I don't know what I'd do if something happened to you."

Rachel brushed an imaginary something off Marvin's shoulders. "I know you're being protective of me, but I'll be alright. Why don't we rejoin the others?"

"Do we have to?" Marvin asked in a serious tone. "I want to hold on to this moment forever."

With a gleam in her eye, Rachel smiled at Marvin. "We have forever." Marvin smiled. "But let's go because I'm sure everyone is wondering what we're doing, especially that crazy Mona."

"I heard that," came Mona's voice from the other side of the door.

"See?" Rachel said. She reached out and touched Marvin's face, sculpting it as she allowed her hands to run the length of it. Then she held the back of his head in the palms of her hands and drew his face to her, moistening his lips with hers.

Encircling her body with his arms, Marvin tasted her lips but let Rachel lead the way as she fanned the flames of passion that had lay dormant. Suddenly, she pulled away, fully aware that they had no privacy. But she was almost grateful for the reprieve because she was on the verge of relinquishing her soul to this man of hers.

They emerged from the room, Rachel's arm looped through Marvin's, startling the busybodies that had camped outside the door. Mona, Sylvia, and Claudette were a funny sight.

"Going home tonight?" Mona asked, following Rachel and Marvin back to the family room.

"Nope. You've got me for one more night." Rachel laughed, as did Sylvia and Claudette.

"So is all this just a pretense?" Mona badgered, laying her hands where Marvin and Rachel's arms were joined together. "You need to go on home with your husband. Tell her, Marvin."

"She's staying another night with you and Michael." Marvin squeezed Rachel's arm. She smiled.

Hand-claps and loud whistles met Rachel and Marvin when they returned to the room where the others were.

"Do you have anything to say?" Tyrone inquired.

"They look pretty happy to me," Trina offered.

"You could say Marvin and Rachel are back on track," Kenny said, not wanting to be left out.

"I'm in love with this woman," Marvin finally said. "She's the love of my life." Rachel smiled and settled into the crook of Marvin's arm.

Trina stood in the middle of the room. "Look everyone, this Friday I'm going to have a little get-together for Kenny and Sylvia." Kenny and Sylvia traded glances. "You are all invited. How does seven o'clock sound?"

"We'll be there!" Mona said on behalf of she and Michael. She waved her hand in the air. "Party over here." There was laughter.

"Count us in," Claudette said on behalf of her and Tyrone.

"Marvin and I will be there, as well," Rachel said.

"We're honored," Sylvia said, grabbing Kenny's hand. They both walked up to Trina and gave her a light hug. "Thank you."

"Good," Trina said, satisfied with the responses.

# CHAPTER FIFTY-FIVE

**M**arvin picked up Rachel's picture from his desk and smiled. She made him happy. Their weekend had started out rocky, but all had ended well. God was smiling on him, and he felt deep within his bones that in the end things were going to be alright. The obstacles were great, but there was no mountain too high for God to conquer. He put the picture back on his desk.

He would make going to church a priority. He'd been a faithful parishioner before all of his success; how did he expect God to be there for him, when he had run out on God? At that moment he remembered his grandmother's words...*a family that prays together stays together*. She was a smart woman.

He pushed the button on the intercom. "Yvonne, dial Mr. Harold Thomas' number for me."

"Right away, Mr. Thomas."

Marvin brought his fingers to his mouth and kissed them, placing them against the picture of Rachel. He couldn't stop looking at her. He sat back in his seat just as the intercom buzzed.

"Mr. Thomas is on line one."

"Thanks, Yvonne." Marvin waited a second before speaking. "Harold, good news."

"You've got a good ring in your voice. What's up?"

"Looks like I won't be needing the private detective. Rachel's friend Sylvia surprised us with a recording of Peaches and the bartender in conversation. Peaches talks loosely about getting money from a man she claims to be her boyfriend who just happens to be married, although things were taking longer than expected. Sylvia also captured the bartender telling Peaches about Kenny and me coming to the bar asking questions about her. Peaches was livid. Kenny's cousin Trina said we may be unable to use the recording in court, but it certainly will serve as ammunition if and when we're able to get something concrete on Peaches. My main concern is her relentless attempt to get money from me."

"We could set her up," Harold began. "I can bank the fifty Gs."

"How would we go about doing it? I don't want anyone hurt, especially my family."

"How did it go with Rachel last night?"

"She's coming home today. We talked some last night, but it was the efforts of her friends that got Rachel to thinking. We've got a lot to work through, but I'm going to do everything I can to make sure that our marriage is not compromised like this ever again."

"A tall order, man, but if anyone can manage it, you're

the one. What do you say to setting a trap for Peaches?"

"Let me think on it. Oh by the way, Kenny's cousin is having a get-together this Friday. She lives in our neighborhood. Come join us and bring Denise. We'll have a babysitter for the kids, so if you want to bring Danica, that will be fine."

"I'll check with Denise and get back to you. Give the Peaches thing some thought, Marv. I'm afraid if you hold that lunatic at bay for too long, she's going to strike again. Just food for thought."

"Right. Okay, Harold. I'll let you know something in a day or so. Hope to see you on Friday."

"I'm out."

Butterflies flitted through Marvin's stomach as he hung up the phone. He looked at his watch for the third time in less than a half hour. It was three o'clock; Rachel was coming home this afternoon. Easing up in his chair, Marvin picked up the receiver again and dialed home. After several rings, he replaced the receiver in its cradle and sighed. Memories of last evening flooded his mind. *She's coming home.*

The phone rang and Marvin snatched up the receiver without giving it a second thought. He smiled. "Hey, baby."

"You got my fifty thousand dollars? And what's this I hear about you harassing Earl? If you wanted information about me, you should've asked yourself. You're barking up the wrong tree."

"Peaches! Bitch, you crossed the line with the picture, and I warned you about staying away from my family. I'm not giving you one red cent, and if you come anywhere near my house or family again, you will have hell to pay."

"Your threats mean nothing to me, Marvin. Now listen, and listen good. I'm shortening your delivery date. You have until the end of the week to get my money. No more excuses. It's not becoming of an executive of your caliber. If you don't have my money, I have no problem taking other measures to see that you do what I ask. I'll be in touch." *Slam!*

Marvin grabbed his ear and rubbed it as the sound of Peaches slamming the phone down vibrated throughout his head. He slammed his own phone down on the cradle and pushed back from his desk. Standing up, Marvin took an empty coffee cup and threw it against the wall. Yvonne rushed in with a worried look on her face.

"You alright, Mr. Thomas?"

Quiet engulfed the neighborhood as Rachel drove into her subdivision. It was just as she'd left it, but it seemed to have a different feel to it.

As Rachel moved toward her street, she realized that it was she who was different. She would no longer take life for granted. God giveth and he taketh away. Life and family were to be cherished, and while she might be living one of the best times in her life, she couldn't ignore the fact that God had blessed her with the things she had. The moon and the stars, the sun and the rain, night and day—they were God's gift to mankind so they would be utilized for man's benefit and His glory.

Rachel pulled into the garage and turned off the engine. Looking over her shoulder, she gazed at a sleeping Serena and smiled. They were home, and this was where she was going to stay. She was going to be a friend, partner, and lover to her husband. She was finally growing up.

# CHAPTER FIFTY-SIX

Wednesday came before he knew it. Cecil placed his notes in the attaché case in preparation for his meeting with Robert Jordan and Regal Resorts. After pondering over the case all weekend, he realized this was a cut-and-dried case. There wasn't a written contract with Marvin's signature on it that stated he had sold his shares to Regal Resorts. It was Marvin's word, through Cecil, against Regal Resorts. Since Cecil was armed, thanks to Yvonne, with a copy of the minutes from the board of directors' meeting at Thomas and Richmond Tecktronics, Inc., indicating that the board was not in agreement with a buyout/merger, Regal Resorts had no leg to stand on.

With great precision, Cecil placed a newly drawn-up document for Regal Resorts to sign relinquishing any claim and interest they might have had in Thomas and Richmond Tecktronics into his attaché case. He stopped in the small bathroom that occupied a small area of his office and checked his tie in the mirror and patted his hair. The light in the bathroom made his Princeton ring and Rolex sparkle. Satisfied, he stepped out of the bathroom, picked up his attaché case, and headed to Jordan's office a few blocks away. He was ready.

Cecil arrived at Jordan's office in fifteen minutes flat. Jordan was a senior partner at Jordan, Whittier, Jacobs, and Black. His name was not only legendary in Atlanta but all across the United States, his having defended some big names in business in several high-profile cases including Enron and WorldCom. Jordan's record of successful wins was higher than the number of floors in the Empire State Building.

A pretty brown-skinned secretary sat at the reception desk when Cecil approached Jordan's office. Her hair was brownish-red with blonde highlights and was pulled back tight in a ponytail, so tight it made her eyes slant. She had a gracious smile for Cecil, and the name on the desk plate read *Cynthia Brown*.

"Good afternoon, Miz Brown," Cecil said, offering a gracious smile in return. "I'm Attorney Cecil Coleman, and I have a twelve o'clock appointment with Robert Jordan."

"He's expecting you," Cynthia said. She got up from her desk and walked around it. "Mr. Jordan is waiting for you in the conference room down the hall." Cynthia pointed. "First door on the right."

It was difficult not to stare at this woman's gorgeous body. Cynthia wore a red St. John two-piece suit with matching red three-inch heels. She was almost as tall as Cecil, and the rest of the package was a head turner with all other assets in the right place. Cecil had to put his hormones in check and redirect his mind and energy to the purpose intended. He thanked Cynthia and headed out the door just as another black female with a short Afro, in her late thirties or early forties, passed him.

"Hi, Peaches," Cynthia said. "I hope this is the right file. You know we needed this a couple of days ago."

Cecil stopped in his tracks. *Peaches. Peaches*, he repeated over in his head. That was the name of the woman Trina was talking about—the woman who was making Marvin's life miserable. What was the likelihood that this could be the same Peaches? It's not a common name, and the Peaches Trina had been talking about lived in Atlanta. He'd have to inquire about her once he finished with Jordan.

"Is there anything wrong, Mr. Coleman?" Cynthia asked.

Cecil straightened up his shoulders. "Uhh, no...no. I thought I had forgotten something, and I was just trying to remember if I put it in my briefcase. First door on the right?"

"Yes, that's it."

The other woman named Peaches stared at him and smiled. "Thank you," Cecil said, and walked out of the office.

Swallowing, Cecil couldn't get Peaches out of his mind. He didn't know much about what was going on, and hadn't paid much attention to Trina's ranting and raving about this part of Marvin's problem. He couldn't wait to finish with Jordan.

Voices could be heard as Cecil entered the conference room. The trio comprised of Vincent Kinyard, David Eason, and Jordan stopped and looked up as Cecil came into the room and found a seat at Jordan's insistence. Cecil tried to gauge their moods, but they were a stoic bunch and gave no hint to what they were thinking.

"I'm not going to prolong this meeting but get right to the point. Coleman, I hope you've had time to re-think the decision to fight us for the shares Marvin Thomas gave up. We can avoid a nasty, drawn-out trial. Kinyard and Eason are prepared to complete the documents necessary to transfer the stock and continue with buyout procedures. I hope your coming here this afternoon means this was what you plan to do, so we can get this over with and have lunch. I wouldn't mind a round of golf. How about you fellas?" Jordan nodded at Kinyard and Eason.

Cecil opened his attaché case and took out his notes but left the contract in the case. He observed the men at the table whose eyes seemed hopeful, waiting for him to concede.

"Gentlemen, I come here this afternoon with the same

mindset as you, and that is to conclude the matter in this case so that we can move on with our lives. However, it has never been my intention to settle the dispute over the shares in your favor. In fact, I find it rather presumptuous of you all to think that I or my client was ever going to give in, no matter how you may perceive this case to be. It is not as cut-and-dried as you may believe.

"I offer for your edification a copy of the minutes of the last board of directors' meeting of Thomas and Richmond Tecktronics, Inc., that was held on Friday, October 24. In the minutes you will find, under Action Items, the text of the board's decision to support Mr. Marvin Thomas in securing his fifty-two shares in Thomas and Richmond as well as their unanimous agreement not to support a buyout. Without the agreement and signature of the board of directors of Thomas and Richmond Tecktronics, Inc., you have no other recourse but to bow out gracefully."

Jordan took the copies of the minutes and passed the other two to Kinyard and Eason. He scanned the document, specifically looking for the Action Item entry. After reading it, he crumpled up the piece of paper and threw it across the table. "I don't know who you think you're trying to fool with this piece of garbage, Cecil, but this document doesn't mean a hill of beans to me. You come in here slinging your fancy rhetoric, but the bottom line is those shares belong to Regal Resorts, Inc."

"You should be held in contempt," Kinyard lashed out. "You were the one who came to us with this offer. And just like that you want to take it back. What kind of lawyer are you?"

"I don't apologize for my actions," Cecil said. "I work on behalf of my clients."

"Well, you should have advised your client against selling his shares before you came to us with the offer. That's what Jordan would have done," Kinyard said.

Cecil was fuming. "Since you weren't there, you don't know how I advised him, but it's none of your damn business. The point remains that there will be no buyout, and since there's no evidence or record of any stocks that belong to Marvin Thomas being sold to Regal Resorts, this case is closed."

"I'm going to have you disbarred, Coleman," Jordan shouted, standing up and pointing his finger at Cecil. "You're not going to get away with this."

Cecil smiled. "I already have." He quickly took out the document that he had drawn up for Regal Resorts to sign. "Jordan, I have a form that I'd like for your clients to sign that relinquishes any claim and interest they might have in Thomas and Richmond Teck-tronics."

"This is bullcrap, Coleman. We're not signing anything." Jordan took the document and tore it into pieces. "You've not heard the last of us."

"Hold up, Jordan," Vincent Kinyard said. "Why don't we make Mr. Coleman an offer?"

"What are you talking about, Kinyard?" Jordan asked with a frown.

"I say that if Mr. Coleman wants us to sign this document and forget about Thomas and Richmond, that his client pay us the sum of one hundred thousand dollars for all the time wasted in pursuing this. Mr. Coleman will retain his reputation, and there won't be any bad feelings."

"Sounds like something I could live with," Jordan said. "How about it, Cecil?"

"Do I look like a fool to you? Paying one hundred thousand dollars is like admitting an offer was tendered, whether it was or not. And I'm sure my client won't agree to this."

"This is our best offer. Take it or leave it," Jordan said with a smug look on his face.

Cecil stood up. He looked from Jordan to Kinyard to Eason. He placed his notes back in his attaché and shut it with force. "I'll get back with you."

"Soon, or else we take it a step further."

"Good day, gentlemen." And Cecil walked out of the conference room and down the hall. He wanted to strangle Jordan. Jordan was pursuing this out of spite. Thomas and Richmond Tecktronics had made a name for itself, but given the history of its origin, Cecil thought Jordan might be more sympathetic and advise his clients accordingly. Well, he had a record, too, and he was going to win this case.

Just as Cecil was about to leave the office, he remembered Peaches. He went back to Cecil's office and was grateful that Ms. Brown was still there and the office was empty. Surprise registered on her face when Cecil re-entered.

"Hi, Mr. Coleman. I didn't expect to see you again. Everything go okay?"

"Well, let's say it was enlightening. We've still got a few things to clear up. But the real reason I came back was to ask you about the lady who came into the office when I was about to leave. I thought I recognized her, but I wasn't sure."

"You mean Peaches. Franklin is her last name; I don't think Peaches is her first name, though."

"Would you do me a favor?"

"What kind of favor, Mr. Coleman?"

Cecil handed Cynthia his business card. "I need you to keep this completely confidential. I believe I know her, but in order for me to know for sure, I need her first name. I want to surprise her if she's who I think she is. When you get it, you can call me at this number."

"Sure, I'll do it. I think that's so cool when people can hook up after years of not seeing each other. She thought you were cute, too, and she didn't seem to recognize you either. I see you have a ring on your finger."

"It may not even be her," Cecil offered. "I think I just want to satisfy my curiosity. Don't go to any trouble."

"No, I'd be happy to do it, Mr. Coleman. I'll do it discreetly."

"Oh, and yes, I'm happily married. You have a good day, and if you can get the information, that would be great."

Cecil walked out, noting the disappointment on Cynthia's face when he told her he was happily married. He was happily married, but if he'd ever slip, he might have to check out Ms. Brown, even though she worked for the enemy. But he did get something out of it—a last name for Ms. Peaches.

# CHAPTER FIFTY-SEVEN

Consumed with her laundry list of things to do today, especially all the heads she was scheduled to shampoo and make pretty for the various high school home-comings, Claudette didn't see Ashley shuffle into the visitors room until she was upon her. Her face lit up when she saw Ashley.

"Hey, Ash," Claudette said, reaching out to give her a hug. Ashley offered her cheek. "So what was so important that you insisted I come today? I'll have to work all night to get heads done for homecoming."

"Thanks, Claudette. I can always count on you. You know, you're my very best friend. Sylvia used to be; we've lost our connection. 'A friend is one who walks in when others walk out.' That is a quote from Walter Winchell. I like his sayings."

"Wow, Ash. Don't make me shed any tears up in here; I'm on the verge. But I will tell you, the girls love you. In fact just this past weekend, Rachel said she wanted to accompany us on our next visit to see you, which will be soon."

"That's good to hear—about the girls, I mean. But to

answer your question, I was wondering how Marvin is doing and what's happening with his company."

"What's with your sudden preoccupation with Marvin and his company?"

"Marvin was so good to me when I was going through my own trials with William. Do you remember how he immediately went to bat for you when Kwame got into trouble because of the fire?"

"How can I forget? It also brought Tyrone back into my life."

"Claudette, whenever I get out of here and I will, I want to settle down, maybe get married again. I want a man just like Marvin. Rachel is so fortunate to have snagged that jewel."

"You don't know how fortunate." Claudette went on to tell Ashley about the recent events, including Rachel's receiving the picture from the brazen Peaches and Claudette's, Mona's, and Sylvia's attempt at being detectives and what they found out. Claudette shared the moment they all came together in Ex-Files fashion, and how it brought Rachel and Marvin back from the brink of splitsville.

Nostalgia led Ashley to shed a tear. "I miss the group. If it weren't for you, Sylvia, Rachel, and that crazy Mona, I wouldn't have made it. My divorce was so devastating, and then to have William walk back into my life, which was what I thought I wanted, and have it go so sour."

"That was in the past, Ash," Claudette said, rubbing her arm. "Look toward the future."

"I know, Claudette, but the future seems so far away."

Claudette put her head down. She couldn't offer any assurances that would make Ashley feel any better about her plight. Possibly, with good behavior, Ashley might get released early, but that was a stretch to say the least.

"Unless there's something else you want to know, I've got to be getting back to the shop. I'll let you know when the girls and I are coming. I'll even bring Reagan, too."

A smile formed on Ashley's face. "I'd like that. Oh, do you have Marvin's address? I'd like to send him a word of encouragement."

"You're lucky I have my address book on me. He'd like that, Ash. You're always thinking of others."

Claudette wrote down Marvin's address, folded the piece of paper, and placed it in the pocket of Ashley's prison outfit. "Give T my love and kiss Reagan for me," Ash said finally.

Claudette stood and waved good-bye to Ashley. She waited until the guard came to escort Ashley back to her cell. After standing there a few minutes, a worker passed by and gave her a Kleenex to wipe her face. That was the first time Claudette had shed tears for Ashley—her best friend.

Ashley stood in line and waited to use the phone. She hadn't heard from her father in almost a week, and it probably was because he didn't take her seriously. Well, she wasn't weak little Ashley. After all, look what she'd done to William. The downside to that was that the people of the State of Georgia had spoken and given her free accommodations for life in a no-frills environment where she didn't have to cook or required a good job to make ends meet.

She'd accepted her fate because she may have deserved it. And according to the judge, William's life was not hers to take, no matter how he may have treated her.

Next in line to use the phone, Ashley tapped her feet. She didn't relish the task of calling her father, who was objecting to her request for money. Mr. Robert Jordan was a hero to many, but to Ashley, he was just Dad. She didn't care if she was in jail, the money was hers, and Attorney Robert Jordan would not dictate to her what she was to do with it.

It was her turn, and Ashley dialed the number she had committed to memory. She waited while the operator sought an acknowledgment that the receiver would accept the charges...then she heard a familiar voice... a weary voice, a voice that accepted the charges, even though he was not equally happy to hear her voice.

"Daddy," Ashley began, "I need you to bring the money to me today—a certified cashier's check. I'd appreciate it very much if you could come within the next couple of hours."

# CHAPTER FIFTY-EIGHT

"Cecil, I'm so looking forward to this party."

"So, you and your cousin are reconnecting. I thought you said he was one of the sorriest black men you knew. This is quite a three-sixty; and a party to boot."

"I judged Kenny wrong. Yes, he had his issues—what black man doesn't—but if I think back, he was always industrious. He just had that other side to him—the partying, the womanizing. It was a shame how he treated some of those women. I'm equally amazed at how he ended up with Sylvia. She seems like she's always been a class act."

"Well, we all have skeletons in our closet, Trina. I'm sure you have a secret or two."

"I don't know what you're trying to imply, Cecil, but one must look at oneself before throwing stones."

"And I guess you're not guilty of that very thing? Yeah, you went to all the right schools and found your way to the right law firm right after college."

Trina smiled at her husband's accolades. Yes, she had done well for herself. She went to the bar and fixed herself a gin and tonic. "Want something to drink?"

Cecil shook his head. "No, I'll save my drinking for the party tonight. We might as well make this into a victory party for Senator Obama. I feel it in my bones that come Tuesday night, we're going to have our very first African-American president."

"I'll drink to that," Trina said.

"By the way, Trina, why did you abort your baby?"

Liquid flew into the air as Trina spit out the gin she had begun to swallow. Protruding eyes dominated her face as Cecil dragged the wool off her secret. His revelation made her uncomfortable, although he remained cool, calm, and collected.

"Wonders never cease. I've done a good job of hiding *your* secret all these years."

Recovering, all Trina could do was gawk until her voice found her. "How long have you known? That happened several years before I knew you even existed."

"How long have we been married?"

"You've known for fifteen years and didn't say anything?"

"More like sixteen years, but who's counting. I knew this day would come—not that I would hold it against you. I'm sure you had your reasons for not sharing it with me. You know how much I wanted children. But the point is, Trina, we all have something to hide; some don't care. It doesn't minimize my love for you.

"Now, why don't we get ready for the party tonight? I think I'm up to meeting our neighbors, friends, and relatives." Cecil smiled. "Oh, and I have a surprise for you, but I'll wait until this evening when I can share it with the whole group."

Words couldn't find their way to Trina's usually glib tongue. It was so unlike Cecil to be talking in riddles. Maybe he was bothered by the fact that Trina made him see what he'd become, but to bring up the fact that she'd been pregnant before? Her secret that had lain dormant for years had come bursting forth like a geyser, opening up old wounds, and now Cecil was talking about a surprise; this was too much. She was the prosecuting attorney, but her case had been cracked wide open. She turned in time to see the smug look on Cecil's face, and she didn't appreciate it one bit. Silently, she went into the kitchen to finish preparations for the night's gathering.

At precisely eight o'clock the doorbell rang. The anxiety of the morning was still with Trina, but she put on her happy face. She opened the door to the honorees, Sylvia and Kenny.

"Hello and come in," Trina said. Sylvia wore a red-belted, sleeveless, iridescent after-five, while Kenny wore a black Yves St. Laurent suit and a black knit turtleneck. "Sylvia, you look absolutely stunning," Trina said to Sylvia, taking the couple's wraps.

"So do you, Trina," Sylvia returned the compliment, giving her an air kiss and admiring the fuchsia silk chemise that accentuated Trina's shapely curves.

Cecil appeared from a long hallway and smiled at the group. "And so this is cousin Kenny Richmond and his lovely wife, Sylvia." Cecil shook Kenny's hand and placed a kiss on Sylvia's knuckles. "My wife has worked hard all day to make this party a success." He winked at Trina. "You all make yourselves comfortable." Trina went into the kitchen.

"Thank you," Kenny and Sylvia said simultaneously.

"Too cool to go outside. During the summer, we sit out on the deck and admire the lake."

"I'm sure it's beautiful," Sylvia offered. "What I can see of your home is absolutely gorgeous. I'm sure Trina spends hours making it look fabulous."

"Not really. So what are you drinking?" Cecil continued.

"Chardonnay," Sylvia said matter-of-factly. "For both of us."

"I like that you speak for your man," Cecil said. Sylvia blushed.

In the kitchen, Trina's nerves were on edge. She was in the dark about Cecil's surprise and when he was going to reveal it. She really wanted to enjoy the party, especially since this was the first time she'd hosted anything at her home. Saved by the bell, she flew to the door.

Mona was also stunning in her blueberry-colored, iridescent silk taffeta wrap dress with ruffled trim accented by a multi-strand bib necklace made of jet black and clear Austrian crystals along with matching earrings. Michael, always immaculate, wore a blue Bob Mackey two-piece suit with a white shimmery knit turtleneck.

"Hey, everyone," Mona said, stepping inside. "This is my husband, Dr. Michael Broussard," she said to Cecil and Trina, although Trina had already met him. She loved flinging Michael's credentials at those who thought they were more uppity than she. "It certainly smells good in here. Claudette and T are right behind us. They were just pulling up when we rang the bell."

"Come on in and make yourselves comfortable," Cecil said, giving Mona an extra stroke with his eyes. "I'm the bartender for the evening, and your wish is my command."

"Whew," Mona said. "I like that, but I'll start off with a glass of wine, if you don't mind."

"Me, too," Michael said.

"Please help yourself to the hors d'oeuvres," Trina said, unveiling the silver platters that held cream cheese-stuffed endive, mini vegetarian egg rolls, stuffed mushrooms, watercress sandwiches, and fruit in season on long wooden skewers just for starters. "I also have smoked salmon, Beef Wellington, and Swedish meatballs that I'll put out in a minute."

The doorbell sounded again and Cecil glided to the door as if he'd performed this task many times before. He opened the door and stood back as he surveyed the three couples that stood there. "Come on in."

"Hi, I'm Tyrone and this is my wife, Claudette." Tyrone extended his hand to Cecil.

"I'm Cecil Coleman and my wife, Trina, is entertaining the others."

"Hey man," Marvin said as he followed Claudette and Tyrone, giving Cecil the brother handshake and hug. "This is my wife, Rachel, and with us is my cousin, Harold, and his fiancée, Denise."

"I don't know how you dudes ended up with these fine women, but you must have the Midas touch. What an attractive bunch you all are. Come on in. Kenny, Sylvia, Mona, and Michael are already here. Is everyone here, now? I see a car circling the block."

"No, I think this is everyone," Marvin said. Cecil shut the door.

Excitement was in the air. Hugs and kisses went around the room. The ladies admired one another's evening dresses, a definite shoo-in for *Ebony* Fashion Fair's evening wear scene on the catwalk, especially Claudette's custom-designed kente cloth ensemble and Rachel's low-cut, sea-blue crinkled chiffon dress with an empire waist and a flowing split front. Denise wore a simple but elegant black, V-neck, form-fitted cocktail dress.

"You're working it, Claudette," Mona said. "You are so cute."

"I think everyone looks lovely tonight," Claudette said. "Tonight feels so right. Feels like love."

"I'll drink to that," Denise said.

"What's this I hear about you and Harold getting married?" Mona asked, taking another sip of wine.

"Yes, we're going to do it in December, and you're all invited." Denise looked at Rachel. "Ladies, I'm truly in love this time."

Rachel smiled. "I'm glad to hear that because Marvin is all mine." The ladies giggled, although Trina had no idea what the joke was. Realizing this, Rachel told Trina that Denise was Marvin's first wife.

"Oh, I see," Trina said, staying far away from that conversation. "Everybody, can we all gather around?" she asked. "Cecil, I need you. It's time to make a toast."

Cecil left the comfort of male conversation and stood by his wife. "Glasses full," Cecil said. Everyone filled their glasses and waited for the toast. "You do the honors, sweetheart."

Trina held up her glass. "This is a special night for me and Cecil because this is the first time that we've entertained in our home. And I can't think of a better way to open up my home than by celebrating finding my cousin, Kenny, and his wife, Sylvia. Mind you, he was never lost, but there was a disconnect that was probably my doing. While I won't go into it, I discovered something about myself when I saw Kenny jogging a few weeks ago. I realized that family is important—that we need family.

"These past few days hanging out with you all, even

though a very serious matter brought us together, has been so special. I guess I've been working so hard that I didn't have time to realize that I had no special friends in my life. Cecil has always been my best friend, but I never thought I'd relish the time with a special girlfriend. You all have something...a chemistry that endears you all to each other. When I saw how the girls went to bat for Rachel and Marvin, and I hear that Kenny, Harold, and Marvin did some investigating on their own, it made me want to be a part of this special something."

Smiles radiated from Rachel's, Sylvia's, Claudette's, and Mona's faces. Sylvia went to Trina. "You're our girl, too. We have some crazy moments, but the beauty of it is that we all love and cherish each other's friendship and will go the last mile for one another. We've been put to the test many times."

"I'm a witness," Denise cut in. "Even though I was not the most likable person in the beginning, when they found out I had breast cancer, these ladies were there for me." Denise pinched her lips together and could no longer contain the tears.

"Get that glass from her before she drops it," Mona said.

Harold went to Denise and hugged her. "I love you."

"I could go on," Trina said, "and although my toast was all over the place, you get what I mean. I love you guys."

"I concur with her," Cecil said. He took Trina in his arms, then kissed her passionately in front of everyone. As if on cue, everyone began to clap and didn't stop until Cecil finally released Trina's lips. "And while we're celebrating, I want to remind all of you to vote on Tuesday if you haven't done so already. Obama for pres-ident. Yes, we can."

"Obama for president," everyone shouted.

"Before we eat," Cecil continued, "I have a big surprise for everyone, since we're family now. I can say that, right?" Trina had a big smile on her face.

"Yeah, man," Kenny said. "You're family." They embraced.

"I can't keep the excitement bottled up anymore. A couple of days ago, I had a meeting with Robert Jordan, who's representing Regal Resorts. Without going into all of the details, I do think we can win this. I don't want to get your hopes up too soon, but I think I've got them backed into a corner. It may take raising some money, but I'll talk to the guys about that later. But here's the real drum roll."

"Baby, hurry up," Trina said. "I've been on pins and needles all afternoon since you mentioned a surprise."

"Well," Cecil began, "you would never believe who works at the law firm where Jordan is the senior partner."

"Who?" Marvin asked.

"I won't make you wait any longer. Peaches, Peaches Franklin."

"What?" Marvin screamed. "You got her last name?"

"She walked into Jordan's secretary's office while I was there, and just before I left the room, the secretary called out her name. How many Peaches are there in Atlanta? From what Trina has told me about her, she seemed to fit the description. I went back later and got Peaches' last name, but the girl was sure that her first name wasn't actually Peaches. She's going to try to see if she can come up with that information for me. How about that?"

Marvin jumped around the room like a kangaroo. He pulled Rachel to him and they began to dance. Soon, everyone joined in. "Where's the music?" Mona crooned. "I feel the party coming on."

Marvin stopped for a second. "God is good." He shook Cecil's hand. "I know we are still far from getting a handle on Peaches, but this is closer than we've ever been. I feel in my heart that God is going to work everything out."

Sylvia went to Marvin. "He has. Just wait on Him to do His thing. I'm so happy for you and Rach."

Rachel took her turn in the spotlight. "If I haven't said it before now, I love you all. I can't thank you enough for putting yourselves out for me and Marvin. I know you love us. You all are my everything." Rachel burst into tears.

"Okay," Mona cut in. "Trina, I know this is your and Cecil's place. But we've got to cut out the sob stories.

This is a party. Now let's celebrate. Thanks for that good news, Cecil. We needed it. With all the goods we've got on Peaches, it's just a matter of time. Now, where's the music?"

"To Kenny and Sylvia," Trina said, lifting her glass once more. "Now we can eat, dance and be merry."

"To Kenny and Sylvia," everyone cheered.

Music floated through the air while everyone got in line to fill their plates with smoked salmon draped with a crème sauce, mini Beef Wellington, Swedish meatballs, chicken and cilantro bites, and other wonderful appetizers.

"Look at Mona checking out the food," Sylvia said to Rachel. "She thinks nobody can cook but her."

"That girl is a trip, but I love her," Rachel said. "Oops, my cell phone is vibrating. I hope nothing's wrong with Serena. She and Danica are next door. Can you believe that Denise and I can really be friends? Hold on a second. Hello."

"Hey, Rachel, this is Holly, your next-door neighbor. Would it be too much to ask you to get Serena's *Dora the Explorer* video? She's whining and keeps saying she wants to see it. I really didn't want to bother you."

"Alright, I'll come home and get it. It'll only take a couple of minutes. If I was anywhere else, Serena would just have to suck it up. She can't always have her way."

"Thanks, Rachel. I just want Serena to be comfortable."

"Okay." And the line was dead.

"Rachel, are you really going to go home just because Serena wants to see a video?"

"I know, Sylvia. I've spoiled that little girl. But that's my love. It will only take a few minutes."

"Why don't I go with you?"

"No, no. It'll only take five minutes. Enjoy the party. After all, it's for you and Kenny. We're just helping you celebrate. If Marvin asks, tell him I'll be right back. The guys are over there in a huddle discussing business, and I don't want to interrupt."

"Okay. You know he'll be mad when he realizes you slipped out. Keep your cell by your side."

"I will."

# CHAPTER FIFTY-NINE

The Colemans melded into the group easily. The ladies were in their corner eating and swapping stories, while the men talked strategies. Every now and then, Mona would sing along with Peabo Bryson and Roberta Flack as they sang "Tonight I Celebrate My Love for You."

Out of the clear blue Claudette got up from her seat, put her plate down, and fetched her purse. "Marvin, I plumb forgot, I guess with all of the excitement. I received a letter in the mail from Ashley today, and she asked me to give it to you. I saw her a couple of days ago, and she asked me for your address. She said something about sending you some encouraging words. I'm not sure why she sent this to me. Oh, here it is," she said, pulling the envelope out of her purse and handing it to Marvin.

All eyes were on Marvin. He searched the group of women. "Where is Rachel?"

"She ran home to get something for Serena," Sylvia volunteered. "The babysitter called. She'll be back in a few minutes."

"I wish she had told me," Marvin said, a little agitated, but all the while opening the envelope. "I don't want her to be out at night by herself with that crazy woman on the loose."

"She'll be alright, Marv," Kenny said, patting Marvin's back. "It's just a few blocks around the corner. She'll be back in no time."

"Okay." An envelope addressed to Marvin was inside the larger one. Marvin ripped it open and took out a sheet of paper that was folded. Unfolding it, Marvin's eyes began to bulge. "What is this?"

"What is it?" Mona asked.

Marvin lifted the cashier's check in the air by the corner. He gulped. "It's five hundred thousand dollars. Oh, my God..."

"Let me see that," Cecil said, taking the check from Marvin. He examined it and ran his fingers across it as if it he was making an expensive purchase. "Man, you must be living right. God has answered your prayer. What does the letter say?"

"Read it for me, Sylvia," Marvin said, handing her the letter and shaking like a leaf. "I can't believe it. I can't believe this is real."

"Okay, I'm going to read the note." Sylvia began to read:

*Dear Marvin,*
*Ever since I heard about your plight, I wanted to do some-*

*thing to help you. And when I realized my father was the opposing attorney on your case, I resolved to do what I could. My father has no idea and probably doesn't give a damn about how you worked hard to establish your business and make it what it has become. His only concern is to win.*

*Claudette kept me up-to-date with what was going on, and I hope that this little token will help you with your defense. You were always there for me when I was going through my trials with William. Rachel is so fortunate to have a man like you. William was a good man in the beginning, but somewhere things went wrong. Again, I hope this helps. I miss my Ex-Files family. Come visit me sometime.*

*Ashley*

Silence choked the air out of the room. Tears flowed from just about everyone who'd been a witness to this miracle. Even Cecil was getting teary-eyed...maybe because he was going to get paid or because the five hundred thousand dollars was what he needed to get Regal Resorts to give up their quest to obtain Thomas and Richmond Tecktronics. "Thank you, Ashley," Marvin said finally.

She sat in the shadows of the darkness, performing her own surveillance service. At least an hour and a half had gone by since the partygoers had entered the house on Lake Front Drive. That's where she should have been.

Peaches wasn't sure why she was sitting in front of this house in this upscale neighborhood. She had followed Marvin but hadn't counted on him leaving the house with a troupe of people. She hadn't formulated a real plan to force him to give her the money she had demanded, but she planned to give Marvin a reminder that his deadline was today. He had ignored her warning.

She saw movement at the lakefront house—a woman was leaving the house alone. Peaches watched as the woman crossed the street and got in Marvin's car. It had to be Rachel.

Rachel started the car, turned on the headlights, and headed away from the house. Peaches waited a minute, not wanting to be detected. After a minute had elapsed, she started her car and headed for Marvin's house, driving slowly. Peaches knew the street by heart and prepared to turn onto it.

As she passed Marvin's house, she noticed Marvin's car in the driveway. Peaches kept driving, proceeding to the end of the street. Turning her headlights off, she quickly made a U-turn and drove right into the driveway of the neighbor two houses down from Marvin's. The long driveway was shielded by a cluster of trees and the house sat back from the street. Peaches had a clear view of Marvin's house. She waited and saw movement again.

Quietly, Peaches opened her car door, got out, and

crouched down so Rachel couldn't see her. Instead of walking to her car, Rachel walked next door. Peaches sighed, her adrenaline flowing out of whack. She moved away from her car and stood by one of the trees that offered no cover, since the leaves had recently fallen to the ground. She waited.

Voices reached Peaches' ears. She opened her purse and pulled out a gun. She heard a door close and crouched down so she wouldn't be detected. Peaches inched forward just as she saw Rachel head toward her car. She'd have to hurry and cross the hundred feet of lawn in order to reach the car before Rachel got in it.

Peaches sprinted across the lawn, dressed from head to toe in black. Just before Rachel could close the door, Peaches nudged up behind her and put the gun to her back.

"What...what's..." Rachel tried to say.

"Shut up, and you won't get hurt. Get in the car. You and I are going for a ride. Don't try anything; I'm getting in on the other side." Peaches hit the unlock button.

"It's you. What do you want?" Rachel snapped.

"I said be quiet if you value your life and you want to see your little girl again. Now I'm going around the car and get in."

Peaches zipped around the car and hopped in the front seat next to Rachel. Rachel turned and looked at Peaches.

Peaches pointed the gun at Rachel. "Drive. Don't do anything stupid. All I want is my money."

"What if Marvin can't get the money?" Rachel's voice quaked.

"Do I have to spell it out?"

"Peaches, I don't know why you're doing this to us. I'm not sure what went on with you and Marvin, but I can tell you this, my husband is a decent man and doesn't deserve this. He's gone through enough. It may take time to raise the money because we just don't have it."

"It sounds like you are in trouble then, but he'll raise the money because he loves you. You're the one link in this equation that's going to make your husband come to his senses. Said he wasn't going to pay, but I guarantee you he will now. Now stop talking and drive."

Frightened, Rachel drove through her neighborhood and took a chance and drove toward Lake Front Drive.

"What do you think you're doing?"

"I'm driving like you told me."

"Think you're smart, don't you? Where do you think I picked up your scent? I followed you all earlier this evening to this street. Party dresses and all. I saw you and your bourgeois girlfriends strutting like you got a million dollars stuck up your behind. Now turn this car around and drive out of this subdivision so I can think. Remember, you want to see your little girl again."

"Let me tell you one thing. I may be a hostage in my own car, but don't mess with my child." Peaches took the butt of the gun and slammed it on Rachel's wrist. "Ouuuuuuuuch!"

"And what were you saying? I didn't think so. Now drive the damn car!"

Fear and anger gripped Rachel as she continued to drive. She glanced over and saw that the gun was still pointed in her direction.

"Where are we going?" Rachel finally asked Peaches.

Peaches cocked her head and sneered at Rachel. "Don't ask me any questions. Drive where I tell you. You'll see when we get there. Just be glad that you'll be alive to see where you're going."

"Well, I wouldn't be good to you dead. Would I?"

"You are a stupid-ass bitch," Peaches ranted. "If I want to know what you think, I'll ask for your opinion. You act as if this gun isn't loaded."

"Why, Peaches? Why Marvin?"

"That's how hostages get killed. They don't listen. Keep your mouth shut."

"But Peaches, I need to know. I've made so many wrong turns in my life, and just when I found the yellow brick road and finally made it home, another tornado hits and my life gets turned upside down again. You can't begin to know what my life has been, but for once I understand why people say they believe in miracles and what living your best life is all about. I have that with Marvin."

Peaches stared at Rachel, her eyes becoming glassy.

"Maybe I do understand. I, too, have made a few wrong turns in my life, but unlike you, I haven't found the yellow brick road." There was a long pause before Peaches spoke again. "I killed my husband because he was abusive."

*Screechhhhhhhhhhhh.* Rachel's hands shook on the wheel. She pulled the car back into her lane just in time. The driver in the next car shook a fist at Rachel.

Unmoved by the near accident, Peaches continued, setting the gun down in her lap. "I only had to do a little time in the slammer because it was not pre-meditated and...he, my late husband, tried to kill me first," Peaches lied. "Since then, I found it hard to have a real relationship with a man, and to compensate for my insecure nature, I prey on those men that I probably can't have."

"Why Marvin?" Rachel ventured.

"He was in the wrong place at the wrong time. An easy target." Peaches stared out the window. "It was evident that he was in a bad way when he came into Earl's. I just know that he was a fine brother who had come in to get drunk and became fodder for Peaches' vast appetite. If it eases your mind, he was too drunk to have sex with me. I made it look as if he did so that I could blackmail him."

Rachel's face relaxed. For the first time in days, she heard some real good news. She'd wanted to believe Marvin when he said that he might have been set up by this woman, but so much had happened in their lives that it was hard to have faith in anything that Marvin said. Rachel looked at Peaches. "So why are you telling me this now?"

Peaches shook her head. "Didn't you just ask me why I chose your husband? That's what kills me about women like you. Got a good man, living large, but got a head for a coat rack. Have you ever done any manual labor?"

"Peaches, I worked hard all my life to obtain the things I owned prior to me becoming Mrs. Rachel Thomas. I paid for the clothes on my back, the food in my refrigerator, the home I lived in, and the car I drove. I paid my own light bill, gas bill, mortgage, hair, and nails. Not until I married Marvin did I experience what it was like for a real man to take care of me."

"You're fortunate. I don't know what that's like."

"Maybe you haven't given love a chance. There's someone out there for you, Peaches." Rachel watched Peaches as she pondered what she had said. Now, if she could talk Peaches into letting her go.

Rachel's cell phone rang. Peaches picked up the gun. "Don't answer it."

"But it's my husband," Rachel said. "I was supposed to be gone only a few minutes. If I don't answer it, he may—"

"I said, don't answer it."

"Where are we going? We've been on Interstate 85

for fifteen minutes. We'll be in South Carolina if we don't stop. You don't have a plan, do you?"

"I'm thinking," Peaches said, irritated.

"Let's try to work this out, Peaches."

"I've let you talk, now hear me. I want my fifty thousand dollars. And so what that I've told you I set Marvin up. He makes a wrong move, his lovely wife won't be around to tell anyone."

The phone rang, startling the two women. *"You have an incoming call."* Rachel hit the Bluetooth button on the roof of the car.

"Rachel?" boomed Marvin's voice. "Are you alright? Where are you?"

"Do you have my fifty thousand dollars?" Peaches asked, taking over the conversation. "I've got a gun on your wife."

"Jesus!" Marvin shouted. "Please don't hurt Rachel. She hasn't done anything to you. Let's talk this out."

"I'm done talking. You underestimated me...didn't take me seriously. I didn't take you for stupid either, but you and your goons just didn't get it."

"Cut the crap, Peaches. Hurt my wife, and you're going to an early grave."

"Say please."

There was a sigh. "Please don't hurt my wife."

"That's more like it," Peaches said with some satisfaction. "Now, when do I get my money?"

"I'll get it. And when I have the money, how will I get it to you?"

"Not so fast. Give me a call when you've got it, and we'll go from there. Oh, if you involve the police, you won't see your precious one again. Ask your wife what happened to my first husband."

Marvin was quiet. "Are you okay, Rachel?" he asked again, worry in his voice.

"Yeah," Rachel said softly. "Serena is at the baby-sitter's and—"

"That's enough," Peaches cut in. "Sorry, we've got to cut you off. Call when you have my money."

"I promise you, Peaches, if you lay a hand on Rachel, you will be a dead woman."

Peaches cut the conversation short. Her nostrils began to flare. "He doesn't have the guts to kill me. Did a sloppy job of trying to kill himself."

Anger swelled up in Rachel. She kept her eyes straight ahead as she continued to navigate the car along Interstate 85, trying to quiet the thoughts that roamed in her head—thoughts about how she was going to get out of the car, even if it meant killing Peaches. Silently, she prayed. *God deliver me from the hands of the enemy.*

"Get off at the next exit. There's a motel up ahead. You're going to pay for a room for the night."

Panic gripped Rachel. She didn't have one credit card on her person, although they wouldn't have done her any good if she had them since they were inactive. As she exited the interstate, she saw a gas station. An idea came to her. "I've got to get some gas, Peaches," Rachel said.

"Don't try to play me. I'm not your fool and, anyway, we won't need any gas because you're going to drive across the street to the motel. You aren't good with numbers, are you?" Peaches teased. "A two-year-old could've figured your game plan."

"I wasn't trying to play you, Peaches. I need some gas; you can see for yourself. What if we have to move out in a hurry?"

"The only reason I would have to move out in a hurry is if that fool husband of yours calls the cops, which will give us a reason to be on the run. I don't buy your story, sister. Now drive to the motel and get us a room."

"It's going to be hard for me to do that now," Rachel said, her bright idea smashed to smithereens. She'd plan to pretend like she was getting gas and then run and get help from inside the store. It might have been too dangerous.

Peaches pointed the gun at Rachel's heart. "I'm being very calm about this. What do you mean by it's hard for you to do? And your answer better be good."

Rachel stared into the barrel of the gun. "I don't have any credit cards, and the few dollars I have in my purse may just get us a couple of gallons of gas."

"Pull over into the gas station. I've had about enough of your stalling. You irritate me to no end. I don't understand what Marvin sees in you."

"I'm everything to him you'll never be. I'm his woman;

his only woman. I'm the mother of his only child. He loves me inside out as I do him. But what Marvin knows that you'd never understand is that I'll always be there for him—through the good times and the bad, and I respect and honor the man that he is because he is worth it all."

"Whatever. Right now, he's the man that's going to make Peaches fifty thousand dollars richer. You can have him. Now pull over to the side and stop the car."

"I might as well get gas since we're here," Rachel said, trying to re-engineer her idea.

"I said pull to the side." Rachel did as she was told. "Give me your purse, and if you've got any credit cards, you're going to be sorry."

Peaches snatched the small black-sequined clutch away from Rachel's hand. Tearing into it, the only contents Peaches found were Rachel's Georgia driver's license and a ten-dollar bill.

Peaches sat back in her seat in defeat. "We'll sit in the car all night if we have to. I've been in a holding pattern all my life, and I can certainly hold out a few hours longer for fifty thousand dollars."

# CHAPTER SIXTY

Everyone gathered around Marvin, anxious to hear word about Rachel. Mona paced the floor, then sat down on the couch and placed her hand under her chin, deep in thought. Claudette stood still like a wooden statue, arms intertwined with Tyrone's, waiting for instructions that would put them into action. Kenny and Harold stood like military soldiers with legs gaped apart, waiting to receive orders before going into battle. Trina and Cecil sat at the bar, sipping on cocktails, accessing the mood of the now somber group, and Sylvia stood behind Marvin, her hand racing up and down his back for support as his face announced that the news he'd just received was not good.

"Where's Rachel?" Sylvia asked quietly, not wanting to get Marvin more upset than he already seemed to be.

"She's been kidnapped."

"What?" was the collective response.

"We've got to help her," Mona shouted as she jumped up from the couch. "We can't just stand around talking about it."

"Hold up, Mona. Rachel's been kidnapped by Peaches. She wants her fifty thousand dollars before she thinks about releasing Rachel. The woman is more clever than I'd given her credit for."

"Look, Marv. I've got your back on this," Harold said, moving over to Marvin and giving him a friendly pat on the shoulder. "I'll finance this and worry about Peaches later. She won't get away with it."

"Thanks, Harold, but there's no need since I've got this check from Ashley. The problem is putting my hands on the cash tonight. I'm afraid that if I don't, Rachel will be at Peaches' mercy."

Trina stood up and took charge. "Okay, guys. We've got to remain calm about this. It's time that we called the police. Peaches and Rachel can't be that far. I don't know how long it takes, but the police can probably trace their location through cell phone records. I say we move fast. They may be able to use a helicopter to search for her."

"You're right, Trina," Marvin said.

"Why don't you make another phone call to Rachel and Peaches just to let them know you're working on getting the money," Cecil said. "We don't know if this woman has a weapon, and this may calm her down, at least for a minute."

"Good idea," Harold said.

"She's armed," Marvin said in a daze. "Peaches has a gun."

"I'll call the police," Sylvia said, pulling out her phone.

"No, let Marvin do it," Trina offered. "He'll have more of the details since he talked to Peaches. I think the rest of us need to pray for Rachel's safe return."

Sylvia put her phone back in her purse, looked at Trina, and smiled. Trina was right; Sylvia bowed her head in silent prayer.

Rachel shuddered. She gripped her forearms, then rubbed the length of them, trying to brace herself against the coolness of the night air that penetrated the car. She and Peaches had been sitting in the car for over twenty minutes, waiting on a phone call that would set them both free.

Cars whizzed by on the interstate below while others pulled in and out of the gas station at two-minute intervals, although no one seemed to notice them parked off to the side. Rachel made noises with her mouth and squirmed in her seat, unable to get comfortable.

Annoyed, Peaches sat up straight, her fingers still wrapped around the gun, and looked at Rachel. "Turn the damn heat on if you're cold. And stop making all those hissing sounds. You shouldn't have come out the house naked in the first place."

Rachel ignored Peaches. She turned the ignition on so they could get some heat.

Rachel's phone rang. They jumped. *"You have an incoming call,"* the Bluetooth recording said.

"Answer it!' Peaches said, waving the gun. "That's probably Marvin with my money. Yes, I'm feeling better already."

Rachel reached up to the roof and opened the line.

"Rachel, this is Marvin. Baby, are you alright?"

"Yeah, Marvin. Under the circumstances, I'm doing the very best I can."

"Hang in there, sweetie."

"Enough," Peaches cut in. "Do you have the money?"

"We're working on getting the cash," Marvin said calmly. "No one has that kind of money lying around. This is Friday night; all banks are closed. Now, if you want to take a check—"

"Would you take a check?" Peaches screamed, waving the gun in Rachel's direction. "Don't play me, Marvin. I won't hesitate to take out your precious little wife." She gave Rachel a look, then sat the gun in her lap.

"You mess with Rachel, and I'll stomp the living daylights out of you."

"And I'll—"

"And you'll what?" Rachel asked, now pointing the gun at Peaches. Peaches' eyes became round as saucers. She hadn't even realized the moment Rachel snatched the gun out of her lap. Now, she was the one staring at the open end of the barrel.

"Get out!" Rachel screamed, continuing to point the gun at Peaches' head.

"What's going on?" Marvin shouted over the car's speaker.

"Open the door and get out, Peaches." Peaches sat without moving. "Don't provoke me, Peaches. I'm not too bourgeoisie to put a bullet in your ass."

"I don't believe you," Peaches replied, keeping her eye on the gun.

*POP, POP.* "I said get your ass out of the car!" *POP, POP.*

"Rachel, what's going on, what's happening?" Marvin kept shouting. Rachel could hear the others in the background shouting, "Call the police! Marvin...call the police!"

Blood oozed from Peaches' arm as she attempted to open the car door.

"Get out!" Rachel screamed again.

Within seconds, a swarm of Georgia State troopers surrounded the car—guns drawn and in position. Peaches tumbled out of the car, pointing at Rachel with her good arm. "That crazy woman tried to kill me. Officer, she tried to kill me. See," Peaches said, pointing to her arm as the blood continued to run down.

"Call an ambulance," one of the officers said.

A state trooper stood at the driver's side of the car, tapped on the window, and shined his flashlight on her. "Ma'am, I want you to put the gun down slowly." Rachel looked up at the officer, then turned away and placed the gun on the passenger seat of the car. "Now, I want you to get out of the car with your hands up. Slowly."

"That nut tried to kill me," Peaches screamed over

and over. "Look at my arm. If I hadn't moved in time, the bullet might have pierced my heart."

"Will you calm her down," the trooper in charge shouted at the other officer. The officer sat Peaches on the ground, took off his shirt, tied it around her arm to stop the blood, and waited for the ambulance to arrive.

Three officers surrounded Rachel with their guns drawn. "Keep your hands up, and lean against the car," the trooper in charge said. "Mattson, get the gun and the purse out of the car."

"Got it," Mattson replied.

The trooper turned Rachel around to face him, her arms still in the air. "Cuff her, Mattson." After Rachel was cuffed the trooper stared at her. His eyes searched hers before finally doing a slow scan over the rest of her body. Then his eyes went back to Rachel's face, moving back and forth as if he were an X-ray machine. Rachel stared back, unashamed of the way the trooper was looking at her. Although it was almost pitch black save for the street lights that illuminated the gas station, Rachel noticed that her captor was a tall, medium brown-skinned officer who was fitting his uniform. She did a slow scan of her own.

"Uhm...umh, Mattson, let me see the purse." Mattson brought it to him. After taking the purse, he looked at Rachel. "Ma'am, your ID?"

"It's in the purse. Go ahead."

The trooper looked in the purse and found Rachel's driver's license. "Purse pretty empty, uh...Rachel Thomas.

Is that your name?" He looked from the picture to Rachel and back to the picture.

"Just as you see it on the license."

"Can you tell me what happened here tonight and why you and the other woman were just sitting in the car?"

"She kidnapped me," Rachel began. The trooper's brows lifted as if he didn't believe what Rachel was saying. "I was attending a party with friends and had to run home to get something for my daughter. When I tried to get into the car, this crazy woman came up behind me, put a gun to my back, and ordered me to get in and drive."

"Do you know of any reason why she would do this to you?"

"Yes, officer, I do. She's extorting fifty thousand dollars from my husband."

The trooper sighed. "Ma'am, do you realize that you were the one found with the gun in your hand and may be charged with attempted murder?"

"Sir, while I do realize that, if I had wanted to kill her I would have. I pulled the trigger four times to scare her so that she would get out of my car. She was arguing with my husband on the phone, and that's when I seized the opportunity to snatch the gun out of her hand. Oh, goodness, can someone call my husband? I'm sure he's wondering if I'm alright because he was on the phone when I fired the gun."

"Okay, Miz Thomas. We're going to call—"

One of the troopers ran up and interrupted the

interrogation. "Jeffries, I just got a call from the station.
They received a call from a man who says his wife had
been kidnapped by a woman who's dangerous and is
trying to extort money from him. The description fits
the wounded woman over there. Her name is Peaches
Franklin. And she has a record."

"Thanks." Jeffries turned to Rachel, who was not
smiling, and gave her another once-over. "I guess you're
telling the truth. Mattson, take off the cuffs. Please
don't go anywhere yet, ma'am. I've got to talk to the
other woman." Jeffries took off his jacket and handed
it to Rachel. "This will keep you warm."

"Thank you," Rachel said, finally offering up a smile.
"Thank you very much."

As the officer walked the few steps in Peaches'
direction a call came across his radio. He took the call,
then turned back toward Rachel. He stood in front of
her. "Your husband is on his way." He looked at her
again as if he was contemplating something. Then he
said, "This may be out of line, but I wish this was
another time, place, and under a different set of circumstances. You take care of yourself."

Rachel watched the back of Trooper Jeffries as he
walked the short distance to where Peaches sat. She
smiled. Even in the dead of night, under duress, and in
her thirty-something body, she was still able to turn
heads. She lost the thought as the wail of the ambulance's siren pierced her ears.

# CHAPTER SIXTY-ONE

Election Day finally arrived. This was the moment that men and women black, white, red and yellow; Democrats; and talk show hosts ages eighteen to one hundred and six had waited for—the promise of a new president who offered hope, and for some, the first African-American president some forty years after Martin Luther King Jr. had said it was possible. Everyone was gathered at the home of Marvin and Rachel waiting for the returns to be splashed across the television screen.

"The food is here," Mona announced, as she and Michael brought in dishes full of Cajun cuisine.

"Just trying to show up Trina," Rachel whispered, helping Mona to set up in the kitchen. Mona winked.

"I hope there's some jambalaya in one of these containers," Trina said, as she came into the kitchen to offer her assistance. "You've got a reputation in Atlanta for having the best Cajun food."

"That rumor is correct," Mona said, moving swiftly about the kitchen to get everything set up so they could eat. "And, I've got Hurricanes for the full effect.

I want you to feel like you're in the French Quarter or anywhere in New Orleans for that matter."

Trina and Rachel laughed. "Trina, this is Mona ninety percent of the time. She always acts as if she's a pillar of strength. She's definitely our queen of comedy, but I've also seen her vulnerable side."

Mona stopped and looked at Rachel. "Let's not go there today, Rach. This is a celebration—a celebration for you coming back from near tragedy and for the next president of the United States, Barack Obama."

"He hasn't been elected yet," Rachel said.

"Oh ye of little faith," Sylvia said as she walked into the room followed by Claudette. "You all having an Ex-Files meeting without the founder?"

Everyone looked at each other and broke out into grins. "We'd never leave you out, Sylvia," Rachel cooed. She looked at each of the ladies in the room. "I couldn't have a better set of friends and supporters. I love you all so much. You stood by me when I wasn't myself because of all I've been going through. That was for you, Sylvia." Sylvia nodded. "I appreciate how you rallied around Marvin and me in our weakest moment. All I want to say is thank you, and I love you all."

"Group hug," Claudette shouted. They all fell together, including Trina, and stood entangled with each other for more than a minute. When they let go, all you could see were smiles on everyone's faces. They were truly sisters.

"There you are," Marvin said, coming into the kitchen.

"You all having an Ex-Files meeting without me?" Everyone busted out laughing. "Why are you all laughing? I remember what happened at the last meeting you didn't invite me to."

"Even the wine and candy were no match for that meeting," Mona howled.

"Baby, that was how many years ago...three, four?" Rachel said. Everyone laughed again. "That meeting was about our first date, when your ex, Denise, showed up at the restaurant. And to think now, Denise and I are friends and you're still the love of my life." Rachel took Marvin's face in her hands and kissed her man square on the lips.

Claps went around the room. "Okay, all that smacking and crap has got to stop. We're getting ready to eat," Mona said.

"Sounds good," Marvin said, "but Cecil wants everyone to come into the family room. He wants to make an announcement."

"Did Barack win?" Mona asked.

"It's too early," Claudette advised. "The West Coast precincts haven't closed yet. That should be in about three hours."

"Listen to Claudette talk politics," Sylvia howled. "We'd better go into the other room before Marvin becomes unglued."

"You all go on," Mona said, licking her fingers. "The food will be ready when you finish talking."

The group headed for the family room where the

rest of the men were assembled—Cecil, Tyrone, Kenny, and Michael. The women found their respective husbands and sat beside them.

Cecil took the floor. "This truly is a day of celebration." There were smiles on Marvin's and Kenny's faces. "Yesterday, Attorney Robert Jordan called me and we met. Regal Resorts decided to give up their pursuit of Thomas and Richmond Tecktronics, Inc."

Everyone jumped to their feet and shouted congratulations all around. Mona ran into the room to see what all the excitement and commotion was all about.

"The fight for Marvin and Kenny's company is over," Michael explained to Mona. "Cecil just gave us the news." Mona stuck her lip out, then clapped her hands along with the others.

"You should have seen Robert Jordan's face. He's not used to losing, and he wanted so badly to win this case just for his record. He didn't care about Marvin or Kenny, just his ego. But the real showstopper was when I told Jordan that I had been prepared to pay Regal Resorts five hundred thousand dollars. He had a weird look on his face when I told him that Marvin had received a check from a supporter named Ashley Lewis. Jordan turned twenty shades of red, slammed his briefcase down, and uttered some unintelligible words. I looked at Vincent Kinyard and David Eason for an answer, but they shrugged their shoulders."

"Robert Jordan is Ashley's father," Claudette said with

a great big smile on her face. "Ashley came through."

"That's what I was about to say," Cecil said. "No one told me."

"I was too far under to have even given it a thought," Marvin said. "I haven't spoken to Ashley in God knows how long. I still might not have connected the two."

"Well, it was a sweet victory. I trust you and Kenny have reorganized and put some measures into place to get back on track. With all this talk about bailouts and company after company either folding or laying off employees, you'll have to be more than on top of it. Your management team has to micro-manage, which may mean daily tweaking."

"We're on top of it, Cecil," Kenny said. "Marvin and I are working very closely with our business and internal auditing departments. We've put into place some measures for streamlining some of our operations without, at the present, having to penalize any of our employees. We just thank you for all that you've done to make this happen. I know the board of directors will be pleased."

"I don't think there's anything I can add to what Kenny has already said except...Cecil, you're the man," Marvin said with confidence. "You deserve that space on the twenty-ninth floor." Cecil smiled.

"Twenty-ninth floor?" Kenny said. "You the man, cousin." They gave each other a fist bump.

"Barack is doing it!" Mona cried out, staring at the

television that the group had temporarily ignored. "He's way ahead of McCain. I can't stand this."

"Keep hope alive!" Tyrone said, finally getting a word in.

"I'd like to make a suggestion," Claudette said out of left field. "I feel that this is in order, and I hope you'll consider it, Marvin."

"What is it, Claudette?"

"I'm so happy about the good news that Thomas and Richmond has been saved. And as for the five hundred thousand dollars that you didn't have to use, I suggest that a portion of it be used to start the Ashley Jordan-Lewis Defense Fund."

"Claudette, you are such a brilliant woman. You don't mind me saying so, do you, T?" Marvin asked.

"Not at all," Tyrone said. "She's brilliant and a whole lot more. And she can hook up some hair." Everyone stared at Tyrone. "Shameless promotion."

"I think that's a great idea," Marvin said. "The board is going to pay Cecil for his work, and I think establishing the defense fund in Ashley's name goes without saying."

"Yes," everyone sang in chorus.

"Oh, Ashley will be so proud," Sylvia said. "I know that we haven't been so good about visiting her, and she's an Ex-Files member—one of us. And I think we need to do something about trying to find a way to get an early release for her."

"That may not be so simple to do," Trina said. "After all, she's been convicted of premeditated murder. Her father is a powerful lawyer right here in Atlanta, and if he wasn't able to call in some favors to get his own daughter released, you may have a tough time doing so. But let me say this on record, I'll work with you and do whatever I can. I'm in."

"This is great," Claudette said. "The hope that Barack Obama brings is infectious. I realize he's only one man, but I can't help but feel a sense of making it to the Promised Land. I say that we all go to see Ashley sometime next week and give her the news. She will be surprised and happy."

"Rachel was talking this morning about those moments when one lets others see their vulnerabilities," Mona said. "This might be it, Trina." Mona fanned herself with her hand, overcome with emotion. "Claudette has always been so giving. She's been there, even if behind the scenes. I remember how Ashley and Claudette's relationship started. Claudette was a mean cuss and wouldn't cut Ashley a break, but something drew the two together. Ashley couldn't have a better friend in you."

"Thanks, Mona," Claudette said. "I appreciate you saying so. Ash loves all of you. She misses us, so establishing a defense fund on her behalf is a way of showing we do care. Thanks for hearing me out, everybody."

"It's a wonderful idea, Claudette," Cecil said. "As I

sat listening to you, I thought about how good I was feeling about winning this case, the fellowship of newfound friends, and how much Trina and I feel that we are part of you all. So many good things have happened in the short time I've known you, even as recently as this past weekend when our sister Rachel was brought back to us unharmed." Everyone clapped. "But I want to give a gift as well. Although I've already received a retainer for my work on the Thomas and Richmond Tecktronics case, I'm donating the rest of my time. Paid in full."

Marvin and Kenny walked over to Cecil and gave him a brotherly hug. "How about a group hug," Tyrone suggested.

"Lord T, you're sounding just like Claudette," Mona said. "You all get your hugs. Then it'll be time to eat."

The ladies got up from their seats and began chatting while Mona went to uncover the dishes in preparation for the group. "Baby, is that your phone ringing?" Rachel said to Marvin.

Marvin pulled away from the group. He looked at the caller ID and frowned. "Hello," Marvin said.

"Yes, is this Marvin Thomas?" the caller asked.

"Yes, it is."

"Well, this is Earl from Earl's Tavern."

"Earl, yeah. What's up? Let me go into another room so I can hear."

"Mr. Thomas, I'm sorry that I didn't come forward

earlier about Peaches. I saw the story on television earlier about the kidnapping. I hope your wife is fine."

"She's doing better than expected under the circumstances. Thank you for asking."

"Well," Earl began, "I did have some information on Peaches that I have since gone to the police with. She murdered her husband some years earlier, and she's extorted money from others beside yourself. I think I called myself protecting her when in truth she needed some help. I just wanted you to know that I've tried to do my civic duty, although it might have been a little late."

"I appreciate you telling me," Marvin said. "I believe I understand where you're coming from, Earl. We all have persons in our lives we want to protect from something or other, but I'm glad it's behind us. I hope Peaches is put away for a long time so that she won't be able to hurt anyone else."

"Well, I just wanted to share that with you, and I hope you don't hold it against me. Anytime you're downtown and feel like stopping by, please do."

"Thanks again, Earl. I appreciate it. Good-bye." Marvin stood in the hallway and then a smile crossed his face as he saw Rachel—his rainbow.

"What's wrong?" Rachel asked, finding Marvin in the hallway.

He pulled Rachel to him and hugged her tight. "God is so good, Rachel. That was Earl from the bar I went to the evening I met Peaches. He told me he spoke with the police about Peaches. Peaches killed her husband. Just think, it could have been you."

"I know. Peaches told me she killed her husband," Rachel said. "Let's not be sad because I have a feeling that Peaches is going to be in jail for a long time."

"I agree. How about joining the others to celebrate our new president-to-be. I can feel it, Rach."

"Let's go."

"You guys got quiet fast," Marvin said, returning to the family room.

"We're eating Mona's good food," Trina said with a mouth full of jambalaya. "You better get some before it's all gone."

"I'm gonna do that," Marvin said with a smile on his face. "I also have some good news."

Everyone turned their faces away from the television to listen to Marvin. He told them about Earl going to the police with the information about Peaches. It was a joyous time.

With all bellies full, the women helped Mona clean up Rachel's kitchen so they could sit together in peace and watch the election returns. The men were having their own private debate about the two-and-a-half-year presidential race while the ladies recapped moments from the last year. Then there was silence as each person became engrossed in their own private thoughts as they watched Obama's electoral votes climb the leader board.

"Mona, darling, we're going to have to get ready to go. It's just about eleven o'clock, and I'm on-call tomorrow. I need to get some rest."

"Okay, babe. Let's watch the news at the top of the hour." Michael sighed and stayed seated.

The top-of-the-hour news came on. The newscaster announced that the West Coast precincts had just closed. Everyone in the room sat up straight. *Barack Obama has just been elected the forty-fourth President of the United States.*

"Oh my God," Sylvia said, jumping from her seat. "Hallelujah!"

"Yes," Cecil and Trina screamed together, giving each other the Obama and Michelle fist bump.

"My president," Claudette said. "President Barack Obama and First Lady Michelle Obama. That has a wonderful ring to it."

"I'm on my way to Washington, D.C.," Mona said. "I'm going to be front and center at the inauguration. I'm going to be able to see the whites of Barack's eyes when he takes the oath. I might even help Michelle hold the Bible."

"When's the last time you held a Bible?" Rachel asked, soliciting laughs all around the room.

"That's our cue to leave," Michael said. "It's been real, people. This was a great day. And to Marv and Kenny, congratulations! And Cecil, keep handling your business."

"Got that, man," Cecil said.

"Sylvia, you ready to go home and celebrate?" Kenny said. "Maya has little Kenny and Serena."

"My king, I think we can do that," Sylvia said, doing a victory dance. "Me, you, Barack and Michelle."

"Kinky," Tyrone said.

"What do you know about kinky?" Claudette asked. "Only thing kinky about you are those knots on your head."

"That's wrong, sister. I've got some moves left. I say we try them out, but we'll let Barack and Michelle watch."

"You guys are so crazy," Marvin said, holding Rachel around the waist. "You must be drunk from Mona's food or those Hurricanes. We love you guys! Thanks for celebrating this historic day with us—in more ways than one."

"We love you all too," everyone said at the same time.

"Marvin, I'll give you a call later in the week to discuss the Peaches thing. I think this is going to be straightforward and simple, especially since Rachel's off the hook for shooting that psycho."

"Sounds like a plan, Trina. Good night."

After all their friends had left and had made it safely to their cars, Rachel and Marvin cuddled up on one of the sofas in the family room. "We're going to make our own music, Mrs. Thomas, just you and I. No Barack, Michelle, Sylvia, Kenny, Mona, Michael, Claudette, T, Trina, or Cecil. Just you and me, baby."

"This night couldn't have turned out any better, Marvin. We're going to be alright. You've got the company back and Peaches is in police custody. I wished that Harold, Denise, and Ashley were here to celebrate with us. I thought that was a wonderful suggestion Claudette made about the defense fund."

"You're absolutely right about everything. And we've got a new president—President Barack Obama, first African American to hold the office. That's awesome. Speaking of Harold and Denise, the wedding invitation came in the mail today. They're getting married on December thirty-first; we'll be there to help them celebrate. I'm glad that Harold and I have mended our fences. It's like having my brother back by my side."

"Me too. So are you ready for our private celebration, Mr. Thomas?"

"Past ready. I love you, Rachel."

"I love you, too, Marvin."

The phone rang. "Who's calling this late?" Rachel asked.

# CHAPTER SIXTY-TWO

Marvin got up and walked to the kitchen and retrieved his cell phone. He didn't recognize the number, but he answered anyway.

"Hello," Marvin said, a little annoyed.

"Yes, Mr. Thomas, this is Captain Jeffries with the state trooper's office. I was just informed by the Georgia State police that Peaches Franklin has just escaped."

"Escaped. How in the hell did that happen? Wasn't she under lock and key? I don't believe this."

"She complained of severe pain in her wounded arm and was taken to the hospital for treatment. This woman is a slick one. She saw an opportunity to slip out of the examining room and unfortunately the officer who was on guard outside the room was talking and had his back turned to the door. He will be reprimanded. Unmarked cars have already been dispatched to your area, but I wanted you to know so you would be on your guard. I'll keep you informed on any updates we receive in this matter. Know that we have heightened our search for Miz Franklin, and we hope to have her back in custody before too long."

"I don't know if that's reassuring at all, but thank you for letting us know." Marvin shut the lid to his cell phone.

When he returned to the living room, the pep had gone out of Marvin's step. "What's wrong?" Rachel asked. "Who was that on the phone?"

Marvin looked at Rachel. "We've got to wait just a little longer."

"For what, Marvin?" Marvin was quiet. "Wait for what? Now you're scaring me."

"Peaches was taken to the hospital and she escaped."

"She did what? How in the world, Marvin, how in the world could that have possibly happened? What kind of police officers do we have running the force?"

"Peaches is clever. The police hope to have her back in custody soon. They have our house under surveillance, but know that I'm in no way leaving you alone until Peaches is caught. I can't believe that bitch had the nerve to interrupt our celebration."

"We can still have our celebration, baby. I don't think Peaches has enough nerve to mess with me again. I put the fear of God in her. You should have seen her eyes when she realized I had the gun instead of her. But I've got something for her just in case."

"What are you talking about, Rachel? You're not talking about a gun."

"I'm not? Just let Miz Peaches step on my property again. It won't be her arm next time. I'll aim straight for her heart. I've got a little something-something to protect myself in the event that girlfriend ever tries to raise up on me again."

# ABOUT THE AUTHOR

Suzetta Perkins is the author of *Behind the Veil;*
*A Love So Deep; EX-Terminator: Life After Marriage;*
*Déjà Vu, Betrayed,* and a contributing author of *My*
*Soul to His Spirit.* A native of Oakland, California,
Suzetta resides in Fayetteville, North Carolina. Suzetta
is the co-founder and president of the Sistahs Book
Club and Secretary of the University at Fayetteville
State University. She is a member of New Visions
Writing Group in Raleigh, North Carolina, and a
mentor for aspiring writers. Visit www.suzettaperkins.
com, www.myspace.com/authorsue, www.facebook.com/
suzetta.perkins, and email nubianqe2@aol.com.

# READER'S DISCUSSION GUIDE

1. The opening scene is the window that allows you to see what is about to transpire in Marvin Thomas' life. You can feel something is amiss; you can feel the tension. What's so heavy on Marvin's mind that he needs to see an old friend?

2. Who is Marvin's business partner?

3. Some secrets can be catastrophic if exposed. Marvin Thomas had two secrets. What were they and whom did they impact before and after they were exposed?

4. As Marvin Thomas' life began to spiral out of control, it impacted members of his family first. What happened while Rachel was out on a spending spree?

5. Do you feel Rachel overreacted?

6. When Marvin was at his wit's end, he finds himself at a local bar. What was strange about him going to the bar? Who did he meet and what happened?

7. As a result of Marvin's indiscretion, what did Peaches tell him he had to do?

8. To what length does Peaches send Marvin messages about paying up or else?

9. What did Rachel receive from Peaches and what were the contents? How would you have handled the information Rachel received?

10. Which two characters mended a broken friendship? How did the one character come to the aid of the other? What was the cause of their broken friendship?

11. What did Sylvia, Mona, and Claudette do to try and salvage Rachel's marriage?

12. What did Ashley do to try and help save Thomas and Richmond Tecktronics? Why?

13. What historic event in our history did Marvin, Rachel, Sylvia, Kenny, Mona, Michael, Claudette, T, Cecil, and Trina witness on television?